Break ME

Break ME

KNIGHTON EQUESTRIAN

TILLIE COLE

Montlake

This is a work of fiction. Names, characters, organizations, places, events, and incidents are either products of the author's imagination or are used fictitiously. Otherwise, any resemblance to actual persons, living or dead, is purely coincidental.

Published by Montlake, Seattle

www.apub.com

EU Product Safety contact:
Amazon Media EU S. à r.l.
38, avenue John F. Kennedy, L-1855 Luxembourg
amazonpublishing-gpsr@amazon.com

ISBN-13: 9781662523441 (paperback)
ISBN-13: 9781662523434 (digital)

Cover design by Emily Mahar
Cover image: © Abramova_Kseniya, © Dimitris66, © Katsumi Murouchi, © Kositskaya Olga / Getty; © DarkMatters / Shutterstock

Printed in the United States of America

To all the horse girls (and people) who spend their days with mud under their fingernails and a burning passion for riding in their hearts.

This one's for you.

PROLOGUE

Hallie

Age 12
Ocala, Florida

The humidity felt different here in Florida. It stuck to my skin like glue, wrapping its wet hands around each strand of my long dark hair, making it curl into ringlets around my face.

My heart fluttered as fast as a hummingbird's wings as I gaped at the humongous equestrian center spread out before me. I knew horses. I'd been raised in the saddle with reins in my hand. I knew how to ride and rope cattle from a mustang's back. I knew how to navigate rough pastures and herd cows into pens with perfect precision. But as a large bay mare passed by me, coat glistening, mane brushed out, hooves oiled and free of dust and mud from a hard day's ride, I may well have been as unfamiliar with these animals as I was with the country clubs and fancy houses I'd seen on the ride from the airport.

The main door in a huge white barn to my left opened, and a woman around my daddy's age came walking out. She looked as pristine as the bay mare that had just passed us by. Her bright-red hair was swept off her freckled face and tied in a bun at the back of her scalp. She wore cream breeches, a polo shirt to match, and polished tall black riding boots. As if feeling my stare, she lifted her head and saw me standing beside the social worker who had brought me here. Her face was as beautiful and put together as her clothes.

And she looked just like Daddy.

A lump sprouted in my throat as she approached, and her hazel eyes glistened with tears as she tracked her wide gaze over me. I glanced down at my well-worn cowboy boots, Wranglers, and favorite pink, long-sleeve button-up. My trusty Stetson was on my head—I had my daddy's packed in a protective box in my luggage.

"Hallie," the lady rasped, throat hoarse, and a tear fell from her eye. Her hands were shaking as she quickly wiped it away. She moved until she was just before me. She smelled like rose petals. Her cheeks matched their red shade too. She crouched until she was eye level with me. Without thinking, I reached out and touched her face. I felt my bottom lip tremble.

"You look just like my daddy," I said. My chest felt tight. I was trying real hard not to cry. I'd cried a ton over the past few days. Ever since my daddy . . .

I sniffed and wiped away a few extra tears.

"You look like him too," the lady said softly.

Aunt Jeanie, I reminded myself. *Her name is Aunt Jeanie.* She was my daddy's younger sister. Daddy never spoke of her much. The only thing he'd ever said was that he'd been real sorry he'd stopped speaking to her when she decided to leave the family ranch before I was born. Said he hadn't understood her choice to move away at the time. And that breaking all ties with her was the biggest mistake of his life.

One he never got to make right.

"You can cry, darlin'," she said, her accent sounding a little like mine.

"Cowgirls don't cry," I said, echoing what Daddy and the cowboys back at the ranch used to tell me if I was hurt or upset.

A flash of what looked like sadness took over her face, like she'd heard that saying before too. "Do you know who I am?" she asked.

"Aunt Jeanie," I said, and pointed at Sally, the social worker. She'd explained where I was going. Aunt Jeanie stood up and shook Sally's hand. They began to talk about me, but movement from my right caught my eye, pulling me away from the conversation. In an outdoor arena across the yard, someone was cantering on a horse—a large gray horse that must have been at least seventeen hands high and then some. The horse was beautiful, all platinum glossy mane, its body thick with muscle.

Before I knew it, my feet began moving, and the next thing I knew, I was watching the rider and horse through the slats in the pretty white fence. Watching as the man steered the horse over huge, brightly colored jumps. My pulse raced and my breath held as, with each one, they seemed to take flight.

I wondered what that would feel like, to ride on horseback over those huge fences.

I watched, transfixed, as the man jumped all the fences, not touching a single pole. He patted the horse's neck as he brought the horse to a slow and steady trot. The man unclipped the chin strap of his fancy helmet and placed it in his lap, tipping his head back toward the sun. His dark hair was sweaty, one thick strand falling over his forehead. It still looked perfect.

Before I knew it, he'd moved closer to where I stood.

"He needs more push on the triple bar. His left hind was dragging." The man snapped his head in my direction. A crooked smile pulled on his lips. He was dressed in all black, the total opposite of his gray horse—they looked like night and day.

Aunt Jeanie came up beside me, resting her arms on the top of the fence. She was the one who had spoken to him. Loosening his reins, the man headed over to us. I looked up at him from under the brim of my hat. When he looked down at me, his smile was blinding.

"Who's this little cowgirl?" His voice was deep, and his accent was strange. He didn't sound American.

Aunt Jeanie turned to me with a big smile on her face. She placed her hand on my shoulder. It was soft and warm. It felt nice. I hadn't been around too many women in my life. "This is my niece, Hallie." It sounded strange being called that. Her *niece*. But . . . I liked it. Aunt Jeanie gestured to the man again. "Hallie, this is Jasper Knighton. He's an Olympian show jumper and currently ranked number one in the world in the Under-25s. And he's still only nineteen!" My eyes widened. That sounded real impressive, and he was younger than I'd thought. Aunt Jeanie turned to Jasper again. "Hallie will be living with me and Luke from now on."

Jasper nodded. "Nice to meet you, Hallie," he said, and I felt my cheeks heat. "Do you ride?" He placed his helmet back on, fastening the strap under his chin.

"Yes, sir," I said, forcing myself to find my voice.

"English?" he asked again, and I looked at the saddle he sat on, all shiny polished black leather with fancy stirrups. At the supple black leather bridle over his horse's head. They looked nothing like the western saddles and bridles I was used to. I shook my head. "Have you jumped before?" He pointed to the fences he had just cleared moments ago. I shook my head again, too shy to speak.

"Jeanie," he said, addressing my aunt. "Make things right with your niece and teach the girl to jump." He looked at me again, throwing me a wider smile. "There's nothing like it." He turned his gray horse back toward the colored fences, kicking him on, calling out, "Nice to meet you, Cowgirl Hallie!"

Jasper began trotting around the arena again, then built to a steady canter and sailed over each jump with ease. When he had cleared the round, another man then entered the arena on a bay horse, and he and Jasper Knighton talked and chatted, taking turns at practicing the jumps. Both were clearly very good, judging by the lack of poles dropped and the number of staff who stopped their stable duties to come and watch them.

I could have watched them all day.

"Come with me, Hallie," Aunt Jeanie said suddenly, taking me away from my newfound fascination. I looked back over my shoulder, just to see Jasper jumping another clear round. Aunt Jeanie nudged my arm, pulling my attention back to her. "Jasper Knighton comes all the way from England."

"Does he live here too?" I asked.

Aunt Jeanie smiled. "No, darlin'. This is a training facility for professional show jumpers." I was so confused. I had no idea what these things were. Her arm wrapped around my shoulders. "All will become clearer in time," she said. "Jasper's home is back in England. He's just here using our facilities for practice while he competes in the US." I nodded, still not sure what kind of sport this was. I only knew about riding horses for ranching purposes, not whatever all this fancy stuff was.

"This okay?" Aunt Jeanie suddenly asked, referring to her arm around me. I nodded. Daddy always walked with me like this too. It felt . . . It was nice but made me miss him too.

Aunt Jeanie stopped at the entrance to another huge white barn. She bent down, meeting my eyes. "I know things are real hard for you right now, darlin'. The world feels strange and unfair, and to make it so much worse, you've had to move away from everything you know. Your friends, your ranch." Her voice cut out, and she looked out over the pastures around us, filled with horses. When she looked back to me, she said, "I may have never met you before today, but you're my *family*, Hallie. I've always loved you. You're my big brother's little girl. I was *made* to adore you."

Aunt Jeanie's bottom lip wobbled. "To know that your daddy, after everything we'd been through, wanted me to be the one to take care of you if anything happened to him . . ." Aunt Jeanie cleared her throat. "That . . . well, that just means the world to me, darlin'." She squeezed my arm affectionately. "And I'm gonna make sure I love you with all my heart and then some."

She took a deep breath, then gestured around us. "This place may be different from the ranch back in Texas, but it's full to the brim with the one thing I know we both love." She stood and opened the barn. A long, wide center aisle was lined with stalls. Inside some of them were horses, but most were empty. "The majority of the horses housed here are either being trained in the arenas or turned out in the fields right now." Then we stopped at a blue roan gelding with a jet-black mane and tail. His coloring reminded me of dusk.

Beautiful.

Aunt Jeanie stroked her hand down his handsome face. "This here is Rocky. He's four and just recently broken in. We are gonna train him up to be a show jumper. His sire was a world champion, so we're expecting great things from him too."

He was *stunning*. Moving closer, I held out my hand, and he immediately nuzzled my palm. I was raised on a ranch, raised around horses, but my love for them, my draw, was always *more*. It was like my soul only calmed if they were near. Riding horses felt more natural to me than walking on my own two feet. It wasn't a choice to be around them; it was a necessity.

"Rocky—show name 'Rocky Mountain View'—only came to us last week from Colorado. He's brand new to Silvercrest." Aunt Jeanie must have seen my confusion. "That's what this equestrian center is called." I took off my hat and pressed my forehead to Rocky's nose. I laughed as his warm breath puffed against my face as though he was saying hello.

Aunt Jeanie laughed too, then said, "I was thinking the pair of y'all could maybe find your feet here together." I turned to my aunt in surprise, pulse racing. "He's yours if you want him, Hallie-girl." My body filled with warmth. *Hallie-girl.* My daddy always called me that.

"I'd like that," I said, feeling the first bit of happiness in days. But that faded when I scanned what Aunt Jeanie was wearing. Then I thought of Jasper Knighton and the pristine black leather saddle he sat upon. "I . . . I don't know how to ride like y'all," I said, pointing to my scuffed and faded cowboy boots that had a small hole in the toe.

"Then we'll just have to remedy that, won't we?" Aunt Jeanie said. And I nodded, feeling a frisson of excitement shimmy through me. Lifting on my tiptoes, I wrapped my arms around Rocky's neck, and like he knew I needed it, he tucked his head into the crook of my neck and shoulder, calming my nerves and soothing my sorrow.

As I held him, I pictured Jasper Knighton and his friend soaring over the fences in the arena. I wanted to know what that felt like, to ride like that. I wanted to learn to jump.

I wanted to learn to fly.

Chapter One

Hallie

Age 25
Surrey, England
Present day

"Holyyyyy shiiitttttt," Sage said as she crushed me, clambering over my lap to look out the window at the most famous and exclusive equestrian training facility in the world.

I pushed on her chest to get her off me, but she was immovable, like a granite boulder. "Sage!" I protested. "I can't breathe!"

Sage huffed in fake annoyance and sat back in her luxurious leather seat. "Hallie. You're so dramatic. Who needs to breathe anyway?"

I raised my eyebrow at my best friend. "Er . . . just the entire human population."

"Pfft," she said, then batted her hand at me. "Semantics."

I rolled my eyes at her, then glanced out the window of the town car that was driving us to Golden Oaks Equine Manor. Fields and fields of horse paddocks met us, only to have the center of the facility come into view. I'd grown up at Silvercrest Equestrian Center in Florida, which was arguably the best training center for show jumping in the entire US. But this . . . I took in barn after barn, miles of perfectly manicured gallops, exercise pens, a mass of both indoor and outdoor arenas, and ancient-looking English cottages that must have been accommodation for the manor's staff, grooms, and riders. Acres and acres of sumptuous land stretched as far as the eye could see, dozens of horses turned out and filling every field.

Even in winter, this part of Surrey was truly an idyllic place, like something out of a Regency-era painting.

"It's so beautiful," Sage whispered as she rested her chin on my shoulder, drinking in the view too. I nodded, only to have to drop it when Sage's awed voice changed to bitterness as she added, "It's a shame that Mr. Douche Canoe lives here."

"Sage," I said, beyond exasperated, drawing out her name to emphasize it. "Can we please go one single day without hearing you bitch about your archnemesis?"

Sage's mouth dropped open in obvious outrage just as we passed through a wrought-iron gate and arrived at the very stately long driveway to Golden Oaks. "As my best friend and nonblood sister, I am *appalled* that you're not on my side."

"Sage, I *am* on your side. You need a getaway driver? I'm there. You need help moving a body? I'm your girl. Need money? I'll rob a damn bank for you. But for the love of God, can we *please* just have one day where you don't mention Atticus Knighto—"

Sage's hand slapped over my mouth, cutting off my words. "Hals. I love you. But do *not* speak his name in my presence. I'll be forced to hurt you if you do."

I bit down on Sage's palm, causing her to rip her hand away on a pained hiss. "Bitch," she snarled, shaking her injured appendage. I smirked and caught Sage's responding smile in my periphery. Sage Miller. My best friend, the finest show jumper I knew, and certifiably insane.

I couldn't love a person more.

Two more ornate iron gates later, we stopped at a large castle-keep-looking building. Sage and I stared up at it through the town car's window. "It has columns, Hallie. *Columns.* I feel like we're at the entrance to a fancy horse-themed Disney World." I nodded, too lost in wonder to use actual words. "And just like Disney movies, this one has a megavillain . . ."

"And I'm done!" I said, ignoring the rest of Sage's tirade, opening the door before the driver could get there. I could not take Sage's hate-filled diatribe about Atticus Knighton one more time. Endless years of ear-torture was long enough.

Sage got out of the car and stood beside me, the ice-cold wind whipping around us. We stared up at the entrance to the building, all gray stone and old-world English architecture. "That was rude," she said, nudging me in the arm.

"Sage, why did you agree to ride Knighton horses when you hate Atticus this much? You're gonna see him here. All the time. He *lives* here. This is his family estate. His DNA is in every brick in the million-dollar stables and in every blade of grass we just passed on their gazillion acres. *This*"—I gestured to the incredible equine setup around us—"is *his* empire. The Knightons are royalty in the horse world, you know this. They're a powerful dynasty. But that's especially true in their home country. They're the gods in the horse world here in England. *You're* the interloper."

"Damn right I am," she said, her Tennessee accent thickening and a sadistic kind of smirk spreading on her stunning face. She looked like an angel but had the spirit of a hellion. With platinum blond hair, olive skin, and the darkest of eyes, Sage Miller turned heads everywhere she went. As well as being a natural beauty, she was the most loyal person I'd ever met. Growing up in the same competitive circuits in the US had brought us close, even closer when she came to board at Silvercrest as a teen, but the respect and love we had for one another was what made us truly inseparable. So much so that most jumping fans saw us as a pair, a twosome. As did sponsors. Hence, we were here in England together.

When you got to know her, Sage was a total sweetheart, but she had a wicked streak that only one man had ever been able to stir in her. And God help Atticus Knighton, because he had no idea what monster he'd awakened back when Sage was only eighteen. "I'm gonna destroy him in the arenas he believes he owns, on the horses his family has bought or bred for millions of dollars." She smirked triumphantly. "Internal destruction."

I sighed and rubbed a throbbing pain at the center of my forehead. We'd been awake for over twenty-four hours at this point. I was exhausted.

Eric—the driver of the town car that picked us up from the airport—placed our luggage beside us. "The estate manager will be here to greet you soon, madams," Eric said, then: "Oh, here she is now."

A lady with a severe blond bob approached us with two young men in tow. The men were dressed in navy-blue breeches, Knighton Equestrian–branded navy-blue polo shirts, and insulated, waterproof jackets, with ball caps to match. I was in my favorite cowboy boots and barn coat. I might be an equestrian now, but I was still a cowgirl through and through. The way I dressed and talked made good fodder for my rivals, but I didn't give a shit. This was who I was. Nothing would change that.

"Sage Miller and Hallie Oakley, lovely to meet you," the lady said when she reached us. Her delicate English accent was in stark contrast to her forest-green power suit and shrewd eyes. "Victoria Smith, Golden Oaks' estate and event manager. Basically, I run this place, so if you need anything, it's probably me who will fix it for you." Victoria held out her hand to me.

"Nice to meet you, ma'am," I said. "Hallie."

"Sage," Sage said, offering her hand too.

Victoria gestured for the guys behind her to take our bags. As they picked up our luggage, Victoria then waved for us to follow her. "This is just the gatehouse to the property." We passed through the open doors of the building. My eyes were wide as I looked around the foyer. The gatehouse had a *foyer*. Large oil paintings of horses filled the dark wood–paneled walls, and suits of armor—for both knights *and* horses—stood proudly in the corners, like they could come to life at any moment and defend Golden Oaks from ancient enemies.

I stopped dead in my tracks in front of an ornate stone fireplace when I came to an oil painting of the most handsome man I had ever seen.

Jasper Knighton.

The day I met Jasper at my aunt's home had changed my life. To say that I became enamored with him later in my teens was an understatement. Jasper Knighton was a show jumping prodigy. Ranked number one in the world for nearly a decade, he had three Olympic golds under his belt. He dominated the sport. He was a once-in-a-generation talent. For years, no one came close to him.

I'd only ever spoken to him once, on what was one of the hardest days of my life. Even when we competed on the same circuits, I watched him from afar or from the safety of the stands. I wasn't a wallflower by anyone's estimation, but Jasper Knighton was an idol to me. He was incredible. *Untouchable.* His fame in our industry unparalleled. Together with his horse, a famous gray stallion named Lord Henry, born and bred from this very equestrian property on their stud.

My own horse, Rocky, had been my pride and joy for over a decade. We'd swept through the Juniors and Under Twenty-Five Grand Prix. He was retired now, back home at Silvercrest with my aunt, enjoying the sun and endless fields of grass. He was the first love of my life. A heart horse. In my eyes, he was perfect. But in the professional equestrian world's eyes, Lord Henry . . . there was none like him. The best jumping horse I'd ever seen—that anyone had ever seen. He was perfectly bred.

"That's Jasper," Victoria said, catching me staring at the painting. I smiled tightly, embarrassed I'd been caught. "But you probably already knew that."

Sage's arm came around my shoulders. "Don't mind Hals, Victoria. She's just got a small case of hero worship for your boss." I wrapped my arm around Sage's waist and discreetly pinched her side. Sage flinched, then backed away with a smug grin. My best friend knew all about my slight obsession with Jasper and liked to torture me as often as she could about my infatuation.

Sage also had zero filter and loved nothing more than embarrassing me in public. Case in point.

Victoria nodded in understanding, oblivious to our silent argument. "He's the best rider there's ever been," she said. "The horse world will never be the same."

Jasper Knighton wasn't dead, even though Victoria's somber tone may have indicated that. About eighteen months ago, after a string of family tragedies, he stepped back from competing and abruptly withdrew from the limelight. Completely. From what I'd heard, he'd always been more reserved anyway, unlike his gregarious cousin. But he'd been quiet, pleasant, and amiable. These days, the horse world's gossip mill talked of him as a moody and bitter man who was best avoided. I had no idea whether that was true, but the man who'd chatted with me that day years ago at my aunt's center became my hero. I couldn't imagine him being bitter and cruel to anyone.

The oil painting must have been fairly recent. Gone was the nineteen-year-old I'd met, the one whose career I'd followed intently throughout the years. Instead I regarded a man of thirty-two with messy, deep brunet hair and heavy stubble covering his face. His eyes were as dark and stormy as the gray English skies in the painted background.

If possible, he was even more handsome in this picture than when he retired. More rough and rugged. But my stomach fell, as he also appeared troubled. Haunted, even. His eyes . . . They screamed of pain.

It made my heart ache.

"If you'd come this way," Victoria said, and we walked out into a courtyard. I stopped dead in my tracks as the true glory of Golden Oaks immediately greeted us. Laid out like an equine paradise was every horse rider's dream: pristine arenas (both indoor and outdoor), and stable blocks that stretched for miles. Even the harsh winter weather failed to make this place look anything less than spectacular.

"Okay, I get why you convinced me to come with you," Sage said from her equally awestruck state beside me. I smirked at my best friend. There had been *no* convincing. Getting the opportunity to compete on a Knighton-bred-and-trained horse was the equivalent of winning the lottery in our industry. Despite her history with Atticus, Sage had jumped (no pun intended) at the chance.

As had I.

The property stretched far and wide. There were trainers working horses in round pens. And they weren't just show jumping trainers; I saw dressage and eventers too. Golden Oaks was unlike any other stable yard in the world. A melting pot of all different disciplines across one extensive property.

Only the best of the best got invited to train here, a blessing I didn't take for granted. I'd worked tirelessly to be where I was in my career. Golden Oaks would only further my drive to be number one in the world.

Victoria turned to us with a smile that softened her prickly approach a little. "Can I just say, we are all so excited that you both have agreed to train here and jump for Knighton Equestrian. I just adore watching you."

Sage winked at Victoria. "Thanks, girl. We're so happy to be here too . . . even if it is cold as balls."

An ATV suddenly arrived before us, thankfully cutting off Sage's balls talk. A girl who looked about twenty-one was driving. She jumped out of the vehicle and wiped her hands on her navy-blue riding tights. "Mila Burton," she said, shaking our hands. She was petite with long, fiery-red hair that fell to the middle of her back. She boasted a pale complexion and an adorable face full of freckles. She was gorgeous. Mila then faced me. "I'm your new groom, Ms. Oakley." She smiled. "I'm a huge fan and so honored to be working with you. You're a true inspiration to me."

"Good to meet you too, Mila," I said, "but please call me Hallie." Mila's face flushed and she nodded with a wide smile on her face, then introduced herself to Sage. We followed Mila into the ATV. Sage sat beside me. Mila leaned around me to speak to her. "Your groom is Horatio. He's a good friend and one of the finest grooms here at Golden Oaks. He's currently settling in the newly acquired Knighton horses after their travel day."

"Perfect," Sage said, and we slowly set off through the equestrian center once our luggage was secured in the back of another ATV. I caught myself yawning, and my eyes watered.

Mila smiled at me. "Jet lag?"

"Jet lag," I confirmed, then let my gaze drift to my surroundings. I'd had the privilege of competing all over the world. I'd been lucky to have visited many amazing countries, but there'd always been something about England for me. In the spring, everything was green, lush, and vibrant in a way that no other country could touch. My aunt told me it was because it rained so much that it was so full and alive. Seeing the overcast, drizzly skies right now, I had no doubt she was correct. But I loved the other seasons too. Even the current gray and moody skies that came with fall and winter.

Strangely, it always gave me a sense of peace.

But this place . . . Golden Oaks . . . It was what I imagined heaven would look like. I'd never seen anything so well thought out. Every section of the center had been planned to perfection and immaculately maintained.

The waning winter sun shone through the windshield, warming my face a bit. I closed my eyes, only to smile when I heard classical music coming from somewhere to my left. I opened my eyes and glanced over to see a man in a nearby dressage arena, perfectly executing an extended trot on a bright-bay warmblood.

I immediately recognized him when he raised his head. "Felix Knighton," I said, and Sage whipped her head toward him too.

"Like silk," Sage said a few seconds later, awe in her voice. "He moves like silk on that stallion." As if he felt us talking about him, he looked directly our way, showcasing the large scar that took up half of his face. Felix had been known as the most handsome of the Knighton men—Jasper and his three cousins, Forrest, Felix, and Atticus—until an accident marred one side of his face and he turned in on himself, completely pulling back from the social side of our sport.

"He's the most beautiful dressage rider I've ever seen," I said, and Mila nodded.

"He's out here every day. He's a better rider now than he ever was before his accident, and he was impossibly good then," Mila said. We passed the dressage practice arenas, and my heart beat in double time when the one-point-six-meter-high show jumps begin to boast their bright colors in the distance. Seeing a well-designed course had an almost Pavlovian effect on me. There wasn't a jump or course I wouldn't try to clear. I was fearless that way.

"The grooms and yard staff all bunk in the staff quarters just over there," Mila said, pointing to the most stunning "bunk-houses" I'd ever seen. "But you both will be staying in the Orchard Cottages." Mila smiled dreamily. "They're beautiful, and just up here." Suddenly, a large mansion began to crest just over a hill of trees to our right.

"What. The. Fuck," Sage muttered, only to add, "Holy shit!" when the full might of the mansion came into view.

Mila giggled. "That's where the Knighton family lives."

"All of them?" I asked.

"Yes. As far as I know they have a wing each," Mila said. "But they're very private people, and the staff and riders don't go inside."

"Stuck-up assholes," Sage uttered under her breath, and I elbowed her in her ribs before Mila overheard. Sage folded her arms across her chest. Her grudge against Atticus Knighton consumed her.

When we were eighteen, Atticus came to Silvercrest to train and compete. The minute they met, they were a collision of flames, always bickering and sniping at one another. It became their favorite game. To be near them was to feel their undeniable chemistry. But when Atticus left my aunt's stable yard to return home, he took all the affection Sage had toward him too. Weeks after he left, when I couldn't take her sullen mood anymore, I dragged her to the hay loft, and we drank our weight in wine. Drunk off her ass, Sage admitted she and Atticus had fucked. When she found out he had fucked another visiting rider only days later, her want for him turned into blind hatred.

I regarded Atticus as a friend back then. I still did. What he did to Sage was wrong, and I wanted to punch him for hurting her. But she was eighteen, and he was only a year older. We were all stupid teens back then. But if you crossed Sage, you would never be granted her forgiveness. And he never had.

I studied the mansion. It certainly looked big enough for a football team of people to live there and barely see one another if they didn't want to. It was so stunning, like Downton Abbey or some period drama, all ancient gray stone, diamond-patterned lead windows, and English ivy devouring its facade. Four towering, ornate columns stood like protective sentinels at the entrance, and an old oak, arched door led the way inside.

"Here we are," Mila said, and I tore my gaze from the mansion to look to my right. A wide smile immediately pulled on my lips. A small grouping of sweet cottages was tucked into what looked like an orchard of fruit trees. Their branches were bare now, but I could only imagine what they'd look like when they were in full bloom.

The cluster of homes were quaint and beautiful and made me think of my childhood books by Beatrix Potter. But these "cottages" were far from small. They were all interlinked, with the same diamond-patterned lead windows, gray stone, and ivy-covered walls as the main house. They were like miniature models of the real thing.

"You each get a home to yourself—bedroom, bathroom, et cetera, but there's a huge communal kitchen and dining area that is the heart of all four properties. For now, there's just you both residing here, but we are expecting two more female riders later in the season."

"Who?" Sage asked, bluntly as always.

Mila smiled excitedly. "Clara Thompson, the great British dressage rider, and Lenora Ackland from the British eventing team."

"We know Lenora, somewhat," Sage said with an approving nod. "She's good people."

It was true. Lenora had been at some of the same training facilities as Sage and me over the past few years. But we had never met Clara Thompson, though I knew who she was. The professional horse world was small once you were in it—a goldfish bowl. Clara was the most beautiful rider to watch in the dressage arena, the only exception being Felix Knighton.

The ATV carrying our luggage pulled up behind us, and the young men who met us at the gatehouse took them to two adjoined cottages. Victoria jumped out of their ATV too. "Sage, you're in Snowdrop," she said and pointed to her cottage. "And Hallie, you're in Buttercup." A small smile pulled on my lips at the cottages' cute names. I glanced at the others, seeing name plates on their respective doors reading "Daisy" and "Daffodil."

Victoria opened the doors, then handed us our keys. "Both have been stocked with new towels, fresh sheets, and toiletries. The kitchen has been stocked with food and drinks too." Sage nudged my arm with hers and shot me an approving nod. In our careers, we'd had some accommodations that could be deemed just above wild camping. I should've known that Knighton Equestrian would only provide the best for their riders. Nothing this famous family did was inferior.

"We put in grocery orders twice a week, so please just fill out the form in the kitchen when you want to add something." Victoria reached into her pocket. She pulled out two car keys. "You also each have a car while you are here." Victoria nudged her head forward, gesturing to a couple of brand-new black Land Rover Defenders in the parking spots to the side of the cottages.

"Now, that's what I'm fucking talking about!" Sage said and rushed across the courtyard to open her car and slide in. She laughed out loud when she realized she was in the passenger seat, then climbed out. "Forgot y'all drive on the other side over here!"

I snorted with humor too, and Sage flicked her middle finger at me before rounding the car and getting in on the correct side.

"Hallie," Victoria said. "Please." She gestured to the now-open door of my cottage.

"Thank you," I said, and entered. The first thing that hit me was the sweet scent of vanilla, then the old-fashioned paneled walls. "Wow," I said, and walked to the living area. A large open redbrick fireplace took up most of one wall, with a huge, comfortable-looking beige-colored couch and TV against the other. Scenic paintings adorned the lavender-painted walls. The floor was made of lightly colored flagstones that carried throughout the cottage. My bedroom upstairs was vast, with a four-poster bed and a large floor-to-ceiling window overlooking one of the grazing paddocks. The field was free of horses right now, but I could only imagine how idyllic it would be when it was full.

I made my way back down the stairs to the kitchen. I couldn't help but laugh when Sage came rushing through from another door (clearly the one to her cottage). "Well, hell's bells, Hals! This place is fucking insane!"

Sage opened every cupboard in the cream-colored, Shaker-style kitchen that was the size of most people's entire homes. There was a huge skylight above us, flooding the place with daylight. Then she came over and looped her arm over my shoulders. "I think this'll do, Hals. What do you think?"

"It'll do," I said sarcastically, as Victoria knocked on the door behind us and peeked her head through.

"Everything okay?" she asked.

"More than," I said.

Victoria smiled proudly, and I could see just how much she loved this place and her job. That was always a good sign, especially as some equestrian facilities could be toxic places. No one would believe half the shit that went down on the professional circuits. Bitching and fighting were just par for the course. "I'll let you both rest and get settled in today. Then tomorrow, we'll have you meet Leon and assign your horses for the season."

"Yes! Bring it on!" Sage said, rubbing her hands together.

"Perfect," I said too, and my heart started racing.

Leon Turner was, hands down, the best show jumping trainer in the world, and I'd be lying if I said he wasn't the main reason Sage and I agreed to ride Knighton horses. He had been the one to personally recruit us. I'd been told by my trainer in the US that the Knightons gave Leon carte blanche on recruitment. If he said you were worthy of a Knighton horse, no one questioned it, even if two women from the wrong side of the tracks got the most coveted spots.

As potential future Team USA riders, both Sage and I had opportunities to ride American-bred horses at some of the best facilities in the States. But like many riders, we were given the chance to train abroad with other trainers. For us, it was Leon Turner who had asked for us personally. That wasn't a chance anyone gave up.

Both Sage and I had already dominated the Under-25s international Grand Prix circuits. But now we'd aged into the big leagues. We were young and hungry, and we wanted to be the best, and Leon Turner, along with Knighton horses, was the trainer to help us achieve that.

"Mila and Horatio will be here in the morning to collect you," Victoria said, then hesitated at the doorway. "I truly am so excited that you're here. You're both some of my favorite riders, and I cannot wait to see you soar even higher."

Victoria exited the cottage, leaving me with a contented, warm glow running through my veins. Sage kissed me on my cheek and leaned her head against mine as we took in the pretty view. "Five-Star Grand Prix champions and Olympic golds are coming our way, Hals. I can just feel it."

I was normally much more cautious than Sage when it came to achievements and our future, never wanting to jinx things. But something about this place, this equestrian "Field of Dreams," made me feel that was possible too.

Chapter Two

Jasper

Golden Oaks, Surrey

"Nothing?" I asked.

"Nothing new," Phillip, my very highly paid private investigator, said through the phone. "But we'll keep digging. We'll get there, Mr. Knighton—we always do in the end. Something will surface."

"Thank you, Phillip," I said and hung up the phone. I threw it down on my desk and leaned back in my seat. The leather of my chair creaked beneath me, and I tipped my head back and closed my eyes. The smoke of last night's cigar still permeated the air, doing nothing to calm the anger burning in my chest.

Another week and another set of unanswered questions. I took a deep breath and opened my eyes. My father's face smiled down at me from his picture above the fire opposite my desk. I met him square in the eyes and said, "I don't know where to go from here, Dad." A lump clogged my throat, and I had to clear it just to rasp out, "I feel like I'm failing you." I rubbed my forehead, trying to keep a hold on my emotions. "I feel like I'm failing the whole family."

Of course, my father didn't appear to console me, to reassure me. Because he was taken from us two years ago. It was deemed an accident by those at the scene, but anyone who saw that wreck knew it wasn't. My father was killed, and I had no idea who did it—or why.

I steepled my hands and stared down at the ever-thickening file I'd been studying for months. Pictures and leads that ultimately had only led to dead ends. Whoever was doing this to us was good and knew how to cover their tracks to perfection.

I closed my eyes again. I was so tired, but insomnia was now my closest friend. I'd have given anything to sleep through just one single night. I spent every hour of every day like a bloody ghost, running through every person that could have a vendetta against my family in my head. (News flash: There were *a lot*.) Questioning how and why somebody was doing this and how the fuck I could stop it.

A knock sounded on my office door, ripping me from my downward spiral. I sat up and ran my hand through my hair, trying to at least look like I'd had some shut-eye of late. "Come in," I called, already knowing who it'd be.

As predicted, Forrest, my cousin and best friend, came through. He silently moved to the bar at the side of the room and poured us both two fingers of Oban, our favorite whisky.

Forrest sat down opposite me and placed my glass down on the desk. "Nothing new?" he asked. I shook my head and knocked back my whisky in one.

"Shit, Jas," he said and tutted at me like I was a misbehaving toddler. "Respect the scotch, will you? You're not a heathen."

I rubbed my lips together as the Oban burned the back of my throat. I blew out a long sigh. "I don't know where the fuck to go from here, Cousin." It pained me to admit that. But this was Forrest. The one person I did open up to. He was the closest to me in age and a lot like me in personality too. We grew up together, side by side, and he'd pretty much been keeping me going these past couple of years when everything went to shit. It wasn't like he hadn't seen some hard times with his parents too.

Forrest sat back in his chair. "You need to step away from this for a while, Jas. It's consuming you."

I glared at my cousin. "My father is dead. My sister is injured, one of our best horses was drugged, and I just know something else is coming our way. So forgive me if I don't want to 'step away for a while,' Forrest."

"*Don't*, Jas. Don't act like I don't give a fuck," he said measuredly, but his green eyes flashed with anger. Forrest may have looked calm and collected on the outside, but he had the bite of a pit bull if he was pushed too far.

All ire seeped from my body, and I sagged in my seat. "I'm sorry," I said, and meant it. Forrest's eyes lost their heat too. "I haven't slept in what feels like months, and I'm all in my head."

Forrest leaned forward. "You don't sleep ever, Jas. I see you haunting the grounds at every hour God sends. You never see your family anymore. Barely show your face in public. You look a mess." Forrest flicked his hand at my overgrown stubble and unkempt, crinkled clothing. "And worse, you've completely given up on everything you love, on any kind of *life*, just to chase answers we may *never* get."

"Not again, Forrest. I'm sick of hearing it," I said.

Forrest shook his head, exasperated, and I knew he was about to let me have it. "You were at the top of the game! You were already smashing what people believed were unbreakable records. You were going to be the greatest show jumper of *all time. All* time, Jas. Only to throw it away for seclusion in this depressing, dark office, which has turned into your personal prison." Forrest sighed. "You want answers. We *all* do. But we don't want to lose you in the process." Forrest's green eyes bored into me. "We've already lost far too much."

My stomach dropped. My family were my everything. And I knew I was theirs too. But I just couldn't step away from finding out who was after us. I just . . . *couldn't* . . .

I was doing all of this for *them*, for *all* of us here at Golden Oaks, so no one got hurt again. I was the eldest of us Knightons, the head of the family. It was my job to be sure everyone was protected. As much as I wish it didn't, my jumping career paled in comparison to that.

My cousin didn't speak for a spell, but then said, "Let Atticus ride Lord Henry, at least." I quickly refocused on Forrest. He was all seriousness now. He held up his hands in reaction to my angered gaze. "I know he's your baby. But he's too good to just sit in the stable or graze in the fields. Ben is doing his best keeping him fit, but that horse is a titan amongst horses, and he deserves to achieve the accolades he was bred for. Don't take him down with you, Cousin. He loves the show ring, and you're depriving him of what he was born to do."

Silence stretched awkwardly between us. Atticus wasn't touching Henry. My youngest cousin was an incredible show jumper, but he was *not* touching my stallion. As if he'd read my mind, Forrest's shoulders sagged. He waited a few tense seconds before he finished off his whisky and stood. He was only an inch shorter than my six-three height. Otherwise, we looked more like paternal twins than cousins. We both had dark-brown hair, short at the sides and longer on top, and scruff on our cheeks and chins. Though admittedly, Forrest looked a damn sight better than me these days. Only our eye color differed.

"Let's go," he said. I raised a questioning eyebrow at him. "It's time you came to family dinner again. It's been too long you've holed yourself up in here, and we're all done with it. You're coming to family dinner to see your cousins and sister, and you don't have a choice." He smirked, trying to break the heavy mood. "And open a damn window. This place stinks of cigars and brooding man."

I laughed, and the action felt strange in my chest. It was true; I hadn't attended family dinner for some time. In fact, I couldn't remember the last time I did. Even with all our touring schedules, whoever was in town would make time for family dinner. It was something our parents had instilled in us growing up. Yet even though I was mostly in town these days, I hadn't attended a single one in God knew how long.

I got to my feet and walked around my desk. Forrest's hand landed on my shoulder. He waited for me to meet his eyes. When I did, he said, "Stop taking all this on by yourself, Jas. We're *Knightons*. We go through the good and the bad *together*. Let us help carry the burden."

I smirked at my cousin. "Firstly, never say anything that cheesy to me again. We're British and that shit doesn't land." Humor flashed in Forrest's wide grin. "And secondly, I'm the eldest here. Stop trying to come for my title and know your place."

Forrest shook his head, understanding my dry humor. "I don't want it, Jas. Believe me. And I'm only one year below your thirty-two, so let's not pretend you have the wisdom here. I'm the brightest of us all, if you'll recall. I was accepted into Mensa at age six, unlike your underachieving self."

I headed for the door to the office and opened it, ushering my "bright" cousin through. I immediately caught a glimpse of myself in the large hallway mirror that hung opposite my office. "Shit," I said, as I ran my hands over my too-long scruff.

I looked terrible.

"That's what I'm *saying*!" Forrest said emphatically, and I fell into step beside him. "You're more grizzly mountain man than English country gentleman these days."

I rolled my eyes, feeling a flicker of calmness settle in my chest. Forrest was good for me like that. Pulling me out of the darkness. All my family had that effect on me. I'd just stopped letting them in quite some time ago and allowed the darkness to pull me down.

"How's training going?" I asked Forrest.

"Good." He nodded his head, but he didn't elaborate. I was sad to say that I hadn't kept up with his practices. Forrest was an international five-star eventer—show jumping, dressage, and cross country. And he was consistently at the top of the league.

"You need to come and watch me when the season starts," Forrest said. "Get out of the house for a while. Lady Aurelia is phenomenal. You need to see her." Lady Aurelia was Forrest's pride and joy, a nine-year-old dark-bay Dutch Warmblood mare who had been bred from his father's prized stallion.

"I'll try," I said, but the lie sat heavily in my stomach. The truth was, I couldn't bear seeing anyone from the horse world these days. Horse sports were our family's entire lives, our *livelihoods*, but I was honest enough with myself to say that the industry was as toxic as it was beautiful, and the gossip mill was unrivaled. I knew I was top of conversation in most circles. Even the many scandals that arose in our sport couldn't compete with my quick exit from the circuit and my past year and a half of reclusiveness.

Just stepping foot out at a show, Forrest's or not, would garner more attention than I could be arsed with. That, and it physically hurt me to be there and not compete. Jumping was all I knew. Not doing it anymore felt like a piece of my soul had been ripped away from me. Seeing people jumping, or even just riding, was like being repeatedly shot in the chest.

The smell of tonight's dinner drifted down the hallway, shaking me from my depressing thoughts. Our home was stately and boasted the most incredible and historic banquet hall. But we cousins preferred our small, informal family/dining room for family dinners. One where we didn't have to shout down the table to talk to one another. We might be rich and privileged, but we weren't pompous arseholes having five-course, silver-service meals every night.

I was sad to say that nerves swam in my stomach as we approached the family room. Forrest side-eyed me at the door. "They're your blood," he reminded me, and I exhaled a long, calming breath. He thought I was nervous because I'd kept myself away for months. But it was more than that. Every time I saw Atticus's smiling face, or worse, Felix's scarred one, I felt like I was letting them down. Even worse when it came to Genny. I could barely meet her eyes without wanting to drop to my knees and beg her forgiveness.

Forrest walked through to the dining room, and keeping my head down, I followed.

"Well, I bloody never!" I heard Atticus say in his loud-as-fuck voice. "Is this a ghost I'm seeing? A mirage? Felix, am I dehydrated?" I looked up to see Atticus dramatically grab hold of Felix's arm. "Did I take a kick to the head at training today? Did Barnaby throw me and I'm in some kind of trauma-induced dream?"

"All right, Atti," I said and shook my head. "For fuck's sake. You can shut up now."

His brown eyes danced as he flew across the room, wrapping his arms around me and lifting me off the floor. "It's good to see you, Jas!" he said.

"Put me down, you dick, before I make you," I said.

Atticus lowered me down, but his famous, too-charming grin remained. "Ah, *there* he is! It's not a good day unless you're threatening me!"

Despite my best efforts, I huffed a laugh at my ridiculous youngest cousin. Forrest and I leaned more serious. Atticus? He was a shit-stirrer, a joker, and a tornado of energy, all rolled into one.

Atticus leaned forward and pressed a kiss to my head. Being the youngest, he was also—*annoyingly*—the tallest of us all. He was six-five, with dark floppy hair and eyes so brown they looked almost black. To say he was a ladies' man was an understatement. He was as much a horny stallion as the treasured horse he rode.

Atticus moved before me, really studying me. "Shit, Jas. You look awful." He smiled wider. "You've lost your looks." He clenched his fists. "Yes! That means even more pussy for me."

Forrest sputtered. "If you're not careful, little brother, your dick will fall off from overuse," he said, slapping his younger brother on the back of his head on the way past. "And keep your sex life to yourself. You humping away breathlessly over a line of random women is an image I never want to think of."

Atticus flexed his arm, showing his muscles through his tightly fitted shirt. "Breathlessly?" Atticus questioned, scowling. "I'm the fittest here, in both looks *and* endurance." He smiled widely. "And I'll have you know I fuck like a god."

Forrest ran a hand down his face. He looked to Felix, who was watching in quiet amusement from his place leaning against the stone fireplace. "Get your boy under control before I muzzle him, Felix."

Felix shook his head and walked toward me. Atticus and Felix were as close as Forrest and I were. Felix held out his hand to me and pulled me close when I offered mine back. With a tight hug, he said, "I'm glad to see you, Jas. Missed you."

I pulled back and studied Felix. His hair was longer these days, falling to his chin in waves and shielding his face. He was as big and imposing as ever. His scar ran down the entire left side of his cheek. He was lucky he hadn't lost his eye in the accident. Instead, our already introverted middle cousin grew quieter, and we hadn't been able to bring him back out of his shell.

The door that led to the family kitchen opened, and Geraldine, our housekeeper, popped her head through. "Five minutes, boys!" she shouted, then her eyes widened when they landed on me. "Jasper! It's so lovely to see you, sweetheart!" Her smile was warm and made me feel like a child again.

Geraldine was in her midseventies and had long since been asked to retire with a very comfortable retirement package. But we *Knightons* were her entire life, and she refused to leave. I'd be lying if that didn't make me happy. This place would lose its heart without her.

"Looking good, Geraldine," I said.

She came toward me, batting away the compliment. She hugged me close, then kissed me on my cheek. In her usual blunt way, she said, "You need a shower and a good shave, my boy. You look terrible."

I laughed, then nodded. "I'll get right on that, Geraldine." She nodded happily, then rushed back into the kitchen. At this point, Geraldine was the only parental figure most of us had left. My uncle Edward—Forrest, Felix, and Atticus's dad—died of cancer when we were younger. Their mother now resided in Jersey, one of the Channel Islands, and rarely came to visit. She had never liked it here at Golden Oaks and actively avoided it.

"Jas?" My heart stuttered as my sister's voice came from behind me, only to fall when I saw her enter the room in her wheelchair.

"Genny," I said, and rushed over to her. She held out her arms, and I wrapped myself around her.

Mouth meeting my ear, she said, "I'm just too tired from physio to use my crutches tonight. Don't panic." I squeezed my sister hard, then pulled back. "I could read the worry in your face."

I blew out a long breath. I would never look at Genevieve and not feel guilty, but I was happy she was improving with her daily physio. Her chances of walking again unaided were fifty-fifty. But as I looked at her light-brown hair and blue eyes, she looked really well. I wasn't sure if that meant anything. We Knightons were good at masking our pain.

"Here we go!" Geraldine's voice came through the kitchen. I helped Genny take her place at the table beside me. My cousins all sat on the opposite side. I glanced to the chair beside Genny.

"Where is . . ." I went to say, when the door to the dining room opened and Leon rushed through.

"Sorry I'm late!" he said and quickly took his seat next to Genny. He dropped a kiss on her cheek, then did a double take when he saw me at the table too. "Jasper!" he said and leaned behind Genny to offer me his hand. When I shook it, he said, "It's so good to see you, man." His eyes brightened. "Ready for training again yet? It's not too late for this season."

I laughed at his vain attempt to get me back on the team. Since I'd stepped back, he hadn't once stopped trying to get me back on board. "I'm not coming back, Leon." I pointed at Forrest, who was busy yanking the serving bowl of mashed potatoes back off Atticus before he consumed the lot. "This one forced me to come to dinner."

Forrest raised an eyebrow at me but was completely unapologetic by the shrug of his shoulders. Genny's hand landed on my arm. "I'm glad he did." Her eyes looked sad when she said, "I miss you. We all do."

I leaned over and kissed the side of her head. Genny then turned to Leon. "Were you busy today?"

"I've been organizing the new show jumping horses for tomorrow. This season's riders have arrived, and we'll assign them their mounts in the morning." I listened to Leon, trying to ignore the pang of jealousy in my chest. "I've been studying past competitions to observe the riders' styles, see anything that we particularly need to work on." Leon nodded his head enthusiastically. "They look good. I think they'll be a great addition to our team."

Leon was the best show jumping trainer on the planet, bar none. He had been here at Golden Oaks since a teen as a boarding rider and was an excellent competitor. But he chose the trainer route, and I thank God he did. I was the rider I was because of him. Same for Genny, Atticus, and Forrest.

"Hallie Oakley and Sage—"

"Miller," Atticus blurted, finishing my sentence for me. All eyes fell on my youngest cousin. A wide smile stretched on his face. "Sage fucking Miller."

I frowned at my cousin's reaction. I had also signed off on Hallie and Sage to be the new faces of Knighton Equestrian, the apparel company I had started years back when I was still competing. I had money that I had inherited, generational wealth that comfortably sat in the billions, but my ever-growing personal brand had made me a multimillionaire in my own right. Hallie Oakley and Sage Miller were two of the most impressive show jumpers on the scene right now. When Leon told me they were coming to ride for us, my artistic director at Knighton Equestrian had convinced me to sign them for modeling my new products too.

I had no idea what they were like as riders, or even what they looked like. I'd been too preoccupied to look. Thankfully, I had a rock-solid team around me who had run Knighton Equestrian for me the past few months whilst I'd been consumed with other things.

"Wait," I said, suddenly recalling an infatuation Atticus had years ago with an American rider during his summer abroad. "Is she the one . . . ?"

"He's obsessed with," Forrest said, in a tone that suggested he was sick of hearing her name. "Yes."

Atticus kept smiling, unbothered by Forrest's dry jab.

Leaning forward, Atticus said, "Sage Miller is living fire, Jas. And she burns with hatred for *me*, and me only." He sighed, but as though the thought turned him on, not upset him. "She's fucking magnificent."

"But back to why they are here," Leon said, a look of censure aimed at Atticus. "Sage Miller is the riskiest rider I've seen in a long while. She's fearless and rides each course like she's storming into battle. Strong, bold, and brave." Atticus nodded in agreement, but his eyes were hooded. I wanted nothing to do with whatever the fuck was happening between them. It sounded like a shit show.

"And Hallie?" I asked.

Leon's face immediately lit up. It was hard to impress Leon, and I could already see stars in his eyes over the younger American rider. "Elegant, poetic, graceful. She rides like she was grown from a saddle. When she jumps, she looks like she's soaring. She has the best seat of anyone I've seen." He gave me a sidelong glance. "Well, *almost*." I waved him off. Leon appeared lost in thought, then said, "A little rebellious, perhaps. Mutuals of ours have described her as stubborn and immoveable when she wants to do something her way." Leon shrugged. "But I respect that."

"She's your favorite, then?" Genny asked. "I've competed against her before in the Under-25s. She—actually, *both* Hallie and Sage—are stunning riders. Hallie always stood out to me as a little wild and untamed, but in all the best ways. Not your typical competitor, that's for sure."

I covered my sister's hand with my own, giving it a slight squeeze. I knew it was probably because I was her brother, but I heard the slight shake in her voice when she mentioned competing. Genny's whole world had been jumping until her accident. In the blink of an eye, the horse world lost both of us from the circuit. And my father too, who had done more for this sport than anyone in recent British history.

Genny gave me a tight smile, and Leon went on to hold court. As we ate, he told us of his goals for this season and just how impressive our team was on paper. By the time Geraldine had served us dessert, I felt better than I had in a while. A little calmer. But I wasn't naive. I knew it was a temporary reprieve from the inner demons that had now become my closest companions.

As we all stood, one by one, my cousins said their good-nights. Forrest hung around until it was just Genny, him, and me. He put his hand on my shoulder. "Was that okay?"

"More than," I said, and pulled him in for a quick hug.

"No more hiding away, okay?" he said when he pulled back, eyes boring into mine, telling me he meant it.

"Yeah," I said. Then sighed.

"Especially over this next week," he added. My stomach fell. I nodded but found myself unable to speak.

Genny was silent as she watched us. Sensing she wanted to speak to me alone, Forrest kissed my sister on her cheek, then said, "I'll leave you both to catch up. See you tomorrow." I watched my cousin leave the family room and wondered again what I would do without them all in my life.

"Come sit beside me," Genny said, and patted the seat that was right by where she'd moved her wheelchair. I sat down and held her hand. "How are you coping with his anniversary coming up?"

The food I'd just eaten curdled in my stomach. "I imagine how you feel too," I said, and watched Genny's pretty face cloud with sadness.

Genny sighed, then said, "No, Jas. You certainly feel it more." I stilled and studied my little sister. She was six years younger than me, and I'd been her self-appointed protector since the day she was born. Even now she was twenty-six, I couldn't shake that responsibility. Genny held my hand tighter. "I miss Dad. More than anything. But we must move on, Jas. You've been living a Groundhog Day for far too long now."

I shook my head. "I can't. Too much has happened. Someone is after us, Genny." I laughed without humor. "They *attacked* you. Drugged Lady Dahlia. You both still have a long recovery ahead of you." A year and a half ago, Genny's horse was drugged in Saint-Tropez during the Sandings Grand Prix Tour. Lady Dahlia went down midjump and landed on Genny, fracturing my sister's spine and a multitude of bones. In that moment, I thought I'd lost my sister. The investigation revealed that someone had pumped the horse so full of ketamine it's a wonder she could even see the fences. Lady Dahlia hadn't recovered well and now couldn't be ridden, as she was so traumatized by the accident. Genny could barely walk, and we had no idea who had done it to us. To her.

"I know, Jas," Genny said with a slight edge to her voice. Her eyes welled with tears. "But even so, I didn't want you to sacrifice everything you loved because of it." She sat up straight. "Do you know how guilty I feel over that? You love riding. Being a horseman *is* you. And you stopped because of me and became reclusive and miserable. A shadow of your former self."

"No," I said, shaking my head, but those words hit me like a crowbar to the chest. "This is *my* choice, Gen. I'm the one who decided to devote my time to all this. There should be no guilt on your part. It's something I feel compelled to do."

Genny lowered her head and said, "I just want this all over with, Jas. And I want you to start living again."

I brought my sister in for a tight hug and said, "I will. When I finally find out who is trying to hurt us." Genny's shoulders sagged in defeat, but I wouldn't be deterred. Genny wanted me to leave it to the police. But this was the horse world. This sport made people exceptionally wealthy. The crazy shit people did to rivals was on another level, and the lengths people would go to bring them down were insane.

And we were now the target.

When I pulled back, I said, "Come on, I'll walk you back to your rooms."

Genny shook her head, just as Geraldine came through the door to the kitchen with a tray of popcorn and drinks. "No need," Genny said, face brightening. "Me and Geraldine have got a night of binge-watching *Love Island* ahead of us." I laughed as they moved to the sofas. I helped Genny get settled, then turned to leave with a wave.

"Night, guys," I said.

"Jas?" Genny called out. I turned back to my sister. "Don't be on your own tomorrow, okay? Come and find me, and we'll get through it together."

I gave her a reassuring smile. "I will," I promised, knowing that was a blatant lie. I left her and Geraldine to their trash TV. As I entered the hallway, I let my head fall back against the door and exhaled a long breath. The lightness that had filled me over dinner vanished the moment I was left alone with my thoughts.

My feet itched to leave the house. Moving down the hallway, I made my way to the back exit through the mudroom. I threw on my flat cap, wellies, and wax jacket and stepped into the freezing night. I let the ice-cold wind hit my face and began the moonlit walk to the only place I ever felt whole. The place no one, not even Forrest, knew I still went to. The only place that reminded me I was still alive.

Chapter Three

Hallie

I squeezed Sage's arm in excitement as two horses were led into the large indoor arena. Mila held one, and a man I assumed to be Horatio, Sage's groom, held another. When they came to a stop before us, Horatio waved at Sage. He was tall and slim, with the most attractive face. All blond hair and blue eyes and wide smiles.

Sage went to go and introduce herself when a man I instantly recognized came rushing into the arena.

Leon Turner.

"Sorry I'm late!" he said, his southern English accent thick. He was dressed in a Knighton Equestrian–branded beanie, a heavy barn jacket, black breeches, and tall riding boots and gloves. He immediately stopped before us. I rubbed my gloved hands together just to feel some warmth in my fingers; the English winter was no joke. This Florida girl was struggling.

"Sage," Leon said, shaking her hand. "It's great to meet you. I'm Leon."

Sage laughed. "We know," she said, and shook his hand back. "Honored to be here, sir." Leon nodded his head in acknowledgment.

Then he moved to me. Leon's smile was wide. "Hallie Oakley, I'm so happy you agreed to join us this season." I shook his hand back.

"The honor is all mine, sir," I said, butterflies whirling in my stomach at having the best trainer in the world standing before us. Was this reality?

Leon then addressed us both. "I've been watching you closely for years. You've done amazing in the Unders, and if we work hard, I know we can get you to the top of the game in the Overs." Leon stepped back to show our grooms, who were still standing with the horses.

"I take it you've met Mila and Horatio?" Leon asked.

"Mila, yes, but not Horatio," I said. Horatio handed the reins of the chestnut mare to Mila, and he came toward us. He shook my hand first. "Hallie. Huge fan," he said, his accent holding a strong lilt.

"Irish," he said, pointing at himself, clearly reading my mind.

"Nice to meet you," I said, and then Horatio turned to Sage. Horatio held out his hand, but Sage wrapped him up in a tight hug.

"No formalities, Horatio. You and I are going to be close friends." Horatio smiled, and his cheeks blushed at Sage's enthusiasm.

"I'm excited to be working with you," he said, then went back to hold the mare. I winked at Mila, and she smiled back with the same excitement. This was a huge moment for us all. We were meeting our horses. The second half to our competitive unit.

Leon nodded to Horatio, and Sage's groom threw on his hat and moved to the mounting block, stepping gracefully into the saddle. Immediately, the chestnut mare began prancing on the spot, filled to the brim with energy. Horatio was clearly a skilled rider, but he struggled to hold her back as they headed to the rail. His arm muscles flexed with the strength he needed to keep her fiery spirit contained.

"Lady Seraphina is a warrior queen," Leon said. "Nine years old, seventeen-three, and an Irish Warmblood. She's from one of the strongest lineages in our stud." Horatio turned the corner of the arena, and it took everything he had to hold Seraphina back from taking off and him losing control. "She needs a rider who can match her spirit," Leon said. "One who is fearless but solid." I cast a glance at Sage, whose eyes were locked on the mare.

The inferno in my best friend's dark eyes told me she had already fallen in love.

"Take her over the fence," Leon shouted to Horatio, who moved Seraphina into a canter and headed for the jump that was set up in the middle of the arena. The moment Seraphina saw it, her ears pricked forward, and you could feel the excitement pulsing off her in waves. Horatio had no choice but to let her go. And go she did. Sage gripped my hand as her mare soared over the vertical jump, clearing it with ease.

"As you can see," Leon said to Sage, "Seraphina is your typical chestnut mare. Feisty, independent—"

"And fucking insane," Sage finished, just as Seraphina tried to throw Horatio off her back in an attempt to jump again. Sage tilted her chin. "Just like me." Sage released my hand and turned to Leon. "I love her."

He smirked. "The minute you signed on with us, Sage, I knew she was yours." Leon shook his head. "We haven't had a rider yet who can handle her." He pointed at Sage. "Perhaps until you."

Horatio brought Seraphina back over, and Sage was donning her helmet in seconds. As soon as she was on the horse's back, my chest swelled. They looked perfect together. Sage turned Seraphina to the track, and within ten minutes was soaring over the jump, holding the exceptionally strong mare back with perfect precision. When she was done, Sage came over to where we watched.

Her face was flushed, and her eyes were sparkling. "She's my horse," Sage said confidently, and I could see them both in my mind, clearing the Grand Prix circuits and dominating the jump-offs, racking up wins one by one.

Leon patted Seraphina on her neck. One rider and horse pairing down. Then he waved at Mila and turned to me. I watched my groom climb on the dark-bay stallion she'd been holding. "Lord Huxley is a seventeen-two Irish Sport Horse. A stallion. Eight years old. A descendant of Lord Edward, one of the first stallions in the Knighton empire, and one of the most sought-after sires here at Golden Oaks."

"I've read about him," I said, awe in my voice as Mila turned the pretty stallion and kicked him on. He had a black mane and tail and every part of him was lean muscle and pure power.

"He's calm for a stallion but still harnesses superb power in his hind end." I was transfixed as Mila began to trot him, then pushed him into a canter before taking him over the jump. My heart was in my throat as he soared over the fence—as he *flew*. Mila brought him back to me, dismounted, and handed me the reins.

I moved in front of Huxley and let him breathe in and out, taking in my scent. "You are a beauty," I said, pressing my forehead to his. I closed my eyes and stroked his wide cheeks. Canyon, my best friend from Texas, always told me to get to know the horse I was working with before I got on. To bond with him. That without that bond, the pairing would never be strong. Canyon was a natural horseman, or what some people referred to as a horse whisperer.

He was the best horseman I knew, so anything he advised, I did.

I stepped back and looked into Huxley's eyes. They were a deep brown framed by long dark lashes. And they were kind. Goose bumps broke out all over my body. I didn't know why, but some gut instinct I harbored told me deep down that this gentleman would look after me if I looked after him. I ran my palm over his topline and down his side. I laid my hand over his heart, closing my eyes as I felt it beat. I smiled when it was strong and steady under my touch. Moving back to Huxley's face, I pressed my forehead to his again and exhaled a long, slow breath.

"Nice to meet you, Huxley."

Mila gently handed me my hat, watching me closely as she did so. Clearly, my somewhat unorthodox introduction to Huxley had fascinated her. I would need to speak to Mila soon. I was a hands-on rider and liked to do much of the warm-ups and prep myself. I knew that wasn't common in this industry, and I'd gotten many a side-eye or degrading whisper on the circuit over the years for lunging my horses myself, dressed in my favorite cowboy boots, barn jacket, and Stetson. I didn't care. The cowgirl in me wouldn't have it any other way. I was here for the horses, not the pomp and ceremony.

"Have a good ride," Mila said.

I squeezed her arm, then used the mounting block to get on Huxley's back. The minute I did, I felt the strength of the stallion beneath me but sensed the calmness within him too. Huxley was a thinker, he was intelligent. He wasn't bottled fire like Seraphina. He was controlled and measured and exactly the kind of horse I loved to ride.

I gently kicked him on and smiled when we moved easily into a trot, then a steady canter. Riding Huxley was like being taken along a lazy river, relaxing and smooth, but you could feel the strength swirling under the surface. A current that could be too strong if not respected.

Turning to the jump, I slackened the reins and let Huxley fly. A low laugh slipped from my throat as we left the ground and landed softly, easily clearing the fence, and I kept my seat perfectly. I pulled Huxley to a reluctant halt in front of Leon, Sage, Mila, and Horatio. Leaning forward, I laid my cheek on Huxley's neck and stroked him a few times. "Good boy," I murmured over and over, loving the sight of Huxley's ears twitching back and forth at the sound of my voice.

"Perfect," Leon said, and I caught the excitement in his eyes. "What did you think?"

"I love him," I said, and Leon nodded his head. I could tell he had felt we were a perfect pair too. Leon showed his might as a trainer with these couplings alone. He'd studied us, and he must have known each of the Knighton horses incredibly well to choose a rider and horse that were so well matched.

"Then we have our pairings," Leon said, and Sage moved Seraphina close to me. "He's beautiful," she said, gesturing to Huxley.

I smiled. "I've never seen a horse suit you more than this firecracker," I said. Almost on cue, Seraphina stomped her front right foot, impatient at standing around doing nothing. This mare needed to constantly move.

Unbothered, Sage ruffled her hands through Seraphina's thick chestnut mane. "Redheads," Sage said, shrugging. "Gotta love 'em!"

I laughed, then spent the next couple of hours on Huxley, getting to know him as he got to know me. And it was strange, because in those two hours, I never felt the bite of the bitter-cold wind once.

I'd never been a good sleeper. I theorized it was from my childhood on the ranch. Early mornings and late nights meant I was used to functioning on very little rest. On top of that, the excitement of meeting Huxley today, mixed with the lingering jet lag, made for a restless night. I glanced at the clock beside me and saw it read just after midnight.

Rather than tossing and turning for hours, I threw back the covers and dressed in thermal jeans, a warm base layer underneath a red plaid shirt, and a thick equine robe. Pulling on my Stetson, gloves, and my well-worn cowboy boots, I slipped out the cottage door and made my way to the barn where Huxley was housed.

Golden Oaks was a stunning equestrian center by anyone's measure, but under the full moonlight, the lawns tipped with frost, and the huge pond with a fountain water feature in the center, it looked truly magical. The grass crunched under my feet as I took the shortcut over two fields to the barn.

The main house was in full view from this vantage point. Low lights glowed on the outside porch, and a few windows were dimly lit behind light drapes. Other than that, the only soundtrack of the night was nocturnal owls in trees and the shuffling of horses' shod feet as they shifted in their stalls, their huffs of breath hitting frozen air.

The barn where Huxley was housed came into view. It was a stunning Dutch barn painted in white with black beams, smaller than many around the property, but big enough to hold around ten horses. Huxley and Seraphina were in this one. An indoor jumping arena was attached to the side for quick access, but that was out of bounds for some reason. We riders used the other arenas just a short walk from the barn.

I entered the barn, and the warmth from the heating system immediately began to thaw my frozen bones. I filled up a feed bowl with chaff and made my way to Huxley's stall. Most of the horses were lying down or sleeping standing up, but as if he sensed my approach, Huxley put his head over the stall door. I smiled as his head bounced up and down in excitement, smelling the food. I opened the stall door and stepped inside, placing the bowl on the ground.

I smoothed my hand over his neck and down to his shoulder under his winter blanket. His coat was shiny and soft, and he felt cozy and warm in his rug. Crouching down, I righted his crooked forelock and said, "I couldn't sleep, baby boy. So I came to see you." His ears twitched at the sound of my voice, but Huxley wouldn't be pulled away from his late-night feast.

Leaving the stall, I then topped up his haylage and made sure his automatic waterer hadn't iced over. I folded my arms over the stall door and watched Huxley. As he finished eating, he moved his head beside mine. I kissed his nose. "We have a tough season ahead of us, Lord Huxley," I said, using his full show name. "But I think we can do it. Don't you agree?" I asked, and as he huffed his nose over my hair, I smiled.

Stepping back, I patted him on the neck. "I'll be back in the morning for training," I said. "Get some rest, beautiful boy."

Not quite ready to go home yet, I turned right instead of my usual left and wandered along the stalls. Every single horse here was exceptional. There were hundreds of stud farms around the world. Aunt Jeanie even had one herself. But when it came to the cream of the crop for international show jumping, dressage, and eventing, there was no higher caliber than a Knighton-bred horse.

Finding myself at a closed door, curiosity got the best of me. The barn was open and airy, and it was clear that something existed behind this door. Never one to mind breaking a few rules, I decided to take a look. Making sure the coast was clear, I slid the barn door open and peeked inside—there were a few more occupied stalls. Perplexed, I wondered why these few horses were housed away from the others, but as I walked along them, it didn't take me long to realize that it was because these were the *Knighton family's* horses.

I first passed by Lord Barnaby, a pitch-black stallion who looked ripped straight from Hades' underworld. He belonged to Atticus. Next was Lady Aurelia, Forrest's five-star-winning eventing horse. After that was Lord Sebastian, Felix's regal dressage horse. But when I turned another corner, everything within me froze, and I lost the ability to breathe.

Staring back at me with pitch-black eyes and a coat so pristine it looked like the purest white silk, was Lord Henry. My heart kicked into a sprint, and a highlight reel whirled in my head of all my teen years spent watching this horse achieve the impossible. Lord Henry flicked his head up and down, seeking my attention, and I moved my feet closer. When I stopped before him, I lifted my hand and in total awe ran it down his thick, muscled neck. It wasn't an exaggeration to say I was starstruck. Most people got flustered at seeing their favorite actor or singer in person. Me? It was this horse. The most impressive one to ever exist.

Lord Henry looked to be still in perfect fitness, even though he'd been retired from the circuit for eighteen months. In fact, he looked like he could join the Sandings Grand Prix tomorrow and dominate in the most prestigious arenas the world had ever seen.

Lord Henry was the lightest gray horse I'd seen in person. He was eighteen hands of pure power, muscle, and grace. I'd always thought that he looked just like Shadowfax from *Lord of the Rings*. Up close, I could confirm that he was his doppelgänger.

"It's an honor to meet you, Lord Henry," I said, removing my huge, robe-style coat now that I'd warmed up, leaving me in my plaid shirt and jeans. I hung my coat and hat on a nearby bridle hook, and then just stood, running my hand gently over Henry's face. "You are the greatest horse I've ever seen jump," I said, like he could understand me.

Canyon would tell me that he could. He was as close to me as a brother, and he always said that horses understood our emotions and tone of voice, rather than the words themselves. I liked to think that was true. I wanted Henry to know how much I admired him.

It was like I was deep in meditation, seeing my dream horse in real life. What I would give to just simply ride him over a course once. Henry stood still and let me fawn over him like the gentleman he was. Suddenly, a loud crash sounded from a nearby door, disturbing the serene moment, making Henry spook and retreat into the safety of his stall. Not wanting to be seen, I ducked into the empty stall beside Henry's, putting myself well out of sight.

The name plate on the stall's door said "Lady Dahlia." My stomach sank. That was Genevieve Knighton's horse, the one that fell on top of her in Saint-Tropez. I hadn't seen or heard of Genny or Dahlia since.

I momentarily wondered where the mare was and whether she was okay when arrhythmic footsteps sounded in this private area of the barn. My heart began to thunder. I wasn't meant to be here, that was for sure. The closed barn door had clearly told me that this section was out of bounds. If I was caught, I knew I'd be in trouble. I pushed myself farther into the stall's corner, trying to blend into the dark.

Then I heard, "Hello, Henry." The softly spoken words were said with a slight slur, but I held my breath when a familiar posh English accent instantly sent goose bumps down my spine.

The sound of Henry's door latch opening echoed off the barn walls, piercing the silence of the night. The shuffling noises of someone stumbling hit me next, then nothing until, "Sorry, boy. I'm not in a good way tonight." Not a part of me moved as I listened to the man I'd idolized for too many years to count talk to his treasured horse.

Jasper Knighton was on the other side of the wall. *The* Jasper Knighton.

"Two years," Jasper said, his voice catching and making my heart squeeze at the pain in his fractured tone. I caught the sound of sloshing liquid hitting glass, then a deep swallow. The smell of whiskey drifted on the frigid air to where I was stood. A long sigh came next. "I haven't been able to find out who it is yet, boy," Jasper said, and the sadness in his voice echoed how I'd felt once too.

After a couple of minutes of quiet, I carefully looked between the metal bars of the stalls and froze when Jasper came into view, dressed in black jeans and a white Aran wool sweater. But what had tears pricking my eyes were his arms wound tightly around Lord Henry's neck. And how the stallion, understanding how broken his rider was, just stood there and let him shatter against his light-gray coat. In one hand, Jasper clutched a half-empty bottle of whiskey. His dark-brown hair was longer than it used to be, falling in messy waves over the side of his face.

Feeling like I was intruding on a very private moment, I began to inch slowly out of the stall. Once in the main section of the barn, I turned to make a beeline for the back door when Henry suddenly moved, the sound of his shod feet scraping on the ground, and Jasper asked, "Is someone there?"

My eyes were wide as I stared straight ahead. My heart began to pound. As much as I didn't mind being caught doing what I shouldn't, I wasn't sure I could face Jasper Knighton. Over the years, I'd built this man up to be a veritable idol in my mind.

The sound of Jasper leaving the stall came from behind me. "Who are you?" His words were slurred, but when I heard the bolt to Henry's stable door open and close, I felt Jasper's approach. Knowing I couldn't get out of explaining myself, I turned slowly and finally met his eyes.

My chest felt like it had been cracked wide open when Jasper Knighton's thirty-two-year-old face came into view. The whites of his eyes were bloodshot from what I presumed was the whiskey, but they were sharp and focused on me. Thick dark scruff covered his cheeks and chin, and his longer hair fell in loose waves over his forehead.

Jasper Knighton was quite literally the handsomest man I had ever seen. He was tall and broad, with lean, toned muscles and a face that was perfect but for a slight scar that ran through his eyebrow from a riding incident years ago. I remembered it like it was yesterday. In Monaco, after jumping a fence, his reins snapped in two—a freak accident. But the buckle of the rein shot upward and sliced through his eyebrow, causing it to bleed. Despite this, Jasper stayed seated on Lord Henry, clearing the last fence of the jump-off by holding on to Henry's platinum mane and trusting his stallion to keep him safe. It won him the Grand Prix. It was the greatest display of horsemanship I'd ever witnessed.

Jasper's lips parted and a slip of breath pushed through, bringing me back to the here and now. My long dark hair was free from a tie and fell to my waist, rather than being held back in my usual daytime braid. His eyes roved over every part of me. I felt completely exposed, but shivers of excitement traveled like lightning over every inch of me.

"You look like an angel," Jasper rasped, and his comment only made me lose my composure even more. "You're stunning."

Years of hero-worshipping this man, and a decade of finding him the most attractive man in the world, came crashing down onto my soul as he uttered those words. I fought the smile that threatened to pull on my lips and could feel heat bursting on my cheeks in a bloom of red blush. I tried to speak, but nerves held me a silent captive.

Jasper stumbled closer. He smelled of a heady mix of sandalwood, mint, and horse. And right now, of whiskey. His eyes glazed as he stepped closer still, and I ceased breathing. Jasper raised his hand and gently took a strand of my hair between his finger and thumb, stroking down its full length.

"So soft," he said, then lost his footing. I reached out and caught him before he hit the floor. Jasper was much heavier than me, but I managed to walk him backward and balance him against the wall between Lord Henry's stall and Lady Dahlia's old one. Like his body couldn't take any more, Jasper slumped to the floor, legs spread out before him, still clutching the whiskey bottle like it was his lifeline. My hands held on to his arms, and the force of his fall had me slumping down before him too. I looked up to see Jasper grinning, and the sight should not have been as hot as it was.

He then proceeded to laugh. My heart skipped at the melodic sound. "Angel," he said, and took hold of my hand. I stared down at our intertwined hands. His were rough and calloused from all his years riding, I presumed. But they were warm and seemed to fit perfectly within mine. "I'm sent an angel to get through tonight, and she finds me like this," he said again, forcing me to meet his dark eyes. He was still chuckling, but the pain that poured from his gaze made my stomach churn in sadness.

Without releasing my hand, Jasper took another swig of his whiskey, shaking his head as he swallowed. He held the bottle out for me, then pulled it back before I could refuse it. "Silly me. Angels don't drink whiskey. Only fucked-up souls do."

"Jasper," I said, searching around me for any sign of help. I needed someone stronger to help me lift him.

"You know my name," he whispered, causing me to face him again. He set his bottle of whiskey down and ran the tips of his fingers down my face. "Such beauty," he said, then stared at my eyes. "Your eyes look turquoise, like a tropical sea."

I tried to stop my foolish heart from melting at his compliments and vowed to keep to the task at hand. "I need to get you home," I said, worried about how the hell that could be done when he could barely walk.

"Not home," Jasper said, firmly, almost panicked, shaking his head and dropping his hand from my face. He took another swig of his whiskey. He looked up to his left at Henry, whose head was over the stable door, watching his owner crumble. "Anyway, *he's* my home," Jasper said, and the softly spoken sentiment brought tears to my eyes. "My proper house is a cell." He huffed a humorless laugh. "A big cell, but a cell nonetheless."

I tried to pull back my hand from his, but he held on to me tighter. "Don't leave me yet, Angel. *Please* . . ." he begged, all playfulness gone and only devastation causing his body to slump. "I . . ." He choked on his words. His head fell back against the wall. "I don't want to be alone tonight."

I warred with what to do. This was *Jasper Knighton*. I had broken into his private stables, and worse than that, he was, in a roundabout way, my employer. I was pretty sure any fraternizing was frowned upon.

"Please, Angel," he begged again, and when I looked to his face, I didn't stand a chance. I'd been this broken once in my life. And I still remembered that pain like it was yesterday.

Pushing my worry aside, I released my hand from Jasper's and got to my feet. Jasper's shoulders slumped, and the sadness that engulfed his perfect face cut through my chest. He watched my every step with his dark-brown eyes, a plea to stay within their chocolate depths.

I rocked on my feet. I needed to leave. I needed to reach the main house and get one of his cousins to help. I didn't know Jasper personally, but I believed he wouldn't want any of the professional riders here seeing him in this state. But then, I didn't want to give away that I'd snuck into the private section of the barn either.

Shit.

Then I looked down at him and saw the silent tears falling down his stubbled cheeks. In that second, I knew I wouldn't be going anywhere.

Jasper watched my every move, like I was gravity, and he was being pulled toward me. Nervously tucking my hair behind my ears, I moved beside him and sat down. I left an inch of space between us, but Jasper shuffled closer until his thigh was flush against my own. The heat from his body almost set me ablaze. More so when Jasper's hand found my own and he entwined our fingers together.

I stared at our joined hands far too long. I blinked a few times just to be sure this was real. I was here, in the Knighton family barn, with Lord Henry behind us and Jasper Knighton holding my hand. I felt like I was hallucinating.

"Did he send you?" Jasper said, pulling me from my thoughts.

I looked up at him, at his beautiful, sorrowful eyes. "Who?" I asked.

Jasper exhaled, his breath deep and stuttered. "Is he disappointed in me? Because I haven't found out who did it?" I frowned, unable to understand what he was talking about. Jasper took another pull of his whiskey. He clutched my hand tighter, then regarded me again. His head tipped to the side. My God, this man was perfect. His face, his stubble, his *accent.*

"Are all angels as beautiful as you?" he asked, and I was sure I wouldn't be able to take much more. Jasper was extremely drunk and somehow believed I wasn't quite real. But hearing him tell me I was beautiful completely derailed me.

"Jasper," I said, and reached for the whiskey with my free hand. "I think you can stop now." Jasper watched me but pulled the bottle to his chest.

"If I stop, the pain comes back," he said, being more candid than I believed he would ever be sober. After all, to him, I was a complete stranger.

"What pain?" I asked, feeling intrusive. But Jasper was broken, and I didn't know how to make it better.

Jasper tapped his hand over his chest. "The pain that lives in here." He placed his hand over his heart. He met my eyes, and his gaze filled with tears. "It never goes away, Angel. It's always here. Bringing me so much pain and guilt that I can't take it." He shook his head as though he was being tortured inside. "And I deserve it. I know I deserve it." He sighed, and his breathing was shaky. Gripping my hand harder, he brought my hand to his cheek, and I stilled. I didn't dare move. Meeting my eyes, he said, "I just wish it would go. Even for a little bit. Just so I could breathe."

"Jasper," I murmured, feeling my eyes filling with tears too. I was soft at heart and couldn't bear to see anyone else in pain. I curled my fingers against his face and ran the tips over his tear tracks, erasing the damp rivulets. He was watching me, like he was waiting for me to save him, to erase the agony in his heart. "You can let go. Don't keep it all inside."

More tears fell over the edges of his eyes, and I wiped them away, all the while Jasper never stopped watching me. "You have an American accent," he said out of the blue. He frowned, and I just knew this was the moment he'd realize I wasn't an angel or a figment of his imagination, but instead his new rider who was grossly overstepping her place.

But Jasper took another drink of the whiskey, then held the bottle out to me. "Take it, Angel," he said, and I released his hand and took the bottle, placing it beside me. Henry blew out a breath above Jasper, and Jasper lifted his hand up to his horse. The stallion nuzzled his nose into Jasper's palm, and I couldn't help but smile. Anyone who didn't believe animals were a true gift from God had clearly never met a horse.

"I'm okay, boy," Jasper slurred. I could see the bone-tiredness overtaking Jasper as he slouched even farther against the wall. He dropped his hand, and then looked to me and added, "I have an American, dark-haired, blue-eyed angel here, looking over me."

I wasn't sure I could take much more of Jasper's compliments without bursting apart, so I got to my feet and retrieved my long robe from the bridle hook. Bending down, I laid it over Jasper. I couldn't move him, and it didn't appear that he could walk, so I thought it was best to make him as comfortable as possible for a night sleeping on the concrete floor.

Glancing to the exit, I made to leave Jasper alone, when familiar fingers wrapped around mine again, and he whispered, "Stay."

I knew I should leave. Everything in my body told me to go now while Jasper was drunk enough that he wouldn't remember me being here. But when he squeezed my fingers again and whispered, "Please, Angel . . ." I was done for.

Rolling my lips together nervously, I sat back down beside Jasper and briefly closed my eyes when he laid his head against my shoulder. The heady scent of sandalwood and mint invaded my senses once more. But those notes were a balm to my soul, and I exhaled in defeat.

It was quiet in the barn, only the soft sighs of sleepy horses and crunching haylage to be heard. Until . . . "Thank you for finding me tonight, Angel," Jasper said, drowsily. "I'm so bloody tired of being alone." Not even understanding the context, just the tone of Jasper's voice, was a stab to the heart.

"Always," I said, and in minutes, I felt Jasper's exhausted body slump harder next to mine and his breathing evened out into slow and steady breaths. I stared straight ahead, Lady Aurelia sleeping in my direct view. My heart was racing, and when I dared look down, it fired off into a fast sprint. My hand was still in his, and he had clutched it to his chest like he would never let go.

I turned, trying my hardest to dislodge myself from his side. But even in sleep, Jasper held on harder, and I had no choice but to stay still. Glancing down, Jasper's face, only minutes ago pained and broken, was now serene and still. Taking a liberty, I ran my fingertips over his forehead, smoothing down the frown lines that broadcasted his pain.

I didn't know what plagued him, but he clearly felt he was to blame for something and that he was failing someone—someone he clearly loved.

"What haunts you?" I let that question disperse above us into the dusty barn as Jasper fell deeper into sleep. And I kept watch. I didn't know this man, but I would stay here for him tonight, allowing him to find some semblance of relief from whatever plagued him.

I blinked my eyes open, an unfamiliar barn coming into view. It took me several slow seconds to clear the fog from my brain and remember where I was. A low groan broke through my stupor, and I looked up to see Jasper Knighton asleep . . . and me draped over his body with my hand clasped in his.

Panic rushed through as potent as electricity, and as silently as I could, I rolled off Jasper, wincing as the morning winter sun flooded through the windows of the barn.

Shit, I thought, as I unthreaded my fingers from Jasper's and he began to stir. Getting to my feet, I barely glanced back as I made a grab for my Stetson and fled for the exit. I had no idea what time it was, but I knew that I had fallen asleep on Jasper at some point last night, and it was only by the grace of God that I hadn't been caught.

Lord! What would have happened if he'd awakened to find his newest rider sprawled all over him? I felt sick just imagining the embarrassment of that situation.

Opening the exit, I allowed myself one last look over my shoulder at Jasper. He was slumped against the wall, my robe still blanketing his body. I should have been panicking about leaving my coat, or any evidence that I'd been here, but I barely spared it a thought. All I could see was Jasper's still outstretched arm, palm upturned as though searching for the hand that had kept his company all night long.

My heart lurched and I thrust myself into the crisp morning air. The cold wind whipped around me, but I ignored the biting chill and began to run from the barn toward the cottage I had been given. From the man who had cried on my shoulder. I ran from the man who had slept in my arms.

But most of all, I ran from the man who had called me beautiful.

The one who had called me Angel.

Chapter Four

Jasper

A relentless tapping hit my foot, causing me to crack my eyes open. I flinched the moment I did, the morning sun piercing me like a million needles into my brain. I groaned and clutched my head, but the tapping on my foot remained. I glanced up, only to see Forrest looking down at me. His arms were crossed over his chest, but his face . . .

Nope, I couldn't cope with his sympathy or censure right now.

I tried to sit up, but there wasn't a part of me that didn't ache. I guessed sleeping on a concrete floor would do that. "Shit," I said when I managed to shuffle myself into a sitting position. I leaned back against the wall and took a deep breath, fighting the nausea that was springing up within me.

I glanced up, only to see Forrest heading into the break room. The smell of coffee brewing immediately drifted into the main body of the barn. A snort and a breath of warm air came from above me. I lifted my hand and immediately found Henry's velvety muzzle. I gritted my teeth against my raging hangover and looked up at him. All I could see were clouds of white air from where his warm breath hit the cold, and his teeth as he nibbled at my fingers, searching for treats.

"Sorry, boy," I said, my voice barely making a sound. "I promise next year will be different." I moved again, exhaling deeply when every part of me protested. Forrest chose that moment to reappear, an insulated coffee cup in his hand.

"Black, just like your soul," he said, a wry smile pulling on his lips. He was dressed in jodhs, a Knighton Equestrian black puffer coat, and riding boots. He had a beanie on his head. He was ready to train. This was what Forrest and I did for years when we were at home and not on tour—trained together every morning. Being an eventer, Forrest was a seasoned show jumper too. Other days, I'd continue to train in the arena, but he would move on to practicing cross country alone, or ride dressage with Felix.

Forrest sat down beside me and tapped his mug to my own. I took a sip of the scalding liquid and sighed as the caffeine hit my tender stomach, giving it a smidgen of life.

Forrest looked beside him and lifted the almost empty bottle of Macallan into the air. "Christ, Jas. Not even Oban?"

I rested my head against the wall and smiled at Lady Aurelia prancing around the stall opposite us to get my cousin's attention. "Your princess awaits," I said, and Forrest smiled.

"Let me just talk to drunken Uncle Jas, darling, and we'll get you ready for jumping," Forrest said to Aurelia. It always made me laugh how much of a soft touch Forrest was with his prize mare. He was an unmovable force with everyone else, a bit closed off and serious, except for when it came to his girl.

A few silent minutes passed, then Forrest said, "You were meant to find me last night, Jas. Or at least Genny." I froze. "We came looking for you." Forrest motioned around the barn. "I don't know why I never thought to check in here." He shrugged. "Maybe it's because it's the middle of winter and it's fucking freezing outside."

"Whisky keeps out the cold," I said, and cleared my throat to try to warm up my voice. My head pounded, and I tried my best to remember what the hell happened last night and how I ended up in here.

I shifted again, and the smell of vanilla and roses drifted up my nose. At that, a slither of memory slipped through from last night, and I felt my fingers tingle. I glanced down at my hand and balled it into a fist. As I did, I clocked the Knighton Equestrian–branded equine robe laying over me like a blanket.

Turquoise eyes and long raven hair swirled in my memory, coming back in dribs and drabs. But I couldn't put those pieces together to form a coherent picture. Then from the depth of my unconscious, I whispered . . . "Angel." My heart seemed to stop in my chest. I searched all around me.

I hadn't been alone last night. I clutched the robe in my hands and brought it to my nose. Rose and vanilla, and a soft hand in mine.

"You okay there, Cousin?" Forrest asked.

"Was I alone this morning? When you found me?" I asked.

Forrest's eyebrow rose. "Oh, tell me more, Cousin," he said, dryly.

I shook my head and pressed a thumb into each of my eyes. I tried to think, but my brain was whisky-fueled mush right now. An angel . . . I shook my head. That couldn't be right, *right?* I shook my head again.

"Jas?" Forrest said. "You okay? You're shaking your head a lot."

I took another sip of my coffee and said, "Pretty sure I hallucinated an angel was here with me last night." My confession was met with pure silence.

I risked a glance at Forrest.

"What the hell, mate? I say this because I love you, Jas. But I think it's about time you get some help. Real help. *Professional* help." He shook his head. I entertained that Forrest was probably right. He sat up straighter. "You didn't add a few shots of absinthe into your bender last night, did you? You know that shit can make you have some really vivid dreams."

I sat forward, resting my arms on my knees. I released a sardonic laugh and remembered taking a few shots of the green fairy in my study before the whisky. "Yeah, I did, now that you mention it." Forrest laughed harder.

I laughed too, but when Forrest's humor died and he put a hand on my shoulder, all hilarity vanished. Forrest squeezed my shoulder and said, "Seriously, Jas. I'm really worried about you. We all are. You're spiraling, Cousin."

"I know," I said, and ran my hand down my heavily stubbled face. The reality was, I wasn't handling shit well. I needed to sort myself out. I had two extremely successful businesses to run, and I couldn't let my family down again.

The barn door suddenly opened, and Felix and Atticus stepped through. Felix's eyes latched on to mine, exuding his concern. But Atticus just laughed out loud, making me wince at his usual booming volume. "Jasper, Jasper, Jasper, what do we have here?" Atticus said and came to stand before where I sat with his older brother.

"Fuck off, Atticus. I can't cope with you today." He was dressed in all black—he always did, to match his horse. Atticus put his hand over his chest like my words had wounded him, but nothing hurt this fucker. He was Teflon.

"Your words," Atticus said, "are like bullets to my heart."

I released an exasperated sigh and ignored his shit-stirring grin.

Felix sat down on my other side, moving the bottle of Macallan out of the way. His gaze met mine, and he nudged my arm. That was Felix-talk for giving me his support. I nodded back at my middle cousin. I was okay.

"So?" Atticus said, standing in front of us all. "Seeing as though we are all here, which is a rarity these days, shall we have a morning hack?" His eyes bored into mine. "Like old times."

I swear Henry whinnied in support. He loved riding out with the other horses. We had acres and acres of trails to keep the horses fit and their toplines strong. I wanted to say yes. Even hungover and feeling like I'd puke at any moment, the thought of just taking a moment of joy for myself clawed at my brain. But then the darkness within me pulled my excitement back down and reminded me that I had more important things to be doing these days.

"I can't," I said, and I swore I felt disappointment pulse off all three of my cousins in a suffocating tidal wave. "I have to go." I got to my feet, still holding on to the robe in my hand.

"Whose is that?" Atticus asked.

I looked to the robe and my pulse fired off into a sprint again. Rose and vanilla . . . "I don't know," I said. "It was over me like a blanket when I woke up this morning."

"Oh, shit," Atticus said, fixing his usual teasing smile back on his face "One of the grooms has seen you passed-the-fuck-out on the barn floor." He laughed. "Good job they've all signed an NDA."

My heart sank. Was that who the angel was? A groom. *Shit.* I worked hard at keeping myself away from the staff and riders. I couldn't be arsed answering the same questions about retiring or being a freak show as the Grand Prix champion who was now a recluse. And I would never fool around with a staff member. That's a scandal I wanted to keep *far* away from.

Forrest and Felix got to their feet too. I held my coffee mug up in a salute and focused on tamping down my dizziness. "I'll see you all later." I gave Henry a kiss on his nose, then headed to the back door.

"Jas! Are you sure you're good?" Forrest called out, and I looked back at my best friend, only to see Felix and Atticus watching me in concern. I hated it. They were my family. My blood. I never wanted them to worry.

"I'm good," I said. "I just have a long day of meetings ahead of me."

It was true. I was in the Knighton Equestrian offices all day today. Meeting after meeting awaited me as we launched the new season. It took me until I was almost back on my wing of the family home to realize I still held on to the robe. And as the scent of rose and vanilla washed over me once more, I knew whoever I saw last night must have been real.

I just had no idea who my mystery angel was.

"Tommy," I said, and my driver looked at me in the rearview mirror as we drove out of Golden Oaks. "Can you stop here, please?"

"Of course, sir," Tommy said, and I opened my car door before he could. Leon was in the outdoor arena to my right, and I needed to tell him of some new mares that were arriving later today. Even though there was a slight chill in the air, one could almost mistake today for a spring day. The sun was bright, and the first signs of winter breaking were creeping in.

"You're too wide on fence three! He can take a sharper corner than that. Circle back and do it again," Leon called to the rider who was cantering around the ring on a dark-bay stallion. I recognized the stallion immediately—Lord Huxley. Even as a foal, he'd shown tremendous potential. I'd been waiting to see what this horse could do in the big leagues after dominating the lower levels for the past couple of years. Even before I took the helm here at Golden Oaks, I'd always had a vested interest in our stud-bred horses maturing and showcasing their skills coming through. My dad brought me up knowing how every part of this place worked. It was our entire life.

I leaned over the fence and watched as the rider brought Huxley back to the third jump and did exactly what Leon had said. The rider then carried on for the rest of the course, and a flare of excitement built in my chest as I watched her. She was good. And she handled Huxley's strength and power perfectly.

Leon clapped when the rider cleared the last fence. "Cool him down for a few now," Leon said, and must have felt me behind him as he looked over his shoulder at where I stood.

"Jas," he said in greeting, and headed toward me. He leaned back against the fence, his attention fixed on the rider.

"She's good," I said, and nodded at her perfect seat as she slowed Huxley from a canter to a trot. Her posture and fluidity were outstanding.

"I think we can really go somewhere with these two, Jas," Leon said. He pulled his gaze away from the rider to face me. "What brings you out here so early?"

"Two new mares are arriving to the stud this afternoon. I wanted you to look at them for me. See which stallions you think would suit them best." Leon nodded, but my eyes found the rider again. For some reason, I couldn't look away. She was walking Huxley now, slowly nearing our position on the rail. She leaned down, patting and hugging Huxley's neck.

Leon followed my gaze. "Hallie!" Leon shouted, and the girl lifted her head. She was too far away to make out from my vantage point. Leon waved her over, and she began to approach. A strange feeling of knowing trickled down my spine as she came closer. Bumps spread on my arms under my tweed jacket and wool jumper. I lifted my flat cap to push back my hair and put it back on my head. *Hallie.* As in Hallie Oakley. Our new rider from the US.

When she stopped before us, her head was slightly bowed, hiding her face under the peak of her riding hat.

"Hallie, I want to introduce you to Jasper Knighton," Leon said, and every inch of Hallie tensed. Huxley, responding to her reaction, stomped on the spot and swished his tail. I frowned at her odd reaction.

I waited for Hallie to look up, but instead, she kept her chin down and said a quick, "Nice to meet you, sir." Her Bible Belt accent was strong, and surprisingly, there was a familiar note to it. Kicking Huxley on, Hallie rode him away.

"That was strange," Leon said, bewildered by Hallie's stiff reaction. He shrugged. "Maybe she's starstruck by *the* Jasper Knighton." I rolled my eyes as Leon laughed, his wide teasing smile showing me he was giving me shit. "Being honest, though, her reaction does strike me as odd. She seems a bit more of a ballbuster to be intimidated simply by little old you."

I slapped him on the back. "I'll leave you to it. The mares will arrive around two. I'm out all day at meetings, but I'll see you tonight at dinner," I said, and moved back to my car. I'd decided to make a concerted effort to attend family dinners again. It'd at least get Forrest off my back for a while. Plus . . . I'd missed my cousins and sister. I hadn't realized how much until I ate with them all again.

I slipped into the back seat but kept watching the arena as Tommy prepared to pull away. I caught Hallie dismounting from Huxley, and from my position in the car, I had a perfect a view of her through the slats in the arena's white perimeter fence. As soon as Hallie was on terra firma, her body came into view. I stared at her perfect curves and the way her riding tights hugged every inch of her toned thighs. Stretching, Hallie reached her arms up to the sky, her base layer creeping up to reveal a slip of her tanned, flat stomach. I shifted in my seat and shook my head. I could not be having these kinds of thoughts toward a rider of mine. Then she turned to loosen Huxley's girth, and her arse came into view. Horse girls' arses were always full and round, and Hallie's was no exception.

I tried to look away, but she had me transfixed. Hallie then lifted her gloved hand to her chin strap. I inhaled in anticipation, and the minute she removed her hat, my stomach dropped right to the ground. Hat-free, a long raven-colored braid was revealed. But that's not what had me holding all my breath captive in my lungs. *No*, that was when Hallie turned, and like she could see me through the fence too, her turquoise eyes met mine through the car's window. Wide, *knowing* eyes.

Jesus.

Hallie Oakley, the newest show jumper for Team Knighton, was the girl who had found me in the barn last night. Was owner of the robe I still had . . . *She* was rose and vanilla.

Hallie Oakley, who had the most perfect seat on a horse I'd ever seen, was the angel who had found me on the worst night of the year. The angel who had sat beside me and stopped me from being so alone.

Fuck.

Chapter Five

Jasper

Tipping my head back as the cold night swirled around me, I jumped on the spot, shaking off the last of today's hangover. Rolling my neck from side to side, I tried to iron out the cricks, then moved the crotch of my joggers away from my dick, urging it to calm the fuck down too.

Ten hours. Ten bloody torturous hours of looking at picture after picture of Hallie Oakley had made me hard as a fucking rock all day. The only reprieve I got was when we looked at color samples for the upcoming Knighton Equestrian shoot and not the models themselves. The shoot that Hallie would be at in a couple of weeks with her long raven hair and turquoise eyes, looking beautiful as fuck and wearing my designs.

Twenty-four hours ago, Hallie Oakley was blissfully absent from my life. She was a name I had swirling somewhere in the back of my mind as a rider who Leon was impressed by. It was a name I'd heard on people's lips on the circuit as an up-and-comer, and someone many were nervous of competing against one day. Now Hallie Oakley was imprinted on my brain as the most beautiful woman I'd ever seen, with an arse I desperately wanted pressed up against my dick and a face that looked like it had been painted by a Renaissance master.

If I hadn't seen her this morning in the arena, if her striking eyes hadn't met mine and revealed who she was, it would have only taken me a second of looking through the test shots my creative team did a few weeks back of this season's models for me to recognize her from the night in the barn. I scanned my desk, image after scattered image of Hallie glancing up at me, her stunning, sea-blue gaze causing my hands to curl into fists. There wasn't a bad picture amongst them. In each, she was beautiful—full lips, dimples, and radiating innocence until you saw the streak of wild that lived in her eyes.

Fuck!

She'd seen me drunk.

She'd seen me broken. *No one* got to see me broken. Fear washed through me. Had I said anything to her? Had I told her anything about what we were going through?

I groaned aloud and ran my hand down my face. I had to get her out of my head. Our riders signed NDAs. Even if I'd stupidly loosened my lips, she couldn't share what she'd heard. But that didn't make me feel any better. I didn't like people seeing me crumble. I didn't like looking weak.

"Fuck!" I called out into the quiet night, clenching my hand into a fist. But when I looked down at that fist, all I could see and *feel* was Hallie's hand firmly gripped in mine.

I thought back to today, of how she couldn't look me in the eye. Of how she kept her hat tipped down so I didn't see her face when we were introduced. She couldn't wait to get the fuck away from me. Good. She needed to. Last night shouldn't have happened.

And why had she even been there? In the family barn? It was out of bounds for anyone but us.

I sighed, trying to clear my head. I'd thought of nothing else all day. With every picture of Hallie that crossed my desk, my dick got harder until I thought that it'd punch through the tabletop. To say she was the most beautiful woman I'd ever seen in my life was an understatement. No wonder in my inebriated state I'd thought she was a fucking angel.

Unable to take any more of my own brain, I set off on one of the riding trails in a jog. The night was dark, but the lamps illuminating the trails and arenas were still lit, allowing me to see the way. I urged my body into a fast run, pushing as far as my legs could take. I might not have been competing on the circuit anymore, but I'd never let go of my fitness routines. I didn't know why. Maybe I still needed to keep myself fit and healthy because I was so used to it. Or maybe—a truth I refused to admit—it was because I wanted to keep myself tour-fit . . . just in case.

Just in case, one day, I found it in me to ride professionally again.

I ran as fast as my legs would go, exorcising the last of the whisky from my system. When I couldn't take any more, I drew to a stop at the fountain on the opposite side of our house and put my hands on my knees.

I sucked in freeing gasps of air, my lungs screaming at the frigid temperature. Sweat poured down my face, and I stood straight, tipping my head back to the view of the crescent moon and blanket of stars above me. I loved that about living in the sticks—no light pollution to rob you of a full and vibrant night sky.

My breathing began to slow when I suddenly heard the crunching of gravel underfoot behind me. I turned around, expecting to find Felix or Forrest, who often came out here to run too, but I froze when a familiar set of turquoise eyes were fixed on me, wide and awkward. I immediately swallowed and ran my eyes down the stunning picture of Hallie Oakley, only feet from where I stood.

She was dressed in purple. A long-sleeve lavender base layer and black yoga pants. White trainers were on her feet, and her long hair was pulled back in a high ponytail on the top of her head.

She pushed a ringlet of hair from her flushed face. "Sorry, I was just out for a run." Her voice was breathless, and her accent thickened into a deep southern twang. "I didn't think anyone would be around."

I stared at her. Fuck me, but she was gorgeous. Her body was all curves—small, dipped waist and perfect flared hips. But my gaze dropped down to her hand, clenching and unclenching at her side. The hand that had held mine all night. The one I still could feel against my palm if I concentrated hard enough.

Flustered, no doubt by my heavy silence, Hallie blew out an exasperated breath and turned to leave. As she did, I said, "You were in my barn last night."

I could be an arsehole. I knew that. In fact, Atticus often called me a surly twat—I knew that too. But even to my own ears my voice was too hard and gruff.

Hallie stiffened. I waited to see what she would say. When she turned back to face me, I crossed my arms over my chest and waited for a reply.

Hallie tucked her loose ringlet behind her ear, but her chin tipped upward, a hint of defiance in her body language. I narrowed my eyes at that show of power. "I'm sorry," she said, her sweet, accented voice immediately flooding me with warmth even though the night was ice cold and bitter. "I couldn't sleep, so I went to see Huxley. I didn't . . ." She trailed off, seeming to try to find some kind of excuse. Sweetness laced her voice again as she said, "I didn't mean to pry into your section of the barn. I didn't know it was closed off until I saw your family's horses and realized who they belonged to."

I clenched my jaw. Something about her apology seemed forced, like she wasn't sorry one bit. All I could picture in my head was Hallie finding me completely wrecked last night. Hell, I didn't even let my own family see me that way, never mind a young rider who we'd just sponsored to ride our horses for the next couple of years. Shit, how old even was she? She could have been anywhere from five to ten years younger than me. I wanted to smack myself in the face at my fuckup.

But apparently, I wasn't done being a moody bastard, and the flare of challenge in her eyes was a red flag to a bull. "You must have opened a closed door to get in there," I said, and heard the venom in my voice.

"A closed door that means *keep out*," I added. I couldn't help it. I was fucking embarrassed. I was the owner and CEO of Golden Oaks and Knighton Equestrian. I was meant to have my shit together, and on her first week here, Hallie had seen me in a total mess.

"I'm sorry, sir," she said, and I studied her face. Was I mistaken, or was there an attitude on the word "sir"? I couldn't be sure, but it had my blood beginning to heat in my veins.

"Hallie, right?" I asked. I knew exactly who she was. At this point, her face was seared into my brain.

"Yes, *sir*," she replied again, only this time with more bite. By the ghost of a smirk on her lips and the crossing of her arms, I knew she wasn't being contrite. But hell if the word "sir" leaving her mouth—shitty attitude or not—wasn't a damn aphrodisiac.

I stepped closer to her. Close enough that I almost choked when the scent of rose and vanilla crept up my nose. Her turquoise eyes practically glowed in the warm lamplight as she watched me, not a hint of shyness about her now. I stood about a foot above her, and she raised her chin higher as her eyes ran over every inch of me.

Fuck. Me.

Hallie waited for me to speak, as still as night. Her cheeks were flushed, whether from jogging, the cold, or my presence. "If a barn door is shut, you don't go in there," I said, rigidly.

"Yes, *sir*," Hallie said again, with that same rebellious inflection to her voice, and fuck, she had no idea what that kind of attitude did to me. It made me want to break her.

I kept my shit together and said, "We're going to forget all about last night, okay? Forget that you saw me being so unprofessional, and I'll forgive your blatant intrusion into my family's private property."

Hallie inhaled slowly, though I caught a hint of fire flare in her tropical sea eyes. "Yes, sir," she said again.

With nowhere else to take this conversation, I nodded again in acceptance.

As her eyes boldly met mine for several strained seconds, I knew I needed to leave. I needed to turn around and leave this woman alone. But the way she stared at me, unabashed even through my censure, had me rooted to the spot. I found myself *wanting* her to push me, to let out whatever ire had built within her. To try my patience. It'd been such a long time since I'd had a worthy adversary. Someone who awoke something inside of me. Something I thought was long dead.

"If that's all, *sir*," Hallie said in a falsely sweet tone, breaking the heavy silence between us, "I'll get myself home."

Hallie took off back toward the row of rider cottages nearest our house. I could have done without knowing she was sleeping only yards away from my own rooms. But I watched her go until she opened her front door and disappeared inside, but not before glaring my way.

I blew out a long breath, getting my shit together, then took off in a steady jog back to the house. As soon as I entered through the back door, I went straight to my study. I was in there all of five minutes before I logged on to my computer and brought up the CCTV cameras from the barn last night. And I watched exactly what had happened. I watched Hallie go to see Huxley, just as she'd said. And I couldn't help but smirk as I watched her stand at the closed door to our family section of the barn and check the coast was clear before she boldly looked inside.

Didn't know it was private, my arse. Little Miss Southern Belle knew exactly what she was doing. Then I watched, fascinated, as she stared at Lord Henry. My heart beat faster, just seeing how taken she was with my stallion. But more than that, I stopped breathing at how Henry let her fuss and fawn over him. Henry was a beautiful horse, but like the prince he knew he was, he could be particular with who he let close to him. But he'd let Hallie love on him instantly, like she'd known him for years.

Seconds later, I groaned when I saw my drunken self stumble into the barn, clutching a bottle of whisky, and Hallie hid away in Dahlia's old stall. Until I heard her trying to leave. Until she helped me lean against the wall. And until she held my hand and sat with me as I cried. And how she blanketed me with her robe, and then fell asleep beside me, her head laying on my chest.

It was over an hour that I sat in my study just watching us both sleep on that floor—a fool plagued with demons and the angel who selflessly stayed by his side.

Slamming the laptop shut, my head fell into my hands. I was stupid, letting Hallie see me that way. And it wouldn't happen again—*couldn't.* No matter how beautiful she was, or how her spark of rebellion had ignited something within my dormant heart, it couldn't happen again.

I had no time to obsess over tropical eyes and long dark hair. Or how good a small hand felt in mine.

I had only one job these days: to find my father's killer and protect my family.

And that was fucking that.

Chapter Six

Hallie

A few days later

"Shit!" I hissed as the pole fell to the ground with a dull thud. I closed my eyes as Huxley cantered around the track, letting the familiar rhythm of his steady motion calm me down. I inhaled through my nose and out through my mouth, but nothing helped. All I could see in my mind's eye was Jasper, skin slick with sweat as he caught his breath from his run. All I could feel were his dark eyes burning into mine as I sassed a "Yes, sir." Heat had flared within them as he'd tried to read whether I was being insolent or not. I held my attitude back just enough to keep some respect, but all I could think of was what if I had been defiant? Something told me that Jasper Knighton *wanted* to be pushed.

"Hallie!" Leon's loud voice broke through my racing thoughts—thoughts I couldn't contain, hadn't been able to for days now. I could still feel Jasper's body heat as he moved before me, scalding me like a flame. I could smell the sandalwood and mint of his cologne.

And I couldn't stop from imagining him crushing his lips to mine or showing me exactly what he did to women who spoke back to him.

"Hallie! Jesus . . ." Leon said, breaking through my Jasper-fueled haze again. When I looked at Leon, I realized I was just circling the track, Huxley keeping me safe with his steady pace.

"Sorry!" I said, and brought Huxley to a walk. Leon headed toward me from his place in the center of the ring. His eyes were narrowed as he assessed me. I smoothed my features. I didn't think *"I've been fantasizing about your boss and almost-brother and all the dirty things he could do to me in bed"* would be a good-enough excuse for why my head had been in the clouds in today's session.

"I'm distracted. I know. I'm sorry," I said, and brought Huxley to a halt. Leon stood beside me, arms crossed.

"We don't have time for distractions, Hallie. Every minute of practice is essential." Leon's head tipped to the side as he regarded me. "You're not normally like this—you're always focused. What's on your mind?"

My heart stopped. Huxley moved restlessly beneath me, clearly feeling my distress. "I haven't been sleeping," I said, lying through my teeth. "I think it's just catching up with me."

"Are you following the training plan?" Leon asked suspiciously. The training plan. What to eat, when and how much sleep, and non-riding-related exercise we riders were to do to keep in top form.

"Of course!" I said with a little too much enthusiasm. I wasn't. At all. Late-night jogs and confrontations with Jasper weren't exactly "sticking to the rules." Nor was the number of times I had fought touching myself while thinking of my boss.

My fucking *boss*. Who was most certainly, absolutely forbidden.

"Why don't I believe you?" Leon said, a whisper of a smirk pulling on his mouth. Leon was a tough nut to crack, but he'd shown flickers of humor under his stern exterior during our sessions. I liked him. Loved training with him. My stomach rolled. I didn't want to let him down.

I sighed and ran my hand down my face.

"Let's call it for today," Leon said, and I snapped my head up.

"No, really, I'll get myself together—"

"Sage will be here soon," Leon said, cutting me off. He ran his hand down Huxley's blaze. "It's not working today. No need to keep going when it doesn't feel right. We don't want Huxley"—Leon met my eyes—"or you unnecessarily stressed."

I sank into my saddle, relaxing and taking note of Huxley beneath me. I closed my eyes and focused on my horse. Leon was right. Huxley was tense, and that was only because of me. I was off, and he sensed it, so the atmosphere was off.

"I'll be better tomorrow," I promised Leon, leaning down to hug Huxley's neck in apology for being a dud of a rider today.

"Rest, sleep, we'll reconvene tomorrow." Leon patted Huxley's neck and walked toward the jump to fix the pole as Sage entered the arena. I clicked my tongue, indicating for Huxley to walk on, and met Sage near the doors to outside.

"What's up your ass?" she asked, clearly reading my face.

I blew out a long, frustrated breath. "Off day," I said. I hadn't told Sage of my run-ins with Jasper. It didn't feel right telling anyone about Jasper being so broken by something. If I'd tried to explain about the fountain incident, it would need context from our night at the barn. So I'd kept things to myself.

"Why're you having an off day?" Sage questioned, because of course she did. She knew me. Her eyes narrowed. "You don't have 'off days.'"

"Well, hell just froze over because I'm having one today."

"Sage, when you're ready!" Leon called from across the arena.

I clucked Huxley on, making my escape, when Sage leaned in close. "If you think I'm leaving it there, darlin', you're sorely mistaken." Sage trotted Seraphina onto the track, and I left through the doors, letting the bite of the winter chill slap at my cheeks.

"Do you want me to take Hux?" Mila said out of nowhere, making me jump. "Sorry!" she said, holding up her hands.

"Not your fault, Mila," I said. "I'm all over the place today." I looked out onto the bridle paths that surrounded the property. "I'm going to hack out on one of these paths for a while, darlin'. I'll turn him out in the field when I'm done."

"You sure?" Mila asked, clearly also sensing something was off with me. At this point, I should have been wearing a neon sign that read, "Approach with caution, I'm having salacious thoughts about my boss."

"I'm good," I said and moved Huxley on, passing by the barns and along a path that led me into a private forest. The minute the trees created a canopy above us, the wind dropped and the only sound was the animals scurrying on the ground and birds flapping their wings in the branches.

Huxley's ears pricked forward in excitement, and I let myself relax. I wanted to slap myself when the first thing that came to mind was Jasper. "I'm fucked, Hux," I told my horse. I'd always admired Jasper. He had always been my inspiration to jump and compete. Over the years, I'd come to find him ridiculously attractive too. I mean, who wouldn't? I knew I'd probably see him here at Golden Oaks. But this past week . . . Hell, I never would have imagined that.

I smiled when we rounded a corner and the woods opened into a field, a herd of deer spread out before us. Stunning. Huxley watched them avidly. Lost in the picture of them grazing, the cold mist surrounding them making the scene look more like a painting, I said to myself, "You must stay away from him, Hallie. He's your boss, and the last thing you want is fellow riders on the circuit thinking you got here on your back and not your merit." My stomach fell at that. I'd worked far too long in this sport for it to be sullied by rumors of anything romantic with Jasper. Not that there would ever be. But I had to hide my attraction toward him.

Turning Huxley onto the trail, I followed the path back to the barn. After I'd untacked Huxley and brushed him down, I blanketed him and put him out in the field to graze.

By the time I'd walked home, I felt more certain of myself. Jasper Knighton was simply my boss. I would give him a wide berth, and any interactions would be purely professional. I had a career to forge, and I couldn't let my attraction toward my employer get in my way.

Ten days later
Knighton Equestrian Warehouse, Surrey

We arrived at a large warehouse at the crack of dawn. The morning was still dark as our car arrived at a back door of a huge white building. Sage was asleep on my arm, and I nudged her when we stopped.

"Wha—?" she mumbled, waking from slumber.

"We're here," I said, and Eric, our driver, opened the door for us. We'd insisted to Victoria that we'd drive ourselves here today, but she'd refused. *It's a long tiring day. Believe me, you'll want the rest on the way back,* she'd said, and ordered us a car.

The Knighton Equestrian warehouse was about an hour outside of Golden Oaks. Sage had used the travel time to catch some more rest. I'd been too wired. As per my vow to myself, I'd kept my head down and gotten shit done. I hadn't once caught sight of Jasper. Sometimes I found myself wondering whether he was avoiding me too. If he was, it was for the best. Not seeing him had given me the reprieve I needed to push him from my mind and focus on the only reason I was here: jumping.

We'd trained like crazy over the past couple of weeks, and I didn't want to jinx things, but Huxley and I were on fire. Like you feel some things are just meant to be, that was me and my stallion. The same went for Sage and her insane mare, Seraphina, or Fefe, as Sage affectionately called her. How anyone could nickname that mare something so sweet and whimsical was beyond me, but no one could deny that Sage and Fefe were a dynamic duo. When it came to competing against Sage in the upcoming Grand Prix, I honestly wasn't sure which of us would win.

But we wouldn't have it any other way. We were best friends and even fiercer competitors, though our rivalry had never affected our friendship like it did most others on the circuit. That was the biggest blessing we had.

A man came to the car. When we stepped out, he held out his hand. "Marco Roberts," he said with a wide smile. "Artistic director for Knighton Equestrian."

"Nice to meet you, Marco," I said and shook his hand.

Sage followed suit, then slapped him on the back and said, "You got coffee in this place, Marco? Because I'm gonna need a kilo of that shit, stat! This country girl needs the bitter taste of java to get my systems firing and my bitch mode swiftly put on silent."

Marco blinked a few times at my filterless best friend but quickly ushered us inside, out of the cold drizzle and into the warm(ish) warehouse. "Right this way," he said, and I smiled as Sage successfully bulldozed another employee.

I turned behind me and saw two cars parked in the reserved spots next to the door. Both had private license plates. One read "APK" and the other "JHK." The cars were top-of-the-line Range Rovers, and my stomach rolled when I realized who one of them most likely belonged to. JHK—Jasper Harold Knighton. I imagined the other belonged to Atticus, but I'd keep that piece of information from Sage until she'd had her coffee. If she knew Atticus was going to be here after two weeks of successfully avoiding him, she would go nuclear.

Straightening my shoulders, I quickly followed Marco and Sage into a large kitchen/break room, and my friend beelined for the tray of coffee pods. She opened the refrigerator, then turned to me, fury on her face. "How does this country still not have proper coffee creamer? Flavored or otherwise?" She pouted like a three-year-old. "I miss my fave cinnamon creamer from Whole Foods."

"We have really good tea bags here in the warehouse," Marco offered as a solution. "I ordered them myself from Harrods. Made from the finest tea leaves money can buy."

Sage smiled sweetly at Marco, but I saw the simmering rage bubbling underneath her surface. "Tea doesn't quite give me the same hit as sugar-laden coffee does, sweetheart. But thanks for the offer." Marco blinked, stunned at Sage's candor as she popped a pod into the machine and practically inhaled it when it was finished.

Sage thrust a cup into my hand, then made a second coffee for herself. I blew a kiss at her in thanks, and Marco gestured for us to sit down at the break-room table.

Marco laid some papers on the tabletop and said, "The shoot will be over the next couple of days. Today will be the still shots here in the warehouse, showcasing the details of the new season's apparel. Tomorrow will be at Golden Oaks, where we'll do action shots of you both on your horses for this year's tour." He looked at each of us. "Is that okay?"

"Yep," I said, and Sage nodded with a mouthful of coffee.

"When you're ready, we'll get you into hair and makeup," Marco said, and we followed him into a room next door.

Sage and I sat down on two makeup chairs to meet Sarah, the makeup artist, and Jamie, our hairstylist. They got to work on us immediately. I always found this part of my career a novelty. We didn't do shoots often, but we'd done them enough to be used to this kind of pampering. It was a welcome change from boots covered in shit and mud. It seemed so far away from my old life it was laughable.

Classic rock played behind us, and I closed my eyes. My pulse immediately raced, and all the work I'd done to forget Jasper over the past several days unraveled when all I could think of was that Range Rover outside. Was he here? I mean, probably? This was his company. But would I see him? Would he even be involved in the shoot? I had no idea how hands-on a brand owner he was.

I felt anxious thinking he would show up. My mind took me back to the fountain, and I squeezed my thighs together. I wasn't proud of myself, but by the time I'd gotten back to my cottage that night, I was in bed in no time with my hand slipped down the front of my pants. I came hard, in mere seconds, and had to bite down on my bottom lip to stop my cry from sailing through the walls to where Sage slept.

Just the idea of him being here today brought goose bumps to my skin. When I didn't see him, I could keep him on the periphery of my mind. If I saw him . . . I had no idea if all my hard work would be blown to smithereens.

"No!" I suddenly heard Sage wail, yanking me from my thoughts. "No, no, *NO*!"

I opened my eyes. My best friend was gripping the arms of her makeup chair and glaring her most vicious glare at the doorway. I looked to my left, only to see Atticus Knighton leaning against the doorframe, shirtless, with a wide smile on his face.

"Nice to see you again, Miller," he said, his voice like silk and his accent thick with humor. If Sage could breathe fire, in this moment, I was sure she would.

"What are you doing here, shithead?" she said through gritted teeth as Sarah kept applying contour to her cheeks. I had to say, even through her rage, Sage's makeup looked incredible.

Atticus stretched his muscled arms over his head and rested them on the top of the doorframe. His abs were cut, and there wasn't an ounce of fat on his body. A fact I'm sure my best friend had noticed but would never admit, even under pain of death.

"Haven't you been told?" Atticus said, "I'm modeling for Knighton Equestrian this year too." Atticus pointed at his chest. "Me, you, and Hallie. Our hot little team." As he said my name, Atticus pushed off the doorframe and bent down and kissed my cheek. "Nice to see you again, Hals," he said, and I smiled. I'd always really liked Atticus. He was cheeky and playful and not an arrogant douchebag like some of the male riders were on the circuit.

"Don't," Sage warned. "Do not call her that." And in that moment, I knew my friend was completely psycho when it came to this man. One tumultuous summer in his bed as a teen had become Atticus's villain origin story in Sage's mind.

"He can call me Hals, Sage. Everyone does," I said, calmly.

"*He* doesn't," Sage snapped, never taking her furious gaze off Atticus, who now leaned against the makeup table. Jamie finished curling my hair and winked at me. He was clearly enjoying the show. Sarah finished applying Sage's lipstick, then she and Jamie swapped places.

The air around us was thick with tension. "Surely you knew I was part of Team Knighton, Miller. We'll be traveling together. *All* season. Living beside each other in the team's hotels. Dining together, doing press together." His eyebrows lifted up and down. "Always together. Just like old times."

"No, definitely *NOT* like old times!" she sputtered incredulously. "I wouldn't touch you if you were the last hard dick on earth and I was drunk on aphrodisiacs. And of course I knew you had this gig," Sage said. "Nepotism is still alive and well."

"Sage," I warned.

She cut me a withering look. The fact was, of course nepotism was involved in this case. The Knightons were horse royalty. But Atticus was also an excellent jumper. And I was sure that was what annoyed Sage more than anything. He had the talent to back up the fact that he rode for the best team in the world—a team he owned part of. Like Sage, Atticus was almost reckless with the risks he took on the course. Never with his horse—anyone could tell he adored Barnaby. But when it came to his self-preservation, he was as crazy as my best friend.

Completely unaffected by Sage's hostility, Atticus turned and looked in the mirror, tousling his hair with his fingers. "Sarah, Jamie," he said to our makeup artist and hairdresser, "I don't think I'll need much prep today." He met Sage's gaze in the mirror. "It's hard to improve perfection."

"Fucking narcissist," Sage muttered under her breath, then stayed in a silent staring match with Atticus until he said, "How are you finding Huxley, Hals?"

I exhaled a relieved breath, happy just to be given a diversion from their bickering. "He's amazing," I said. "I can't wait for Doha." Our first

Grand Prix of the tour began in a couple of weeks in Qatar. I was more than ready to go. I liked being on the move.

"Good," Atticus said, then asked, "You like Golden Oaks?" I cast a glance to Sage. She was quietly fuming in the makeup chair, but her eyes were closed while Jamie did her beachy waves. I just prayed she was finding some kind of Zen.

"Adore it," I said, and in my mind, instantly replayed holding Jasper in the barn, getting reprimanded by the fountain, and the fact that, only a short time later, I orgasmed to the thought of Jasper's pissed-off, stupidly handsome face.

"You're done, sweetie," Sarah said, and I looked in the mirror.

My smile was wide, for both the glam and the turn in conversation. "I love it, thank you."

Marco popped his head in the room. "Hallie? Oh, perfect, you're done. Let's get you in wardrobe." I'd never left a room so fast, laughing to myself when Atticus jumped into the chair I'd just vacated and smiled provocatively at Sage right next to him.

Dressed in a white robe, I followed Marco into the room next door. My mouth dropped, just seeing all the clothes hanging on the rack with my name on it. There were base layers of all different colors, riding tights, breeches, show jackets and shirts, riding boots, and all the casual attire one could think of. I ran my hand over the nearest set, trailing my fingertips over the embroidered Knighton Equestrian logo—a horse with a crown on his head. And not just any horse, but the profile of Lord Henry.

It made me fill with warmth. Jasper had loved his stallion enough to make him his brand's entire aesthetic.

"I'll be back in just a second," Marco said. He was a whirlwind, ducking in and out of all the rooms with his clipboard in his hand. I had just lifted a black, flared-waist base layer off the rack, admiring the ultrafeminine design, when someone entered the room.

I turned and froze when I saw it was Jasper. He stopped dead in the doorway when his gaze collided with my own. My heart kicked into a sprint the minute our eyes met, and ice shards trickled down my spine as his dark-brown gaze began to rove hungrily over my face and my freshly styled hair. Jasper licked his lips and appeared completely unabashed that he liked what he saw.

No, no, no . . . All my resolve I'd built against him of late began to fall away.

I flicked my hair off my shoulder, and finding my voice, tried to greet him normally. "Jasper." I discreetly let myself drink in my fill too—I couldn't help it. He was dressed in dark jeans and a plaid shirt with a KE-branded fleece gilet over the top. The outfit was effortlessly stylish and screamed country gentleman. I, however, became suddenly aware of being only in a dressing gown. A thin one at that.

In my dreams of late, in a scenario like this, this man would be pushing me against the wall, loosening the gown's tie around my waist, and wrapping my legs around his hips.

He is your boss. He is your boss, I chanted to myself. *Keep it professional.*

"Ms. Oakley," he eventually greeted, although tightly. It seemed keeping things professional between us was his goal too.

He stiffly nodded his head to leave when I couldn't help but blurt out, "Hallie." Jasper stopped dead and looked at me over his shoulder. That was okay, right? Ms. Oakley just seemed so . . . cold. We could remain professional and still be on a first-name basis. *Right?* It seemed weird *not* to be. "Call me Hallie," I repeated, confidently. Jasper stalled for a second, whether in shock or something else, I didn't know. But he eventually gave me a single nod again and left, just as Sage walked in. Her eyes bugged out of her head when she saw who had passed by.

"Jasper Knighton!?" she said, half question, half surprise. I had forgotten that Sage hadn't seen Jasper at Golden Oaks yet.

"Jasper," I echoed in confirmation, and busied myself looking at the clothes. Sage wasn't having any of that bullshit and grabbed my arm.

"Um . . . Why aren't you freaking out?" Her dark eyes searched mine. "You just met your icon and teen crush, and you play it off nonchalantly?" I opened my mouth to say something when a knowing look came over her face. "You've already met him! Before today." It wasn't a question. The problem with having such a close friend was that, at times, they knew you better than you knew yourself. Sage pulled me away from the door and into the privacy of a corner. "Spill."

Sage had her arms folded across her chest in her I'm-taking-no-shit-from-you stance. "I briefly met him the other week when I was training with Leon."

Her eyes narrowed at me and her head tipped to the side in assessment. "And why am I just hearing about this now?" She was right to be suspicious. If I had just met him then, I would have told Sage immediately.

"You need to tone down your animosity toward Atticus," I fired at her. It was a shit move and I knew it. "Don't jeopardize your place here because of your sour history with him."

A pissed-off smirk was etched on Sage's perfectly made-up face. "Oh, interesting. You don't want to talk, so you're using my wrath toward Dickface against *me*." Her eyes narrowed in suspicion, and she cocked her hip at me. "I'll let you keep your secrets for now, lady, as we're in a public place. But I'm onto you, and you *will* be telling me everything." Sage leaned in so close I could smell every note of her sweet perfume. "*All* of it, Hals."

"Okay," I said in defeat. It had only been a matter of time anyway.

Marco came back into the room, followed by another member of the team. I'd met so many staff members of late my head was spinning—the Knighton family had a dizzying number of people in their employ. This lady was the KE head stylist, Audrey.

Ten minutes later and dressed in a butter-yellow, long-sleeve base layer and matching riding tights and black boots, I was led to the studio. Sage was behind me, dressed in the same outfit but in scarlet. The color suited her dark eyes and blond hair so well. Atticus was already there, dressed in his signature black. The photographer called us over and arranged us with Atticus in the center, Sage and me on either side of him.

"A rose between two thorns," Atticus said when we were in position.

"Careful, fuckface, or I'll prick you," Sage replied between her teeth while smiling for the camera like a professional model.

"Oof. Is that a promise?" Atticus said, under his breath.

Sage growled.

It was gonna be a long day.

I told myself I'd never think modeling was an easy job again. Nine hours in and a billion outfit changes later, every muscle was screaming more than it ever had sitting in a saddle. My cheeks ached from smiling, and I wasn't sure how I'd ride Hux tomorrow for the action shots.

Sarah refreshed my makeup for the billionth time while Jamie fluffed Sage's hair and added another squirt of hair spray. Even Atticus's never-ending energy seemed to be waning. He and Sage seemed to have agreed on a temporary ceasefire to their incessant bickering a couple of hours ago when we'd all begun to flag.

"Almost done," Marco said, ticking something off his clipboard. It looked to be near the bottom of his list, which made me beyond relieved.

We crawled up from the break section sofas and posed one more time. This time it was just me and Sage. Atticus was excluded from this shot, as we were dressed in the Team USA KE apparel. We weren't Team USA members yet, but as Americans, it made more sense to model those outfits. Atticus already rode for Team GB, another notch on Sage's rivalry checklist.

"I think that's it," Steve, the photographer, said.

I exhaled a long, relieved breath, when a voice from the back said, "No. I want Hallie on her own again."

I squinted over the studio lights to a dark corner. But I didn't need to see into that darkness to know who was there.

How long has he been watching?

Jasper stepped forward into the light. He'd lost his gilet and was in his jeans and plaid shirt, his sleeves rolled up to the elbows, showcasing his muscled forearms. That sight shouldn't have been as hot as it was.

Everyone in the room locked in on his commanding presence. He had an aura about him that made everyone stand up and listen. Marco cleared his throat, obviously intimidated. "We have gone through all the listed shots, sir," he said nervously.

Jasper still hadn't removed his piercing stare from me. I felt flushed and wasn't sure if it was the heat of the lights or his attention. My heart kicked into a sprint, and I breathed slowly to try to calm it down. "I want single shots of Hallie," he said, his voice brooking no argument.

Marco went a little pale as he said, "We only have Steve booked for the day and his hours are pretty much done."

Jasper turned to Steve. "I'll pay you double if you stay."

Steve looked elated. "I can stay."

"The car is outside for Hallie and Sage. To take them home," Marco said, almost apologetically. "The driver can't wait, as he has another booking tonight for a nearby wedding."

Sage opened her mouth to say something when Jasper beat her to it and said, "I'll take Hallie home. Sage can leave now as scheduled."

My heart practically lurched out of my chest as he said that. Jasper's arms were crossed over his chest and his jaw clenched, as if he was internally warring with himself over his out-of-the-blue offer. I'd noticed around me, his hands tended to tighten into fists. As though he fought himself about any interaction with me. Was he feeling similar feelings to me? At times, I thought I saw heat in his stare, but . . .

No. I couldn't go there.

"Great!" Sage said overbrightly. I snapped my head to my best friend to find her grinning like the Cheshire cat. She squeezed my arm. "I'm wiped, Hals. You stay and get the extra shots, and Jasper can take you home when you're done." She discreetly winked at me.

I was going to kill her. I was actually going to murder my best friend.

"You can catch a ride with me, Miller. I have my car here too," Atticus said.

Sage patted him on his hard chest as she passed him. "I'd rather eat a bowl full of horse shit than ride with you, darlin', but thanks for the offer!" Sage left to get changed. Atticus watched her go, molten lava in his eyes.

"Catch you at home, Jas," Atticus said with a wave, and made his exit too.

Then it was just the few of us left. My head was spinning. I stayed rooted to the spot, no idea what to do. *I can do this,* I told myself. *Just get the shots and get home. He's your boss. That's it. This is just work. There's nothing more to it.*

Marco went to Jasper, and I heard him say, "What shot are you wanting to get, sir?"

"The main campaign shot," Jasper said after a few silent seconds' pause, and my eyes snapped to his. The main campaign? As in the *lead* shot that would be on billboards and magazines. On my own? I'd understood it would have been the three of us for the main shot when we were briefed.

Clearly Marco did too, as he said, "I thought that was the group shot? We got that a few hours ago."

"I've changed my mind," Jasper said, with all the authority of a crazy rich man who got whatever he wanted when it came to his brand.

"Okay," Marco said, then asked, "And what will Hallie be wearing? We've used all the allotted garments."

"All but one," Jasper said. Marco frowned in confusion. "The new sample has just come in. I want her in that."

"I didn't know you'd commissioned a new colorway, sir." Marco headed to another storeroom. He stopped before he got to the door, turned back to Jasper, and asked, "What color is it, sir?"

"Turquoise," Jasper said without stalling, and my heart thudded to a complete stop. Jasper met my eyes and ran his tongue over his lips. "I want her wearing turquoise."

It was pitch black by the time we finished. I was bone tired, but energy flowed through me with the force of a million cups of coffee as Jasper pulled up to the back door in his Range Rover. I went to rush through the pouring rain to get in when he opened the driver's-side door and dashed around to open the passenger door for me instead. He didn't say anything, but gestured for me to get in. The sight made me a little weak at the knees.

I was dressed in gym leggings and an oversize Knighton Equestrian sweater that Marco had handed us to wear when we got cold in between shots. I felt I looked too rough and underdressed to step into a car that likely cost more than many people's homes. But when Jasper said tightly, "Ms. Oakley," and flicked his head—an instruction to get in—my legs moved of their own accord, and I jumped into the seat.

I almost groaned as I sank into the butter-soft leather. Jasper was in the driver's side in seconds, pushing his hand through his now-wet hair. It was so dark with the rain it looked like strands of black ink.

As Jasper put on his seat belt, I said, "Hallie."

Jasper looked up through heavy dark lashes and pinned me with his midnight gaze. I swallowed under his heavy attention. He raised an eyebrow. He looked so dominant in that moment, I almost had to look away. But I held strong. I swallowed. "You keep calling me Ms. Oakley," I said, my voice sounding too loud in the quiet car. "I'd prefer it if you called me Hallie."

He stared at me as I put that to him again. I was trying to keep a distance, keep professional, but Jasper referring to me by my formal name just seemed strange. We could be civil and friendly without crossing any lines.

We had to.

"*You'd* prefer it," he said, not a question, just a murmur to himself.

"Yes, please," I replied plainly, ignoring the hint of authority in his voice, then shivered as the rain and cold from today seemed to sink into my soul.

Jasper must have noticed, as he began pressing buttons, and in seconds my car seat warmed up and the vents directly opposite me on the dashboard blew hot air over my frozen frame. I settled back, enjoying the warmth thawing the chill, when the seat began to vibrate and I realized it was giving me a massage.

I moaned a little in surprise, and Jasper's grip became so tight on the steering wheel that the leather creaked under his hands. The heat from the chair and vents must have been too hot, because suddenly, every part of me felt alight.

Jasper pulled out of the parking lot and onto the back roads that led to Golden Oaks. It had taken us an hour to get here this morning, and it quickly dawned on me: I was stuck in this car with Jasper for that long going home. And he wasn't saying anything. There was no music playing, and the heavy silence was making my head spin.

This was awkward. I knew it was going to be awkward, but I couldn't take an hour of this. He was too sullen, too silent . . . too goddamn *close* to me. I cast him a sideways glance. His mouth was tight, his hands gripped the wheel even tighter, causing the muscles in his forearms to ripple and veins to push from his skin. It shouldn't have been that attractive. But it was maddeningly hot, and I snapped my focus out the windshield to think of anything else.

After another five minutes of unbearable, strained silence, I blurted, "Thank you for taking me home." I had to say something, or I was going to scream. I wasn't the loudest person by any stretch, but being in a car with someone I not only admired but was also highly attracted to—even though his attitude was less than desired—was too much for me to take.

Jasper glanced at me from the side of his eye. "I made you stay late."

Okaayyy. He didn't want to talk. Great. Maybe I'd mistaken the heat in his gaze at the fountain. Maybe I'd been wrong about it all and he really was just pissed at me for invading his family's barn and seeing him upset.

I stared out the window, trying to take in the views, but the rain was lashing at the glass, and it was too black outside to see a thing anyway. All I saw was my reflection and my cheeks deflating when exhaling a long breath. But it felt like there was a crackle in the air between us, even more so, when in that same reflection, I saw Jasper look over to me and his tongue lick along his lips as he did.

I almost groaned again. I was so confused and overthinking every little thing.

"Can I put some music on?" I asked suddenly and turned to face him. It was that or ask him to pull over and put his tongue to other uses.

Jasper flicked the icon on his dash for music, and I began scrolling through the thousands of stations it offered. I smiled when I landed on a favorite.

As Lainey Wilson's beautiful voice began pouring from the speakers, I couldn't help my knee bouncing to the beat and singing along in a very low tone. Every time I heard this song, a pang of homesickness hit me. Not for Silvercrest, but for the ranch I only got to visit once a year if I was lucky. Three Hill Ranch. My true home.

I felt Jasper's eyes on me. This time, when I turned to him, he didn't look away. "Where in the south are you from?" His voice was tight and strained, like he'd had to force himself to speak to me. It made me smile a little, knowing that he clearly couldn't take the tension of our weird standoff we'd found ourselves in either.

"Originally, Texas," I said, and my mind instantly conjured up the magical glow of an orange sunset, the sound of crickets in the long grass and the dust from the cattle fields that would stick to your skin after a hard day's ranching. Lainey sang of wildflowers and wild horses, and I understood the lyrics in a visceral sense. I knew what it was to be raised on those hardworking ranches and working dawn until dusk.

"Originally?" Jasper asked, taking me from my pangs of homesickness. His hands were still tight on the steering wheel, but he was talking, which was more than I thought I'd get on this journey.

"I moved to Florida when I was twelve." I left it at that.

Jasper exhaled slowly, like he was allowing himself to lessen the pressure he had on keeping himself locked up tight, and said, "I've spent some time in Florida." I was taken back to another memory as he said that. "Where in Florida are you from?"

"Ocala."

"That's where I once stayed," he said, a hint of a question in his words. I watched him search my face, I assumed double-checking whether he knew me.

"I know," I said, and Jasper's suspicious expression demanded answers. I wiped my palms down the thighs of my leggings. "My aunt owns Silvercrest."

Jasper frowned. "Jeanie?"

I nodded. "I went to live with her when I was twelve." Silence met me. When I looked to Jasper, this time, his expression was softer, sympathetic. He got it. A kid didn't leave their home in Texas to live with a relative in a completely different state unless there was tragedy involved.

"I like Jeanie. She knew my father well. I spoke to her on the circuit from time to time when she was there to check on the horses Silvercrest had trained," he said. His uptight frame screamed that he kept a tight lid on everything. Every word he said seemed weighed and measured. It made me want to crack him open and see what was inside. To break the towering wall he kept himself hidden behind.

And to understand *why*.

But nevertheless, I smiled as he brought up my aunt. "She's the best," I said. "I miss her like crazy."

Chris Stapleton came on the radio next, and I tapped my finger on my knee to the beat. I loved this song. "So from age twelve, you grew up at Silvercrest?" Jasper asked.

"Yeah," I said.

"It's an incredible facility," Jasper said, and that made me happy. My aunt had worked so hard to make it what it was.

"It is. The best in the US," I said, proudly.

There was hesitation in Jasper's frame, until he asked quietly, "What do you think of Golden Oaks?" There seemed to be an echo of vulnerability in his tone. It warmed my heart for some reason. Maybe it was because he always seemed so cold and closed off. Apart from seeing him with Henry the night he was drunk, and how affectionate he was to his stallion, he never gave off any warmth.

I smiled, and the force of it made my cheeks ache after today's shoot. Jasper sucked in a quick breath as it did. "I love it. Everything about it is perfection." Jasper nodded, and his body lost some of its tension. "It's truly an honor to ride for y'all." This time it was Jasper's turn to smile. A little. A hint of a smile. It was barely there, but I caught it, regardless.

I eyed him with humor. "Watch out. I get real country when I'm tired."

"Noted," he said, dryly, but the ghost of his smile was still there.

The atmosphere in the car seemed lighter after we spoke. The tension had eased somehow. There were a million things I wanted to ask. But I'd only just gotten him to stop scowling at me, so I thought it best to tread carefully.

"I spoke to you at Silvercrest, you know," I said, and Jasper turned to me in surprise, like he was trying to place it.

"You were training in an outdoor arena." I fought the pang of pain that still filled my chest when I thought back to that day. "I had just arrived at Silvercrest from Texas. Literally. That day. Within the first ten minutes on its grounds, I saw you in a nearby arena, jumping Henry."

Jasper frowned, clearly trying to recall it. I turned my body toward him. I was so tired, but I didn't want Jasper to stop talking to me. The unease between us had finally ebbed, and it almost felt surreal to be here with him, in this car, just him and me talking. Younger me would have been screaming. "I don't remember it. What did we talk about?" he asked.

Tucking a damp strand of my hair behind my ear, I said, "I'd never seen anyone ride English before. I wandered over to the arena and watched you jump." I shook my head, still remembering the butterflies that accosted me, watching him sail over the spread fence with such regality. "I was mesmerized." Jasper waited for me to continue. "You asked me if I'd jumped before. I told you I hadn't, and you told Aunt Jeanie to teach me."

"So you started riding quite late?" he said, a sliver of awe in his voice. Like he couldn't believe I was a professional now after only starting in my early teens. Most people in our industry were brought up in the saddle and were competing as young children.

"I've always ridden. But I only knew western, Jasper. I was brought up on a cattle ranch." Jasper's eyes flared a little, and I allowed myself to entertain the thought that he was imagining me in my chaps and cowboy hat and nothing else.

No, Hallie. Don't go there.

"Wait," he said, eyes on the road ahead but tight, as though he was trying to recall something. "I think I *might* remember it," he said, and my heart thudded faster in my chest. He looked over and caught my stare with his own. "It's hazy. But I remember Jeanie introducing me to you. I think?" He blinked, like he couldn't wrap his head around it. "The little cowgirl? That was you, huh?"

I lifted one of my feet, showing I was wearing my old Ariats. I tipped my pretend hat. "Nice to make your acquaintance, sir."

My heart missed a beat the moment that "sir" left my mouth. But it confirmed something for me: The flash of heat I'd wondered if I'd misread in Jasper's eyes earlier? I hadn't. It was there now, blazing as he roved his gaze over my lifted leg and to my boots. I slowly lowered my leg back down, only for us to be plunged back into tense silence. This was torture.

The air between us felt awkward again now. But I wanted to tell him what that meeting had done for me. I went back and forth on whether to mention it, but I had to. People should know if they've had a positive influence on your life. "It was *you*, Jasper. *You* were the one who inspired me to jump." He swallowed, his Adam's apple bobbing up and down in his throat. He stayed silent. But I pushed harder when I said, "You inspired an entire generation to ride."

A flicker of softness took over Jasper's face, so handsome in that moment it made me breathless. But then, inch by inch, his face frosted over to his usual stoic expression, sucking up any warmth that had built between us. "Well, those days are gone now."

His voice hardened, and I could tell by his rigid posture that the topic of his riding was off limits. So I backed off. The massage chair was lulling me to sleep, and I hated the tension that had built back between us, so I said, "But I have to confess that, as much as I admired you, it was Lord Henry who truly stole my heart."

The minute I mentioned Henry, Jasper's walls crumbled, and a proud expression engulfed his face. A throaty, raspy laugh slipped from between his full lips. "That sounds about right." Jasper looked at me, a loving smile on his face and my heart clenched. "Henry is always the one to steal hearts."

Not just Henry, I wanted to add but thought better of it. He probably knew he could walk into any room and command everyone's attention.

"He's beautiful," I said. "The best horse there's ever been."

Jasper nodded, as Jordan Davis next crooned from the speakers. Then, "He let you fuss him," Jasper said, almost in wonder.

"What?" I asked, confused.

"Henry," Jasper said, briefly looking at me as he turned the car right. I realized most of the hour had passed. It had felt like five minutes. I suddenly wanted the journey to last a lot longer. "He's a loving horse, especially for a stallion. But only to people he lets in." Jasper cast me a wry grin, as if he knew he could have been talking about himself.

Jasper sighed. "I've never seen Henry allow someone to pet him as quickly as he did you."

Two things destroyed me in that moment: the first was just how soft and tender Jasper's voice got when talking about his beloved horse. And secondly, that Henry had taken a shine to me.

"Well, that's just made my life, right there," I said, and I laughed. Jasper watched me laugh, and he swallowed deeply again. But this time, his eyes heated as they fell on me, and every part of me sparked with life.

I turned my head to the window and fought to keep my heart from bursting from my chest.

Too close. That felt *too* close.

The car fell into a peaceful silence after that, and I closed my eyes as the perfect dulcet tones of "Neon Moon" came sailing from the radio. I didn't even realize I'd fallen asleep until I felt a fingertip lightly tap my shoulder. I blinked, my body snug and warm in the soft seat.

"Hallie," a gravelly, deep voice said, the most perfect-sounding voice I'd ever heard. "We're home," the voice said again. I didn't want to move. I was comfortable, and I felt safe.

Suddenly, I was weightless. In my subconscious, I heard a door unlocking, and then I was on a soft surface again. A blanket was laid over me, but I didn't open my eyes. My body was fighting to stay asleep, but my brain was screaming at me to wake up. My body won, shivering as that ghost of a touch slid over my cheek.

"'Night, Angel," that perfect voice said again, and I caught the sounds of a door locking and a car pulling away over gravel.

Angel . . . angel . . . angel . . . replayed in my head, like a mantra. Then, *I've never seen Henry allow someone to pet him as quickly as he did you . . .*

My eyes suddenly snapped open, and I fought to breathe. I was *wide* awake now.

He knew Henry let me fuss over him. He knew Henry hadn't fought me. How did Jasper know that, unless . . . ?

The cameras.

Jasper had clearly played back the CCTV. Goose bumps broke out on my skin again when I thought of why. But now I knew that he'd seen us. He'd seen me help him. Saw us holding hands . . . Seen me sleeping on his chest, his arm wrapped tightly around me.

All my hard work to keep Jasper from my mind immediately crashed into rubble. He'd smiled at me, chosen me to lead his apparel's campaign.

And he called me angel.

Chapter Seven

Jasper

Golden Oaks, Surrey

Stupid, stupid, stupid, I chastised myself as I let the waterfall shower rain over my head. What the fuck was I thinking, driving her home like that? Seeing her curled up in my passenger seat, watching me with those sleepy fucking turquoise eyes.

Turquoise.

Shit. In my madness, I'd called in a new colorway for this season's collection last minute. I'd pawed and pawed through the Pantone swatches until I found the color that had been seared into my brain after that night in the barn.

Hallie-fucking-turquoise.

And rather than just leave it there, I left my office in the warehouse to go to the photo shoot and watched Hallie's tight, curved body showcase Knighton Equestrian clothes in a way no one else could, her dark hair falling like a silk curtain over her perfect tits and hips. And like I'd been possessed, I'd demanded to see her in that damn new turquoise set.

The one that was now, suddenly, headlining the entire collection.

The water pelted down on my head, but it didn't stop the visions of Hallie in my car from assaulting my brain. Second by second, my cock grew harder until I clenched my fist against the shower wall with one hand, and with the other, I slipped it around my too-hard dick, hissing when Hallie's smiling face was all I could see in my mind. I pumped my dick up and down, faster and faster until I grit my teeth to hold back my shout and spilled on the shower floor.

That moan she'd emitted in the passenger seat when I'd turned on the massage function . . . Christ, it was burned into my brain. I wanted to hear her moan like that under my tongue while I made her fall apart.

No! Stop.

But my brain didn't want to listen.

Breathless, I tipped back my head and tried to forget the fact that Hallie had said she'd started to jump because of me (and Henry). That she'd met me before I was jaded and permanently angry. That was the person she admired, not the fucking arsehole I was right now. She probably couldn't stand me now. I wasn't a good person to be around these days. My stomach turned. I *hated* how much the thought of Hallie disliking me affected me.

Fuck!

I turned off the shower and climbed out. I'd kept the bathroom window open, and the cold air bit at my bare skin. Determined to put an end to this obsession with my new, young, fucking stunning rider—because shit, she was *seven* years younger than me—I vowed to stay away from her. I just needed distance. She would leave on tour soon, and I could get back to finding out who was trying to destroy the Knightons.

Dressing in jeans and an olive-green wool jumper, I threw on my padded wax jacket and my flat cap. I wouldn't go to the arena today where Atticus, Hallie, and Sage were shooting the action shots. I'd leave it to Marco. Leon was going to be there to ensure the jumps were correct and adequate. Plus, I had a meeting with Alexis Hobbs, for my sins. Daughter of Richard Hobbs, the biggest horse dealer in our sport. For years he and my father had done business. The Hobbs bought many of our foals for foreign markets.

They were some of our biggest buyers. Like me, Alexis had taken the reins of the family business after her father had a heart attack and decided to retire. But where Richard was a gentleman—ruthless, yet a man of his word and honest—Alexis was anything but.

Not a week after my father died, Alexis had offered to buy the entire Knighton enterprise. I'd flat-out refused, of course. That only made her more tenacious. Alexis Hobbs was money mad and drunk off power due to her now-elevated status in our industry. She was ruthless in business.

And she'd been trying to fuck me since I was twenty years old.

Ten years my senior, she'd borderline stalked me in my early years on the circuit. My resistance only seemed to make her more determined. There wasn't a deal that Alexis didn't land once she set her mind on it, and with me, she had been denied my business and my cock. A woman like that didn't take too kindly to rejection.

Despite our history, I couldn't afford to alienate one of the biggest buyers in the UK, so today's meeting was a necessary evil. I left my home and followed the path to the Knighton stud farm acreage. We had a family office there too, and all breeding and horse-buying business was done from there. The main house was strictly for family.

Twenty minutes later, I was sat at my desk in the family office, a coffee in hand, when there was a knock on the door. "Come in," I called, and Charlotte, the stud farm's manager, opened the door and cast me a tight smile.

"Mr. Knighton, Ms. Hobbs is here for your meeting," Charlotte said, but was pushed aside as Alexis stepped through like a woman who never had a door closed to her.

I gave Charlotte an apologetic look, and she shut the door, leaving us alone.

"Jasper," Alexis said, dressed head to toe in designer country attire—a tight tweed trench coat, belt pulled tightly at the waist. Her long burgundy leather boots disappeared under the hem of her jacket, and her hair was fastened in a tight bun. Alexis Hobbs was a prime example of how a very attractive person could be made ugly by their fucking appalling personality.

I got to my feet to greet her, but Alexis waved me off and sat down opposite me like she owned the room. I took a deep breath and sat down too. Her eyes were immediately fixed on me. "Can I offer you a drink, Alexis?" I said, trying to keep things cordial.

"No, I'm fine," she said, and placed her vintage Birkin at her feet. Alexis's head tipped to the side as she regarded me. "You look like shit, darling," she said with her usual directness.

I huffed a laugh. "Don't hold back on my account, Alexis," I said dryly. I truly did not care what she thought of me.

"I'd still fuck you, though," she said bluntly and sat back in her chair. Her eyes hooded, she crossed her legs, and I was sure it was her attempt at seduction.

"And yet it's still a no," I said, just as direct. "I don't mix business with pleasure, Alexis. You know this."

She rolled her eyes. "Darling, you've fucked a million women on the circuit, so let's not tell fibs."

"Anyone I've fucked on the circuit was a fellow competitor, not an employee or someone I do business with. I keep things professional when it comes to Golden Oaks." I took a sip of my coffee to stop myself from telling Alexis to fuck off and take her business elsewhere. "Plus, that version of me is a far cry from the man I am now." Alexis's smug smile fell, and I could see the residual annoyance in her eyes. "Now, how are you? You're here to see the newest foals, yes?"

Alexis smoothed down the arm of her coat and said, "I'm great, Jasper, and my business is doing better than ever, as you probably know." Alexis reached into her bag. Pulling out a bound A4 document, she placed it on my desk before me. "Speaking of, I have another offer for you," she said and sat back, exuding the confidence of a businesswoman who was sure she had already secured a deal.

"Alexis," I said, curtly, "my business is not for sale—any of them."

Alexis crossed her arms over her chest and nodded at the document, urging me to take a look anyway. Anger surged through my veins, but clenching my jaw, I opened the document and read the offer. I held in my surprise, kept my expression neutral. Alexis really wasn't here to play games. She'd offered more than I'd expected, probably over what Golden Oaks and our stud farm was worth if we ever had it appraised for a sale.

"I want Golden Oaks, Jasper. I want this place, and I want the stud farm and all that entails." Alexis leaned forward and looked me square in the eye. "You've had a rough couple of years, Jasper." I tensed at her faux-empathetic tone. "That money will set up your family for several lifetimes." She waved her hand toward the contract. "Take it, Jasper. You'd be a fool not to. Leave the strife of the past behind and start again." She shrugged. "Work on getting Genny better, whatever you want."

"Don't," I snarled, my voice deep and laced with venom. "Do not bring Genny and her accident into this. Ever."

At my reaction, Alexis fought a smirk. I swore this woman didn't feel empathy. Taking the contract, I tossed it back, the document slapping on the desktop in front of her. "We're not for sale, Alexis. I won't tell you again. Now," I said, and got to my feet, "do you want to see the foals or not? I have more meetings to get to today. Believe it or not, you're not the only one who is busy."

Alexis left the offer on the desk—a power move if ever I saw one—but got to her feet. I opened the door to outside and gestured for her to go first. As she passed, she placed her hand on my arm and squeezed my biceps. "So sullen, Jasper," she said, and I fought the urge to physically recoil from her touch. "And yet still so enticing." She lifted that same hand toward my face, but I pushed it away from me before she could touch me.

"Don't," I warned.

Alexis's eyes narrowed in anger. Good, I was glad I'd pissed her off. She'd done that to me the minute she pushed my stud manager out of the way like Charlotte was beneath her. "Your loss," she said, and sauntered past me and out into the yard of the stud farm. I took another deep breath and followed her out into the smack of cold air.

"The foals are in the field with their mothers," I said, and gestured toward the golf buggy nearby. "I'll drive us there."

Alexis slid into the passenger seat, and I slipped behind the wheel. We were too close for comfort, so I got moving to shorten the time I had to spend in her company. We had only just moved a meter, before she asked, "Where's Forrest? Is he around today?"

My patience was now wafer-thin with this woman. "He's away today," I said. If it wasn't my dick she was after, it was Forrest's. Unlucky for her, my cousin felt the same about Alexis as I did.

"How's Richard?" I asked, inquiring about her father, changing the subject.

"Still alive," she said coldly. I looked at her from the side of my eye. She was staring out into the fields around us, assessing the many mares and stallions of the stud grazing on grass.

"You're blessed he's still here," I found myself saying. Alexis turned to me and stared at me, expressionless. Ice cold. She was ice cold.

"Now I've taken over the business it's better than ever. Daddy's soft heart was going to run us into the ground." I fought the urge to shake my head in disgust. Who the hell talked of their father that way? She forgot that I knew Richard. He was a good man, and their business had been successful; it had been respected. The way she talked of him did him a disservice. "That's probably why his heart gave out." She shrugged. "He spends his days on the golf course now, and I'm growing our empire. It all worked out in the end."

The idea of seeing my father for just one more minute made my soul ache. I'd give *anything* to have him back. Alexis acted like she didn't even care if Richard had lived or died.

I pulled to a stop at the cluster of fenced-off fields holding the foals. I could hear voices in the near distance and knew if I followed the path around the small wood, I would see the photoshoot taking place down below.

Hearing voices, Alexis turned in that direction too. But I led her to the field before she could take a nosey. "Four foals. All Dutch Warmbloods. Strong lineage, fine form, will make excellent eventers and/or jumpers."

"Fine, I'll take them," Alexis said, barely glancing their way. She hadn't been interested in seeing the foals up close, of course; she never was. She only ever came here to fucking torture me, to prove that although I'd withdrawn from public life, *she* still had access to me.

Voices raised behind us again, and Alexis walked toward them.

"What's happening down there?" she asked, but didn't wait for me. Instead, she walked through the short path in the wood until she reached the other side. I followed, wanting nothing more than to send her on her way. I had to play the game, though. I couldn't stand the woman, but I liked her father and would uphold our working relationship for his sake.

Alexis stood and watched the arena below us like a hawk. From up here we had a perfect view of the arena where Atticus, Sage, and Hallie were shooting the outdoor shots. My eyes immediately tracked the arena and the people around it for Hallie. She was sat on Huxley's back outside of the arena, talking to Mila and Horatio.

Sage was in the ring. My eyes strayed back to Hallie. Even from my vantage point, I could see she looked incredible in her competition wear.

"Knighton Equestrian apparel?" Alexis asked.

"The new season's collection," I said, nodding, and tried to focus on anything but the American cowgirl I couldn't rinse from my brain. But her face was too fresh in my mind—I'd come this morning just imagining her insane curves and turquoise eyes, so I wasn't succeeding too well right now.

Sage cleared a jump for Steve's camera, and Alexis snorted. "Of course!" she said dryly. "These are your new *Americans*—barring Atticus, of course." The shitty tone of her voice had my muscles tensing.

"Sage Miller and Hallie Oakley." I turned to look at her with a raised brow. She smirked. "There's not a person on the circuit, new or old, that I don't know about, Jasper," she said.

What she really meant was there wasn't a person she wasn't trying to get gossip on. The equestrian world was renowned for its toxicity, and people like Alexis Hobbs were the reason why. She liked to have something on everyone in our industry. Although she hadn't tried it on me yet, I'd heard rumors of Alexis using blackmail to get whatever she wanted.

Sage left the arena on Seraphina, pulling my attention, and Hallie was called in next by Marco. Hallie walked Huxley into the arena, breaking straight into a trot. I was transfixed as I watched her rising trot, only for that admiration to be interrupted by Alexis's snort. "Here she is," Alexis said, rolling her eyes. "Little Orphan Annie." Instant fire infused my every cell as those words left her poisonous mouth. Alexis nudged me like I was a close pal. "Tell me, does she parade around here in her cowboy boots and hat like she does when she's competing?" Alexis huffed out a degrading laugh. "She's lauded as the next big thing, the poor little cowgirl that could," she added, then shrugged. "Everyone falls at her feet because of her pathetic childhood tragedy, but she looks completely average to me. There's nothing outstanding about her at all."

Something inside of me exploded, completely burst into flames, and I had to hold myself back from insulting Alexis where she stood. Instead, I reined myself in and simply said, "Hallie Oakley is the best rider I've ever seen walk through these gates." Just at that moment, Hallie soared over an oxer with perfect form and precision, easily clearing the fence. It was as though she was proving my point. "And anyone with an ounce of equestrian knowledge would see that a mile off."

A rush of warmth swept through me as Hallie turned to Marco, who was giving her a thumbs-up. Her responding smile was wide and absolutely breathtaking.

"Oh, no," Alexis said from beside me, yanking me from my admiration. Alexis was wearing a smug expression on her face as she looked from me to Hallie and back again.

"What?" I snapped, perhaps too aggressively. Though it didn't seem to have affected Alexis in the slightest.

"*Jasper* Knighton," Alexis said, turning her body to face me head-on. "Mr. 'I Keep Things Professional' wants to fuck his newest rider. His *employee.*"

My chest tightened until it was almost painful, and a wide, victorious smile spread on Alexis's mouth. "Don't be absurd," I said in response.

"Darling, it's written all over your face," she said, then pressed her hand over my cock. "And your cock is half hard just looking at her."

I gripped her wrist and threw her hand away from my crotch. "Don't fucking touch me." Alexis's eyes flared at my anger. She liked me scolding her this way. She was so fucked up. "You're dangerously close to me breaking all contracts with you, Alexis. Know your fucking place and back the fuck down."

Alexis licked her lips, but I could see an excited spark in her eye. Like she had landed some kind of exclusive scoop. Like she now had something she could hold over my head. She stepped closer to me. "Word on the street is that your run of bad luck of late might not be pure happenstance, Jasper. I'd *suggest* you don't push away the allies you still have."

My heart seemed to stop beating, and my lungs froze. I leaned down and glared into her eyes. "And what would you know about my so-called bad luck, Alexis?"

Unintimidated, she simply shrugged. "All I'm saying is that you should respect those loyal to you, Jasper. It seems like you might already have an impressive enemy."

Shivers sliced down my spine. Alexis was a bitch, potentially a stone-cold psychopath, but before this I'd never considered she was behind any of the threats, the accidents. Yes, she wanted my businesses, but I'd never believed her capable of setting up my family's misfortune to get what she wanted.

"It's time for you to leave," I said, and began walking back to the golf buggy. It was that or I would toss Alexis over the fucking hill that had given us such a good view of the arena.

I sat in the driver's seat, and Alexis sauntered out of the woods like she had all the time in the world. I fucking detested this woman. My hands balled into fists on my thighs. I'd stupidly given away my attraction to Hallie.

I was a bloody idiot.

Alexis sat beside me, and we rode back to the yard in silence. When we reached it, her driver was waiting for her outside her brand-new Bentley. Once out of the buggy, I rounded the cart, and Alexis stood before me. She held out her hand. Reluctantly, I shook it. I went to pull away, when Alexis held on, pulling me close. "I'll keep an eye out for your new riders on the circuit, Jasper. Especially your cowgirl."

"Don't even think about it, Alexis. There's no gossip here for you. Hallie is riding my horse, I'm her sponsor, and that's all there is to it. You're fishing for a story that doesn't exist."

Alexis leaned in until her mouth reached my ear. "Eyes don't lie, Jasper"—she smirked—"and neither does the blood that filled your cock just looking at her." Alexis pulled her hand back and tapped my chest. "Consider the offer I've left on your desk, Jasper. If I want something, I won't stop until I've got it. You know this."

With that, Alexis turned and got into her car, leaving me fuming on the spot. Staff members watched her leave, showing obvious disdain for her on their faces. Alexis seemed to inspire hatred wherever she went, and clearly, she gave no fucks about it.

But I was a veritable inferno. Every part of me was a live wire. Alexis had seen me look at Hallie like I wanted her—because I fucking *did.* But that information could not be in the hands of someone like Alexis Hobbs. She followed the Sandings Tour, was at every single stop, "taking care" of her clients. She was a wolf, and I'd just made Hallie a sacrificial lamb.

Exhaling in frustration, I scrubbed my hands down my face and fucking hated myself when I felt them shaking. I saw the taillights of Alexis's Bentley exit the long road out of the property and couldn't shake the twist in my gut her words had given me.

Word on the street is that your run of bad luck of late might not be purely happenstance . . .

What did that *mean*? What had she heard? Did she know something? Could she be involved somehow? Surely not. But what if . . .

My head throbbed from all the racing thoughts. Would Alexis go as far as to resort to threats and violence against my loved ones to get her hands on Golden Oaks? The fact that I now wasn't sure was alarming. It wasn't like people hadn't done this type of shit for decades in this industry.

Or worse.

I began to walk, to fucking *anywhere*, just to stop the slamming of my heart from breaking my ribs, my racing thoughts from shifting to a migraine. My mind was a whirlwind. All I saw were rapid images of pain and sadness—my father's accident, his broken body, eyes frozen open with death, staring up at me as I clutched his still hand, as the scent of his blood invaded my senses. Next came Genny and Dahlia falling in Saint-Tropez, my sister being crushed, and me watching it all, believing she was dead too—more still hands, lying empty like they were searching for my help. Cold shivers stabbed down my back.

Then there was Hallie. Lively, rebellious, beautiful Hallie, whose reputation may have just been ruined because of the way I looked at her in front of a woman hell-bent on destroying any rival she believed she had. All because I got fucking hard watching Hallie jump.

I couldn't seem to do shit about the threats to my family and business just yet, but I *could* make sure that any rumors about Hallie and me would be put to rest. The last thing she needed as a new rider on the circuit was snide whispers about her fucking her boss. She was too good of a rider to be the subject of ridicule for her private life. And if Alexis smelled blood in the water, she would attack. Like any apex predator seeking dominance, she couldn't seem to help herself.

"Jas!" I looked behind me to find Forrest running to catch up with me. Unbeknownst to me, I'd been heading in the direction of the outdoor arena where the Knighton Equestrian shoot was taking place. Seemed I really couldn't fucking keep away from Hallie right now.

I schooled my features so my cousin wouldn't suspect anything and waved my hand at him. Forrest fell into step with me. "You heading to the shoot?" Forrest asked. "Atticus has been there a while now."

"On my way," I said, without stopping.

Forrest grabbed my arm. "What's up your arse?"

My heart was still beating erratically, but I just said, "Alexis Hobbs just left."

Forrest grimaced. "Shit. That'll do it," he said. "Is she taking the new foals when they're ready?"

I nodded. Then just to give him some explanation for my shitty mood, said, "She offered to buy Golden Oaks again and practically offered to ride my cock too, so just another regular meeting with the infamous Hobbs heir."

Forrest sighed. I felt my cousin's gaze boring into me. I swear, I felt his grin aimed my way, like there was a disturbance in the air. I swung around and faced him. "What?"

Forrest folded his arms over his chest. He shrugged. "Nothing. I'm just disappointed that I haven't found you in a better mood." I glared at Forrest harder. That used to work on him when we were kids, but now we were grown, I didn't intimidate him at all. "I'd heard a bit of information I thought might have put a spring in your step."

I stayed glaring at him. Forrest eventually cracked. "Thought it was interesting that apparently you sent Sage Miller and Atticus on their merry way last night, only to have Hallie Oakley model some solo shots for you. Alone. In the warehouse. Unplanned." I exhaled slowly through my nose. *"And,"* Forrest said, not bothering hiding his shitty, smug smile this time, "you gave her a ride home. Just the two of you. For an hour. On all those dark roads . . ."

"Is there a question in there, dickhead?" I snapped. My pulse raced. I'd been so stupid with Hallie. So fucking stupid. What the hell was I thinking? I was being too obvious with her. I was a grown fucking man, not a teen with a crush. I had to put an end to this.

Now.

Forrest studied me closely, making me feel like a rat in a lab. "What's going on, Jas? Do you like her?" His humor had ebbed, clearly seeing my icy response, and now he was truly looking into my fucking soul like only a loved one could.

I turned and walked away. Forrest followed. I had to stop this. I looked over my shoulder. Forrest put his hand on my arm and spun me around. He was frowning. "No one would begrudge you some happiness, you know?" I rolled my eyes. He was talking about Hallie, and I literally couldn't listen to this anymore.

To knock him off the scent, I said, "I'm not the hearts-and-flowers type, Forrest. And neither are you, so don't be giving me shit over something you know isn't in our DNA."

"Jas—"

"Leave it!" I snapped, cutting him off.

Of course, he didn't. "You know, Atticus has been telling me that both Hallie and Sage have a lot of admirers on the circuit. She leaves for Doha in a couple of weeks." He shrugged. "There's a lot of rich, good-looking bastards who'll be interested in her. You'd be okay with that?"

That shouldn't have bothered me as much as it did, but the tidal wave of jealousy that crashed through me at Forrest's teasing words was all-consuming. But it didn't matter. Nothing could happen.

With every step to the arena, I grew increasingly agitated. Why, in a matter of weeks, was I letting all my perfectly constructed walls crumble? It only took my phone ringing to push me completely over the edge.

"Yes?" I answered, curtly.

"The new lead we had has gone dead." Phillip, my PI. Instead of feeling let down, my blood tipped to boiling temperatures.

"Perfect," I snapped, and went to hang up, when he said, "The Franklin Stud farm in Yorkshire has been hit." I stopped dead and looked up to find Forrest watching me. All teasing drained from his face. He could tell something was seriously wrong.

"Hit in what way?" I asked.

"Someone injected their stallions with 1-Androsterone. They've failed the drug tests for the upcoming Grand Prix, and there was also a break-in where someone tried to get to the weaned foals that were ready for sale. Luckily, they were interrupted and fled before they could. But it's yet another hit on a stud farm in the past twenty-four months. I'm trying to determine whether the incidents are related, and if they were getting threats beforehand too."

What the fuck? Forrest had clearly heard Phillip as his lips tightened in anger and concern.

"You think whoever did it could be the same person targeting us?"

"Don't know, but it's a possibility," Phillip said. "The crime has just been reported. I have an in at the police who let me know. It'll hit the equestrian gossip mill by the end of the day, I'm sure."

I rubbed my forehead with my hand. "Keep me updated," I said, and hung up. I would call Phillip back later and put him on Alexis Hobbs's scent. Something about the shit she said to me had my alarm bells ringing.

"It's nothing new, Jas," Forrest said, trying to placate me. "It's not like we don't see this often." And he was right. This shit had been happening to studs for years. Rivalry, jealousy, money . . . It all played a role in this industry. Good studs raked in millions, if not billions of pounds a year. Foul play was common.

I didn't speak, instead letting what Phillip said add to the burn Alexis had already kindled inside of me. It was laughable—from the outside, the horse world looked gentrified and proper, all perfect manners and class. In truth, it was like a bad reality show, filled with scandals and a whole lot of fucking behind people's backs.

When we got to the arena, Atticus was on Barnaby. He was midflight over a jump, Steve, the photographer, capturing the motion. We stopped at the perimeter fence. I immediately searched around me and saw Sage and Hallie in the outdoor arena behind us, keeping their horses warm. My lungs seized when I saw Hallie was now dressed in the turquoise set I'd requested her in yesterday. Huxley was wearing the matching saddle pad and ear bonnet, as well as the brushing boots on his legs to keep them safe should he hit a pole. The color was in stark contrast to his dark-brown coat.

And then there was Hallie. She cantered Huxley around the arena, then lined up for the approach. There wasn't anything I could fault with her seat or technique as she took Hux over the 150 cm fence. In the base layer and riding tights, the clingy material showcased her hourglass figure.

I couldn't fucking want her.

I couldn't.

For the second time that day, I was saved from my wayward thoughts by my phone. Tim Franklin from the Franklin Stud was calling.

I walked a few feet away from the arena, seeing Atticus head for the gate. His part of the shoot seemed done for now. "Tim," I said in greeting.

"We've been hit" was all he said. Tim was my dad's best friend and had been the same age too. His stud in Yorkshire was world renowned.

His children were big show jumpers on the circuit—his son, Spencer, had always been one of my rivals since our teens. But we were good friends, as much as two competitors could be.

"What happened?" I said. I knew, of course, but I couldn't let him know that. Phillip was the best at what he did. I paid him a shit ton of money to keep him working for me. Including keeping things he told me under wraps.

"Anabolics. Performance enhancers on my Grand Prix stallions," Tim said. I could hear the rasp of devastation on his voice. "The pricks broke in, dismantled my top-of-the-range security system, and injected all my superstars for this season." Tim sighed. "We interrupted the bastards doing it and scared them off, but the few CCTV cameras they missed only showed men dressed in all black with ski masks hiding their faces."

The sound of the arena gate opening caught my attention, and I watched Hallie enter the ring.

"Have any leads?" I asked.

"None yet. But I will," Tim said, as Steve explained what he wanted Hallie to do in the background. The fence for the shoot had Knighton Equestrian fillers on it, my Lord Henry logo plastered on the wings. "I just wanted to give you a heads-up, son," Tim said. "If there's someone targeting studs, I wanted to let you know first. Your dad would have done the same for me."

My heart fell a little at that. He would have. My dad may have been a ruthless businessman at times, but he was always good to people in our industry. Our stud farm had, of course, always had rivals. But it had never been nefarious.

Hallie walked Huxley around the edges of the arena and moved him into a trot. As she rose up and down, I had to turn away from the sight of her perfect arse when I felt my traitorous cock begin to swell again.

"Do you think the McGowens could be up to their old tricks?" Tim asked in a hushed tone.

Even at the sound of the name, anger took me in its hold. Five years ago, the McGowen Stud, a hugely successful farm in the Cotswolds, was caught drugging rival studs' Grand Prix horses, some so much that they never recovered. It was the biggest scandal to hit the horse world in years. The owner of the stud, Charlie McGowen, was sentenced to time in prison. Was still there. We all found out later that he had made some bad gambling decisions on the circuit and needed to make some of his cash back, quickly. He thought taking down other studs was his answer.

His son, Jacob McGowen, a professional show jumper and the rider I hated most in our world, took the helm and swore to turn the stud around. He had, it seemed. But while I admired him for picking up the pieces his father left behind, I still hated the arrogant fucker. He was the one I wanted to beat most of all on the circuits, but as much as I thought he was a smarmy bastard with little to no morals, I didn't think he was corrupt like his old man. Then again, I had begun to wonder if I was a crap judge of people these days.

"We'll keep an eye out," I said. "Let me know what you learn."

"Will do, son. Keep safe." Tim was about to hang up when I asked, "Just out of curiosity, Tim, has Alexis Hobbs ever made you an offer on your business?"

"That bloody woman is like a dog with a bone," Tim said, and my blood iced over. "She was up here just a week ago flashing her cheque book at me and offering me obscene money for my land and my business—the lot! I told her to sling her hook." Tim paused, then asked, "Why?"

"No real reason," I said, trying not to imply anything before I had more information about my suspicions. "I just had the pleasure of her company this morning, and she made me an offer for Golden Oaks too."

Tim tutted. "More money than sense, that one." Then he made my spine straighten when he said, "I'm pretty sure your old man mentioned something about her trying to buy your place just before he passed. I blame her father. He indulged her too much as a kid. Thinks she can get whatever she wants." Someone spoke to Tim in the background, and he said, "I must go, Jasper. This place will be like King's Cross today. I'll speak to you soon, kid."

Tim hung up, and I tipped my head back and closed my eyes. Alexis had met with my dad? I let the winter sun warm my face and wished spring would just hurry up and fucking arrive. Everything seemed better in the sun.

I sucked in a deep breath, but nothing would calm the fire inside. It was taking hold of me, and my mood turned sour. Forrest was watching me with narrow eyes. I reached the arena just in time to see Hallie taking to the air, perfect jumping stance and clearing it with ease. As she landed, her eyes found mine and a smile etched on her lips.

Fuck me, but she was beautiful.

You can't, a voice said at the back of my head. *You can't put her in danger. You can't do anything to harm the stud. The horses. But especially Hallie . . .*

Hallie trotted past, smiling wider at me. "Your legs were too far forward," I said. Even to my own ears, I caught the arsehole tone of my voice. Hallie's smile slipped off her face, and I hated myself in that moment. But I kept going. "Your reins were too short. Huxley almost hit a pole because you were holding him back." I flicked my hand to Steve, who was frowning at me. He checked the last shot he got on the camera, and by his expression, he must have known I was talking utter shite. I waved my hand at Hallie. "Again."

Hallie took a deep breath, calming herself down, and nudged Huxley into a trot. When she had him in canter, she led him over the jump again. She was perfect. It was perfect. Her eyes fell on me as she landed, and I shook my head.

I hated it. I hated being this prick, but I couldn't allow her to like me. I couldn't like her back. Just look what was happening in our industry, the suspicions I had set off in Alexis. "You're too fast on the approach. He's too under the jump, and on the circuit, that'll cost you time or points." I waved my hand again. "Do it again," I snapped, and this time I saw ire flare on Hallie's face at my censure. As expected, her short fuse had been blown.

But she did as I said. In fact, she did it three more times. As she landed on the fourth, she drew Huxley to a stop. She was only meters away from me. "You need to practice more," I said, my words tasting like acid coming off my tongue. Hallie undid the chin strap of her hat and pulled it off. Her hair was in a braid, and she looked unworldly. But her kind, turquoise eyes were no longer soft, they were like granite as they scored into mine.

"I practice all the time," she said, her accent holding a pissed-off tone. "I lunge Huxley, work out, and leave no stone unturned. I can't possibly practice more."

"This isn't the Under-25s," I said. "This is the mainstage. With the most experienced riders in the world all clawing for the top prize money." I pointed at Huxley. "You're riding our horse and you're representing our brand, so you need to measure up. And quickly."

"Fuck, Jas," Forrest muttered beside me. "Enough. It's a bloody photo shoot. She's jumping for a damn picture, not competing." His voice was hard. Good. He was pissed at me too. That'd be three this morning alone.

Leon, who had been on the other side of the arena, came over. He was scowling at me. He'd clearly heard everything too. "Take a walk, Jasper," he said.

One thing was for sure, I was the owner of this stud farm and the CEO of Golden Oaks, but the training arenas were Leon's. And right now, I was fucking over his most promising rider. The fact he was like another cousin to me was the only reason he *could* speak to me like this on the land I owned.

I could feel the heat of anger pulsing off Hallie as I stayed rooted to the spot for a few more seconds. When I turned to her, her face was flushed, and her breathing was heavy. I hated myself. And I was pretty sure Hallie Oakley now hated me too.

Good. That was what *had* to happen. When Alexis sniffed around now, all she would hear is how much of a dick I was to Hallie. Zero romantic interest.

"Fix it," I snapped at Hallie, and turned away.

Even Forrest didn't follow me this time. I practically ran to my home study, slamming the door behind me and immediately pouring myself a large whisky. I slumped down to my chair and tossed my hat on the desk, knocking the whisky back in one. I stared at the oak top of the desk, my eyes blurring as I became lost to my thoughts.

Who the fuck have I become?

It was amazing how fear and pain could curdle a soul. I wanted my old life back. I wanted morning hacks with my cousins and chasing wins at the Grand Prix. I wanted family dinners and traveling with family. I wanted Lord Henry being in center spotlight where he belonged.

I wanted my sister to be okay.

I wanted my dad to be alive.

Blinking, I wiped away the tear that slipped from my eye. I clenched my jaw and chased my self-pity away. But when I pictured Hallie's hurt, her angry face, I just wanted to go to sleep and wake up when all this shit was done.

But I had to protect her, and being close to me, in any way, shape, or form, only brought people bad luck.

Opening the desk drawer I always kept locked, I brought out today's offering. Unfolding the letter that had arrived in this morning's post, I read the typed words:

> All you love will be destroyed.
> Everything you built will be torn down.
> You will have no one left, and no empire to rule.
> I will destroy you, like your father did me.

Taking out a file from the same drawer, I placed the newest letter inside. The file was getting full. Flipping to the back of the pile,

I found the letters my father had kept hidden in the same place. Threats just like this, but more personal. Ones against his life, Genevieve, and me.

My cousins knew about my father's letters. But they didn't know they had never stopped after he had died or that they were now coming to me. I didn't want them to worry more than they already were. And Genevieve, I'd kept *everything* from her. She had the kindest, purest heart I knew, and I didn't want anything to change that.

But then the threat against her had come true, and it had been all my fault. She didn't know her big brother had kept things from her, didn't know she had to be vigilant for people trying to hurt her. She didn't know I'd failed to stop her getting injured. Her and her precious horse, who was so spooked she now had to be housed alone and away from a herd.

The guilt that wrapped around my heart over that was so stifling, most days I didn't even know how I breathed.

What the fuck had Dad done to inspire such a vendetta against our family? He was my *dad*, so I had a view of him no one else did, but he was a nice, kind man. He hadn't ever hurt anyone to my knowledge. When our mother died, Dad took the helm without a thought. He didn't foist us off on nannies or send us to a boarding school. He was *there* for us. So what could he possibly have done to make someone want to kill him? To hurt me and Genny and anyone who has any affiliation with us? The letters addressed to him made out as though he was almost *evil*. What they said about him was a far cry from the man I knew and loved. But I refused to believe my view of him was incorrect.

I knew him, damn it.

I *knew* him.

I wanted to be like him. Even though my attitude of late was anything but. Hallie's hurt expression sprang to my mind, making my heart feel like lead. Forrest wanted me to be happy. He thought I liked Hallie—and he wasn't wrong.

But it was best that she hated me.

I refused to be an albatross to anyone else.

It was better this way, with her despising the ground that I walked on. I'd admire her from afar and watch her soar on the tour. Because despite everything I said today, she was the best natural rider I'd ever seen.

She was incredible.

And she deserved to be kept safe.

Chapter Eight

Hallie

I rubbed my chest again, then shoveled another scoop of Ben & Jerry's Phish Food into my mouth.

It felt like I'd been punched. In a way I had, but with Jasper's words instead of fists. His venomous, nasty words. I followed the ice cream with a sip of rosé and said, "My leg wasn't too far forward. I saw the photo Steve took. My position was perfect."

"It was," Sage said, holding up her middle finger. "Fuck him and his sexy eyes." I turned my head to Sage. She held up her hands in surrender. "He's a douchebag for speaking to you like that, Hals, but he's still a *hot* douchebag." I'd told Sage all about my interactions with Jasper. I could never keep anything from her for long. In true Sage fashion, she had lapped up every detail with vigor, whooping and hollering with every spilled word.

I sighed, and my head fell back against the couch. "He was today, and he made me feel about an inch tall in front of everyone in the arena." I cast my eyes out the window, at the fields that led to the main house. "But I don't think he is usually." I curled onto the couch and faced Sage.

"Last night in the car, he was stiff and unapproachable, until he wasn't." I blew out a frustrated raspberry, and Sage laughed. "He swings back and forth so much I have whiplash." It was true. Last night, I thought we'd finally gotten somewhere. He'd mellowed toward me. Today . . . Shit, that was *rough*.

"He's had a tough couple of years," Sage said. "Maybe that's why he's gone from Smiley to Moody Jasper."

I glanced down at my outfit. I was still dressed in the turquoise set from the shoot. The one he'd picked out especially for me. I didn't understand the man. And despite the fact I should keep the hell away from him and his epic mood swings, him pushing me away made me want to know him more. I wanted to find out where the Jasper of old had gone.

I was a glutton for punishment. But I didn't want him to be sad, and some kind of Spidey sense within me told me he was. That the way he was acting toward me was a front, a ruse. Perhaps maybe a shield. A way to keep anyone from getting too close.

"You need to just focus on the riding, Hals. It's what we're here to do. No distractions," Sage said with a firm nod. She shoved a big spoon of ice cream in her mouth to cement her point.

I raised an eyebrow at Sage. "What?" she said at my knowing expression.

"No distractions?" I questioned.

Sage pointed her spoon at me like a weapon. "Don't you dare. Do not even dare mention that heathen in my presence." For the first time since my reprimand this afternoon, I felt a spark of humor ignite inside of me.

I held up my hands in surrender this time. "I'm shutting up," I said, smugly. But Sage watched me with narrowed eyes.

Turning on the TV, Sage snuggled beside me and said, "Now, put something on with hot, muscled men. I've fed my stomach with sugar and now need some for my eyes and spank bank later."

"Thanks for that visual, Sage," I said, dryly.

"You're welcome, sweetie," she said, and patted my hand.

We settled on *Lord of the Rings* because, well, Aragorn, but I could barely focus on the film. Instead, I racked my brain about what had happened between last night and today to make Jasper turn so cold. At the arena, he was wicked. It took every ounce of self-restraint I had not to dismount and slap him across his beautifully stubbled cheek. But I kept my shit together and did my job, despite my clawing need to argue back. It wasn't easy for me to keep my mouth shut, but I'd endured it today. Jasper seemed off kilter, shaken somehow.

He reminded me of how Canyon spoke of troubled or hurt horses. They seemed violent and aggressive on the surface, but it was pure fear driving them. It just took someone understanding for their true selves to shine through. I wondered whether Jasper Knighton was the same.

Still, his words today *hurt.*

I was currently in Sage's cottage, but her couch was the same as mine. I closed my eyes and remembered when Jasper had carried me back to my cottage from his car and laid me on the couch.

Night, Angel.

He'd called me angel. I was sure of it. And this time he hadn't been drunk off whiskey. *No,* he'd been stone-cold sober and ran his fingers down my face and called me fucking *angel.* I may have been half asleep, but I was 100 percent sure of those things. And suddenly, today I couldn't ride? My jumping was subpar? My leg position was wrong?

They weren't. I wasn't being cocky, but I had worked damn hard over the years to ensure I was the best, and Jasper Knighton in a savage mood was not going to derail me.

The longer I sat watching elves, hobbits, and men fight to save Middle Earth, the more the anger in me grew and grew until I needed to get up and move.

I shifted and Sage flopped to the couch, passed out from her sugar crash, no doubt. I covered her with a knitted throw from the back of the couch and kissed her good night on the cheek.

Locking Sage's door, I grabbed my equirobe from my cottage's entranceway and made my way across the fields to the barn, checking my pockets to make sure I had some Polos for Huxley. The mints were his favorite treat, and after the way we'd both been unfairly spoken to today, he deserved them.

Ten minutes later, I entered the barn and made a beeline for Huxley. My stallion was busy eating his hay but stopped when he saw me approaching with his snack.

I laid my hand flat and laughed as Huxley practically sucked up the mint like a vacuum. He crunched it quickly and immediately nudged my arm to give him more. I kissed his blaze and tickled his cheek. "You're a sweetheart, baby," I said, and gave him a cuddle, slipping him one more Polo for good measure.

I moved to Fefe next, who just scowled at me from the back of her stall. I held out my hand, showing her the mint. "Come on, princess. It's for you." She looked at me as though I was a lowly peasant and didn't deserve any of her time. Rolling my eyes at her attitude, I dropped the mint to the ground in her stall. "I'll leave it there for you, Moody."

I walked away and smiled when I heard her munching it up. Sage had a real sassy pants there.

I found myself at the closed-off private Knighton part of the barn. I now knew I shouldn't have been there. Jasper had told me so. But after today's tongue lashing, *fuck* Jasper.

Undoing the bolt, I threw back the metal handle and slid the door open. Barnaby and Sebastian immediately came into view. I gave them each a Polo, then moved to Lady Aurelia. I slipped her a Polo too, and she was kind and appreciative, unlike Fefe.

I turned toward Lord Henry to give my favorite horse some love and treats, only to find his stall empty. My stomach fell and I rushed over to check he wasn't lying on the floor with colic or worse.

My heart slammed in my chest, seeing it empty, and I began to panic. It was one in the freakin' morning. Where could he be? I searched all over the barn, and with every empty stall and corner, true panic built within me.

Has someone stolen him? That dark thought had me running toward the exit, but I came up short when my brain registered the thudding sound of hooves. The Knightons had a private indoor arena that was solely for their use, and it was attached to this section of the barn. I moved over to the closed doors and heard the unmistakable thuds of a horse in motion.

There was a pedestrian door built into the main barn door, and as quietly as I could, I turned the knob and opened it. I snuck inside, only for my mouth to drop open at what I found.

A flash of white passed by me, and before my very eyes, Lord Henry was sailing over jumps. Not just jumps, but a tricky and challenging course that looked like it had been created by the best course designer on the tour. The fences had to be at least 160 cm in height, bigger than the standard Grand Prix course. Henry sailed over them like they were only a foot tall. But that's not what had me so enraptured. No, that honor belonged to Jasper, who was jumping his stallion with as much proficiency and beauty as he had a year ago when he was still on the circuit.

As he turned Henry to take another fence, the joy on Jasper's face made me breathless. *This* was Jasper Knighton. *This* was the man I had met all those years ago. This moment was an echo to the past. I was once again the inexperienced twelve-year-old cowgirl, watching a man take flight on an almost mythically talented horse.

The sight brought tears to my eyes.

Jasper hadn't given up like he'd led everyone to believe.

I'd assumed that Lord Henry was ridden by Jasper's groom, Benjamin, and that was why he was still so fit and muscular. But Jasper clearly rode him when no one was around, in secret, but with as much talent—if not more—than before.

As they took the final spread fence, I audibly gasped as Henry cleared it with room to spare—a perfectly clear round. But in the quiet arena, that gasp gave me away. Jasper pulled Henry to a halt and whipped his head in my direction. Jasper was breathing hard, well exercised from the course. Henry had barely broken a sweat.

The happiness I'd seen on Jasper's face evaporated into a hard scowl under the brim of his helmet. He was dressed in all black, the Knighton Equestrian base layer and breeches fitting him like a second skin. *Hell*, his body was perfection. He was tall and toned and muscled, and perched on Henry, he commanded such power it was aphrodisiacal to simply watch.

And I watched him like a hawk. Jasper walked Henry to where I stood. As he stilled before me, towering high on Henry's eighteen hands, he said, "What are you doing here?"

His voice and attitude were just as harsh and demeaning as they were earlier today, but I pushed that aside to say, "You still ride." I caught the awe in my voice, but I didn't care. Jasper hadn't quit. I shook my head. "You are incredible."

"You shouldn't be here," Jasper bit out, but I noticed a slight softening in his tone.

I lifted my hand and ran it along Henry's nose. The champion stallion let me pet him. "You're better than ever, Henry," I said, like the horse could understand my compliment.

Jasper pulled on Henry's reins and he stepped back, away from my touch. As quick as a breath, Jasper kicked his legs over the saddle and dismounted. When he hit the arena floor, he took hold of the reins below Henry's mouth and walked his prize stallion through the big barn doors. "Leave," he hissed at me as he passed. *"Now."*

But I couldn't move. I was still in shock, in awe, in wonder of this man and his incredible horse. Instead, I watched him go. In his all-black getup, Jasper looked imposing and mysterious. He quickly untacked Henry and let his horse into his stall with fresh hay. Jasper whipped off his hat, and after he'd put all his equipment away in the tack room, he came out and saw me still standing here.

His face became a thundercloud. "I *told* you to leave," he said through clenched teeth. He walked to where I stood, power and dominance in his every step. His long black riding boots cocooned his muscled calves, and his thigh muscles flexed as he moved.

I walked back a few steps until my back hit a nearby wall. Jasper crowded me, and I was instantly accosted by his sandalwood and mint scent. It made me heady. He was scowling at me. But this time, I wasn't backing down.

"Leave!" he said, more aggressively.

But I tipped my chin to his command and said, "Why are you hiding the fact you still ride?"

He stepped closer still, until his palms flattened on the wall behind me, caging me in. The air between us seemed to crackle, and I imagined lifting my hands, untying his belt, and dropping to my knees. Heat rushed through my veins and goose bumps broke out over my skin.

"Look at me!" he barked, and my eyes immediately snapped to his. His jaw clenched when I obeyed. His voice gravelly when he said, "Why do you keep breaking all the rules?"

I ignored him. I was a rule breaker. Sue me. I'd been called a lot worse. "You were incredible," I said, my voice wrapped in awe. "I've never seen anyone jump like you on Henry." I shook my head. "Your talent is being *wasted*, Jasper."

His responding laugh was cold. His cheeks were heavily stubbled, and his hair was damp from where he'd sweated under his helmet. His hands balled into fists against the wall above me—he looked unhinged.

Beautifully unhinged. "Get out, Ms. Oakley. And do not tell anyone I was here."

"Hallie," I bit back, feeling my blood begin to rise to boiling temperatures. "You only ever call me Ms. Oakley when you're trying to create distance between us."

"There is *only* distance between us!" he hissed, then laughed patronizingly. "Do not fool yourself into thinking there is anything happening here."

I pushed on his chest, *hard,* but Jasper didn't budge. He was granite. "I wouldn't *dare,*" I snapped back. "You're a miserable prick who doesn't deserve my attention."

I didn't let my surprise show on my face, but I was startled by my vitriol. I wasn't a wallflower, I spoke my mind often, but when Jasper acted like this, like some overbearing and elitist asshole, some untapped warrior instinct inside of my soul rose up, battle ready and preparing to fight him like I'd never fought anyone before.

We breathed hard, eyes fixed on one another as our bodies were tense and taut. This moment shouldn't have been sexy, it shouldn't have created air so thick between us that felt like it had its own pulse. It shouldn't have drawn us closer, but like a rope tied around our chests, it pulled us in, inch by inch, until I could feel his body heat against my breasts. Shivers ran down my spine and gathered between my legs.

"Why do you keep *looking* at me like that?" Jasper asked, his voice cut like glass. "Why do your pupils dilate? Why do your nipples harden?" My shallow breaths became trapped in my throat. "Why does your skin flush and paint your cheeks with red?"

A hungry expression built on his face that I knew reflected my own, and I wished I could take a picture of him exactly like this. Untamed, broken, and all his untethered need and lust for me laid bare. My hands itched to touch him, to splay on his chest and feel his hard muscles shifting beneath. I wanted him to lose all his careful control, rip off my clothes, and fuck me against the wall.

My need must have shown on my face, as Jasper's teeth clenched, his jaw tensing like it was taking all the inner strength he had to hold himself back from doing just that. His eyes closed, and he inhaled a deep breath. When they opened again, he edged closer, so close that my tits brushed against his chest. I swallowed a moan and squeezed my thighs together to stop my traitorous clit from torturing me further by this treatment. Jasper was breathless at our proximity; I was too. "Tell me how much you like to watch me ride," he said, his mouth near my ear. *"Yes,"* I wanted to call out. *"Let go. Let go of your self-imposed restraints and just feel. Stop fighting whatever this is."* "Tell me how much you want your legs wrapped around my waist as I push inside you." He laughed one single husky laugh, and just at the sound I almost came on the spot. "Tell me how much you want to feel my tongue between your legs, licking at your pussy until you're screaming my name."

I was scalding to the touch. Sweat was trickling down my back, and I was so wet between my legs that if he pulled my riding tights down, he would be able to slip straight inside.

My cheeks felt on fire, and I was immobile, wanting him to dominate me, unleash the man he was inside . . . until Jasper's lip traced the shell of my ear and he said, "But it will never fucking happen, *Hallie*. You came here to ride my horses, not me."

Like a bucket of ice water had been dumped on my head, it took several seconds for his words to filter through me. *The asshole!* My anger came over me swiftly and strongly and I wanted to tear him apart. But instead, I forced my legs to move. I pushed past him with force, and this time, Jasper let me.

I rushed to the exit, feeling both livid and humiliated, when something made me turn to face him and say, "I can't believe I was so wrong about you." I let those words circle around us, filling every inch of space with disappointment. "I have idolized you for years, have only heard your reputation to be one of a gentleman. But this—" I waved my hand up and down his frozen frame. "*This?*

This version of you isn't someone to admire." Jasper's eyes widened and his nostrils flared. "You are cruel, and you are bitter, and to discover the man who inspired me to ride is such a fucking *dick* . . ." I laughed sardonically now. "*That* is the real tragedy here."

With that, I spun on my heels and rushed out into the cold night, ignoring the few stray tears that tracked down my cheeks and the sudden ache of emptiness that had burrowed into my heart.

Chapter Nine

Hallie

The sun beat down from above, warming my old Stetson and keeping my head warm. This kind of weather had come to be my favorite in England—the brisk coolness of a winter's day, but with a clear blue sky, the sun beaming brightly above, casting the mass of green fields in a stunning golden hue.

Clicking my tongue, I smiled as Huxley immediately moved from a trot to a canter as we worked at liberty. His dark coat glistened in the bright light as he circled around me, highlighting each of the muscles that'd been honed and defined from all our training.

"Good boy," I praised, and Huxley's ears pricked back and forth at the compliment. We were outside in an arena away from the main body of the estate. Yesterday, an insane number of security guards had turned up at Golden Oaks and were staying for the foreseeable future. Word in the yard was that Jasper had hired more guards due to a string of stud farm break-ins that were happening up and down the country. I understood the reasoning for the extra protection, but seeing a guard everywhere you turned was a little unnerving.

Today, I wasn't riding. This morning was just Huxley and me bonding, something I'd been doing with him since we'd been assigned as a team. Taking out my cell, I video-called the one person who'd appreciate this.

When Canyon's face came on my screen, I smiled despite the lingering ache that had been there for the past couple of days, one that had cast a shadow over my happiness, regardless of my best efforts to put it behind me.

"Hallie-girl!" Canyon said, and the rising Texas sunrise behind him made homesickness crash over my heart. Canyon was clearly on horseback if the bobbing of the camera was any indication. It was about 5:00 a.m. on the ranch, but I knew Canyon already would have been up. Ranchers awoke at the crack of dawn.

"How's the ranch today?" I asked. I kept my arm out to signal to Huxley to keep going. I wanted him to do his final rounds of this exercise, then we'd call it a day.

Canyon lifted his steel coffee mug to the camera. "Good, Hals. Havin' my mornin' ride around the perimeter with Rosie." Canyon moved the camera down so I could see his old, treasured quarter horse beneath him. She didn't work cattle these days, but she still loved to hack around the land. My chest squeezed tightly. I loved my life now, what I did for a living, but there was something about ranch life that called to me like a siren's song. I wiggled my toes in my cowboy boots and felt the heavy denim of my trusted jeans pressed against my thighs. Wearing these clothes, if I closed my eyes, I could almost taste Texas. Could almost trick myself into believing I was back there with him.

The way I'd been feeling these past couple of days, I wished I was. Just for a small reprieve from the cave that had burrowed into my heart.

"Hals?" Canyon said, suspicion in his voice. "What's wrong? I know that face."

I opened my eyes and forced a smile. I turned the camera so Canyon could see Huxley being lunged without a line. Our liberty work was coming along nicely, and my beautiful stallion trusted me increasingly each day.

"He's a beauty," Canyon said. I turned the camera back to me and *whoa*ed in a gentle voice, signaling Huxley to come down to a walk. He did exactly as I wanted. "He trusts you," Canyon said approvingly, and I could see the pride on his face. "We'll make a horse whisperer out of you yet."

I laughed. "I'll leave that to you and your magical touch, but I like the bond Hux and I have built up. I'm really getting to know what makes him tick." I held up my hand, and Hux came over to where I stood. I laughed again when he laid his head over my shoulder, his beautiful face filling up the screen of my phone. I kissed his nose and said to Canyon, "I've almost got him jumping bitless. After that, I want to see if I can do it with just a neck rope."

"You're doing that on the circuit?" Canyon asked, surprised.

"Not yet, just in private. My trainer knows I do it, but there's no plans to take it to tour. Maybe one day, if Hux and I stay as a team for a while." My stomach turned. I would be devastated if I lost the ride on Huxley.

With that thought, my mind drifted to Jasper and how he so cruelly shot me down the other night. God, I loved it here at Golden Oaks, but things between Jasper and me were strange, and it was casting an eclipse over my future.

"What's happening, Hals?" Canyon asked, seriously this time. His brows were drawn down, and I knew I wasn't getting away with not saying something about my mood.

"Homesick, I guess," I said, not wanting to disclose the truth. Canyon was practically my brother. Even though he was only a few years older than me, he had always been my protector. He was wiser than his years. My daddy would say he believed Canyon had been on this earth before this lifetime. That he was an old soul who felt and thought deeper than most.

Canyon raised an eyebrow. "That's the story you're sticking to?"

A smile pulled on my lips. "It is," I said with a firm nod.

“That tells me it’s guy business, therefore none of *my* business. That ’bout right?” he asked, and I couldn’t help but laugh.

“Let’s go with that,” I said, and Canyon shook his head playfully.

I kissed Huxley again as Canyon said, “You just remember whose daughter you are, Hallie-girl. You’re Texan, and we Texans don’t take shit from anyone.”

“I’ll remember that,” I said, feeling warmer inside than I was before. The sound of cows bleating in the background of Canyon’s cell sailed through my phone.

“Aw, hell,” Canyon said, groaning and giving me an apologetic smile. “Duty calls. A fence on the west side just came down and the cattle are making a run for it.” Canyon turned Rosie toward the broken fence, then held up the cell and showed me the view. My heart swelled in my chest, seeing the sun rise over the fields I knew so well, and in this moment, I could almost mistake Huxley’s head over my shoulder for my daddy’s heavenly hug as I looked out at our land, the land that meant so much to him.

“Texas misses you, Hallie-girl,” Canyon said, and tears built in my eyes. Canyon’s face appeared again. “And so does your family.”

“Love y’all,” I said, and wiped at my eyes. “Tell your mama and daddy I’ll call this weekend.” I spent some time every Saturday and Sunday calling Canyon’s mama and daddy and my aunt Jeanie and uncle Luke, telling them about my progress over here in England.

“Will do,” Canyon said, and I hung up the phone just as Canyon began racing Rosie toward the fleeing cows. I looked up and saw a robin on a nearby tree take to the sky above us. I put my cell back in my barn jacket and fixed my Stetson. I had work to do.

Turning, I stepped away from Huxley, seeing his ears prick and his tail swish in excitement. “Are you ready?” I said. Laughing, I started to run around the arena, and like the playful boy he was, Huxley gave chase. I was a huge believer in the fact that if you wanted a horse to perform for you, that you also had to give them what they needed. For

Hux, that was grazing in fields, treats, and playtime. Horses were just big dogs in my opinion. They had personalities and loved silliness too.

As I ran around the arena, Huxley bucking in excitement as he chased me, I allowed the fun and levity to cast away the residual hurt in my heart. Breathless, I took off my hat and used it to fan my face. My cheeks were hot from the exercise, and Huxley came to stand beside me. I ran my hand down his neck and laid it over his heart to feel it thumping.

Reaching into my pocket, I pulled out a Polo, held it to his mouth, and he gobbled it right up. I tipped my head back to the sky to catch my next breath when I heard, "That was wonderful to see!"

I snapped my head to the left, not realizing I had company. When I glimpsed over the fence, Genny Knighton was there in her wheelchair, a bright smile on her pretty face. My instant happiness at seeing her again was immediately washed away when I saw Jasper behind her, dressed in his usual barn jacket and flat cap.

My gaze flicked to his. His expression was tight, and his hands gripped the wheelchair handles so hard I thought he might break them. But Genny was all smiles, and I made myself ignore Jasper and walk toward them.

"Genny!" I said, and climbed over the arena fence. I landed in front of her and bent down to give her a hug. Genny's embrace was warm. When I drew back, I nodded at Jasper. "Mr. Knighton," I said, and heard the creak of the plastic handles under his hands.

Good. I'm glad the use of his formal name pissed him off.

"Pfft," Genny said, and laughed. "Mr. Knighton!" She held up her hand. "Call him Jasper, Hallie. He's too uptight as it is to be called Mr. Knighton too. It'll go to his head."

I nodded to Genny and gave her a tight smile. "How are you doing, darlin'?" I said, hoping I wasn't being too forward.

"Better," Genny said, positively. "It's been a rough road, but I'm getting there," she said and took a deep breath. "Slowly." That strained breath told me just how hard it had been for her—still was.

I took hold of her hand and squeezed. "You're missed."

"Thank you," Genny said, and I noticed Jasper's hands loosen on the wheelchair's handles a little. Like he was a touch more relaxed. Huxley chose that moment to put his head over the fence and nudge my arm of the hand that was in my pocket.

I rolled my eyes and handed him another mint. He crunched away contently, and Genny said, "It was so nice to see him with you like that." She cocked her head to the side. "You seem like the perfect pairing." She added, "Leon said that you're both training really well and he's excited to see you in action. He thinks you could go far at Sandings."

I laid my hand on Huxley's neck, then shifted my gaze to Jasper, who was silent and statue still. "That's nice of him," I said, but couldn't hold my tongue enough to also say, "Your brother disagrees, though." Okay, apparently I was still more than pissed. Jasper tensed, and unable to stop my tongue I added, "He gave me a grocery list of issues I had the other day. Made me wonder what I was even doing here."

"Jasper!" Genny said and turned to look up at her brother, angry on my behalf. I should have felt guilty about my words, but I didn't. Not one single part of me felt bad. If he could be a prick, I could be one too. And his harsh words had made me question my ability.

"What?" he said, incredulously. "All our riders need to be as prepared as possible. The Sandings Grand Prix is the big leagues, and these are Knighton horses." He gestured to Huxley. "The pressure on the circuit is intense. We must be as faultless as we can." Jasper shrugged, and that movement incensed me. "No one is perfect."

"You're right," I said after a few strained seconds. "*No one* is. And *no one* should act as though they are either."

Genny's brow furrowed, and she looked from Jasper to me and back again. In that moment, I considered that maybe I'd gone too far. Jasper was technically my boss and had the power to cut my sponsorship whenever he wanted. But I just couldn't help myself where he was concerned. Rationality left my body, and only the need to fight back remained.

After a few strained seconds, Genny went to open her mouth to speak again, when suddenly an alarm sounded, piercing the air, and Jasper whipped his head to look behind us—in the direction they'd just come from.

Genny turned too, and I placed my hand on Huxley's neck to calm him down when the shrill sound made his head throw back in surprise. "*Ssh,* boy," I soothed, then made sure the gate to the arena was locked. He was safe inside there.

"Stay here," Jasper said, and took off running in the direction of a nearby barn. There were raised voices and the sound of something breaking.

"Dahlia," Genny whispered, and the color drained from her face.

"Dahlia?" I questioned, keeping my eyes fixed on the barn. Grooms and yard staff rushed to try to shut the barn gates manually that had opened automatically when the alarm sounded.

"That's Dahlia's barn," Genny said. "It's all electronically controlled." Genny swallowed, and my heart began slamming in my chest. "She needs extra care as she spooks so easily now. We had to install extra-strength stalls to hold her." Genny looked to me. "The alarm . . . It only makes that sound when the electrics have gone down or someone has opened the gates manually."

On cue, there was a flurry of panicked, raised voices, and then a horse I recognized as Dahlia burst from the gap they'd been unable to close in the barn doors. The anxious mare was covered in sweat, and her eyes were wide as she galloped down the path.

"Dahlia!" Genny cried, and I heard the fear in her voice. I searched the area around us. It was all gated and there was nowhere for Dahlia to go. She reached a fenced-off area and turned, galloping like a bat out of hell. She headed for a nearby grass paddock, and I held my breath as she stormed toward the high fence that surrounded it.

"She's going to jump it," Genny said, panicked, her hand reaching out to grab on to my arm. Her fingers squeezed it so tightly I knew they'd leave a bruise. "Hallie, she's going to jump it!" Just as Genny feared, Dahlia, nostrils flared and eyes wide, jumped the fence, clipping her back right hoof as she did. I winced as Genny cried out at the sound.

Jasper came barreling from the back of the barn and climbed over the fence, a halter and rope in his hand. Even with a slight limp, Dahlia didn't stop her hurricanelike run. Trees lined the perimeter of the field, wired fencing the only thing stopping Dahlia from clearing that too and escaping into the woods.

I didn't even think, my body acted of its own accord, and in seconds I was running toward the field, climbing the fence to get there too. A few more grooms and yard staff were hot on Jasper's tail, but I had my eyes firmly on Dahlia. Froth landed on the ground from her mouth, and even from the other side of the field, I could hear the heaviness of her breathing.

Jesus. I knew Dahlia had been affected by the accident, but this poor mare . . . She was absolutely terrified and didn't resemble her former self at all. Sadness propelled me forward toward where she was clearly hoping to jump the wire fence. But the closer I got to the tree line, the more I realized just how high the fence was.

"She won't clear it," I said to myself, feeling my heart fall to my feet. Dahlia's limp was bad now, but if she tried to jump that fence, she could break a leg. I looked behind me to see Genny watching from the other side of the fence. Even from this distance, I could see tears tracking down her face.

Dahlia was her heart horse. They'd survived an awful accident together. She'd kept her alive when most other riders I knew would have destroyed her or cast her aside as a lost cause. Genny was still trying to help her. But if Dahlia tried to jump this fence . . .

"Come here, Dahlia." I heard Jasper talking to Dahlia in a soft, gentle voice. "Steady, girl," he said, and I slowed my pace until I stood behind him. Dahlia had stopped running but was pacing back and forth along the fence, like she was searching for a way through. I scanned my eyes over her. Her fetlock was bleeding and swelling from where she'd knocked it on the fence. She was thick with sweat, and her breathing was erratic. Her ears were pinned back, her mouth was frothing, and her breathing was too quick. She wasn't going to stop, and she clearly had no intention of listening to Jasper.

"Get back," I said to the grooms that were approaching. Jasper glanced at me but quickly refocused on Dahlia when she whinnied in a painful tone. It was only a second that Jasper looked away, but it was all Dahlia needed to circle where she stood and attempt the fence.

"No!" I called, just as Dahlia leapt into the wired fence. I saw her front legs slip through the square gaps, my throat closing in fear. Realizing she was stuck, Dahlia began to thrash. In my periphery, I saw one of the grooms run back toward the barn, but I kept focused on Dahlia. Another had wire cutters in his hand. I tried to formulate a plan.

Jasper rushed forward, dodging Dahlia's writhing body. "Careful," I said as he narrowly missed her back hoof hitting his ribs.

"Get back, Hallie," he said, and when he turned to look at me, I saw everything on his face laid bare. Fear, sadness, panic . . . his sister. He knew if we didn't do something, and quickly, Dahlia was going to irreparably hurt herself. It was written there on his face for me to see in plain sight.

Jasper tried to approach the mare again. "Dahlia, calm," he said, but I could hear the nerves breaking in his voice. His tone was pleading, like he knew what Dahlia's death would do to his sister and couldn't bear to face it.

I looked back over the field, and Genny was still there, face fixed our way as her hands gripped the fence posts.

"Shit," Jasper hissed. When I turned to him, he was holding his arm where Dahlia's hoof must have clipped him. The groom that had run for the barn was coming back over, and my stomach dropped when I saw what he held in his hand.

A rifle.

No.

That wasn't happening on my watch.

Moving to Jasper, I placed my hand on his shoulder. He whipped his head around. His eyes were wide, and there was so much dread and distress in his brown gaze that I wanted to cry for him.

"Step back," I said, taking a long, deep breath. Dahlia thrashed again, making the fence posts on either side of her groan. I winced when I saw the wire had cut into her leg, and if she wasn't calmed, she was going to bring the whole thing down. She was bleeding and she was terrified, and I needed to get her out.

"Hallie . . ." Jasper went to argue with me.

"Step *back*, Jasper!" I said more sternly.

My heart was beating at a million miles an hour, but knowing I had to help Dahlia, I found a well of peace within me and let it wash over me. Taking off my Stetson, I placed it on the ground and kept my body low. Dahlia paused in her thrashing momentarily, and I used that pause to slowly approach. Her wide, dark eyes fixed on me.

They were pitch black—all dilated pupils.

"Ssh," I said, softly. Not wanting to look away from her, I racked my brain for every lesson that Canyon had ever taught me when it came to natural horsemanship. I'd seen this before. I'd seen horses caught up in wire on the ranch. I thought of Canyon and how he approached them. It went against my effort that Dahlia didn't know me from Adam, and she was already a stressed and fearful horse, but if I didn't try . . . I wouldn't even entertain the alternative.

Inch by inch, I drew closer. Dahlia didn't take her eyes off me. "That's it, girl," I said, in a smooth, soft, feather-weight tone. "You're all caught up, and we just want to get you out." Her ears were jumping in all directions. I could smell the metallic scent of blood invading my senses and had to school my reactions when I moved close to her hoof. My hands were held out in a nonaggressive manner, showing her I wasn't going to cause her more pain.

"Shh," I said, again, and stopped at her stomach. Her front two legs were stretched out and trapped in the wire. She was now lying on her side, and she was losing the energy to hold up her head. As gently as a

butterfly's wings, I laid my hand over her heart. It was too fast under my palm. Dahlia flinched as I touched her, and her back legs kicked out, aiming to hit me.

"Hallie," I heard Jasper hiss from behind me. But I didn't take my eyes off Dahlia's to look to him. He didn't like me, I got it. But in this moment, I needed him to trust me and leave me the hell alone.

"I'm not going to hurt you," I said to Dahlia again. Her breathing grew slower, and her head fell back to the ground. She was exhausted. She was in pain. But the poor thing didn't know how to trust anyone anymore. I inched closer and closed my eyes. In my mind's eye I saw Canyon with a young mustang colt a few years back. I remembered him moving his hand along the horse's neck and back, gently massaging to calm him down. Leaning over Dahlia, I kept one hand over her heart and placed the other on her neck. Gently, I kneaded the muscle. "You're okay," I said softly. "You're going to be okay, girl. We just need to get you out."

Canyon had taught me to look for cues, subtle signs that the horse was relaxing, was trusting you. Right now, Dahlia was taut, a coiled spring—anything but calm. But after several minutes of talking to her soothingly and running my hand over her tight muscles, Dahlia's ears relaxed a little, her breathing evened, and she broke our gaze.

I wanted to jump for joy as she looked away, head tipping up and her hind legs losing their tension. *There,* I thought.

Now.

I glanced over my shoulder, only to see Jasper watching me, chest rising and falling with nervous anticipation—eyes wide and shock on his face. "Wire cutters," I said in the same tone I'd been using this whole time, so to not spook Dahlia.

One of the grooms carefully handed them to Jasper, and I indicated for him to move past me and try to cut the wires. I kept my hands roving over Dahlia's body, praying I'd done enough to keep her in this neutral, calmed state. Her head flicked up when Jasper made the first cut of the wire.

"Shh," I soothed again. Jasper made quick but careful work of the wires and then slowly stepped back. Always leaving one hand on Dahlia's neck, or her flank, her back, I ran my hand down her front right leg and gently coaxed it back out of the fence. I made sure I kept breathing, not wanting to alarm Dahlia in any way that would make her panic.

Moving to the other leg, I did the same, exhaling in relief when both legs were freed. My hands were coated in blood, but her legs were *free*.

"The halter," I said to Jasper, and held out my hand. I didn't take my gaze off Dahlia, who had begun to move her legs, the realization that she was free beginning to register. As she lifted her head, I threaded the halter over her nose and ears, only to get it fastened in time for her to roll to her belly, then hoist herself off the ground.

She was breathing hard, completely exhausted. She began to pull back, ready to bolt, but I held on to the rope and went with her. "*Shh,* girl. You're still okay." I placed my hand on her neck again and just breathed in and out near her face. Dahlia flinched at my closeness but didn't try to run. Her body was trembling, and she needed immediate medical help.

"I'm going to walk her back to the barn," I said to Jasper, but in the same voice I'd been using on Dahlia so she thought I was speaking to her. "Keep everyone back and make sure the barn is empty."

"Careful, Hallie," Jasper said, barely above a whisper, but I walked beside Dahlia, and thankfully, she walked beside me. She flinched, she jumped, and she was tense and scared, but when we made it back to the barn, Jasper had cleared it, and Dahlia allowed me to put her in a stall.

Unclipping her rope but leaving her halter on, I carefully backed out, uttering, "You did amazing, girl. What a good girl." When I reached the stall door, I slipped through, never taking my eyes off the mare. She was blood stained and limping . . . but she was *alive*. The minute I'd seen the groom run over the field with the gun, my heart had shattered. I couldn't have let that happen. I couldn't have let Genny lose all she had left.

The stall's door was manually bolted shut, failed electrics clearly the culprit of Dahlia's escape and, seconds later, a vet came through the barn doors carrying her bag and a panicked expression on her face. She was clearly known to Dahlia as she let the vet go to her. The room came into view, and I noticed a few people who had entered the barn staring at me. At first, I wasn't sure why, until I realized it was in *awe*.

"Thank you," a female groom said, breaking from the cluster of people, and I numbly nodded. "I don't know what Genny would have done if Dahlia had been seriously hurt . . . or worse." Genny's groom, I realized. The tears in her eyes told me she was close to Dahlia too. Almost on cue, Genny came into the barn, Forrest Knighton pushing her in her chair.

Genny's cheeks were tear-stained and pale, but she exhaled a long sigh of relief seeing her treasured horse with the vet. My heart was beating too fast, and I knew it was the built-up adrenaline suddenly leaving my body in one fell swoop.

I closed my eyes when I felt a shaky hand take hold of mine. I opened them to find Genny looking up at me. "Thank you, Hallie," she said, and I heard the depth of that thanks in her gravelly tone. She pressed the back of my hand to her forehead. "Just . . . *thank you*."

I nodded but was unable to speak. Forrest caught my eyes next. I hadn't been formally introduced to him before this, but I knew who he was from seeing him compete over the years.

"Thank you," he said. "I was nearby and a groom called me over." He shook his head. "I've never seen anything like that before." Forrest tipped his head to the side. "Natural horsemanship?" I nodded again. Forrest must have seen I couldn't speak, as he moved aside to let me past. "Thank you again. Dahlia means the world to us all." He cut me a sad smile. "Sorry for how we are being introduced. I'm Forrest."

"Hello," I said, robotically. He must have seen I was struggling, as he gave me a sympathetic smile, then he and Genny went to the stall to see Dahlia.

I kept my head down as I rushed from the barn. I had to get to Huxley. I'd left him in the arena alone, and he needed to be put out into the field. I heard the whispers around me as I passed by the staff—all good things—but my hands had started to shake, and I felt a rush of emotion crash through me.

How silly, I thought as I pushed falling tears off my cheeks. But my breathing was choppy, and in this moment, I realized how scared I'd been. Scared that I couldn't save Dahlia. That I couldn't do anything to help and would have to see a much-loved horse put down.

Finding Huxley still in the arena, calm and waiting for me, I opened the gate and slipped inside. He came straight over to me, and I found myself wrapping my arms around his neck. I let the peace I always felt around horses seep into my bones and allowed a few stray tears to fall into his coat. I didn't know how Canyon did it. How he could work with horses that were so emotionally damaged, so afraid of people and life.

I wasn't sure how *I* had just done that.

"Hallie?" I quickly wiped my eyes and moved around Huxley to see Jasper approaching the arena.

I sniffed and cleared my throat. "Is everything okay?" I asked, worried, and Jasper's shoulders sagged.

"Thanks to you," he said, and it took me a few moments to realize his words were kind and not filled with censure or bad news. Jasper shook his head while my chest lifted from some unknown weight. "I . . . I don't know how to thank you," he added. Jasper's voice was rough, hoarse. He sounded so tired. He had dark circles under his eyes, and in this moment looked as if he carried the weight of the world on his shoulders.

"It was nothing," I said, stroking down Huxley's neck, only to stop when I saw that my hands were covered in blood. I needed to wash it off.

"It was *everything*," Jasper said, cutting through my thoughts and causing me to snap my head up to face him. His gaze was boring into mine. "It was *everything*," he said again, and I felt every word sink into my soul. "Because of you, Dahlia is going to be okay."

Unable to find words again, I nodded. Putting Huxley's halter on, I headed for the gate. Jasper opened it for me. "I'll take him out into the field," I said, then added, "I'm glad Dahlia is good. For Genny."

Jasper watched me closely, and unable to take the heaviness of his stare, I put my head down to walk past him, only for his hand to wrap around mine, causing me to stop dead. I looked down at his hand, at his fingers threading through mine, then up at Jasper's face. He was staring at our hands intensely too, and goose bumps broke out all over my body. When his gaze lifted to meet mine, he swallowed, then gently freed his hand from mine.

He nodded in goodbye and headed back toward Dahlia's barn. I watched him walk away, back stiff and shoulders tense. And as I guided Huxley along the path and to his field in the next section of the property, I could still feel Jasper's fingers entwined with mine.

I could still feel his warmth.

I stared at the clock on the wall. It was 3:00 a.m. I had showered and watched numbly as Dahlia's blood had circled the drain at my feet. Two brandies and a bar of chocolate came next. But none had allowed me to rid myself of the image of Dahlia on the ground, her frightened eyes begging me to help her but being so afraid to let me.

I blew out a frustrated breath and kicked off my quilt. I rubbed my hands over my face and looked out the window. The moon was high in the sky, and the night was crystal clear, making the stars look like scattered glitter particles resting on a black velvet cloth.

I leaned out my window to see the light in Sage's cottage was off. Of course it was, she didn't suffer from insomnia like I did. My chest swelled when I thought of how she had come barreling into my living room earlier. Word had spread quickly of the incident. When she'd finished her training session, the grooms had been telling her how I helped Dahlia. Sage came straight to find me.

"You're a living legend here at Golden Oaks now," she'd said, nudging me, only to read the anxiousness that was still on my face and wrap me in a hug.

"I was so scared," I said into her hair.

"You saved that mare today." Sage kissed my cheek. "Everyone said how calm and strong you were. Canyon would be proud of you."

"He was," I said.

I'd spoken to Canyon afterward. I'd needed to know why I felt so shaken. He told me that he often did too. Helping a living being in distress was always tough on the soul. Sage told me that they had sedated Dahlia for her safety and taken her to the veterinarian barn on site. It was open twenty-four hours, with a resident team of equine veterinarians who only tended to Golden Oaks horses.

Knowing I wouldn't get any more sleep right now, I dressed in my jeans, sweater, and jacket. I threw on my cowboy boots and stepped into the night. I had only made it a few steps when a flashlight shone before me. I jumped in surprise.

"Sorry, Miss," the man holding the flashlight said. "Didn't mean to scare you." I placed my hand over my heart and calmed down when I saw it was one of the new security guards. He was in an ATV and must have stopped his patrol when he saw me.

"You okay?" he said. "It's pretty late to be out."

"Yeah," I said. "Couldn't sleep. I'm going to the veterinarian barn to check on a horse."

"Miss . . . Oakley?" he asked, looking at a clipboard on the seat beside him. I frowned that he knew my name. He pointed at the cottage. "I have you down as staying here."

I exhaled a relieved breath. God, I was so jumpy tonight.

"Yeah, I'm Hallie," I said.

"Stanley," the guard said, introducing himself. "You want a ride to the vet barn?"

"No thanks, I'll walk," I said.

"You might see a few more guards around," Stanley said. "So don't worry if you do. We're here for your protection."

"Thanks," I said, and began to walk in the direction of the veterinarian barn. I used the walk to breathe in and out and try to settle my frayed nerves, attempting some meditation breathing techniques Aunt Jeanie had taught me when I was younger. They worked a little.

But then my thoughts drifted to Dahlia, then Genny Knighton. I recalled in vivid color the incident in Saint-Tropez when Dahlia fell on top of Genny. The details of that incident were never made public. The rumor mill was rife with guesses—drugs, foul play, and even that an internal injury might have ruptured within Dahlia midcourse. Whatever it was, the Knightons had certainly had their fair share of bad luck of late.

Another guard was positioned in the distance, the sound of walkie-talkies turning on and off as the team communicated. The woman gave me a wave, and I assumed Stanley had already prepared her for my appearance.

Next, I thought of Jasper. If I were being honest with myself, I'd thought of him nonstop since I'd returned to the cottage earlier this evening. How, when he had seen me training in the arena with Huxley, he had been his cold and aloof self but had thawed some when his sister spoke to me, as though he *liked* the sight of us getting along.

But my stomach tightened when I recalled the blatant fear in his eyes, seeing Dahlia on the ground in that field, legs tied up in wire. The dark circles under his eyes. I hadn't really noticed it before, but as I remembered his face today, there was a heavy dose of defeat there. A flicker of helplessness that I hadn't noted before. It made me want to hold him, despite the barriers between us. What burdens was he shouldering? More than people knew, I was sure.

I lifted my hand and studied my fingers in the light of the lamp posts surrounding the pathway. *Thank you.* The sound of his voice when he came to find me after we got Dahlia stabled played on a loop in my head. The feel of his fingers wrapping around mine were a tattoo on my skin.

"Jasper fucking Knighton," I said under my breath, frustration in my tone. This man was an enigma to me. He was hot with me one minute and cold the next. I had no idea whether he was toxic or just misunderstood.

Or was he so damaged that he didn't know how to open himself up?

I shook my head, unable to decide, when I realized I'd arrived at the veterinarian barn. There was an illuminated green cross on the side of the building. I opened the doors, and a woman around my age was busy stocking shelves. She looked up. "Hi," I said, "I know this is unusual, and it's very late, but I'm a rider here and helped a horse today—"

"Hallie?" the woman said.

I blinked in surprise. "Yes?" I replied, a question in my tone asking how she knew my name.

The small blonde came to me and held out her hand. "I'm Katie, a veterinary assistant here at Golden Oaks. Firstly, I'm a huge fan and can't wait to see you on the tour in a couple of weeks." That made me smile. "And secondly, the place is abuzz with your name and how you helped Dahlia today."

My eyebrows shot up in surprise. "Really?"

"Really," Katie said, and let go of my hand, only to squeeze my arm. "We all love Genny around here, and that horse is her life. The thought of anything else happening to them . . ." Katie shook her head. "We'd been told you might show up to see Dahlia, and to let you in so you can see she's okay."

"You were told that?" I asked, perplexed, wondering who the hell might have suspected I'd come here.

Katie nodded. "Dahlia's section of the barn is closed off to everyone but Genny, Jasper, the Knighton family, and *you*." My heart slammed in my chest. It couldn't have been Jasper who said I'd turn up, could it? I thought back on the way I'd broken into his family barn—twice. The way he often commented that I always broke the rules, and realized it just might be him.

"She's this way," Katie said, and I followed her through double doors and down a hallway that led to a row of sectioned, private stalls. When we got to Dahlia's stall, my heart lodged in my throat. She was bandaged and cut in several places, but she was clean, and she looked a damn sight better than she did earlier today.

Dahlia was currently sleeping, and I almost cried at how peaceful she looked. Katie laid her hand on my back, a soothing gesture. "I'll leave you to it. Dahlia should sleep awhile yet. If you need me, I'll be out front."

"Thank you," I said, never taking my eyes off Dahlia. The emotions that had plagued me for the last several hours began to drift away the more I watched her. She was alive. She was healing. Everything was okay.

My shoulders sagged, releasing all my pent-up tension, and I laid my arms on the top of the stall door, dropping my forehead on them, and just breathed. I could release the anxiety now; it was over.

I wasn't sure how long I had been standing there when I heard the faint sound of a door opening and closing behind me. I didn't even have to raise my head to look. I knew who had just stepped into this private section of the barn with me. The hairs on the back of my neck only stood up that way for one person.

Without turning I said, "I didn't break in this time. I have it on good authority from Katie that my visit was preapproved."

Jasper didn't respond, and the silence had me twisting to face him. I wanted to scream when I did, because it didn't matter how many times I saw this man, my body responded in the same way—heart racing, pulse pounding, and me finding him the most attractive person on the entire planet. Even now, with his dark hair disheveled and free from his flat cap, dressed in his well-worn Barbour jacket, jeans, and boots, he looked like he could have just walked off a runway.

But that's not what had me most captivated. It was his eyes. His midnight eyes that right now were fixed on me, the intensity of his stare sending shivers down my spine. I cleared my throat. "Was it?" I said, trying to get him to talk. "Was it you who gave me permission to be in here?"

Jasper was leaning against the closed barn door, but I saw the tug of a smile pull on his upper lip. "I thought it best, because God knows you never do as you're told."

In this moment, I let go of the anger I held toward him. Whatever ill thoughts I harbored for my "boss," the tired expression on his face and defeated body language told me no one felt worse about him than he did himself.

"True," I said, and turned back to the stall when Dahlia moved. I scanned over her body and relaxed when it became clear she was just shifting in her sleep. Suddenly, the scent of sandalwood and mint came from behind me, and I closed my eyes. I'd never smelled anything better.

"Hallie?" Jasper said, his voice only inches from me. I schooled my features and glanced back at him over my shoulder. Jasper rubbed the back of his neck, seeming uncomfortable. "Can we talk?"

I furrowed my brow in confusion, wondering what he wanted to discuss. I worried this was dangerous territory for us. We'd never been much good at talking without it ending up explosive. But curiosity won out, and I nodded, following him to the bench that was opposite the stall. I sat down beside him, leaving a suitable distance between us. The barn was completely quiet but for Dahlia's steady breathing and the distant sound of Katie stacking shelves at the barn's reception.

Jasper stared down at his clasped hands for a moment, then on a fortified breath, met my eyes and said, "I'm sorry, Hallie." Those softly spoken words seemed to take flight and land right inside my heart. My lips parted and shock trickled over me slowly.

Jasper must have seen my surprise, as his eyes appeared pained and he rubbed his hand over his face. He laid his elbows on his knees and said, "The man I've been of late . . ." He shook his head, then looked me dead in the eye. "You probably won't believe me, but it's not who I am."

His voice was so broken and laced with sadness that it made my chest ache. I clutched on to the edge of the bench seat like was a lifeline. I didn't say anything in response. As harsh as it sounded, I needed him to give me more than that. He had been hot and cold since I'd come here, kind and then cruel. I was done with the back-and-forth. I was far from a pushover, and I wasn't going to start with him, even though this man got to me like no one had before.

He must have read that on my face, as he sighed and said, "Things have just been . . ." His words trailed off, and he stared at the floor, lost in thought. When he turned his attention back on mine again, he said, "A fucking shit show," and his terminology made my lips twitch in humor. Jasper was so well spoken, so posh, that those words didn't seem right coming out of his mouth.

Swallowing my mirth, I refocused and asked, "Why?"

Jasper froze, and I could tell by his tight expression that he was debating whether to tell me. That was fine. It was his choice. But I wasn't going to play this game again.

Getting to my feet, I faced him and said, "Jasper, I appreciate your apology. And I accept it. Truly." He was watching me like a hawk. "But I think we need to leave our relationship as simply professional." I hated saying those words, an ache actually pulled in my chest, but it was true. "For some reason, we trigger something in one another, and it always ends badly." I met his eyes. The dark-brown color held a hint of red under the fluorescent ceiling light in the barn. "I am thankful you came here tonight to apologize. But I think this is where we draw a line under . . . whatever this is. I leave soon, and we can put all this behind us."

I cast Dahlia's stall one last look and decided it was time for me to go home. Head down, I moved past him, when he took hold of my hand to stop me. It was déjà vu to earlier today, and just like his touch had done then, it sent sparks through my body and rooted my feet to the spot. I looked down at his hand in mine. He was gripping my fingers so tightly it almost hurt. He looked up and met my eyes, silently begging me not to go.

I exhaled a shaky breath, but Jasper coaxed me to sit back down beside him on the bench with a soft tug on my arm. In that moment, I was weak, as I went without a fight. I expected him to release my hand as soon as I sat down, but he kept a tight hold. Right now, I felt he was holding my heart in his hand too.

Jasper swallowed hard, seemingly warring with himself about lowering his high walls, when he closed his eyes and said, "The night you found me in the barn . . . The night I was drunk, was the second anniversary of my father's death."

And just like that, my heart fractured into pieces and understanding filled in the cracks. In this moment, Jasper looked broken. And when he opened his eyes and turned to me, his beautiful face implored me to forgive him, to understand why he'd been the way he had.

Jasper tipped his head back, taking in three deep breaths. When he faced me again, he looked terrified that he'd admitted that. Dahlia's wide, fearful eyes sprang to my mind, and I couldn't help but see the similarities between hers and Jasper's in this moment. I didn't feel like horses and people were so dissimilar. When horses were happy, you could see it in their gait. They were approachable and affectionate. When they were scared, they would run away, or worse, charge and kick out, become aggressive and aloof.

I replayed all of Jasper's harsh words to me of late and peeled back the veil of what they must have hidden—pain, agony . . . anguish. I realized then that I didn't really know him, not deep down. Didn't know the secrets and silent hardships he harbored.

Like I had with Dahlia, I kept my tone soft and placed my free hand over his so both of mine were safely wrapped around his fingers. I felt Jasper relax, and hope sprung in my chest. I wanted him to open up to me. I wanted him to confide in me. Keeping in pain would only destroy a person in time, keeping too much agony inside was cancer to the soul, poison to happiness.

"You can talk to me," I said, gently, rubbing the top of his hand with my palm. "I'm someone you can trust."

Jasper stared at me for so long that I didn't think he would, when his lips parted, and he said, "Since my dad died, I feel like I've been unraveling. And I don't know how to put myself back together again." His grip on my fingers tightened, and I could tell how much that had cost him to admit.

I squeezed his fingers in empathy and said, "I lost my dad when I was twelve." Jasper nodded and searched my face. I knew he'd suspected it from our conversation on the way back from the shoot. But I wanted him to know that I understood him. I understood what losing a parent felt like. Even now, thirteen years on, the loss still hurt. Grief for a loved one never went away—it was a constant roller coaster of feeling, like a part of you was missing and knowing the devastation that it would never be filled.

"Hallie . . ." Jasper said, and I could see guilt on his face. I assumed he was regretting the way he had treated me even more now.

"I'm okay," I said, though my voice told another story. "It was a long time ago. And Aunt Jeanie and Uncle Luke took me in and gave me a loving family and a home. I still have people at my daddy's ranch who are my family too. I never yearned for belonging and affection." I shifted a little closer and put a hand on his shoulder, keeping hold of his hand with the other. "But I know what it's like to lose a loved one." I huffed a laugh. "Two, really. My mom passed away when I was a toddler. She was sick. I don't remember her or her passing, but I mourn her nonetheless."

"My mother died too," Jasper said, and a strange feeling of *knowing* one another wrapped around us. "Cancer. I was twelve." His grip on my hand shifted, and we were now palm to palm, fully holding hands. "The same age you were when you lost your father."

"I'm sorry," I said.

"I'm sorry too," he echoed. I knew he was saying it as more than condolences. He was sorry for the way he had been.

"How did your father pass?" he asked, and there was a hint of something else in his voice. Something I couldn't decipher. Like that topic was almost too fragile for him.

"Heart attack," I said, and tried to push that day from my head.

Daddy? Daddy! Wake up! Wake up, please! Why aren't you waking up?

My cry to his unmoving body still kept me up some nights. Jasper squeezed my hand in support. "I found him," I said.

"Oh, Hallie . . ." Jasper wrapped his arm around me. He pulled me to his chest, and I sank into his embrace. He was warm despite it being cold outside, and his addictive scent was as cozy as roasted hazelnuts and pumpkin-spice lattes.

After a few seconds, I pulled back. "Ranching is hard," I said, and Jasper listened intently. "He was far too overworked and tired, especially for his age." I smiled sadly. "He never got over my mom's death, at least that's what his best friend and the old ranch hands told me." I released a shaky breath. "In all honesty, I think he died of a broken heart. It just took a few years to take him down, is all." I wiped away a stray tear but pulled myself together. "At least I know their love was real while they had it." I laughed, mainly to break through the sadness. "Something to aspire to, I suppose."

"It sounds like it," Jasper said. Then his face fell, and he said, "Do you know how my dad died?"

I did. Of course I did. The news had rocked the equestrian world. "Yes. I'm so sorry." It had been a car accident. It was a wet, cold night, and his car veered off the road, killing Mr. Knighton instantly.

Jasper grew silent. I felt like he was going to say something else, but whatever it was must have been too hard for him to express. After a minute of contemplative silence, he said, "When Genny had her accident, I thought that was it. That I was going to be the only remaining member of my nuclear family." My stomach sank. It was like the energy seeped from Jasper's body . . . No, not energy—hurt feelings he'd needed to share. "I'm fortunate in life, I know that. I have more money than I could ever ask for, and I love the industry we're in. But watching my sister struggle with her recovery and Dahlia . . ." Jasper's attention went to the stall. I could still hear Dahlia's steady breathing. Jasper turned to me, and I swallowed a lump in my throat at the sincerity in his eyes. "What you did today for Dahlia, for *Genny* . . ." Jasper became at a loss for words.

"It was nothing," I said, and tried to wave him off. It didn't work.

"It *wasn't* nothing," he said, voice stern, the gruff and dominant Jasper returning to the surface. He squeezed my hand tighter. "It wasn't nothing, Hallie. It was a gift, one that I didn't deserve after how I've treated you." I didn't know how to respond to his candor. Jasper tipped his head to the side, studying me. "You truly have a gift, Hallie. I've never seen anyone work that kind of magic with horses." He pointed at the stall. "Especially with Dahlia."

"Just a few tips I picked up on my daddy's ranch. People write off ranchers and horse farmers as though they aren't impressive. But I've never seen people work with horses as well as cowboys do." I thought of Canyon. "I have a brother of sorts, Canyon. He's amazing with horses. If you talk of someone having a gift? That's him. It's almost magical." I shrugged. "I just imitated him today. Thankfully it worked."

"Thankfully," Jasper said, but the way he was now looking at me made it difficult to breathe. I wasn't sure if it was in awe or in censure.

"What?" I asked, my usual sassy attitude slowly rising back to the surface.

"You're one impressive woman, Hallie Oakley," he said, and I felt my cheeks burst with redness. Awe. He was looking at me in awe.

I nudged Jasper's shoulder. "You're not so bad yourself," I said, then stared him down. "When you're not being a moody prick." I expected him to laugh, or at least crack a smile, but he didn't. "I was joking, Jasper. Kind of . . ." I went to say, because he *had* been a moody prick, but he interrupted and said, "I came here tonight because I couldn't bear you thinking so ill of me."

I swallowed, trying to warn my heart not to explode at his confession. "I wasn't always this person, Hallie," he said, brokenly. "I wasn't always such a prick." I knew he wasn't. I'd met him when he was lighter, freer.

Unburdened. "I took out all my stress on you because you saw me at my lowest. My newest rider"—he exhaled a stuttered breath and shook his head in shame—"the most beautiful woman I've ever seen, saw me drunk on whiskey and unraveled on my family's barn floor." He paused, then said, "I'm the head of my family. I *can't* unravel. Especially when someone else could witness it."

A mix of emotions swirled within me. I wanted to cry for how broken and alone he was, I wanted to hold him and tell him everything would be okay, even if I didn't know it was true. But mostly, I couldn't stop replaying the words *the most beautiful woman I've ever seen* in my head. I couldn't stop them from sinking into my soul.

"When it gets too much. In here . . ." He tapped his head. "I become someone even *I* can't stand." Jasper released his hold on my hand on his chest to push back my hair from my face, and I thought I might combust. "I didn't even care about how much I had plunged into the dark until you arrived and called me out. Until you saved my sister's horse today, just out of the kindness of your heart because that's the type of person you are. Despite my being awful to you, you helped me and didn't think twice about doing so."

Flattered, a smile pulled on my lips. Jasper mirrored it. "You didn't deserve to be spoken to like that," he said, then added, "That's why I wanted to speak to you. To apologize and tell you that I appreciate your help today more than I can ever express."

"Thank you," I said, my body so light that I felt like I could float away. Jasper's hand in mine was the only thing that kept me grounded.

"How's Genny?" I asked.

"Good, thanks to you," he said, and I wasn't sure I could take Jasper being this kind to me. I was already struggling to keep him at arm's length as it was. Sweet Jasper had the potential to destroy me.

Perhaps feeling we were on dangerous territory too, Jasper released my hand. "I'd better get home," he said, and got to his feet.

Before he could move, I stood in his path and said, "Thank you." Jasper frowned in confusion. "For swallowing your pride and coming to say sorry to me." I shrugged. "I know it's not always easy, especially for moody souls like you." I was joking—partly—and I just hoped he knew it.

Then Jasper smiled widely, and the beautiful sight nearly knocked me off my feet. "It was tough, but I got through it."

I laughed loudly when I realized he was joking in return. "You're so brave," I said, sarcastically, but making sure he heard the thread of truth in that statement too. He had a lot on his plate, and he *was* brave for taking it all on.

Jasper stepped closer and closer until he was almost pressed against me. Shivers ran down my spine at breakneck speed when he cupped my face and said, "If I don't see you before you go to Doha, good luck." My lips parted, and Jasper's heavy gaze dropped to my mouth. I held still as his head leaned in, until at the very last minute, Jasper pressed a soft kiss on my forehead. "Despite what I said to you the other day, you are the best rider I have seen in a long time . . . maybe ever."

Shock held me in its grip because his voice never wavered. He was telling the truth. Jasper moved around me and left for the door, but I snapped out of my stupor enough to say, "What do I need to work on?" Jasper Knighton was a global champion several times over. His advice was like gold dust. Of course I had weaknesses, everyone did. And I truly did want his opinion.

"Leon will support you with all that," he said. "He's the best at what he does."

"But I'm asking *you*," I said back, boldly. Something Jasper seemed to like if the subtle flaring of his eyes was anything to go by.

He was silent for a beat, before he said, "You hold your breath on the approach to a jump. It affects your balance." I did do that. He was right. I tried to change it, but in the moment, often forgot.

"What else?" I pushed, feeling like the twelve-year-old wannabe rider getting coached from her hero.

"Your hands are too high, especially in the jump-offs when you're pushing your horse to the brink." My cheek twitched at just how easily

Jasper gave feedback. Ever the perfectionist. "That's what I'd work on between now and Doha."

"Thank you," I said, and meant it. Jasper nodded his head, then I asked, "What are your weaknesses?"

His expression was serious as he studied my face. I wanted to know that a world champion had things to work on too. I wanted him to talk to me like I'd told him he could. Jasper folded his arms over his chest, then said, "These days?" he asked, and I nodded eagerly. "I just have one," he said, cryptically. "One I'm not sure I'll be able to overcome."

With that, Jasper left through the barn doors, but I was sure I heard "'Night, Angel" as he walked down the hallway. My heart kicked into a heady sprint, and my body filled with lightness, a far cry from where I'd been only hours ago.

Lifting my shaking hand to my forehead, I traced the spot Jasper's lips had just kissed. He had come to apologize to me. He was in a dark place because of all he'd gone through of late. And I was pretty sure that weakness he was referring to? Had nothing to do with his riding skills.

I dropped down to the bench and stared into space.

Jasper Knighton was a deeply layered man. A man I had vowed to stay away from. Only now the thought of leaving him to go on tour brought pangs of pain to my heart.

But it was probably for the best. I had vowed to be here with no distractions. To ride with the sole intent of being top of the rankings. If Jasper came with us, I wasn't sure I could stay focused.

Him not coming on tour was certainly for the best.

I just wished I could convince my soul of that fact too.

Chapter Ten

Jasper

Golden Oaks
Two weeks later

My hands shook as I held the letter in my hand. I had read it, and read it again.

> How is Dahlia?
> If you take measures to protect things I want to destroy, I will always find a way around them.

I rubbed my hand over my face. The state-of-the-art electric barn we'd had built for Dahlia had been hacked. Dahlia escaped and almost broke her legs because this prick was pissed off that we'd managed to keep her in a secure place and he couldn't get to her.

But how did he know? Only the close members of staff knew, and we'd questioned them all. They had worked with us for years and were trusted. It wasn't them, something inside of me just felt it. The company providing the state-of-the-art electric stables had never been hacked before and were now changing their security to make it bulletproof.

Who the fuck was this person?

> The tour begins soon, and I will be watching.
>
> Your father made sure to destroy my life, so I will destroy yours in return.
>
> You worshipped your father but didn't know the secrets he took to the grave.
>
> He wasn't the man you thought, and now the son shall pay for the sins of the father.

I slammed the letter down and gripped my hair. I took a deep breath and replayed all the measures I had to keep everyone safe on the tour—the horses, the staff, the riders . . . *Hallie.*

I had contacts all over the world in this industry, friends in all the high places, and I was using every one of them to ensure there was no drama, no issues for my team this year. But still, I felt helpless, knowing they were going to be traveling around the world, while I was here, having to trust that I'd done enough.

You worshipped your father but didn't know the secrets he took to the grave. He wasn't the man you thought, and now the son shall pay for the sins of the father . . .

The threats in the letters were nothing new, but the letters of late seemed to be getting more personal, like I could feel the anger toward my father growing stronger, more unhinged.

I looked up at my father's picture. My stomach rolled. He was a good man, I knew . . . wasn't he?

"Tell me you were, Dad," I whispered to the man I held up on a pedestal. "You were the man I thought, right?" Eyes the carbon copy of mine stared back at me. I shook my head. He was. I knew it. These letters were just a way to unnerve me. I didn't believe my father was a morally corrupt man. And some unhinged stalker wouldn't make me begin to doubt that now.

I placed the letter in the file with all the others and put them in my drawer. I had barely powered up my computer to work on some Knighton Equestrian contracts when there was a knock on the door and Leon poked his head through.

He held a to-go mug of tea in his hands and said, "I come bearing gifts."

"You're a lifesaver," I said. I accepted the tea from him and took a sip, letting the scalding, milky brew relax my tight throat. Leon dropped into the seat opposite me.

"The horses have landed and have been taken to the venue's stable yard," Leon said as he made himself comfortable. "The grooms and staff are all there and set up in the hotel."

I nodded, but my leg bounced under the table. That letter had left more than a bad taste in my mouth. "Security are there too and have cleared the stables, hotel, and venue," I said, which gave me some peace. "I've spoken to the owner of the arena. They've told me no one will go near our horses, and they are in the most secure section with both our men and the arena's added security."

Atticus, Sage, and Hallie, as well as our other riders, were flying out to Doha, Qatar, tomorrow for the opening of the Sandings Grand Prix and the start of the season. Everything they had been working for began in a few days' time.

Forrest and Felix were still in training here at Golden Oaks. Genny was concentrating on her recovery, and I would be staying here, of course.

Leon shook his head, smirking. "How does it feel to still be king of the circuit even after over a year away?" I rolled my eyes at my friend. He held up his hands in surrender. "Hey, you being worshipped makes it so the rest of us get the best treatment and the best facilities. I'm not complaining!"

A knock sounded on my door. Atticus stuck his head through. Leon got to his feet when he saw my younger cousin. "I registered Lord Henry, remember," he said, and I exhaled an exaggerated sigh. Leon put his hands up again. "Just saying, there's still space for the returning world champion to join us. Your rankings still stand from previous years."

I held out my hand for Leon to shake, ignoring his offer, as tempting as it might be. He shook my hand back, and I said, "Keep safe out there, okay? Keep me informed of everything."

"I will, Jas." Leon cocked his head to the side. "Come see us sometime, yeah? It's not the same being out there without you." A pang of homesickness hit me. Because that circuit was my home. Leon had trained me for years. I felt terrible not going this year. But the letter that had come this morning had me all in my head and told me I was doing the right thing. I swayed between whether my presence on the tour would bring danger or security. But I hadn't shown my face on the circuit for an age, so in the end I felt it best to stay put.

Leon waved and left. Atticus strutted over to the chair Leon had just vacated and sat down. He threw his feet up on the desk, his arms behind his head. "Make yourself at home, Cousin," I said dryly.

"Always do," Atticus said, then threw a mint imperial in his mouth from the bowl Geraldine always put out on my desk. Atticus sucked on the mint and said, "You wanted to see me. What's up?"

"Look after them all, okay?" I said, straight to the point, causing Atticus to still and narrow his eyes on me. "If you feel anything is amiss, you contact me. Immediately."

"What's happened?" he asked, all playfulness forgotten. Atticus was a clown most of the time, but he was loyal to the nth degree and would protect anyone he cared about with a fierce determination. "Have we been threatened again?"

"I'm just being vigilant," I said, evading the question. He was about to go and compete; he didn't need to worry about anything else but the team doing well. Atticus hung on my every word. "Security is already over there, but I want you to be my eyes and ears on the tour." Atticus tipped his head to the side, assessing.

"This doesn't have anything to do with our resident cowgirl-come-show-jumper, does it?" I glared at my cousin, but as usual, it did nothing to intimidate him. He leaned forward and put his elbows on my desk. "You know," he said, his voice slipping into a singsong tone, "you could just, I don't know, *come*." He shrugged. "That way, you wouldn't need me to be your eyes and ears," he said, air-quoting my words. "You wouldn't have to parade yourself around. You could keep to yourself. But at least you'd be there to keep watch over us all and put your mind at ease . . ." He smirked. "And make sure a certain blue-eyed hottie was fully intact."

"I have to stay here," I said, annoyance slipping into every word. "I must look after things here in England. And Knighton Equestrian is busier than ever."

Atticus rolled his eyes. "Forrest's season doesn't begin for a while yet, and if possible, he has a bigger pole shoved up his arse than you, so I call bullshit on that. And you have a laptop. Knighton Equestrian can be managed remotely. That's how you've always done it in years past."

"Genny is here too—"

"Again, so are Felix and Forrest," Atticus cut in. "She also has Geraldine, and by the looks of it, you've hired the SAS to protect Golden Oaks and our team abroad, so I'm not sure what you think you could do to protect them all more than trained specialists could."

Sometimes my younger family members were the blight of my life. And more than annoying when they ripped your reasons for not going somewhere wide open. I'd spent days convincing myself I was better off here. And in walks Atticus, smashing all my excuses to smithereens.

Atticus got to his feet. "I need to pack. The private jet is tires up at ten tomorrow morning. I hope to see you there." He walked to the door.

"You won't," I said sternly.

"Okay. Then see you when I get back," he said, and left the office with his usual dramatic flair.

When he was gone, I locked the door behind him, then moved back to my desk. I replayed the last line of today's letter in my head.

I am watching you.

I ran my hand over my forehead and stared out the window. The place was a rush of activity. Everyone had either already left for Doha or were prepping to go.

I hadn't seen Hallie since the night in the vet barn. My pulse fucking raced as I recalled how she looked in her cowgirl getup, that long, raven hair wild around her. Her stunning turquoise eyes as they fell on me behind her.

I'd fought going. I'd fought the apology I gave her. It was *better* that she disliked me. It was better that we didn't get too close. But after what she had done for Dahlia, there was no way I wasn't going to thank her in person. By saving Dahlia that day, she had saved my sister. I didn't want to even imagine what would have happened if Dahlia had had to be destroyed.

Genny would have been destroyed too.

Hallie didn't understand the gravity of her help that day.

But I did. I also understood the gravity of the hold she had on my heart. Right now, that was the bigger battle for me to overcome. A ghost of a smile pulled on my lips as I thought back to finding her in the vet barn. I knew she'd be there. If there was one thing I knew about Hallie, it was that she cared for horses more than anything. She was a night owl and didn't care about breaking the rules. My gut told me she would have sneaked into the barn to see Dahlia even if she hadn't been allowed. When I entered the barn and Katie told me she was already there, it was the first full breath I'd taken that day.

When we'd begun talking, my suspicion that Dad's accident wasn't an accident at all had been on the tip of my tongue. In that moment, I'd wanted to tell her everything. But I'd refrained. She was here to ride, not shoulder my problems. I didn't want to drag her down with me.

But I had wanted to open up to her. I had *wanted* to. For me, someone so closed off and insular, that had shocked me to my core.

My body relaxed and a smile graced my face when I thought of Hallie's training the past couple of weeks. While I was around the property, I found myself watching her train from far-off vantage points so she wouldn't spot me. I watched her practicing her breathing on the approach and lowering her hands when she jumped at speed.

Hallie had taken the advice I'd given her to heart until she'd mastered it. She could not have been more prepared for the big leagues. She had worked hard, and if I was being honest with myself, going to watch her train on Huxley had become the highlight of my day.

I was in real danger, I knew it. Because after our talk in the vet barn, after the way I'd kissed her forehead, she had consumed my every waking hour.

The thought of not seeing her around Golden Oaks for a while made a pain shoot through my chest and ignited every instinct I had to follow her. I thought of the letter again. I was worried if I went on tour, then whoever was threatening me would see my fondness for Hallie. Worried about the likes of Alexis Hobbs, who had already latched on to the fact I liked my rider. Worried about the leeches like Camille Dubois and all the other rivals I had gathered over the years who would do anything to see my reputation sullied.

But you could protect her better if you were with her, a traitorous voice said in the back of my mind. *You could fend off the wolves.*

Fuck.

Just the thought of her going on tour and only coming back occasionally . . . I hated it. I *shouldn't* want it. I should be stronger; I should resist her. But there was a pull between us that I couldn't explain, one that I couldn't release no matter how hard I tried.

I could never have anything with her. I couldn't risk her that way. But I *could* be there in the background, watching over her.

And I'd love to watch her compete.

Shit, watching her jump was like a religious experience. I had no doubt she and Huxley were going to be contenders for the top spot at each Grand Prix. And the thought of only watching her on TV and not from the arenas themselves made me spitting mad. I wanted to see the footing kick up and cloud as she landed. I wanted to hear the gasps from the crowd as she won the jump-offs. I wanted to see Huxley puffing for breath and Hallie's flushed cheeks as they finished another round victorious.

Unable to sit still, I rose from my desk, threw on my coat, and went to our barn. It always brought me solace. Within minutes I had Henry brushed down and tacked up. I grabbed my hat and led him to our private arena. Henry stood perfectly still as I mounted him. "Walk on, boy," I said, and immediately felt the excitement in my horse at simply being near the course of fences before us.

It had become a kind of game at this point, between me and Leon. He knew I still rode. All my family did. And Leon, an epic course designer in his own right, would sneak in each day while I was in my office and rejig the jumping course for my nightly training sessions.

I clicked my tongue and Henry moved to a trot. "Good boy," I said as I worked out the course. It was difficult, as hard as it would be in any Grand Prix, and just being on my stallion, sussing out the order of fences, made goose bumps accost my body.

Nothing else made me feel this way. The thrill and excitement that came with the challenge of a new course. Of pushing me and Henry to see just how far we could go, what our ceiling actually was. We hadn't reached it yet. And that was the most devastating part of it all.

We still had ladders to climb and accolades to win. But I wouldn't put my horse in danger. Or myself. Genny needed me. As did my cousins.

And Henry . . . I would never have my heart horse hurt.

For the past year and a half I had worried I would never find this feeling again. I moved Henry into a canter and turned toward the first fence. Henry's strides were perfect, and we flew over the first oxer, a brightly colored set of neon-green-and-pink poles. Henry never shied from a fence, even when the fillers and poles were gaudy or the pictures upon them were spooky to most horses. The goal of every course designer was to make the horse and rider collect faults. Over the years, the poles and fences had gotten brighter and more patterned to put the horses off. The fillers and wings had too, showcasing logos or garish branding or even things such as Land Rovers or miniature houses.

Locally, a replica of Tower Bridge was a favorite. Where most horses would hesitate, unsure whether they should approach it, Henry never flinched. I was sure at this point he could jump a moving tornado and not even bat an eye.

I had to hold Henry steady to keep him from racing over the next fence. He lived for the arena, and I felt awful that I was depriving him of what he loved most. He loved this; *I* loved it. There'd been nothing like it for the past eighteen months, nothing came close . . . until I watched Hallie jump the first day I saw her on Huxley. And all the times I'd watched her since.

"Again, boy," I said as we jumped all but the last three.

Henry turned to a spread fence—his favorite—and cleared it perfectly. I smiled as we cleared the next, then went for the last, a small puissance-type mock-brick wall—but still high for a regular jump.

Henry's ears flicked forward and he picked up speed. Then in the way only Henry could, he took flight. The breeze whipped past my head, and I crouched forward, loosening the reins, giving him the freedom he needed to carry us over smoothly. When his hooves hit the ground, I wrapped my arms around his neck. "You never miss, boy," I said, and ran my hand through his platinum mane. In the past five years, Henry and I had won over eight Puissance competitions. It was mostly what we were famous for. Then just like that, my previously full heart fell, and guilt assaulted me.

Bringing Henry to a steady trot, then a walk, I rested my cheek on his neck and said, "I'm so sorry, boy. I'm sorry you've been grounded from what you love. It's my fault. I've failed you." My throat felt thick, and I stayed in the arena a while longer, letting him jump again, just to give him some kind of enjoyment. Resolve built within me. "I'll make it right," I said to Henry. "Somehow, I'll make it right and get you airborne again."

As we cooled down, I noticed a figure in the doorway. My heart slammed into my rib cage until I noticed it wasn't the petite, raven-haired beauty I'd hoped it was.

Forrest was watching us. I waved at my cousin, and as I approached, he said, "I'm getting Aurelia tacked up. I want a go at this course."

I raised my eyebrow. "You think you can clear it?"

Forrest ran his hand down Henry's nose when we came to a stop in front of him. "My queen can do anything she sets her mind to," he said, and I dismounted. After Henry was turned out in the field, I joined Forrest back in the barn. He was brushing down Aurelia. We had many grooms at Golden Oaks who could do this for us, but none of us had ever gotten tired of grooming or tacking up our horses ourselves. Plus, this section of the barn was our private sanctuary. A place only we family members came . . .

Well, us, and a certain Texan cowgirl who had a penchant for breaking in.

Forrest took a curry comb from his brush box and began clearing the mud from Aurelia's coat after her day rolling in the wet field. "I'd ride him, you know." Forrest said, never missing a beat. I frowned at my cousin. "If you went on the tour, I mean." Forrest changed brushes to one for Aurelia's mane. As he pulled through her knotty strands, he said, "You know I'd take care of him. I love all our horses as if they were my own."

I sighed. "Have you been talking to Atticus by any chance?"

"No," Forrest said. Bluntly. And I knew he meant it. He turned to me. "Get away from this place for a bit, Jas. Go to Doha." He placed his hand on my shoulder. "Remind yourself of the joy of this business and not just the threats and tragedy you've been blinded by." A smirk pulled on his lips. "Go and watch your girl jump."

"She's not my girl," I said, clearly too emphatically, if Forrest's responding sarcastic chuckle was anything to go by.

"I am capable of watching this place. *And* Genny," he said, when I opened my mouth to say just that. "Just go on the first leg of the tour. You can micromanage everything there the way you love to here."

I moved to Aurelia's head and ran my hand along her cheek. She was so soft natured for a mare, and her eyes were closing under my touch, content to be pampered. My cousin spoiled her rotten. Said often that she was the only reliable female in his life.

"I don't know what's best to do," I confessed, letting my cousin in a little to how I'd been feeling.

Forrest stopped brushing Aurelia and faced me. "Go. Fucking hell, Cousin. Give yourself a few weeks away. You won't settle knowing our riders are over there alone without their leader." He smiled sadly. "You were always meant to be on those tours. And it'll put your mind at ease seeing that everything is in place with the new security you've hired. And that Atticus and the girls are as safe as they can be."

I turned to Aurelia and began fussing her again. I was being pulled from pillar to post inside. I had no idea what the right thing was to do. But when I thought about not seeing our riders compete in person, and about not seeing Hallie for weeks on end . . .

I gave up fighting.

Clutching my briefcase in my hand, I practically dived from the car in the family hangar and ran for the stairs to my jet. The engines were on, and I could hear the staff readying for takeoff.

Emma, the lead air hostess, startled when I reached the top step. She was preparing the drinks. "Mr. Knighton!" she said. "I didn't expect to see you on board today." Emma had been the leading air hostess for us for years now. She was in her late fifties, and it was good to see her. I treasured loyalty more than ever these days.

Emma's eyes brightened. "Are you competing again?"

I shook my head. I wondered if the pain I felt whenever I answered this question would ever be less agonizing. "No. Strictly here to make sure my team is looked after."

Emma squeezed my arm and said, "Then please take a seat, sir."

Pulling back the curtain divider to the main body of the plane, I stepped through. Sage and Hallie were sitting beside one another in the front row. Sage saw me first. She fought a smile, then nudged Hallie, who had her head buried in a book.

"What now?" Hallie asked, clearly pissed off at being disturbed. Sage nodded her head my way, and I felt strange shivers run down my back as Hallie's bright eyes landed on me and a blush burst onto her cheeks. She opened her mouth to speak, but nothing came out. I'd clearly shocked her, and I decided I liked this look on the sexy cowgirl. Never one to shy away from how she felt, it was good to know I could make her speechless.

"Hallie," I greeted, something in my chest shifting, some weight I'd been carrying lifted with relief that I'd decided to travel to Doha too. Then I addressed her friend. "Sage." I didn't know Sage that well, but anyone could tell that she and Hallie were as thick as thieves.

Atticus must have been in the bathroom, as he walked from the back of the plane and laughed out loud at seeing me standing there—the fucker. "Well, look what the cat dragged in," he said, humor lacing his voice, then came straight for me. He slapped my back in greeting.

"Atti," I returned, through clenched teeth. My shitty attitude toward him only humored him more.

Sage and Hallie's attention was firmly fixed on us when Atticus said, "What changed your mind about coming?"

I was going to murder him. I was. Twenty-five years in prison didn't sound too bad right now.

Atticus grinned, waiting for my answer, when Emma approached and saved me. "Could you all take your seats for takeoff, please? Our window is approaching soon."

I walked to the back of the plane and took my usual seat. Atticus, forgoing his normal place near me, sat across the aisle from Hallie and Sage at the front.

"What are you doing up here, dickhead?" I heard Sage hiss at him.

"Just giving you a good view for the six-hour journey, Miller." I shook my head in exasperation and vowed to talk to my cousin about harassment when we landed. I slipped my AirPods in and let Chris Stapleton croon through my ears. When the next song came on, Zach Bryan singing a guttural tune about burning, I found my gaze drifting to the front of the plane.

I wasn't an avid country music fan. In fact, I'd never really paid it any mind. But since a certain rider of mine tuned my Range Rover's radio to a country station, it was all I'd been listening to. Just hearing these songs made me think of Hallie curled up on my passenger seat, singing along to the music, her sweet Texas twang filling up my car.

Every time I got in the car now, it felt empty.

Retrieving my laptop, I waded straight into my ridiculous workload, only lifting my head when Emma placed a steaming-hot beef Wellington in front of me. I took out my AirPods and stretched my arms, realizing we were airborne. "Thank you, Emma," I said. Before I began to eat, I got up and went into the back section of the plane. There was a king-size bed in the private bedroom and a full bathroom in there too.

Washing my hands, I stared at myself in the mirror. I was dressed in my usual checked shirt and jeans with a Knighton Equestrian–branded olive fleece gilet on top. Even I could see there was a little more life in my eyes here on this plane than there'd been back home. Forrest had been right. Getting away from Golden Oaks would be good for me. I would function better after this break.

As I walked out of the bathroom, I immediately collided with someone. Grabbing their arms to stop them from stumbling, a heady rose and vanilla scent burst all around me, and I instantly knew who it was.

"Shit! Sorry!" Hallie said, and I looked down at her, fighting a laugh at her outburst. Her hair was tied back in her usual French plait. She wore leggings and a long Knighton Equestrian hoodie in pink. A silhouette of Henry was embroidered on the front of this one. Hallie followed my gaze, and said, "I have a change of clothes for when we land." She smirked. "Atticus wants us all to wear our team jackets to represent Golden Oaks."

As well as competing individually, Atticus, Sage, and Hallie would be entering the team events. Riding in the Global Champions Tour for the "Knighton Cavaliers," Knighton Equestrian's sponsored team. It helped promote our stud farm but was also good for prize money and team unity.

"Of course he does," I said, humor in my voice. That sounded just like Atticus. He loved to showboat. "I'm surprised he hasn't given you all full-blown choreography to announce your arrival too."

Hallie laughed and it felt as warm as a shot of whisky hitting my chest. I took a step closer to her. I had to. Her smile faded a little as I did, and heat filled her eyes. Before I knew what I was doing, I took hold of the hoodie's string around her neck, rubbing it between my fingers. "This outfit may be casual, but I'm sure you could wear a hessian sack and still look beautiful."

Hallie exhaled a rushed breath. The air grew to thick static between us. Hallie cleared her throat and gestured around us. "Y'all have yourselves a fancy getup with this plane, Jasper," she said, her country accent thick and strong.

It was nerves, I realized. My proximity, bringing out the cowgirl in her. I shouldn't have loved that as much as I did.

Averting my attention, I glanced around at the wood, gold, and cream finishes of the Gulfstream I bought a few years ago. I didn't know whether Hallie would find this private plane too excessive or impressive. For some reason, I needed it to be the former. "You think it's a waste of money?"

Hallie rolled her eyes and sputtered an incredulous laugh. "Fuck, no," she said, "I spent the first fifteen minutes on board checking the place out like a kid at a new playground. This plane is insane. And it sure as shit beats waiting in line at the TSA or being crammed in economy class next to someone who doesn't understand basic hygiene."

I fought a laugh. "Well, I'm glad you approve."

Hallie nudged her chin in the direction of the bedroom. "That's an interesting feature." My blood went from warm to scalding in naught point two seconds when the image of Hallie, naked and on all fours in the middle of my bed, came to mind. She must have seen the heat on my face as her eyelids lowered and she said, "Use it much?"

We held each other's stares for several beats, the air pulsing between us. With this turn in conversation, we were treading into dangerous waters. Hallie reached out and plucked a piece of lint that had gathered on the shoulder of my gilet. I fought back a vision of grabbing her hand, putting it over my stirring dick, and crushing her mouth to mine. But I behaved myself. "If I travel at night, I will," I said.

Hallie nodded, then, "That's all? You only use it for sleep? How . . . *vanilla*." A playful smirk pulled on her full red lips.

I was fucked. I'd never met this level of temptation before in my entire thirty-two years. Hallie Oakley was my living-fucking-wet dream, and now she was asking me if I fucked in my plane's private bedroom.

I inched closer until Hallie's back hit the wall behind her. Her breathing was rough. "Vanilla?" I said, catching the rasp in my voice. "I've been called a lot of things in my life, Hallie, but never that." I pushed back a fallen strand of her dark hair from her cheek. Hallie sucked in a stuttered breath. "*Never* that."

One night. I would need just one night, one fucking hour with this woman, and I'd show her I was far from vanilla. I'd wreck her for fucking life. And she'd be a good adversary for me. I liked control, craved it. Hallie would fight back, giving me the challenge of a lifetime.

I almost groaned aloud just picturing it. Hallie's eyes fixed on mine and didn't shift. We were close, very close, but if I just leaned in, just a little bit more . . .

"Hals! *Never* fucking leave me with that prick again . . ." Sage came barreling through the curtain, shattering the moment. She immediately froze, seeing us pressed against the wall, and I instantly stepped back and cleared my throat. Sage smiled smugly. "Sorry to interrupt."

I waved her off. "Nothing to interrupt," I said, and pushed past them. "Have a nice flight, ladies," I added, and quickly sat down. I could hear heated whispers from Sage and Hallie, so I put my AirPods back in my ears and ate my meal, ignoring the hammering of my heart in my chest and the fact that my cock was now as hard as nails.

Sage and Hallie eventually moved past me, back to their seats, and I picked up my laptop and briefcase and took myself to the bedroom. I locked myself inside and slumped down on the side of the bed. I ran my hands through my hair.

Watching over Hallie on this trip would test every limit I had. I could still smell her rose and vanilla perfume on my shirt. My dick hardened to a painful degree, and all I could see were her piercing blue eyes as she stared up at me.

But she was in the cabin with Sage and my cousin, where she belonged. And not in here with me.

I ran my finger over my lip. In a perfect world, I would have kissed her there and then. I would have steered her back to this room, thrown her to the bed, bound her hands and licked that woman from head to foot before slamming inside her and making her scream. I'd have spent every hour of this journey making her fall apart, not giving one single fuck as to who heard her.

But this wasn't a perfect world. This was the one I'd been given.

My only job was to protect her.

I just wished I could convince my heart of that too.

Chapter Eleven

Hallie

Doha, Qatar

"Shut. The. Fuck. Up," Sage said as we arrived in my room on the top floor of the hotel Jasper had booked for us. Five star, of course. "It has a living room and a kitchen, Hals."

I laughed at my best friend. "We've stayed in hotels like this before," I said.

Sage eyed me incredulously. "*No,* we haven't, Hals." She walked to an intercom near the kitchen. "We have a butler here. A fucking *butler*."

"True," I said, then went into the bedroom. I sank onto the bed and groaned. It was like lying on a cloud. Sage ran from the doorway and dived on the bed beside me. "Sage!" I squealed as the bed bounced, and I pushed her away when she licked my cheek. "What's with you?" I asked, wiping my face.

Sage turned, propping her chin on her hand. "We're *here*, Hals. We're here, entered in our first five-star Grand Prix and riding epic horses. All those years qualifying in the Unders, getting in the FEI, fighting for the top spots. And we're finally *here*. In a couple of days, we'll be on the main stage and then we're off."

Sage's eyes glistened and her emotional speech made mine water too. "Yeah," I said in a hushed tone. I reached out between us on the pristine white quilt. Sage put her hand in mine. "We'll have a good season, then it's on to Team USA. *Together,*" I said.

"Together," she echoed. Sage and I had ridden for Team USA juniors, but now we wanted in the big show. We wanted to wear the iconic red jackets, and we wanted to compete in the Olympics on our home turf two years from now. California.

"Sage?" I asked, after a few minutes of silence.

"Yeah?"

"Why are you in my room?"

She rolled her eyes. "Because I saw Atticus going to his suite, and mine is right next door to his. I didn't want him to know it."

"He wouldn't do anything, Sage. Yes, you have history, but all his antics are just playful."

"I know . . ." she said, then looked around my room. "Hey! Do you wanna swap?"

I laughed. "Nope!"

"Hals!" Sage groaned pathetically.

"No. Be a big girl and put your history with Atticus to bed. Call a fucking truce. We need to be a team here, and for that y'all need to stop bickering like a ninety-year-old married couple." Sage huffed, in a mood. But I knew my best friend, and by the slumping of her shoulders, she'd heard me and agreed.

"Don't be moody," I said, poking her in the ribs. "You know I'm right." Sage squealed, but then knocked my hand away to lean forward, searching my face.

"What?" I asked.

"Are we going to talk about a certain hot moment on the plane?" she said mischievously.

"Nope!" I said, feeling tingles run up my thighs just remembering Jasper's hard body pressed against them. He had towered above me, and when he told me he was far from vanilla, I didn't care if he took me then and fucked me up against that wall. Fuck the private bedroom; who needed a bed when you had Jasper Knighton pressed against you and a sturdy surface to be devoured against?

"Shit," Sage said, pulling me from my heated thoughts.

I blinked and tried to calm down. "What?"

"Oh, darlin'," Sage said, Tennessee accent coming in strong. "You're screwed." She fanned my flushed face. "You want to drop to your knees for our boss and suck him until he blows."

"Sage!" I said, and hit her on her arm. She rolled over, laughing. I pushed at her and tried to get off the bed. She grabbed my arm. "You won't swap rooms with me because a certain alpha male brooding hunk is right next door to you," she said. "Am I right?"

I was going to kill her. "No," I said, but Sage laughed even harder. Clearly, I wasn't good at bluffing.

"Well, that was convincing, Hals," she said. Facing me again, she said, "Can you just fuck him already? I can't take the tension between y'all. It's like seeing a slow-burn novel being played out in real life. It's driving me fucking insane! Ride that man like he's Seabiscuit. Then tell me all about it. Every. Last. Detail."

"Sage!"

"What?" she said, incredulously. "Have you *seen* that man ride a horse? The power in his legs? He'll fuck you all night and not even lose his breath," she said, and I got off the bed.

Vanilla . . . I've been called a lot of things in my life, Hallie, but never that . . . Jasper's hot confession was on a loop in my head. What did that mean? What was he into? And how did I give it a try?

Feeling like I would combust, I pulled on Sage's arm and yanked her off the cloudlike mattress. "Get back to your room," I ordered. "We're going to see the horses in an hour, and I want to get cleaned up first."

Sage held up her hands. "All I'm saying is that you could go next door and get dirty with our boss instead." I slapped her ass, and Sage cackled as I pushed her out of the hotel room, slamming the door behind her. But I leaned against the door when she'd left and tried to calm myself down.

Jasper was in the suite next door. I would never sleep on this entire leg of the tour, knowing that we shared a wall. I played back our moment on the plane. I wanted him to lean down and kiss me, then drag me back to the bedroom and fuck me against the wall.

Was that too much to ask?

I beelined for the bathroom and turned on the shower. The fact was, all this tension with Jasper had me so turned on that my head was spinning. The competition in a couple of days was high stakes and high pressure. Usually, my hand did the trick to relieve me of that tension, but since Jasper, that was as satisfying as eating an overcooked steak when you'd asked for it rare.

I opened the window in the bathroom a few inches and welcomed the breeze. It was humid and warm, and the fresh air filled my lungs, helping me breathe. But the pulsing between my legs was getting worse.

Leaving the window ajar, I climbed into the shower and let the water fall over my head when I noticed a second handheld shower on the side. Taking it from the holder, I turned it on, twisting the nozzle until the water setting was on "Jet." Nipples hard, I lifted my leg to the ledge of the shower and let the spray flow against my clit. I groaned as my legs instantly started to shake, and like every time I touched myself, I pictured Jasper there with me. This time, he was walking into the shower behind me.

I closed my eyes, and as if it was real, felt Jasper's hands running over my ribs until they cupped my breasts. I moaned as his rough palms caused shivers to travel straight from my nipples to my clit. "Jasper," I moaned, as one of his hands slipped down my stomach, dropping farther until he cupped my pussy and pushed a finger inside me. I moaned loudly, the sound echoing in the shower stall, and my hand slapped against the slick tile wall.

"Fuck," I hissed as my hands began to shake. *"More,"* I said, only for Jasper to bend me forward, pushing on my back. Then in one swift move, he slammed inside of me. I screamed as he filled me completely. He gave me no time for reprieve; instead, he used his muscled, strong legs to take me apart.

Jasper pounded into me so quickly that he had to keep me standing by wrapping one hand in my braid, holding me up with the other around my stomach.

"Fucking take it, Hallie," he rasped into my ear, and I felt pressure building at the bottom of my spine. My face flushed and goose bumps ran over every part of my body as Jasper and his unrelenting movements broke me into pieces. Screaming, I came so hard that my legs collapsed from under me, and I dropped to the shower floor. My hand steadied my fall as my orgasm continued to play out.

I came back to the present in drips and drabs. Blinking into the water cascading from above, I dropped the handheld shower and sat down. Breathless, I stayed there for several minutes, just catching my breath.

"Fuck," I said, placing my hand over my pounding chest. That was intense. Closing my eyes, I still felt the fantasy of Jasper around me, *inside* of me. I laughed to myself. If that's what my imagination could conjure up, what the hell would the reality be like?

"I wouldn't recover," I said aloud into the steamy bathroom. "I wouldn't fucking recover." I had to get up and get ready, but in the aftermath of daydream-Jasper screwing me into oblivion, I grabbed for the handheld shower again and got back to my feet.

I had time for one more.

"Hello, my baby boy!" I said and ran straight for Huxley, who was watching me approach his stall. "Have you been okay? Was the flight comfortable for you? Are the other horses being nice to you?" I wrapped my arms around his neck and kissed him on his nose. Stepping back, I checked over his dark coat and body to be sure he was still in one piece.

This boy had utterly stolen my heart.

"He's good, I promise," I heard from behind me. I turned to see Mila walking up our private section of the yard with a bucket of Huxley's specialized feed in her hands. Near the competition, we changed his grain ration to give him more energy and spark on the course.

"Mila!" I said and wrapped her up in a hug. I'd bonded well with Mila. She was the best groom I'd ever had. She was efficient, an excellent rider, and didn't feel put out that I was more hands-on than most. In fact, she wanted to learn from me, which I loved. Plus, she was a total sweetheart, so that was a relief too.

Sage came next to us after checking on Fefe, her arm linking through Horatio's. Just like Mila and me, Sage and Horatio were joined at the hip. "Tell Hallie," Sage said to Horatio.

"What?" I asked.

Horatio went to open his mouth, but Sage beat him to it and said, "Dillon Matthews from Team USA fucked Mary Van Dousen from Holland two nights ago."

"Isn't Matthews married with kids and about fifty years old?" I asked. "And Mary is only, what? Twenty-eight?"

Sage batted her hand. "Who cares about age gaps?" she said, winking at me. *Bitch.* She tapped Horatio's arm again. "And tell her about Stephanie from France making a play for the CEO of Sandings Bank."

Sage reeled off every bit of gossip Horatio had gathered in the week they'd been here without us. Sage was careful to keep her name out of the gossip mill, but she sure as hell loved hearing about everyone else. The fact was, equestrian competitions could be as dramatic as any reality TV show. When you were on the road for the better part of a year, far away from family and your home, things happened. Often scandalous things, and perfect fodder for rivals.

"And how have you learned all of this?" I asked Horatio. "That's a lot of information for being here all of five minutes."

"We were at a bar last night, and Alexis Hobbs was there. The horse dealer." I'd heard of her—and it hadn't been positive. She was known to be ruthless and would do anything to get her own way. "She was telling us all over drinks."

She was also known to have the biggest fucking mouth in the industry. I'd never met the woman, but I already didn't like her for her shitty morals alone.

"Be careful," I said to Horatio. He stilled at my serious tone. "People like Alexis Hobbs ply staff with drinks to get them to spill secrets about their sponsors and bosses that people like her have no business knowing." I squeezed his arm. I didn't want to reprimand him, but I'd seen how private Jasper and his family were and didn't want anything to get out into the rumor mill.

"I know," Horatio said. "Leon and Mr. Knighton have already warned us off her." I nodded, hating that, in this moment, I sounded like the fun police. But we were here to win and win honestly. I'd seen enough Alexis Hobbs types growing up with my aunt.

"Protect yourself," Sage said to Horatio, backing me up. But then she turned to her groom and whispered, "But keep funneling me the gossip you get about everyone else." She was fucking hopeless.

I turned to Mila and rolled my eyes at our friends. Mila headed to Huxley, and I followed her. When Sage and Horatio were embroiled in another no doubt juicy story, Mila said, "I knew Horatio wouldn't have been able to keep that all to himself. He's been busting at the gut for Sage to get here." I sighed, and Mila said, "He seems a bit daft and immature, but Horatio has his head screwed on. He's been in this game for a while now, and he loves Golden Oaks and the Knighton family. He wouldn't put himself in the position to hurt them in any way. I promise."

I trusted Mila, so I nodded and pushed it from my mind. Turning to my horse, I ran my hand down Huxley's neck as he bent down to eat.

When Mila shut the stable door and bolted my stallion inside, I said, "Are we prepared for the trot up tomorrow?"

"Yes," she said, then grimaced. "He'll be ready to impress!"

"Perfect. Thank you," I said.

"Are you nervous?" Mila asked.

I shook my head. "I love the trot ups." It was true. It was where I found my footing. Where my feet hit the show's ground and centered me. "It puts me in competition mode."

Trot ups were inspections, where the horses registered in the Grand Prix were led around an area for the judges to ensure they were fit to compete.

A commotion suddenly came from my right, hushed whispers from the staff in our section of the stable yard and beyond. When I turned, my gaze slammed into Jasper Knighton's. The minute our eyes met, fire suffused my body.

Jasper's attention was solely on me, even though he spoke to a man dressed in traditional Qatari clothes. Jasper nodded his head, giving the illusion that he was listening to whatever the man said, but his chocolate-brown eyes were locked on me. His jaw was clenched, and he was staring at me like he was ready to fuck propriety, throw me down on the stable floor, and fuck me to oblivion.

This was more intense than yesterday in the plane. Right now, he looked unhinged. I didn't think this man could get any more good looking. I was wrong.

My breathing stuttered, and I broke away from his focus, busying myself by ducking into Huxley's stall and checking him over again. Hiding behind my horse, I leaned on the stall's wall and tried to cool down.

What the hell was that? Why was Jasper staring at me like that?

Then I stilled. There was no way . . . I blinked and peered through the metal sides of the stall. Jasper was still there. He was facing the man now, but every now and then, his gaze would drift to this stall, brows pulled down as he searched for me. I pushed myself back against the wooden wall some more and felt lightheaded.

The shower.

The shower where I'd come, screaming his name. There was no way he'd heard me, right? Surely the walls were thick enough that it would be soundproof. Yeah. I was thinking too much of it. Maybe he'd been recalling our little run-in on the plane. Yeah, that was it . . .

Then the blood drained from my face. The window. I'd left the window open in my hotel bathroom . . . where I'd screamed as I'd come . . . screaming Jasper's name.

No, I told myself. He couldn't have heard anything. I was sure.

I did a good job convincing myself of my lie and left Huxley's stall. The minute I came out, I felt Jasper watching me again. I didn't turn to look, because if I did, I might have to really entertain the possibility that Jasper heard me getting myself off in the shower, to the thoughts of him pounding into me.

Nope. I wouldn't go there.

"Jasper Knighton," I heard someone say, a tone of mockery in his voice.

I tried not to turn around, but when Jasper said, "McGowen," in a tight tone, I couldn't help myself. Jake McGowen stood on the other side of the gate that separated our horses from the next stable block.

Jake was tall and blond with blue eyes. He was conventionally good looking, but the fact was, he had nothing on Jasper. That stood for the competition too. A huge deal was always made of the rivalry between them, but Jake wasn't a fraction of the rider Jasper was, and when they were on the circuit, competing in teams or in the Olympics, Jasper dominated on Henry.

Jasper crossed his arms over his chest. Everything in his stance screamed "back the fuck off." That didn't deter Jake. "I didn't see your name on the rider's list," Jake said.

"Because it's not," Jasper said. His voice was cold and brutal, like an arctic blast. Hatred for this man pulsed off him in icy waves. Jake smiled wide, and I had the sudden urge to walk over and punch him in the face.

"Shame," McGowen said. "I have a mare this year who is going to eat this competition up."

Jasper laughed sardonically and said, "This mare . . . is she pumped full of PEDs, or is she natural?"

Jake's cocky smile fell off his face. "That's low, even for you," he snapped.

Jake moved to walk away but then caught me watching the heated exchange. "Hallie Oakley!" he said, his toned laced with excitement. "Welcome to the tour. It's about time you joined the big leagues. I've been keeping an eye on you in the Unders."

Jasper blocked me from Jake's view and said, "Don't fucking harass my riders." I'd never heard Jasper be so unkind, so unfeeling as I did in that moment.

I peeked around Jasper's broad body to see Jake's hands held up, but the cocky smirk on his face was back in place. "I wasn't aware saying hello was harassment." Jake found me again, and he said, "Nice to finally meet you, Hallie. We'll speak more when your jailer isn't around."

"Leave," Jasper said and turned to the man from Qatar he'd been speaking to before. "Is he stabled near us?"

"No," the man said. "He's on the other end of the yard." That seemed to appease Jasper somewhat, if the relaxing of his shoulders was anything to go by. But Jasper watched Jake walk away, only continuing his talk with the man once Jake was well out of sight.

"My panties are wet," Sage whispered into my ear as she came to stand beside me. "Fuck me, Hals. That was so hot." She nudged me. "Jasper is a total alpha." I turned to Sage, begging her with my gaze to stop talking. Sage ignored me, of course. "You won't be able to walk for days after he's done with you."

"He won't be 'done with me,' as you say. That can't happen."

Sage laughed, hard, and said, "Okay, Hals. Keep pretending that if it makes you feel better."

Fefe chose that moment to whinny and kick her stable door. "Baby girl, you need to chill," Sage said, and went straight over to her high-maintenance mare to calm her down.

"That's one of the owners of this venue," Mila said, pointing to the man Jasper was now walking away with. "Abdul Hashim. He and his family are huge fans of horse sports." I nodded, but I couldn't get the way Jasper reacted to Jake out of my head.

Turning back to Huxley, I grabbed a brush and began to groom him. He didn't really need it, but I had to keep myself busy.

"Head in the game, Hals," I said to myself in regard to Jasper. "Focus on the competition. No distractions. You're here to compete. To make it to the top."

But just hearing Jasper be so dominant was impossible to forget. *Don't harass my riders . . .* His harsh tone, his taut body, and his smooth accent all wrapped around my heart.

Lord, give me strength.

Chapter Twelve

Jasper

Doha, Qatar

Jasper . . . Jasper . . . JASPER!

I would overcome it, I thought as my hands fisted at my sides again. The bones in my fingers were close to breaking in my stress. Well, stress might not be the word. Frustration? The fucking impossible temptation I was under after hearing Hallie in her shower, getting herself off and screaming my name as she did. I'd opened the bathroom window to get some fresh air. Little did I know that Hallie had done the same, giving me the perfect soundtrack to her time in the shower.

I would have given anything to have seen what she was picturing in that moment. I'd heard the running of water, the breathless moans, and then the cry of my name as she came and splintered apart.

I was a strong man. I had resisted her this far, but Jesus fucking Christ, I was only human, and knowing the woman you were obsessing over was finding release to a fantasy of you was more than any man could take. I wanted to see her in the shower. I wanted to watch her make herself come. Had she used her hand? A toy? The showerhead?

I didn't care. I just wanted to fucking see it.

Jumping in the shower myself, I got so hard that I'd barely stroked my hand down my cock once before I spilled against the wall, coming so hard that I had to slam my hand against the tile to stop from losing my footing.

Then I'd seen her at the yard, a yellow Knighton Equestrian base layer and riding tights set hugging her every perfect curve. Abdul, an old friend, had been showing me all the improvements he'd made this year to the Doha venue, but I could hardly focus. Hallie's cheeks were flushed due to the humidity in the air, and I wanted to make her sweat more. Peel those clothes off her tight, toned body and hear her scream my name in person.

My private car was bringing me to the arena, and I forced myself to calm down so I didn't get out of the car with a hard-on. Atticus had informed me everyone was here for the trot up. I'd had meetings with my apparel buyers all morning, but I didn't want to miss seeing our horses being shown to the judges.

Making sure my lanyard was around my neck, I got out of the car and walked in the back entrance to the arena. Abdul understood my need for privacy and ensured I could move about the venue mostly unseen. I walked through the long corridors to a private section in the stands where I could watch the inspection in person.

When I got to the box that had been reserved for me, Atticus was already inside. "What are you doing here? Don't you have to go and get ready with Barnaby?" I asked, as I moved to the balcony that overlooked the trot up and leaned over the rail as horses from Belgium began their display. They looked good.

"I have time. And Abdul told me you'd be here." Atticus smiled. "He didn't think you'd mind me popping in to say hi."

"He thought wrong," I said dryly. But Atticus knew I didn't mean it. I loved the little wanker, despite myself.

Atticus came to stand beside me as I watched more inspections. It was good to suss out the competition. *"Sooo,"* he said, and every part of me stilled. Just the inflection of Atticus's voice told me I wasn't going to like whatever he was going to say. "There may or may not be a rumor that the great and almighty Jasper Knighton is here to watch over his team and is particularly possessive of one of his riders."

My hands balled into fists again, and I bit out, "Jake fucking McGowen."

Atticus nodded. "Jake fucking McGowen." He gave me a side-eye. "And Alexis Hobbs." I froze. Looking at Atticus, I raised an eyebrow, waiting for him to continue. Atticus exhaled. "Apparently, McGowen mentioned your possessive nature over Hallie last night at a brand dinner, and Alexis Hobbs, who was also in attendance, mentioned how she caught you pining over her when she came to Golden Oaks."

I clenched my jaw so tight I feared my teeth would crack. Closing my eyes, I took a deep breath to calm the fuck down. It didn't help. I knew the minute Alexis Hobbs saw something that day, she would bide her time to use it against me.

Hallie had only just stepped onto the circuit, and there were already rumors about her. Fuck!

I'd fix this. I'd make sure Alexis shut her mouth.

"The rumor will cool down when there's no fuel given to it," I said. "I'm not planning to be social here, so there'll be no room for gossip." I nodded as the next lot of horses were lined up to come in. Australia. I caught sight of Mila, Horatio, and Chris, Atticus's groom, checking the board for who was next. I pointed to indicate to my cousin that he better go down and get prepared soon.

I scanned the entrance to the arena and saw Hallie and Sage watching the Australian riders from the tunnel. Today, she was dressed in navy blue, the dark color making her turquoise eyes pop, even from this far away.

There were lots of other riders milling around, sussing out the competition. But my blood instantly spiked to boiling temperatures when I saw Jake McGowen making a beeline for Hallie and Sage.

"Fucking dick," I said, and went to run toward them when Atticus grabbed my arm.

"Don't fall for his tricks, Jas. You know he's only doing this to piss you off." Atticus's grip tightened on my biceps as I watched Jake hold out his hand to Hallie and she shook it. She smiled at him, and I wanted to commit murder.

"Arsehole," Atticus muttered when he next shook Sage's hand. Atticus released me and crossed his arms over his chest. "He knows we have better horses than him, and better riders. His stud is still struggling to get quality riders on their horses. No one trusts him one hundred percent yet, and no one wants to risk competing on a drugged-up horse."

I contemplated what Atticus said, and reluctantly confessed, "I hate him. I truly hate him. But I do think he's legitimate. I believe he didn't know what his father was doing, and he's been clean and professional since he took the helm. I may hate him, but I can respect what he's trying to do."

Atticus snorted with laughter after a few seconds. He put his hand on my shoulder and said, "How hard was that to say, Cousin?"

I smirked. "Climbing-Everest difficult," I said, then boiled some more when Hallie laughed at something he said. "I fucking loathe him." That was an understatement. Jake had tried to best me for years, in and out of the arena. If I fucked a woman, he would fuck her next. If I broke a record, he would almost kill himself to try to break mine.

He never could, and that was the crux of it.

Even with a drug-enhanced horse, he still couldn't beat me and Henry. Now, he couldn't compete directly against me, so he was going to try to do it off the field. I'd stupidly shown my cards when it came to Hallie. I knew that was a red flag to a bull in his case. Somehow, I had to let it not get to me.

"She's smart," Atticus said, referring to Hallie. "She'll see through his shit." All talking ceased when Chris, Mila, and Horatio left to get our horses ready.

"Perfect," Atticus said, and nudged me again. "I have a good feeling about this year."

"Don't jinx it," I said, feeling that pit of fear sink inside of me.

"Believe it," Atticus said, always the most upbeat out of all of us cousins. "Sage is insane on Seraphina, and she will be a force of nature when it comes to the jump-offs. Hallie is a natural and one of the most gifted talents I've seen in years." Atticus waggled his eyebrows. "And we have me. And we know I'm set to be the champion of the entire tour."

"If only you had more confidence," I said sarcastically.

"We can but pray for that," Atticus said, and turned to leave when he paused at the door to say, "Are you coming to the welcome dinner tonight?"

I raised my eyebrow at him. "Do you think I'll be at the dinner?"

Atticus held up his hands. "Just saying, Hallie and Sage will be there, all glammed up. As the newbies, all eyes will be on them." Atticus shrugged. "And I'm sure Jake will be dressed to the nines and making his play." Atticus sighed. "If you're not there to watch him . . ."

"Then *you* will," I said, through gritted teeth.

Atticus laughed. "Jas, tonight I'll be getting my dick wet. I can't compete tomorrow without getting some relief first." Atticus opened the door, but said, "Black tie as usual. *If* you decide to shed your reclusiveness and come to protect Hallie's virtue."

"And who will watch Sage's virtue?" I argued, trying to hit my mark this time. Atticus could talk of me and Hallie all he wanted, but he was like a lapdog, following Sage Miller around like a lovestruck idiot.

"That lady can take care of herself," he said, heat flaring in his eyes. He bit his bottom lip, then said, "She's fuckably vicious."

Atticus shut the door, and I looked back out over the balcony to see Hallie and Sage walking away, presumably to get ready for their turn in front of the inspectors. Jake McGowen watched them go. I ran my hand down my face. I wasn't going tonight. Going would mean every single person on the circuit would know I was here and would ask a billion questions that I had no intention of answering.

But just the thought of Jake McGowen chasing after Hallie . . .

I got myself a bottle of water from the room's fridge and kept my eyes glued on the arena. Two more teams completed their trot ups, and it was time for ours. Sage ran first, impressing the fuck out of me as she managed to keep Seraphina in a straight line so the judges could see her physique. I don't know how she did it, but she'd managed to get that mare to respect her, a mighty feat if there ever was one. I'd written Seraphina off as untrainable. Leon had believed he could find a rider to harness her level of crazy. I had to give it to my friend: He'd done it.

I couldn't help but smirk when Atticus came out next, dressed in a checked shirt, jeans, and boots. Barnaby was as impressive as always, and Atticus smiled and winked his way past fellow riders, spectators, and inspectors, giving them the grin that meant he rarely slept alone. Taking out my phone, I took a video, zooming in on his face and sent it to the cousin's group chat.

It was only seconds later when my phone buzzed in my hand.

FORREST: I was just eating, and the sight of my brother's ugly face has just spoiled it. Thanks.

FELIX: I hope you're not near his room tonight, Jas. You know Atti gets loud the night before a competition.

ME: Not near his room but have earplugs just in case.

I slipped my phone away when I saw Hallie walk Huxley into the tunnel to await her turn. An assistant gestured for her to join a lane, and I stopped breathing as she began to trot. Dressed in a Knighton checked shirt, jeans, and brown suede, knee-length country boots, she looked incredible. Her raven hair fell down her back in waves, but it was the smile on her face that I couldn't look away from. Huxley was perfect, keeping pace with Hallie's every step. I could see her mouth moving as they turned and trotted back. She was talking to him, and it reminded me of the day I saw her training him in the arena when Dahlia got loose.

Hallie had a God-given gift where horses were concerned. I wasn't sure she quite saw it, but from the way people were watching her, everyone else could. A smile crept onto my face as I watched the inspectors nodding and conversing among themselves. They were impressed. My years of doing this told me so.

But that happiness quickly fell away when I spotted Alexis Hobbs near the tunnel, watching from the stands. I leaned forward, and anger surged through me when I saw she was watching Hallie. My fury only increased when Jake McGowen and Camille Dubois joined her.

Camille Dubois, a French rider, wasn't quite in the same narcissistic lane as Alexis, but it was close. She and I had history—something I was glad was in the past. She, unfortunately, was not. The fact that Camille and Alexis were friends, and now seemingly cozying up to McGowen too, wasn't ideal. *No,* it was a fucking shit show. These three were the biggest antagonists in the sport, and nothing good would come of their allying with one another on this tour.

Hallie slowed Huxley from a trot to a walk, and my fists clenched when Camille pointed to Hallie from the stands and said something to Alexis that made them both laugh. Hallie was none the wiser to their cruelty and walked Huxley from the arena and back to the stables. Mila joined her, but I fixed my eyes back on the nightmare trio to keep an eye on them.

I was suddenly happy that I was here. Hallie, as feisty as she was, was a newbie on this tour, and it was my job to keep these people from treating her like shit.

I had to protect her, as her boss, but also because I couldn't stand her name being sullied because of me.

I needed to get out of here. It was a heady mix, being pissed at Alexis, Camille, and McGowen but so turned on by the sight of Hallie that I felt like I was being pulled in a million different directions. Leaving the box, I walked out of the executive stands to calm myself down.

Flashbacks of my youth circled my mind, Camille Dubois beneath me. Next, Alexis's knowing glint in her eye when she caught me watching Hallie at Golden Oaks, and finally, McGowen seeking her out just now.

Then, *Jasper . . . JASPER!* I heard Hallie moan in my mind. I exited the stand and went to the large trailer that held my Knighton Equestrian samples for the teams and sponsors to browse and to order our apparel as their official riding attire next season.

I began to sort through bridles, reins, saddle pads, and bits, just to try to not focus on the fact that at the dinner tonight, the fuckers on this tour would be circling my pretty new riders like sharks smelling fresh blood. I lifted a saddle off the saddle rack and placed it on the mannequin horse. Leaning against it, I said to myself, "You can't go. You don't *want* to go." But then I pictured what Hallie might be wearing, and that prick McGowen making his play, Alexis and Camille making their move, and it made me spitting mad.

But I *would* stay away.

I didn't want to cause a commotion. And I didn't want to be seen.

My decision was made.

As I knotted my bow tie, I met my reflection in the mirror and spat, "Pathetic."

Dinner had been going on for ninety minutes, and a single glimpse of Hallie in a floor-length gold dress, her raven hair falling down her back in soft waves, had me abandoning my desk and throwing on the tux I'd brought with me just in case. Atticus had "felt" the need to keep me up to date on my team.

Wanker.

I looked at the picture that now filled my phone screen. In it, Hallie was smiling at Sage, drinking champagne, and looking like she was thoroughly enjoying herself.

When I looked at her, I was fucking breathless. She was stunning. But it was the men in the background subtly checking her out that had my arse moving. Yeah, I was a jealous fucker tonight. And color me surprised because I'd never felt like this before. Toward *anyone*. But one picture of Hallie Oakley had me dressed in ten minutes flat and taking the elevator down to my private car, ready to smash all my self-imposed rules to smithereens.

I wasn't even thinking of all the gossip my appearance would cause, the questions that would be pressed upon me. All I could see was raven hair, a golden dress, and a woman that was no fucking one else's but *mine*.

In this moment, I was actually questioning my sanity. But the need to be there and make sure no one fucked with her had taken the reins, and I was simply going along for the ride.

Traffic was light, and twenty minutes later, I was walking into the foyer of the arena's party room. There was only one person out here—Gordon Greenwood, the coach of Team GB, who did a double take when he saw me approaching.

"Jasper?" he said and beelined for me. I shook his hand but readied myself to bypass his questions. "It's so good to see you, son," he said, but all I could see was the double doors that hid the dining room from sight.

Atticus had told me the meal had ended, and the mingling and dancing portion of the night had begun. He'd also sent me a line of laughing emojis when I'd told him I was on the way.

"What are you doing here?" Gordon asked.

"I flew out with the team. I wanted to make sure everything was set up and okay."

He sighed. "No sign of you coming back to us then?" I could hear the edge of hope in his voice. I wanted to say yes, but I'd hardened myself to these questions tonight. I'd prepared myself to not feel pain every time I had to declare I was still retired. One thing I was good at was building high walls around myself to keep people out.

"Afraid not," I said. I gestured to the door. "Excuse me, Gordon, but I'm needed inside. We can talk soon, okay?"

"Okay, son. Good to see you," he said, and I could see by his expression that he had another bunch of questions to ask me. I supposed that happened when you mysteriously retired from the circuit at the peak of your career.

I tapped Gordon on his arm and, on a deep breath, walked through the double doors. Music was blaring and there were round tables scattered around the room, where riders from all over the globe were sitting. I caught the hushed, shocked whispers from those nearby.

My name floated in the air around me, but I didn't pay anyone any mind, my gaze roving over the crowd, looking for a certain angel in gold. A couple moved off the dance floor, and behind them, Hallie and Sage came into view. They were sitting at a table, talking to other riders from Germany and Belgium, if my memory served me well.

I cut through the crowd, making a beeline for Hallie, only for Atticus to walk into my path. "Hello, Cousin," he said, with an arrogant smirk on his lips.

"Atticus," I said on a sigh. He glanced around us. I didn't follow his journey. "Looks like you've caused quite the stir." I finally flicked my gaze around me, to see hundreds of eyes focused on me. Anger filled my veins when Alexis Hobbs stopped in her tracks on the way back from the bar and a smirk pulled on her red-painted lips. I made sure to keep my eyes on Atticus and just watch Hallie from my peripheral.

"Jasper!" Spencer Franklin, from the Franklin Stud, slapped me on the back. "Long time no see, friend!" I smiled as Spence stood before me. He looked good. I hadn't seen him in ages.

"Good to see you, Spence," I said, and his sister Lucy appeared next. I hugged her too. When I was competing, Spencer was who I spent most of my time with outside of Atticus. He was a great guy and fierce competitor.

"I'm so sorry about the attack on your stud," I said, and Spencer and Lucy nodded solemnly.

"At least whoever did it was stopped." Spencer shook his head. "I don't want to imagine what would have happened if they'd succeeded."

"Is your dad okay?" I asked.

"He's getting there," Lucy said. And smiled. "More determined than ever to protect his business and find out if the people responsible run deeper than the one random man who was caught and refuses to talk." She shrugged. "You know what Dad's like; he's a bulldog with a bone now."

Spencer looked behind us and said, "It doesn't help that vipers like Alexis Hobbs are circling." Alexis was now draped over Colin Ross, a competitor from Scotland. He looked about as happy to have her touch him as everyone else was. Spencer turned back to me. "The minute she saw us yesterday at the stables she asked us how our yard was recovering." Spencer snarled. "But it was the way she asked it. Like she would have rejoiced if the loss of our stallion semen sales had buried us."

Lucy nodded. "She told us to remind our father of her offer. And that our family had done enough for the industry and deserved to retire." Lucy's face frosted over. "Bitch." I huffed a laugh at the venom in her voice. Lucy smiled too. "I can't help it, Jas. I like to think of myself as a nice person, but around her I become violent."

"It's not just you, Luce," I said, and she smiled in relief.

"I can't prove it, but she's up to something," Spencer said. "I know she's been bold with business since she took over from her old man, but she's gone from level five to ten the past couple of years. She seems to want every yard in Britain." He shook his head in annoyance. "Like an English Rockefeller."

I cast my eyes around us and made sure no one was listening in. Turning back to Spencer and Lucy, I said, "Our state-of-the-art electric stabling system was hacked recently." Spencer and Lucy stilled. "Dahlia got out and got stuck in a fence. I didn't think she would make it out alive. Luckily, she did. But someone knew Dahlia was there. I can only surmise that they wanted to cause maximum damage."

"Genny . . ." Lucy said, gripping my arm. "Is she okay? She never told me last time we talked." Lucy and Genny were close friends. I knew Genny hadn't told anyone. We hadn't wanted it leaving the yard so agreed to keep it to ourselves. The NDAs of our staff forbade them from talking outside our walls too.

"More foul play," Spencer said, then looked to Alexis again. "I bloody hope I'm wrong, but I'm starting to think all these refused sales of stud farms and then the sudden attacks may not be a coincidence."

I took a deep breath and stopped myself from losing my shit about Alexis in public, but I was thinking exactly the same thing. Instead, I just nodded at my friend, silently telling him I agreed.

"I'll warn Dad to keep a closer eye on her and any business that's done. I might not have proof of anything, but my gut is telling me to be suspicious," Spencer said.

"Agreed," I said. I squeezed Spencer's arm. "Thankfully you both compete on mares, and they weren't targeted with the drugs."

"Thank God," Lucy said. "That would have really tipped Dad over the edge. He's a veritable Inspector Clouseau at the minute, Jas. His office looks like a police wall with all the suspects he's putting together."

That made me chuckle. But Tim was a good man. He was tenacious and driven, a good person to have on the scent for whoever was targeting other studs, including my own.

"I can't believe you're here," Spencer said, turning the conversation to something happier. He pointed over at the table where Hallie and Sage were sat. The feisty cowgirl still hadn't seen me. "We've been speaking to Hallie and Sage." Spencer smiled. "They're excellent riders. They seem like great people too."

"True, but I'm kind of scared to go up against them," Lucy admitted, and I laughed. Lucy was thirty-five, and Spencer was my age. They were seasoned jumping professionals and regular winners in the Grand Prix circuits, but any rider would be lying if they said they didn't fear a new, younger—better—rider joining the tour. The fact was, the Grand Prix prize money made rivals out of everyone. One could become very wealthy in one season if they were talented enough.

"They're brilliant," I said, referring to Hallie and Sage, and stared across the dance floor at Hallie. As if she could feel my stare, she tore her attention away from Sage and searched the crowd. Her glass of champagne stilled en route to her mouth as her eyes met mine. Just like earlier, my body immediately heated, and all I could hear was her moaning my name in the shower.

Hallie's eyes widened and she swallowed deeply. Sage followed the trail of whatever had garnered her best friend's attention, and a cocky smirk pulled on her mouth when she saw me stood here like a fucking stalker.

That smirk reminded me so much of Atticus's, and I wondered why those two weren't as thick as thieves instead of being mortal enemies. Together, they'd be a fucked-up, impossible-to-deal-with team.

"Jas?" I tore my attention from Hallie and turned to Lucy again. "Make sure you keep them from the vultures, yes?" Lucy said. She nudged her head at Alexis again, along with some of the cronies that trailed along in her wake. "You know what they can be like with new blood."

"I hear you," I said, the reminder to keep my distance slapping me around the face.

"Let's have dinner while you're out here," Spencer said. "I've missed your ugly mug. It's not the same on the tour without you. There's no one here who makes me look more of a novice than you. I'm looking positively professional now." He shook his head. "It doesn't feel right."

I placed my hand on Spencer's shoulder and said, "You ride just fine. But definitely, we'll set up that meal. It'll be good to catch up." I saw the flicker of more questions in Spencer's gaze. But he was a good friend and would never push me to open up if I didn't want to. I shared the most with him, Tim, and Lucy out of everyone here. Many of the other riders were acquaintances at best. Some, I didn't know at all but for a passing hello.

"I don't believe it!" Leon came to stand beside me, slapping me on the back good-naturedly, then shook hands with Spencer.

Spencer winked at me. "I promise, in your absence I haven't been offering Leon an extortionate amount of money to leave Golden Oaks and come up north to work for me instead," he said. I laughed, but I also knew there wasn't a horse owner or stud farm in this room who wouldn't murder me to get a chance at having Leon in their employ.

"He's family," I said about Leon. "You don't fuck with family. Especially mine," I said, jokingly, but rose my voice a little when I said those words, just in case whoever was taking it upon themselves to try to hurt us was nearby.

"On that note," Spencer said, but leaned in and hugged me. "Don't be a stranger, Jas. I'm sick of talking to your voicemail." That made me suddenly feel like shit, and I made a promise to myself to be better with those who genuinely cared for me.

"I promise," I said, and my friends walked away.

Atticus's attention was suddenly swayed by a woman in blue, and he stepped away from me and Leon. I turned toward my friend to try to ward off any unwanted guests. Leon leaned in close. "I'm proud of you. Putting yourself back out there like this." He frowned. "Is that a weird thing for me to say?"

Huffing a laugh, I said, "Maybe? No? I don't know." I sighed. I played with the tie around my throat. Had I always found these things so stifling?

"You need this," Leon continued. "Even if you're not riding competitively anymore, you *are* Golden Oaks and you *are* Knighton Equestrian. You should have a place at this table after all you've done for the community."

I smiled at Leon. "I'm starting to think I need to add 'hype man' to your job description."

Leon laughed. "Nah, that's a freebie." It was true, though—whenever I lost faith in myself, it was Leon and Forrest who built me back up. Both quieter in personality, but tenacious and protective to a fault.

"Be honest," I said. "How many job offers have you gotten tonight?"

Leon winced. "I've lost count, Jas. But I think about twelve so far?" Leon stepped closer. "Including one to join Team USA."

"Fuck off," I said and shook my head. "The nerve."

Leon smirked and put his hand over his heart. "Don't worry, my everlasting loyalty is still to Golden Oaks." Heat rose a little on his cheeks. "It's home, you know?" Leon was about as good at expressing his feelings as I was. So his declaration was practically a signed contract for life.

"We'd be lost without you," I said, putting my hand on his shoulder, "and not just as our trainer. You're family."

Leon nudged my arm and flicked his chin toward the bar. "Right, enough with that mushy shit; let's get a drink." I cast my eyes to Hallie again. She was already watching me, and I fought the need to march right over there and slam my lips to hers to show every horny fucker in this room that she was taken. Even if she technically wasn't.

"A drink would be good," I said to Leon, and joined him at the bar.

As I waited for my scotch, a hand rubbed up my back. And it was not a friendly touch, but one that spoke of intimacy. For a moment, I entertained it was Hallie, only to realize that was daft. I immediately turned around, only for annoyance to fill my every cell as Camille Dubois from Team France stood there.

"Camille," I said, pulling away from her. But Camille wouldn't be deterred. One thing I'd say for her, she was as tenacious off a horse as she was in the saddle.

"Jasper," she said, her tone all breathless seduction. Camille was a highly attractive woman. Red hair, green eyes, tall and slender. But she was also a man-eater. Foolishly, in my early twenties, I'd fucked her. To me, it was a one-night thing. It was for her too, until I made it clear I didn't want anything further, and that sparked some kind of internal competition within her. When she befriended Alexis, it was like they made a game of who could wear me down first.

Almost as though I'd conjured her to my side, Alexis sidled up next to me too. Fucking great. I peeled Camille's hand from my chest, keeping her away from me by her wrist. "Hands to yourself, Camille," I said forcefully, but not raising my voice. The last thing I wanted was to make more of a scene. Alexis smoothed her hand down my back.

"Jasper. I had it on good authority you weren't attending the tour." I caught Alexis flicking her glance in Hallie's direction. "I wonder what caused this sudden change of heart?"

I pushed Alexis's hand off me too and stepped out of both their grips. "Business, Alexis," I said coldly. "Nothing more. You should know about that. You seem to be trying to acquire as many of them as you can." I stopped myself from saying more. Excitement lit Alexis's eyes, loving the fact that she seemed to have an opponent.

"You were fun once," Camille said, interrupting Alexis and me from a stare-off, holding her glass of champagne out to the side. There was a pissed-off edge to her fake smile—strained and determined.

"You're right. I was once," I said in agreement. "Unfortunately for you, now I'm a miserable fucker."

Camille came closer again just as Leon handed me my scotch, reaching between me and Camille and blocking off Alexis completely. I wanted to fucking kiss him in that moment. Alexis stormed away, but Camille brushed Leon's arm aside and wrapped hers around my neck.

I tried to push her away, but her lips met my ear, and she said, "I'm staying in the Regent. Room two hundred and four."

"I don't fucking care," I said through gritted teeth. I looked up and saw Hallie on the dance floor with Sage. I was momentarily dumbstruck to see her body moving so perfectly to the beat. But when she turned in my direction and saw Camille wrapped around me, pain and hurt immediately radiated from her shocked expression.

Hallie blinked, and momentarily stopped dancing, only for Jake fucking McGowen to sidle up beside her and place his hands on her hips. Hallie spun, looking suddenly so small on that dance floor, but she smiled at Jake and, tearing her gaze from me, began dancing with him.

Fury, thick and strong, overcame me. "Get off me," I said to Camille. When she didn't, I wrenched her arm from around my neck with force. "I told you to get the fuck off me!" I said loudly and pushed her back. People stopped talking around us and stared our way.

"Prick," Camille said in her heavy accent, and strutted away from me.

I ran my hand down my face. What the fuck was I doing here? When I saw the head of the FEI approaching me and Douglas McNulty, from an Edinburgh-based stud coming up from my right, I just needed to get the hell out of here.

I glanced to the dance floor again, and Hallie was still there, Jake holding her hand and spinning her around. She was laughing. The sight was breathtaking. Hallie rarely laughed around me. I was a cold fucker to her, and more often than not, I was either pushing her away or blowing hot and cold. I fought the need to storm over there and let my fist fly at McGowen's face. But I wouldn't. This was Hallie's big chance, the start of her high-flying career. One I knew she would excel at. I couldn't thrust her into the rumor mill, especially with the likes of Alexis and Camille here witnessing it. They'd make Hallie's life on tour hell.

Plus, I was fucked up. My life was fucked up. And I couldn't stand in her way, though as I headed for the exit, I fought every urge within me to turn back. As I burst into the thick humidity outside, I walked toward the Knighton Equestrian stock trailer. I just needed some fucking space.

As I threw the door open, I went inside and started kicking piles of saddle pads out of my way. When I'd exhausted myself, I crouched down and put my hands on my head.

Then the door opened behind me.

Chapter Thirteen

Hallie

Seeing Camille Dubois hanging all over Jasper brought a streak of jealousy to my heart so strong it was staggering. "Bitch," Sage hissed as we stopped dancing to see the redheaded beauty wrap her arm around Jasper's neck and whisper something into his ear.

"I'll tear her hair off her head," Sage said, meaning every word. She made to walk over to Camille, but I grabbed her arm and yanked her back.

"We're not together," I said, and the worst part of that was it was true. I had no claim on Jasper. He'd made it clear there would be nothing between us. He was free to sleep with whoever he wanted.

Camille Dubois had a reputation. Even in the Under-25s, we'd heard of her more than adventurous sex life. It surprised me that Jasper and she were close. I had never met Alexis Hobbs. But one of the newer riders from Belgium, Sofia, warned me about her. Alexis had spent last year's tour trying to find any dirt she could on Sofia, only backing off when there was none to be had.

But the way Camille touched Jasper spoke of intimacy which, frankly, made me sick. So when Jake sidled up to me, I decided to drop my pain and dance instead. But as he spun me around, I caught sight of Jasper watching me with as much jealousy in his gaze as I knew I had in mine.

Shaking his head in frustration, he turned and fled, and without thinking, I followed him. Lifting my golden dress off the floor, I kicked off my heels, knowing Sage would grab them, and ran to find him, only to see a dark figure storming out the door and past the barn toward the business center where I knew Jasper was having lots of meetings this week.

I saw him enter the Knighton Equestrian trailer, and checking the coast was clear, I ran up the steps, opened the door, and slipped inside. The door slammed behind me, instantly locking me in. The first thing I saw was piles of saddle pads strewn around the room, then in the back, Jasper, crouched down low with his messy dark hair tumbling over his fingers as he buried his head in his hands.

Hearing my entrance, he snapped his attention my way and immediately got to his feet. His face was hard, and I knew I was back with the cold Jasper who had chastised me in the barn—the one intent on pushing me away.

Were we really back there?

"Why are you here?" he said, between gritted teeth. His hands were balled into fists at his sides and, even from across the large trailer, I could see they were shaking.

"I came to see if you are okay?" I said, and crossed my arms over my chest. The trailer was hot, the air-conditioning turned off and only the emergency low lighting illuminating the space. In the orange glow, Jasper looked like a god. A fallen, domineering god with stubble on his cheeks and fury in his midnight eyes.

"Am I okay?" he said, repeating my words. There was a mocking tone to his voice. Then he said, "I made it perfectly clear that you need to stay away from McGowen. And I arrive at dinner to find you on the dance floor, spinning in his arms."

His words were fuel to my fire. "Excuse me?" I said. "I *need* to stay away from him?"

"He's bad news," he bit out. "And he's only paying you attention to fuck with me."

I laughed incredulously. I was so done with this shit. "So no one could be genuinely interested in me, is that it?"

"Don't fucking put words in my mouth," Jasper snapped, his hands opening, fingers stretching before closing into fists again. Even in the dim light I could see that his cheeks were flushed and his pupils dilated.

"But it's okay for Camille Dubois to hang all over you like some cheap decoration?" I stepped closer and then closer still, until I was mere feet from where Jasper stood. "Tell me, *Mr. Knighton*," I said, mockingly using his surname. "Have you fucked her? Have you let down your walls enough to screw Camille?"

"Careful," he warned me. But I was past warnings now. This was one wild horse he couldn't break.

"Why? 'Cause it's true?" When all I got back was stony silence, pain sliced through my heart. So I laughed. I laughed right in Jasper's face. "*Perfect.* You chastise me for dancing with a man I have zero interest in, all the while a woman you've screwed paws all over you and *that's* acceptable?" I shook my head. "*Fuck. This.* I'm done!"

I turned and walked to the exit, full to the brim with anger, when Jasper commanded, "Do not *dare* leave this trailer!"

I whipped around, the hot-blooded Texan cowgirl rising up in me. Even as a child, I never let a bull or colt get the best of me, so I sure as fuck wasn't letting Jasper Knighton. "What did you say?" I said calmly, measuredly. *Threateningly.*

Jasper rolled his lips together and his eyes roved over every inch of my body. My traitorous nipples hardened under his heavily lidded stare, but I wasn't backing down. "I *said*, what did you *say*?"

Jasper stepped closer and his sandalwood and mint scent ghosted over me. "I fucked her years ago. *Once.* In my early twenties when we were at the Horse of the Year Show and I was drunk off my arse." He laughed without humor. "Believe me, I wish I could be interested in her now. It would be a lot fucking simpler."

"What does that mean?" I snapped.

Jasper turned, his head tipping back. I watched his broad back move up and down as he took a deep breath, then exhaled. "Because then I wouldn't be thinking of *you* twenty-four-fucking-seven! I wouldn't be convincing myself day and night to stay the fuck away from you. That you're too young for me, that you're my employee, that being in any way attached to me puts you in too much danger!" Jasper was breathless, his chocolate gaze wild. "God, I wish I hadn't heard you *come* with my fucking name on your lips—*twice!* I wish I hadn't heard you scream my name just *imagining* me fucking you!"

Deathly silence stretched between us. I'd been right. He'd heard me somehow, he'd actually fucking heard me . . .

I wasn't sure who moved first, but one minute we were glaring at one another, thick static sparking between us, and the next our lips slammed together, and Jasper's hands threaded into my hair. His fingers wrapped around my thick strands as he pulled me even closer. This wasn't a soft, sensitive kiss. This was rough, raw, and passionate and the culmination of weeks upon weeks of endless wanting and pushing and pulling.

It was fucking explosive.

I moaned loudly, and Jasper used that moment to push his tongue inside my mouth. My legs weakened as his tongue slid against mine, hot and strong, and I was sure I'd never be able to be kissed by anyone else again. Jasper consumed me. I clung to his jacket as he walked me backward toward the wall, slamming me against it. Jasper's tall frame crowded me so much that I was covered by him.

Jasper broke from the kiss, only to pepper more down my neck. He groaned with every nip at my skin, and every fantasy I'd ever had of what Jasper would be like if he kissed me, if he fucked me, were tossed out the window. He was more, *so* much more than I could have ever imagined.

I squeezed my legs together, my clit pulsing. My hips rolled forward, looking for any kind of friction. But Jasper kept me away from him, completely controlling the moment.

"Jasper!" I groaned in frustration.

He reared back and stared into my eyes. Jasper looked ruined, untamed. His cheeks were flushed, and his nostrils were flaring. He lifted his hand and ran his thumb over my bottom lip. "You've fucking teased me for weeks, Angel," he said, voice so gruff it brought goose bumps to my skin. I rolled my hips again, searching for release, when Jasper took hold of my arms and spun me, pushing me to the center of the room where a padded wooden saddle rack stood.

Jasper turned me in his arms, leaning me against it, and, taking hold of the cowl neck of my silky dress, he yanked it down to my waist, revealing my nude strapless bra. He reached behind me, and in less than a second, my bra fell to the floor, putting my breasts fully on display.

Jasper groaned as I was bared to him, his tongue peeking out to run along his lips. "Perfect," he murmured, then bent his head, taking my right nipple in his mouth. "Jasper!" I screamed, my head tilting back as shards of electricity zipped from my breasts to my already dripping pussy. I gripped the back of his head and pushed him harder into my flesh, crying out when he bit down on my nipple before moving to my next one, giving it the same rough and ecstatic treatment.

I was spinning. With my eyes closed and Jasper's mouth finally on my body, I was a live wire. Every part of me was radiating raw need and heat. Jasper pulled back from my breasts, then meeting my eyes, he kept his stare locked on me as he grabbed my dress that was gathered around my waist and began pulling it over my hips.

His mouth never left me. Jasper kissed down my torso, licking his tongue over my stomach until my dress was flung to the floor and he began kissing along the edge of my panties. I thrust my hips forward, searching for his mouth, his tongue, fucking anything to relieve the building pressure between my legs.

But Jasper didn't comply. His heated stare told me exactly who was in charge right now—and it wasn't me. It wasn't like me to submit, but right now, with *this* version of Jasper, I'd willingly drop to my knees and do anything he wanted if he'd just finally give in and make me come.

Breathless, I watched as Jasper hooked his fingers under the thin string of my thong and began to pull it down. "Do you want me to touch your pussy, Angel?" he said, and I almost came just from that sentence leaving his lips. *Angel.* He was calling me angel again, and that endearment spilling from his mouth was the headiest aphrodisiac.

"Yes," I whispered, moving my hips again. Jasper stilled, and I stopped moving too. His commanding chocolate eyes told me to shut up and obey. I was hot, so fucking hot. Then Jasper began to pull down my thong, so slowly it was torturous, and I moaned so loudly that I wouldn't have been surprised if they could hear it all the way in the ballroom.

"Quiet, Angel," Jasper said, shaking his head. "Don't make me gag you."

The thought of that alone made me want to push my luck. I wanted him to do whatever he wanted to do to me. I wanted to see this man fall from his perfectly protected pedestal. I wanted to see him descend into the most primal, untethered version of him. I wanted wild and I wanted Jasper tearing me apart in the most ungentlemanly way possible.

Threading my thong and dress over my feet, Jasper placed his hands on the sides of my calves and began to smooth his way up my legs. "Fucking perfection," he said, drinking in my naked state. When he got to my hips, he pulled me forward, licking along where my upper thighs met my pussy.

"Jasper," I moaned, and he looked up at me again.

"I'm gonna taste this pussy," he said, and I nodded in agreement. Anything. *Please!* I was fully waxed, and he kissed over my bare skin. I pushed his head down, trying to get him to go lower, but instead, Jasper got to his feet. I leaned back against the saddle rack and never took my eyes off him, watching his every move. Jasper kept our gazes locked as he began to unbutton his black tux jacket. Each move he made was slow and purposeful, and he was driving me goddamn insane.

But I held my tongue. I knew he'd only go slower if I pushed it. But *shit*, he was handsome. Olive skin, dark features with stubble covering his cheeks. He was lust personified, a deadly sin I was happily committing.

His bow tie came next, then his shirt. When he peeled them from his body, I was breathless. Jasper Knighton in clothes was perfection. Topless . . . he was unearthly. Cut abdominal muscles, firm pecs, and a dusting of dark hair covering his chest. Then he began to unclasp his belt, and my mouth grew dry. I wanted to see him revealed. I wanted to see his cock. I wanted to kiss it and take it into my mouth. My eyes fell to the bulge that was protruding from his pants.

"Eyes on me, Angel," he ordered, and I snapped my gaze up to meet his. "You look when I tell you to look," he added, and I kept his stare as I heard his zipper being pulled down. His arm moved, and I knew when I looked down, he'd be holding himself.

I moaned again. He smirked, knowing he was fully in control of me. He was. I couldn't deny it. My fingers dug into the wood of the saddle rack, and I was so frustrated that I imagined I'd left welts in their place.

"Look," Jasper suddenly commanded, and my eyes fell to his crotch. I squeezed my thighs together seeing Jasper revealed. He stroked his length up and down. He was long, thick, and uncut, and I went to drop to my knees. Reading what I intended to do, Jasper stepped closer to me and said, "Don't fucking move."

I was statue still, and under his heavy command, more turned on than I'd ever been in my life. I had no idea letting go would feel this good. Jasper lifted his hand to my face and ran his fingertip down my cheek. It was a moment of softness, of gentleness, before he leaned forward and replaced his finger with his lips, whispering, "I'm going to destroy you for anyone else, Angel," he said, and I shivered from head to toe. "I'm going to make you scream so hard that you won't be able to talk. I'm going to fuck you so hard you won't be able to take a single step without feeling me inside you."

"Yes," I whispered, turning my head to drop light kisses along his stubbled jaw. Jasper turned too, and then he was kissing me again. My bare breasts were pressed to his naked chest. The feel of him was electric, euphoric.

Then Jasper pulled back, and placing his hand on my waist, he spun me around so fast that I cried out in surprise. Before I knew what was happening, he pressed my chest to the saddle rack, my ass and pussy spread open and exposed to his eyes. I clutched the wooden legs of the rack, its padded cushion cool against my breasts.

Jasper's hands were immediately on my ass, kneading the flesh. "Look at this pussy," he said, and I shook from need. "That's it, baby. Your hole is clenching for me."

I moaned, unable to take it anymore. The way he spoke, the way he took control, it was every fantasy I never knew I wanted to come true. My body tensed when Jasper's finger ran down over the seam of my ass and moved down until he circled my clit. Scalding flames licked over my skin, and then I heard Jasper drop to his knees and he pulled my pussy lips apart. The humid air kissed at my exposed flesh.

I was wet, so fucking wet.

My cheek was flat against the rack, but I looked behind me, only to see Jasper's savage gaze locked between my legs. I moaned again just seeing the overt lust in his eyes. Then Jasper moved forward, and his tongue licked me from my clit to my entrance, and I screamed. It took everything I had to not come on the spot. I was so turned on I could barely breathe. My fingers bit into the rack's wooden legs as I held on tight and my eyes rolled back, closed, when Jasper's tongue began lapping at my pussy.

"Jasper . . ." I moaned as my thighs shook, and I felt the pressure already building at the bottom of my spine. But Jasper didn't stop; instead, he moved to my clit, sucking it into his mouth with such vigor that I cried out as I broke apart and a million stars glittered behind my eyes. My body jerked, but Jasper gave me no reprieve.

"Jasper, *please!*" I begged, unsure what I was asking for. But Jasper licked me up and down, pushing a finger inside me instead. He lifted off the floor as I gasped for breath, body clenching and unclenching around his finger that was still inside me. Then he laid over my bent body, his chest to my back, and asked, "Are you on birth control?"

"Y-yes," I stuttered. "I'm clear."

"So am I," he said.

"Please," I said, giving a final consent, then with his hands on my hips, he slammed inside me so fast that my yell echoed off the trailer's metal walls. Jasper grunted this time, his perfect control slipping, and his fingers dug into the flesh of my hips. When he thrust, he moved so deeply and expertly that I felt the building of another orgasm.

The friction from the saddle rack beneath me made my nipples pebble, and when one of Jasper's hands slid up to grip the nape of my neck, never missing a beat as he pounded inside of me, I couldn't help but lie still and be fucked.

"Fuck, Angel," he groaned. "You're so tight." I moaned in response. "So fucking *good*," he said, then pushed in from another angle, pressing against the spot inside of me that made me fall apart.

"Yes," I said, as he became relentless. Shivers chased up and down my spine in relays and my pussy began to squeeze so much that Jasper uttered a tortured groan.

"*Come*, Angel," he commanded, and I could feel it there, on the precipice. Jasper was going to make me come again. I was wet, and the explicit sound of Jasper fucking me into the rack ricocheted off the walls around us.

Jasper gripped my hip and neck tighter and barked out, "COME!" As if my body was under his command, I cried out as I came, so hard that tears fell from my eyes. And it didn't stop, because Jasper didn't. He pushed into me over and over, faster and faster, until my cry became an everlasting, tortured moan. Until my body shook and shivered so hard, I could barely keep balance on the rack.

Clearly seeing this, Jasper pulled me off the rack like a rag doll, lifting me and wrapping my legs around his waist as he carried me across the room. Jasper's pants had been removed at some point, and he slammed me against the wall. I was wrecked. My body was used and exhausted, but when Jasper set my feet down on the floor, he reached beside him and pulled a new set of reins from an unopened package.

Grabbing hold of both of my wrists, he wrapped the reins around them, then lifted, the leather straps pulling my arms above my head. I fought for breath as Jasper tied them to a bridle hook above me. He stepped back to admire his handiwork, his eyes roving over my strung-up body. My pussy still throbbed from coming twice, but the way Jasper looked at me, with hunger and want in his gaze, I felt my clit pulse again, impossibly needing more.

Jasper shook his head in awe. "Incredible," he said, then approached my bound body. Running his hands over my arms and sides, Jasper then took hold of my chin and smashed his mouth to mine. His kiss was slightly tamer this time, but I could feel his rock-hard cock pressing between my legs. He rocked back and forth, his rigid length rubbing against my clit. I moaned again, loudly, so loud that Jasper lifted his head and pressed his finger against my lips.

"Shush, Angel," he said, softly but with an edge of an order. "We don't want security to hear." The idea that the security Jasper had hired was outside—because they would be, they followed us everywhere, but at a distance—made everything so much more heightened. If that was even possible.

"I can't help it," I said, moaning loudly again when Jasper sucked on my right nipple as he palmed my left breast. He raised his head and shook it from side to side.

"We can't have that, Angel," he said, then looked beside him. His eyes brightened, and I heard the rustling of plastic again before Jasper held up a rubber bit. My heart pounded harder at what I knew he intended. Jasper pressed his body against mine, and I was almost set alight. This time when I moaned, Jasper slipped the bit between my teeth, immediately muting the noise.

"Bite down like a good girl," Jasper whispered into my ear. Then, wrapping my legs around him until I was suspended from the metal hook above us, he slammed into me. I threw my head back and bit down on the rubber bar, the bit capturing my scream so it existed only in the space between us.

"That's it, baby," Jasper said, angling my body until I was a foot off the wall, Jasper ramming his cock inside of me. I was delirious. I shook my head when I felt another orgasm building. "I can't," I mumbled around the bit. It came out muffled.

But Jasper understood what I was saying, as he looked me dead in the eye and said, "One more, Angel. I want one more from you." I shook my head, tears slipping from my eyes. But Jasper only built up his speed, his cheeks flushing from exertion as a bead of sweat built on his forehead and ran down his cheek. I wanted to lean forward and lick it off his skin.

Jasper's movements became more erratic, and his breath changed—stuttered and deep. "One more, Hals. You can give me one more."

I shook my head, *no, no, no* . . . but my body didn't listen, and my thighs tensed as Jasper found my G-spot again and pushed against it until my hips involuntarily rolled back against his.

"Come for me," Jasper hissed, and his teeth clenched together as I felt his cock swell inside me. *"Come!"* he ordered, and I shattered apart, my scream swallowed by the rubber casing of the bit, and my body tensed and the last of the energy waned with my final orgasm. My muscles twitched and my pussy felt so utterly fucked . . . Then Jasper growled loudly, spilling inside of me.

I opened my eyes and watched him come. His jaw was clenched, teeth gritted together. His fingers dug into my hips, and he thrust inside of me, once, twice, three times, before he threw his head back, lips parting with ecstasy.

I'd never seen anything so beautiful in my life.

In the aftermath, Jasper was breathless, and even minutes after we'd come, Jasper didn't pull out. He still pulsed inside of me, his cock twitching. He closed his eyes and breathed. Then he opened them again, and his gaze collided with mine. Heat and something else I couldn't read shone on his face—disbelief? Wonder? Awe?

"Hallie," he murmured, stepping closer to me, still inside me, until my back rested against the wall and his hold on my legs relieved the pressure of the reins that held me upright. Jasper leaned in and kissed the side of my neck. He licked at the beads of sweat that were running over my skin, and he kissed under my ear and the side of my face. "Angel," he murmured softly, peppering kisses all over my face. Gone was the dominant lover, and in his place was a loving and kind man.

One who was caring for me.

As Jasper slipped out of me at last, he kept my legs firmly around his waist and met my eyes with his. "Angel," he said again, that term of endearment destroying any resolve I had about not letting him in. He took the bit from my mouth, dropping it to the floor with a thud. This time, when he kissed me, it was on my lips. But this kiss wasn't hard or rough or raw. This was soft, featherlight . . . *sweet.* Too lost in the sensual kiss, I didn't feel Jasper reach up to untie the reins until my arms fell to my sides.

I groaned as they ached, blood rushing back to fill my muscles. But Jasper's mouth never broke from mine, and when my arms regained feeling once more, I threaded my hands through his thick hair. After several minutes of just kissing, Jasper broke from my mouth, pressing his forehead to mine. "Fuck, Angel," he whispered, and thoroughly fucked and spent, the endearment made me chuckle.

Jasper's dark eyes lit with the same happiness I knew shone in mine, and it knocked me breathless. Running my hand down his cheek, I sighed. "Yeah, baby," I whispered, marveling at what had just happened between us. *"Fuck."*

Chapter Fourteen

Hallie

Sandings Grand Prix, Doha
Two days later

Butterflies swarmed in my stomach as we reached the mouth of the arena. The place where, in only a couple of hours, Huxley and I would enter our first ever five-star Grand Prix competition.

I turned to the stands, already filling with spectators. I especially looked to the corporate box at the end, where Leon had told us Jasper would be watching. The secret of his presence was all over the show grounds by now—Jasper Knighton was here in Doha, watching this leg of the tour. But he still tried to keep out of view. Leon told us he said he didn't want today to be about him.

He wanted his riders and horses to shine.

The butterflies in my stomach darted north to my heart, simply at the thought of Jasper. Two days. It had been two days since we'd made love. I was calling it that. Because even though what we did was the most mind-blowing and explosive sex I thought a person could ever have, my feelings for Jasper . . . *Hell.* I was skirting into dangerous territory. And the worst part of it was that I hadn't seen him since. He'd been in back-to-back meetings with buyers and breeders and Lord knew who else for the past few days. He hadn't even called me. No text, and no knocking on my suite that was right next door to his.

Just . . . silence.

I had no idea where we stood. Was our night in the trailer a one-night thing? Did he want more? Did *I* want more? I had no idea. I didn't want whatever I had with Jasper to get in the way of my career, but at the same time, now that I knew what it was like to be with him, to be taken in such an animalistic way, I craved more.

What a mindfuck.

When people on the circuit found out Jasper was here in Doha, his schedule quickly filled up. Atticus told us that Jasper's secretary from England was constantly refreshing his calendar with a myriad of meetings. And that was fine . . . *good.* At least that's what I'd told myself. I had a course to prepare for. One I was intending to clear. And looking at the jumps before me, it was going to be a harder feat than I'd ever imagined.

Welcome to the big show, I suppose.

"Earth to Hallie!" Sage said from beside me and nudged my arm. I shook my head and took myself from my wandering thoughts. *Focus, Hallie.* "Are you ready?" Sage asked and pointed to the arena. We were here to walk the course. To familiarize ourselves with the order of jumps, the ideal striding, the best and tightest turns, and anything else they wanted to throw at us. From here, I could already see there was a Liverpool underneath an almost neon-colored oxer. That didn't faze me. Huxley wasn't fazed by the sight of water.

Sage was silent as we walked to the first fence. She was staring straight ahead with a forced-neutral expression on her face. I looked to what had pulled her attention. Atticus. Because of course it was. He was already way ahead of us, walking with Spencer and Lucy Franklin from Team GB, who I knew were close family friends. There were other riders around us too from all over the globe, but no one in earshot. She and

Atticus had agreed on a ceasefire of sorts during this tour. No bickering, no jabs at one another. Even their history meant nothing when it came to our team. Here, they were colleagues and had to be professional. I could see the strain it put on Sage to not call Atticus a prick or asshole daily, but she was taking one for the team.

Unfortunately, now that she wasn't allowed to verbally spar with her archnemesis, she'd directed her attention to me. Sage turned from staring at Atticus, then gave me the side-eye with a cocky smirk.

"You're still thinking about your freaky night, huh?" she asked.

"Shush!" I hissed, and looked around me to make sure she wasn't overheard.

Sage rolled her eyes. "Oh, shut up, Hals. No one can hear." She shook her head. "But, jeez, girl, if I looked as ruined as you did the other night, I'd still be reliving that epic fuck too."

I sighed. I wished Sage hadn't seen me that night. But not long after Jasper had dropped me back at my hotel room, there was a knock at my door. I'd thought it was Jasper again, and like I'd been conditioned to his cock, rushed to open it. But it was Sage, and when she saw me, hair mussed, lipstick smudged, dress askew, and rein marks on my wrists, she burst through the door and demanded to know everything.

So I told her. *Every* detail. Sage, for once in her life, was silent and slack jawed. Until . . . "Who knew Jasper Knighton was such a fucking beast in bed?" she'd said, fanning her face with her hand. I'd flopped back on the bed and groaned.

"I like him, Sage," I said, almost inaudibly. Sage lay beside me, sympathy on her face. "I *dangerously* like him."

"I know" was all she said. Then she ran me a bath, filling it with scented and soothing oils, and had Tariq, our personal butler, bring up some chamomile tea to help me sleep. It hadn't worked. In fact, I'd barely slept since. Not because I didn't like the sex, or that I regretted it.

Exactly the opposite. I craved *more.* I craved *Jasper*—his touch, his kiss, his control in bed.

But I didn't know how things stood between us.

He'd brought me home after we'd fucked in the trailer. He was sweet and attentive and had kissed me good night at my door, like a true gentleman. Then . . . silence. I understood he was busy. But I couldn't get a read on him after our night together.

"Hals!" Sage's voice pulled me back to the here and now, and I realized I'd zoned out again. *Shit.* Sage tapped my cheek with her hand (not softly), and I narrowed my eyes at my best friend. She ignored my pissed-off stare. "Girl, *focus.*" Her hands moved to rest on my shoulders. Staring me dead in my face, she said, "I know you're cock-stunned, but you need to forget about your ravishing of a lifetime and switch to your fierce competitor self. Get your head in the game. Do not let one night of ravenous domination ruin your big chance!"

As crass as Sage's words were, they hit the mark. "On it," I said with a firm nod, and kissed her cheek. Sage winked at me and linked her arm through mine. "Now, fence one," she said, and we began measuring and counting the strides between each jump.

"Sadists," Sage said as we moved from jump five to six. The fillers were gaudy and bright with moving parts designed to spook. She shook her head. "Gonna be a rough one, Hals. This course is insane."

"We can do it," I said, and tried not to get starstruck as Austin Marks from Canada walked fence seven.

When Leni Klein from Germany walked past us and said, "Good luck, ladies. I'm excited to see you ride," I almost passed out. It was a strange feeling to suddenly "make it" after years of climbing the ranks. Finding that your heroes were suddenly your peers and fellow competitors was a head rush.

It also taught you that your heroes were just people. *Ordinary* people who just happened to achieve extraordinary things. And my biggest hero, my biggest inspiration in life . . . well, I could still feel him between my legs.

As if I'd conjured him into real life, I looked over my shoulder and caught sight of Jasper watching from the balcony of a private box, arms crossed over his chest. He wore a light-blue button-down and navy slacks. His sleeves were rolled up to his elbows, showcasing his forearms, and that alone sent my heart into a sprint.

Then his lips kicked up into a hint of a smile as he caught me watching him, and I was done. What did that mean? What did that smile mean?

Not now. I couldn't think of this right now. Inhaling deeply, I refocused and counted the strides between jumps eight and nine, and knew I would nail these two jumps, even if that's all I managed to clear. And despite myself, knowing Jasper was this close energized me. I wanted to show him how good I was. How amazing Huxley was. I wanted his respect as a rider.

"Fucking Liverpool," Sage muttered as we reached fence ten. Fefe, her hell-born horse, didn't like water and liked to refuse fences including them whenever she could—a lake of fire was probably more her thing. I knew Sage would be a little off-put by this, but like my best friend always did, she shrugged and said, "Looks like me and my precious mare may have a fight on the course today." She smiled. "Those are always the most memorable rounds. The battle of the bitches."

I laughed, and we finished the rest of the course. Once we were sure we had the route down pat, we walked back to the stalls where Huxley and Fefe were already tacked up.

"You good?" Mila asked me as she handed me my navy-colored hat. I was dressed in a navy show jacket, a crisp white show shirt, and white show breeches with pristinely polished tall riding boots on my feet. All Knighton Equestrian–branded, of course. Then again, most would be wearing some article from Jasper's line today. His was the highest grossing and most worn equestrian brand in the world. My head spun if I thought about that too much. The man was more than impressive.

As I slid my helmet on, Atticus came over to us. "Ready, team?" he said chipperly, and Sage discreetly rolled her eyes at him. She was trying, really, she was. But no one was perfect.

"The team comp is tomorrow." Sage smiled sweetly at her biggest rival. "Today is every man for themselves."

A heated spark burst in Atticus's eyes. "You can't beat me, Miller," he said with all the confidence of a seasoned competitor and an Olympic gold medalist. Even though Atticus was our age, he'd joined the five-star ranks much earlier than me and Sage. He really was amazing. Only one rider had ever kept him in second place, and that man was now hidden away in a private box, far removed from the competitive circuit.

"We'll see about that," Sage sang as she clipped her chin strap closed. Dressed in the same outfit as me, but for her jacket being burgundy, Sage looked more stunning than ever. A fact Atticus hadn't missed, if the slow rove of his eyes over my best friend was any indication.

"Then how about a wager?" Atticus said. He shrugged. "Just between us teammates, of course."

Sage went to snap back at Atticus but caught my eye. I shook my head. These two would be the death of me. Sage breathed slowly through her nose, then simply shook her head. She then turned toward Horatio, who was walking out of the stall with Fefe. She hadn't made it four steps before she reluctantly turned around and questioned, "What stakes?"

I sighed. *Truce, my ass.* I knew she wouldn't be able to resist his offer. Sage was the most competitive person I knew.

Mila brought the mounting block beside Huxley. I moved in front of my horse and looked him dead in the eye. "Well, milord," I said, a fun little ritual I'd developed with the stallion. His ears flicked back and forward as he listened to me talk. "You and I have quite the task to achieve today." I ran my hand over his nose, then his cheek, and dropped a kiss over his white blaze. "We'll start off steady," I said. "Being our first course, our biggest goal is a clear." I smiled in excitement. "We may be against the clock, but we're gonna have a smooth start, okay, beautiful boy? Today is about getting used to this new arena. We can pick up speed the more the tour progresses. Slow and steady wins the race."

I kissed him again, then moved to my mounting block only to hear, "I think not, fucker!" I climbed on Huxley and looked to Sage, who was storming away from Atticus, who was laughing as he put on his hat. Chris, his groom, had Lord Barnaby ready at his side. Atticus was in all white too, but for his jet-black jacket and boots. I had to say, as a team we looked good.

"What did I miss?" I asked Mila, as I bent down and tightened my girth.

"Atticus's first offer to Sage was a kiss, with tongue," Mila said, fighting a chuckle. "When Sage refused that, he offered that whoever won out of the two of them, when interviewed after the ride, had to say how much they admired the other, and just how good of a rider they were."

"Ouch," I said, grimacing. If Sage had to wax lyrical about Atticus, I feared she would throw up in the process.

"You just know you're going to lose, Miller!" Atticus shouted to Sage and jumped on Barnaby, no mounting block needed. He looked like a beautiful demonic soldier on his pitch-black horse with his long black hair and dark Knighton eyes.

Sage rage-tightened her chin strap, then as she clicked to steer Fefe out of the stalls and toward the practice ring, she passed by Atticus and said, "Fine, you're on. Prepare to kiss my ass!"

"Is that a real offer? Because your wish will be my command," he shouted back, and Sage flicked her middle finger at him as she walked away.

I halted Huxley next to Atticus and said, "You're playing with fire with Sage." I smirked at Atticus, who shrugged.

"Hals, fucking with her has quite literally become my favorite thing to do in life." He threw me his panty-melting smile, the one that had girls swooning in the stands. It didn't work on me, of course. I apparently liked my Knightons less friendly and more dictatorial. Atticus was too approachable and amiable. I preferred aloof and tortured.

Atticus's eyes closed, then he bit his bottom lip and groaned. "And we have all tour together, Hals. *All. Bloody. Tour. Mmpf.*" He shook his head and opened his eyes. "What a year we're going to have."

I laughed, shaking my head, and we walked from the stalls side by side. Just as we hit the warm-up ring, Atticus must have seen a glimmer of nerves on my face, as he said, "You've got this, you know?" I looked at him, and all his teasing humor had faded; only confidence was in his expression. He nodded his head at Sage, who was walking Fefe on a loose rein, warming her up. "You both do."

"Thank you," I said. "That means a lot, coming from you." I leaned closer. "But let's not tell Sage you think she'll kick ass. It'll only make her see you as weak." Atticus winked at me, and Leon came to stand at my side.

Our trainer's game face was on. "Tough course," he said.

"Yes, sir."

He patted Huxley's neck. "Slow and steady. You know the drill. You can do it," he said, and opened the gate to the practice ring. Two jumps were in the center, each approaching the maximum height we'd see on the course. I nodded in greeting at the other riders warming up. A large screen on the wall displayed the action in the main arena. The commentators were talking, then the camera zoomed in on a familiar face in a private box—Jasper, standing next to Abdul Hashim. Jasper looked beautiful. I couldn't take my eyes off the screen, and my heart skipped a beat.

I really was pathetic for this man.

I barely heard what the commentators were saying about him, but when footage from this event two years ago here in Doha came up, Jasper winning the jump-off on Henry, I couldn't help but watch in awe.

Like flying . . .

When it cut back to Jasper, he was laughing at something Abdul said. The camera caught him in a rare moment of lightness, and he was stunning. Then the view moved from Jasper to the main arena, where none other than Jake McGowen trotted into the ring on his sixteen-three-hand mare. The order of jumpers was picked at random. One thing was for sure: Jake, as much as his reputation was battered, was a hell of a rider and would no doubt set the tone for the rest of the class.

I drew my attention from the screen and focused on warming Huxley up enough that I could begin to jump the practice fences. A hush from the arena descended, and when I looked at the screen, Jake was just clearing the last fence. The audience lifted in applause and Jake leaned down to pat his mare's neck. He'd jumped a clear and his smile was wide. Atticus trotted up beside me and said, "His time is beatable. Head down and git 'er done." I raised my eyebrow at Atticus, fighting a laugh. "What?" he said, all innocence. "That's what you Texans say, right?"

"Something like that," I said, and pushed Huxley into a canter. I was riding fourteenth out of fifteenth. Sage was tenth, and Atticus was last. So I got my head down and made sure Huxley was warm and supple. I kept my breaths steady and listened to every instruction Leon gave me.

When the ninth jumper left the practice ring, Sage walked up to me on her way out of the gate. I put my hand on her arm. "Ride strong, babe," I said, a little mantra we had started as teens. We'd never not said it to one another before a competition.

"You know it," Sage said, and as I watched her go, I had to blink away moisture from my eyes. Sage and I had been through *everything* together. To see her walking into the arena on Fefe, Leon giving last-minute instructions as he walked beside them . . . I was so happy for her I could burst.

A collective, *"Ooo . . ."* suddenly came from the arena. As I looked up, Tristan Meyer from Austria had just knocked down poles on the double, both jumps—eight faults. When his horse, Blueberry Note, refused the next fence, he waved his hand, retiring them both from the course.

This was Blueberry's first time in a five-star Grand Prix, and clearly the uberchallenging course and packed audience had her spooked. She was only eight. I patted Huxley's neck and kissed his soft and perfectly groomed mane. "Just keep focused, milord. Ignore the crowd, just listen to me." Huxley liked me talking to him around the course. If I was ever too quiet in practice, I noticed a dip in his attention, and that's when he would make mistakes. I would make sure my voice was loud enough to keep him focused.

A round of applause sounded, and I stopped Huxley to watch the big screen. Sage trotted Fefe out into the arena. I smiled in pride. She looked incredible, so confident. Atticus halted Barnaby beside me, eyes glued to my best friend. The announcer read out her name and Fefe's, and I felt chills break out all over my body.

She was doing it.

We both were.

The horn sounded, and Sage began the course. My body was tense as I watched her clear the first several jumps. Fefe was spritely, nostrils flaring, wanting to storm the course like the crazy mare she was, but Sage kept her steady. I heard the creaking of leather and looked to my right to see Atticus's hands tightening on his reins. I fought a smirk. He could pretend he wanted to beat her all he wanted, but the way his midnight eyes were glued to the screen, he wanted Sage to soar.

I kind of adored Atticus. I always felt he and I could be good friends, but the truth was, his and Sage's animosity toward one another had put a wall between us. Sage was my best friend, and as much as she seemed like a tough cookie, Atticus had really hurt her, and she hadn't been able to move on from it. Sage had to be my priority. But you couldn't help but like Atticus. He was like an electric heater, being around him made you feel warm.

As Sage approached fence ten, the one with the Liverpool, I could see determination on her face. But as predicted, as soon as Fefe spotted the water, the mare balked, thrashing around, looking for freedom.

"A strong reaction to the water there," the commentator said. I held my breath as Sage fought with Fefe to get her under control. Fefe did everything in her power on the approach to run out and avoid the fence, but Sage was cool, calm, and collected. She succeeded in getting her over without a refusal, but *"That will cost Miller some time on the clock,"* the commentator said, taking the words straight from my mouth.

Once she was past the Liverpool, Sage calmed Fefe down, and when she cleared the final fence, I couldn't help but cheer and clap.

"Well played, Miller," Atticus said under his breath, but I could hear the genuine happiness in his tone. The camera panned to Leon, who was cheering from the viewing point. Sage's smile was infectious, and she patted Fefe on the neck, leaning down to kiss her. Jasper came on the screen next, smiling as he clapped too, then Leon from the viewing plinth, nodding his head in satisfaction.

She'd done it. Sage had gotten a clear on her first Grand Prix five-star course. The first from Team Knighton to ride, and ride she had!

I waited for her at the entrance to the practice ring. I jumped off Huxley and wrapped my arms around her when she dismounted from Fefe and saw me standing there waiting. "You were amazing, girl!" I said and crushed Sage to my chest.

Sage pulled back. "It's electric out there, Hals," she said, and butterflies swooped in my stomach again. "I can't wait to do it again!"

Leon came toward us and tapped me on the back. "Back on Huxley. Keep him warm," he said, and I climbed back onto my horse. Atticus came over. Sage smirked. "You see that?"

Atticus shrugged. "I saw you nearly lose it on the water," he said, then cantered off and cleared the higher practice fence with ease.

Sage muttered something unintelligible under her breath.

I focused on the practice ring, then when Julie O'Shay from Ireland entered the main arena, I was up next.

Leon opened the practice ring's gate, and I was lost to a fog in my head as I walked Huxley to the in-gate. "Not too sharp a turn on fence five," Leon was saying. I nodded but was only half listening. I watched Julie turn into fence ten, and her horse bucked as it saw the Liverpool. Unable to keep her seat (which was usually exceptional), Julie fell, crashing through poles to land in the water with a loud thud. Emerald Hill, her prize-winning gelding, took off around the arena. I held my breath as I waited to see if she was okay. Medics ran toward her, but Julie quickly got to her feet, holding her hand in the air to signal to the crowd she was good.

"That fucking water," Leon said. It was true; out of all the fences today, it was the water jump that had caused the most problems. A flare of panic sparked in my chest, but I tried to quell it. Horses sensed your emotions, and I didn't want Huxley spooked. But it was harder to regain calm than I'd expected.

A flash of movement from my left suddenly pulled my attention. I sucked in a shocked breath when I noticed a familiar crop of dark hair and stubble on chiseled cheeks. Jasper looked up at me as Julie walked out of the arena, her groom having caught her gelding and led him out too.

Shards of ice trickled through my veins when I smelled sandalwood and mint. His scent alone was enough to soothe my frayed nerves. What was he doing here? What did this mean?

Focus.

"Huxley likes the water," he said, and I caught Leon nod in agreement at him over my saddle. Jasper's dark eyes locked on mine, bringing another wave of calm to my nerves. "You're going to nail this, Angel. Trust me. I'm rarely wrong about these things."

I nodded, unable to speak. *Angel . . .* Jasper had left the safety of his private box to stand beside me and talk me through this. I opened my mouth, wanting to say something, *anything*, just to hear him speak again, but Leon patted Huxley's rear, and said, "You're up, Hallie. Best of luck."

I tore my gaze off Jasper and back to the arena. Completing my own prejumping ritual, I checked my chin strap, checked the girth, pressed my heels down in my stirrups, then looked to Mila, who was already waiting with my water. Smiling, she handed me the bottle, and I took a long drink. Taking it back from me, she patted Huxley's neck and said, "Fly, boy!" before giving me a good luck nod.

Taking a deep breath, I straightened my posture, and said, "Walk on, baby boy," to Huxley, only for Jasper to squeeze my calf in support as I passed. Shivers broke out all over my body. His simple touch filled me with confidence.

As I walked through the tunnel to the arena, hearing the announcer saying my name and credentials and Huxley's statistics, I felt like I was having an out-of-body experience. Leon walked beside me, peeling off at the in-gate to watch from the viewing plinth. My heart thundered when I saw Jasper go with him.

He left the box to watch me.

What did it mean?

As I entered the arena, my heart jumped in my chest. Taking another deep breath, I moved Huxley into a trot and circled the arena to get my bearings. I focused on the jumps, going through the course in my mind. "Are you ready, milord?" I said to Huxley, the audience melting away to nothing around me. I listened to the sound of Huxley's steady breath as we broke into a canter.

Then my nerves fell away. It was just me, Huxley, and the jumps right now. I'd visualized this course while in the practice ring, something I'd done my entire career. In my head, I'd already achieved a clear. Now I just had to bring it to fruition.

The horn sounded, telling us to begin. "We're off, milord," I said, as I turned into the first fence. "You can do this, baby boy." I gave him rein and let my boy do what he did best. As we landed, any nerves I had left turned into pure excitement. "Amazing, milord, now we need another," I said, as we turned to fence two. Sage was right. It was electric out here.

As Huxley launched into the air, three, four, five times, a wide smile was etched onto my face. The sound of Huxley's hooves on the sand was rhythmic and soothing. The hoofbeats were telling me we were actually here, living out our dream.

As we landed fences eight and nine, I leaned forward and said, "This is the Liverpool, Hux. Most other horses haven't liked this one, but I know you can do it." As we cantered toward fence ten, you could feel the tension from the audience as they braced for a refusal. But as Huxley landed, not even batting an eye at the water, we turned to the triple combination. Clearing those with ease, we turned to the final fence. "Now, baby boy, if we clear this fence, we will have our first ever five-star clear. I know you want that as much as I do. Let's show these people what an amazing boy you are, hey?" Approaching the final fence, I held my breath and let Huxley fly. As his hooves hit the ground and the audience broke into a loud round of applause, I whooped out a happy shout, throwing my fist into the air, then wrapped my arms around his neck, peppering kisses over as much of him as I could reach.

"Good boy!" I said, letting Huxley canter around the arena. *"Her first ever clear in a five-star Grand Prix . . ."* I heard the commentator say, *". . . which puts her in first place . . ."* My head whipped up to the scoreboard. We'd beaten Sage by two seconds, putting her in second place and us in first.

"Huxley!" I said, unable to stop from smiling. "You superstar!"

I headed out of the arena, only to pass by Atticus as he entered the ring. "Git 'er done, Hals!" he said, smiling, and I laughed.

"Good luck," I said to Atticus. He winked at me and entered the ring.

Leon nodded at me in congratulations as I passed him on the plinth but stayed where he was to watch Atticus jump next. Sage was in the tunnel, waiting for me. I dismounted and she wrapped me in her arms. "Incredible," she said, and kissed my cheek. Mila had taken hold of Huxley but hugged me with her free arm.

I turned to watch Atticus, only to startle when Jasper appeared before me. He turned to watch his cousin, but leaned in close to say, "You were brilliant, Hallie." He looked at me from the corner of his eye. "You should be proud." He paused, like he was fighting saying something else, before he said, "I am. So proud."

My heart melted. Jasper stood with his arms over his chest, eyes on Atticus and Barnaby. In that moment, I wanted him to hold me, wrap me in his embrace. I felt a little cold when he didn't.

It was a heady mix in my body, adrenaline from my first five-star Grand Prix, followed by the disappointment of Jasper not holding me in his arms. But I knew he wouldn't. He was too controlled, too reserved, and frankly, we weren't together like that. We'd fucked, once. Perhaps that was all it ever would be. I tried to focus on Atticus too, but too many thoughts circled my head. Why had he come to see me? What did it mean?

I was annoying myself with all the internal questions. I wasn't shy at coming forward. When we were alone, I would just outright ask him. But even me, with my take-no-prisoners attitude, couldn't help but admit it made me nervous. What if he said it was just a single night? The ache in my heart told me I wished it could be more.

Suddenly, the audience broke into rapturous applause. I blinked and brought myself back to the here and now. "Great," Sage said, defeatedly, and I looked to the scoreboard. Atticus's name went straight to the top. He had won. Convincingly.

I didn't even feel sad. My goal was a clear round. I had done that and managed to secure second place too. With Sage in third, we'd achieved a Knighton sweep.

It felt like a dream.

Atticus came trotting toward us. Leon clapped, for once wearing a wide smile on his face. "Top three!" he said and shook Jasper's hand. I watched Jasper's face. He smirked. He was happy, but I caught a flash of sadness in his eyes too.

My heart cracked for him. I just knew he wanted to be in that ring with us. Our fourth member of Team Knighton. He should be. Simply recalling him on Henry back at Golden Oaks . . . He would have wiped the floor with all of us today. Of that I was convinced.

Atticus dismounted, handing Barnaby to Chris after kissing his stallion on the nose. Jasper hugged his cousin, as did Leon. Atticus then faced me. "Sorry, Hals. No hard feelings."

I laughed but then hugged him too. I was proud of him. "You're not sorry in the slightest, but congratulations anyway."

Then he moved to Sage. She was raging. "Miller," Atticus said, smiling, all his teeth showing.

"Atticus," she said tightly, and Atticus's face lit up. I shook my head. At least Sage was being civil in front of Leon and Jasper.

The organizers came over and led us to the podium. Atticus waved at the crowd as we walked past them. I smiled and waved too, but it all felt surreal.

When the interviewers came over, we talked of how we found the course, and just how successful a competition it was for Golden Oaks Stud, with us taking the top three positions. When an interviewer asked Sage, "And what do you think of how well your teammates have done, Sage?"

Sage's smile was wide and obviously fake to anyone who knew her well. "I already knew Hallie was amazing," she said, and I flicked a glance at Atticus to see his expectant grin aimed at my friend. "And . . ." Sage said through clenched teeth, "Atticus is one of the best riders I've ever seen. He deserved today's win."

"Wow. High praise indeed," the interviewer said. As soon as we were free Sage quickly walked off. Atticus began flirtatiously whispering into our interviewer's ear, making her blush, ignoring my defeated best friend.

I searched around me, looking for Jasper, but I only found Leon. I walked to my trainer, who hugged me to his side. "That was a hell of a start, Hallie," he said, which made me beam. Leon wasn't very forthcoming with compliments or affection, so for him this was practically euphoric.

"Thank you," I said, but I searched all around us again. Clearly noticing who I was looking for, Leon said, "Jas had to leave." He motioned to all the cameras, members of the press, and the professional riders milling around us. "The vultures were circling."

"Oh, I wasn't . . ." I tried to say. But when Leon was pulled aside by another newspaper for comment, I realized whatever was happening between Jasper and me had clearly not escaped his eagle eye. The man was known to pick up on the finest details of the sport, so it made sense that he'd seen something between us.

But what that something was . . . I had no idea.

"Hallie," Leon said as I made my way to the stalls after Sage. "Remember the team dinner tonight to talk strategy for tomorrow." I nodded. I had completely forgotten. Tomorrow, the Knighton Cavaliers competed in the team event. As I arrived at our aisle, Huxley was already washed down and enjoying a large hay net. Sage was chatting with Dillon Matthews from Team USA, and every rider I passed shook my hand in congratulations.

Ducking into Huxley's stall, I dropped to the ground and closed my eyes. I had done it. I couldn't believe it. Huxley finished his food and turned his head toward me, lowering his head so I could stroke his face. "You're such a superstar, baby boy," I said, kissing his blaze. Huxley snorted as though he was telling me that he knew it. I smiled but found my happiness fall just a touch.

Jasper had come out from the private box to watch me. But now he was gone, without even a goodbye, and I had no idea when I'd see him again.

Getting to my feet, I dusted the sawdust off my white breeches and went to meet Sage. We had a dinner tonight, and a team event to win tomorrow.

I had to put Jasper from my head.

I just wished I knew how.

Chapter Fifteen

Jasper

"Jas, we're fine. Henry is fine. Dahlia is good. She's healed well. She's safe in her new stable block. There've been no developments with Phillip, the security you've hired is working out, and nothing of consequence has occurred," Forrest said as I called him for the third time in forty-eight hours. "Now, piss off and go do something other than stalk me." He paused. "You do realize we've dominated so far this weekend, yeah? You should be celebrating with my little brother. He's no doubt up to his usual debauchery."

"I know," I said. But since my night with Hallie—which absolutely could be classed as debauched—I'd been doing anything but. I recalled the many meetings that have taken up my time in the days since I'd been here. As much as my head hadn't been in them, I'd walked away with several new contracts for Knighton Equestrian as well as many inquiries into the stud. Huxley, Barnaby, and Seraphina all delivering this weekend had only increased interest in our horses.

"Our team is riding in an hour. Why aren't you at the arena?" I stared out the window that overlooked downtown Doha. I could see the arena lit up in the distance. The team event was being held tonight. I hadn't gone to the dinner with Leon and the riders last night. I fucking couldn't. If I was even close to Hallie, I wouldn't be able to stay away from her. So I'd eaten room service alone and tried to work out what the hell to do about her.

Multicolored city lights stared back at me, my reflection coming into focus in the full-length window. The place was stunning, but all I could see, think of, and hear was Hallie. We hadn't spoken about where we go from here. It should be just one night. It had to be. But I was being a pussy and couldn't bring myself to say that to her. Or bear to hear it if she agreed.

I felt like fucking screaming. I ran my hand down my face. "I fucked her," I suddenly blurted into my phone and was met with a wall of hard silence from my cousin. I cleared my throat, waiting for Forrest to speak.

"I'm assuming you mean Hallie?"

I nodded. "Yes."

"Shit, Jas," he said and sighed. "And what? Now she wants more, and you don't?"

I laughed a sardonic laugh. I *wish* that was true. "Not quite," I said, and Forrest was silent once more until . . .

"Shit. *You* want more." My head dropped onto the glass, and I closed my eyes. I gripped my phone so hard the plastic creaked under my hold. "Jas?"

"I don't know!" I said a bit too loudly. Lowering my voice, I said, "I don't fucking know, okay? It can't happen. I know it can't. I'm too old for her, too fucked up, don't want to put her in the center of the gossip mill, and don't want to put her in danger with all the shite that we're facing at home. There's a million fucking reasons why this can't be more than one night."

"Jas," Forrest said after several silent seconds. "I get what you're saying. But I think you're being too hard . . ."

"No," I snapped. "Do *not* give me permission. Do *not* give me the excuse I need to seek her out again." I clenched my hand into a fist. "I've managed to stay away these past few days, *forced* myself to. She's

too fucking pure for our life. Too innocent to get wrapped up in all our family drama."

"She's a twenty-five-year-old woman who can make her own damn decisions, Jas. Let *her* decide what she wants to do. How much does she know about everything?"

"Not much," I said.

"For fuck's sake, Jas. Is this how you're going to live your life? Alone and rejecting anything you like, want, or love because you're scared?"

"Of course I'm fucking scared!" I shouted. "My dad is dead, Genny can't walk, Dahlia was a championship-winning horse who now can't even accept a lead rope around her neck. I'm getting threatening letters almost *daily*, and—"

"You're *what?!*" Forrest interrupted.

Shit. I replayed what I'd just said, and my stomach fell.

"You better tell me what the fuck you're talking about, right now," Forrest said, calmly, but I recognized my cousin's ice-cold tone. I opened my eyes and defeat ran through me. I was sick and tired of doing all this alone. *"Jasper,"* Forrest pushed.

"I didn't want to worry you all," I said, voice hushed but strained. I moved to my bed and slumped down on the end. Forrest waited for me to continue. Sighing, I said, "I've been getting letters sent to me for a while now. Threatening letters," I confessed.

"Where are they?" Forrest said, and I could hear him moving around the house.

"In a hidden drawer in the desk in my study. Above the top drawer there's a secret latch where I've stashed them."

"Where's the key?" Forrest said minutes later, and I knew he was in my study, looking for a way to open it. I told him, and I heard the rustling of papers.

"Fuck, Jas," Forrest said after a few tense minutes. "Why the hell didn't you say something?"

"You've all gone through enough," I said.

"And you haven't?" Forrest snapped. He took a deep breath. "Has Phillip seen these? Tried to trace them?"

"Yeah, but he couldn't find anything," I said.

"You have a pile of new mail." By the sound of shuffling paper, I knew Forrest was rummaging through those too. I waited until Forrest spat, "Motherfucker!"

"How many?" I asked. Even to my own ears I sounded exhausted.

"Three," Forrest said. I could hear paper in his hands. "Why the fuck are they targeting you? What the hell have you done?"

"No idea," I said, and dropped my head. "For a long time, I thought it was McGowen. But I don't think that anymore. As much as I hate the prick, he's turned his stud around after his dad nearly ruined them, and he's winning more now I'm not on the circuit."

"That's *exactly* why he could be the one responsible," Forrest said. "To keep you from competing so he can clean up all the prize money."

I shook my head. "Phillip said he's clean. It isn't him." I could feel a headache building at the base of my skull. "I suspect Alexis Hobbs, as do the Franklins, but again, Phillip found nothing on her, and without evidence, we have nothing." I hated Alexis, believed she was capable of sabotaging stud farms up and down the country. But the evidence suggested otherwise. "We have no idea who it could be, Forrest. They're completely untraceable."

"Fuck, Jas," Forrest said. I heard my office chair creaking and knew he'd sat down. "No more," Forrest said after a while. I hadn't even asked him what the letters said. It would be the same old bullshit. *I'm going to destroy you, your family, and everything you love . . .*

"You're not dealing with this on your own anymore," Forrest said. "We're telling my brothers and Leon. If it must stop there, fine. We can keep this from Genny if you want. But we all need to do this together. You shouldn't have been shouldering this alone."

My vision blurred and I realized moisture had flooded my eyes. My throat was clogged, and as tears fell down my cheeks, all I could see was the blurred lights of the arena in the distance.

Hallie.

She had been the one bright spot in this shit show of a year. The night in the trailer . . . I wiped the tears from my cheeks. *Fuck,* that night . . . I couldn't stop reliving it. The way she responded to me so well. How she tasted, felt, sounded . . .

She'd made me forget. For that window of time being inside her, I'd forgotten everything but her.

"We'll get through this, Jas," Forrest said quietly, and it was obvious he knew I'd just broken down, turned in on myself as I always did.

"Thank you," I said. "I'll . . ." I took a deep breath. "I'll call later. I'm going to . . ." I trailed off.

"Go watch them," Forrest said, interrupting my spiral. "This is *our* fucking world, Cousin. Some arsehole with a chip on his shoulder isn't going to take all we love from us." I nodded again, like he could see me all the way from England. Forrest was right; I'd been running for so fucking long. That wasn't the Knighton way. We faced things head-on.

I ended the call and left, feeling a little lighter. But only one person would make my heavy thoughts completely lift. Will, my new personal security guard, nodded at me and followed me down the elevator and into my private car.

As the night lights of Doha passed me by, my leg bounced. The minute I got to the arena, I went to the private box that Abdul had set aside for me. I arrived just in time to see Sage clear the final fence. I looked to the scoreboard. Four faults—she'd knocked down a pole on fence five. Atticus had gotten a clear round with a great time. He was killing it.

"Next, representing the Knighton Cavaliers, is Hallie Oakley of Ocala, Florida, US, riding Lord Huxley!" the commentator announced, and something inside of my fucking dark soul was soothed as she trotted out on Huxley. The entire team was wearing olive-green KE show jackets. I moved to the very edge of the box, ignoring a few nearby whispers of my name from the stands.

Hallie picked up a canter, and I couldn't take my eyes from her. Her shoulders were relaxed, and her fluidity held a grace that every equestrian would be jealous of.

She was born to ride.

The horn sounded and Hallie jumped the first fence. I folded my arms over my chest. With every obstacle, my body strained to jump the fences with her. The entire time she tackled the course, I barely breathed. As she approached the final fence, every muscle in my body grew taut.

When Huxley landed, a perfect clear in his wake, I fought back the smile that was forcing itself onto my face. The camera focused on Hallie, and my heart stopped dead. Fuck, but she was stunning. She was smiling wide and speaking to Huxley. She showered him with praise and kissed his neck. She was a true horsewoman. Praised the horse after a round, just like I did Henry. Believed in the fifty-fifty partnership that was horse and rider in this sport.

I watched her as she left the arena and wanted nothing more than to go to her in the stalls, pull her to me, and kiss the fuck out of her. I could still taste strawberries on my lips. But instead of running to meet her in the barn, I retreated into the privacy of the box and sat down on the plush leather sofa, staring at nothing as the remainder of the riders jumped their rounds.

If I'd been asked who'd ridden, I wouldn't have been able to say. All I knew was at the end of the competition, our team placed third. The trophies were handed out, and that brought an end to the Grand Prix at Doha. But I didn't move. As the spectators filed out and the tractors and workers appeared to clear the jumps and rake the ring, I still stayed seated.

The truth was, I didn't dare move. If I did, I would head straight for Hallie and damn the consequences. I'd pull her to me and kiss her. I'd stake my fucking claim. My soul knew she was mine and mine alone, but . . . fuck. I was sick of this roller coaster between wanting her and feeling like I was putting her in danger. But the letters were still coming;

the attacks, and the thought of seeing her pinned under Huxley the way I'd had to see Genny, was unbearable.

My hand balled into a fist, so tight my bones clicked with the pressure. I recalled her jumping. The freedom she held in her body as she left the ground, the partnership she had with Huxley, and her quiet grace as she rode around the ring was like nothing I'd ever seen.

Suddenly an image of her riding Henry popped into my head. He'd let her fuss him. I'd never seen anyone work with horses like she did. And I could only imagine the hidden talents she could pull from Henry if she rode him.

My head pounded. I was trapped in an impossible situation. I wanted Hallie more than I wanted to fucking breathe. Now I'd had a taste of her, I needed more. I craved her in a way I hadn't craved anything in my life. I wanted to taste her again, fuck her and feel her pulse around me, hear her scream as I tied her up and made her fall apart. But I also wanted to feel her soft hair in my hands, to kiss her softly. For fuck's sake, I wanted to fall asleep beside her. Wake up next to her.

I'd never felt that before in my entire life.

But what if being with me hurt her?

But what if being close to her meant you could protect her more? my internal voice asked.

I'd watched her yesterday on the big screen. Before she jumped, the jumbotron had shown her waiting to ride next. The fear on her face had been my undoing. Like she had a damn lasso tied round my heart, I'd run to her. Said *Fuck you* to my anonymity and gone to her side. And I'd seen what my presence did for her—it calmed her, soothed her. Just like she did to me.

Are you going to spend all your life being scared? Forrest's words circled my head. I had been. For as much as I liked to be in charge, living like nothing much fazed me, I had spent the past year being shit-scared of life. Of losing anyone else I loved.

The thought of Hallie being hurt because of me . . . I jumped to my feet, unable to sit there anymore. I was crawling out of my skin.

I started when I saw the arena lights had been switched off while I'd been spiraling. Will was waiting outside the private box when I opened the door. Due to the many meetings I'd been having and moving around Doha more than expected, Will had been assigned to trail me personally. It was probably a wise move, considering all that was happening. I fucking hated that I had to have private security, but that was just the way it was.

"I'm going back to the hotel," I said, and Will nodded, murmuring into his radio for the car to be brought around. I just needed to get back to my room and think. I needed space, and I needed to do what was right.

I stopped in the hallway midstep and asked, "Has there been any sign of trouble since we arrived in Doha, Will? Any threats?"

"None, sir," he said, and that settled something in my chest. I nodded, then headed down the elevator to the car. The entire drive back, I tried to convince myself that being with Hallie wasn't the right thing to do. She had just exploded onto the scene. In the past few days, I'd seen article upon article about her and Sage and the future of Golden Oaks and Team Knighton with the arrival of such flawless talents.

I didn't want to affect that in any way.

As I entered the hotel, a familiar laugh had me turning to the bar. Atticus was there, talking to a gaggle of women as per usual. My cousin was crack to eager pussy. Walking toward him, I placed a hand on his shoulder. He turned and his face split into a happy smile. "Jasper!" He hugged me.

For just one fucking day, I would love to be Atticus. The way he viewed life . . . All of us Knightons took the piss out of his extroverted, easygoing nature, but the truth was, I envied him. To Atti, life was just one big party.

"Good ride tonight," I said.

"You came?" he asked, eyebrow raised. Atticus signaled to the bartender, and in seconds, a scotch was in my hands. "You know," Atticus said, "having you gone from the circuit means I'm going to clean up!" He clinked his glass to mine in celebration, the little shit. I rolled my eyes and knocked back my scotch, feeling its burn ache in my esophagus and slamming the empty glass back on the bar top.

Atticus frowned, losing his humor, then said, "I'm joking, you know? I'm just taking the piss." He sighed, and in a rare moment of seriousness, Atticus leaned in close and said, "Truth is, Jas, I miss you. It was always me, you, and Genny on the circuit. For as long as I can remember." I saw the pain shining in his dark eyes. "I love Hals and Sage, but . . . it felt different today, not having you guys beside me. My *family*. My blood. It was always us Knightons, riding together, you know? I'm a friggin' lone wolf now."

It was why he was at the bar, I realized.

Sighing, I kissed Atticus on his temple. I *did* know what he meant, but it didn't change our situation. Genny couldn't ride and I wouldn't. We were entering a new era. "I'm heading to bed," I said, then backed away, saying, "If I don't see you before I leave, good luck in Mexico City."

"You're going home to England?" Atticus asked, still looking a little sad.

I nodded. I had to get back. I couldn't . . . I couldn't stay on the circuit and be around Hallie. It would be fucking torture.

Atticus cast me a sad smile, then Vivian Cross, an interviewer for *Horse & Rider TV*, grabbed hold of my cousin's sleeve and began pawing at his chest. Atticus seemed only too happy to be touched and got back to his first love: women.

I headed up to my suite, Will taking his spot by the elevator once we made it to our floor. "'Night, Will," I said with a wave, then headed to my room. As I passed by Hallie's suite, my feet slowed. I checked my watch. It was well past midnight. She was probably in bed.

I tried to make my feet move, to leave her alone, but I stared at her door and wondered whether I should say goodbye to her. I was taking a commercial flight back home tomorrow, leaving the team with my jet to get to Mexico. And I wanted her to know I was proud of her. That she was a great addition to the team.

I'd keep it professional. I'd just say goodbye. I could do that.

Before I knew it, I'd knocked on her door. My heart pounded against my chest as I waited for her to answer. "You fucking idiot," I told myself under my breath. Then Hallie appeared, and I bit my lip, holding in a groan . . .

Her dark hair looked freshly washed, flowing down to her waist, and she was dressed in a matching cream silk tank top and shorts. Her long, tanned legs seemed to go on for miles, her toned arms glistened with some kind of oil or cream she'd applied, and her tits . . . *fuck*, the top barely held them in.

"Jasper?" she said, surprise in her voice, searching the area around us.

I was stock still, dumbfounded. My lungs had stopped working, and my cock began to twitch. She was fucking stunning. No makeup, flushed cheeks. Bright-turquoise eyes framed by long, thick dark lashes. She lifted her hand and nervously ran it through her hair. I fought back a deep, guttural groan when I glimpsed the faded marks of where I'd hung her up by the reins as I'd fucked her until she'd screamed just nights ago.

Hallie followed what held my attention and a blush burst on her cheeks. But her eyes grew leaden too, like she was remembering the trailer as much as me.

"I . . ." I said, gruffly and cleared my throat. I leaned on the doorframe just to stop myself from pushing her back into the room and throwing her on the bed. "You were great this weekend," I finally managed, then clenched my jaw.

Hallie's responding smile nearly knocked me off my feet. "Thank you," she said, and she cast me a shy look that almost knocked me on my arse. Hallie was *not* shy, and her sudden innocent appearance was like a hit of Viagra to my cock. In her white nightwear, with her hair down and that sweet smile, she looked every inch the angel I'd believed her to be that night in the barn. "You know, coming from you that means the world to me." Hallie dipped her head. "These past few days . . . They've been a dream come true."

Every word she spoke was sincere, but when she ran her right hand over her left wrist, over the fucking marks I'd put there, I gripped the doorframe so hard I feared the wood would splinter.

I needed to leave. I couldn't take the scent of rose and vanilla that was flooding my nose. I couldn't take her glistening skin, those fuck-me eyes, and her mouth that was just begging to be kissed.

"I'm leaving," I said, finding my voice. Hallie froze. "Tomorrow."

"Oh," she said, her body tensed and her happiness faded away.

I stepped back from the door. I *had* to leave. "I just came to say well done, and goodbye." I nodded and went to turn away when Hallie's fingers wrapped around my forearm. I stared down at those fingers. Her nails were natural but neat, and her touch made a million fucking nerve endings spark to life. I looked up at the girl that was wrapping me around her fingers as much as her fingers were wrapped around my arm.

"So that's it, then?" she said, a bite to her voice, but there was a hint of sadness in her tone too. "You fuck me, we dance around each other for days, not bringing it up, and then you leave?" As serious as this moment was, the take-no-shit cowgirl within Hallie rising to the surface made heat burst in my chest.

"What the fuck can I offer you?" I said, then met her eyes. Her turquoise gaze was blazing. "My life is shit right now, Hallie. No, it's fucking dangerous." I shook my head. "If I even look at you the wrong way, the likes of Camillie Dubois and Alexis Hobbs will smear your name among our peers. Are you prepared for that?"

"I haven't mixed with them once here in Doha," she said back. "And I don't give a shit what they think of me."

"You say that now, but when they're relentlessly accusing you of getting to the top by fucking me, you'll change your tune."

"Fucking you hasn't made me a winner. I did that on my own," she argued.

"*Exactly.* And you deserve to have that be known." I laughed without humor. "I'm not a victim. I don't feel sorry for myself. How could I? I'm rich beyond measure and run businesses that I love. But I have shit happening in my life that you don't want to be around. You don't want to hitch your wagon to this horse. That night in the trailer . . . It's all we can ever have."

"What shit? Why are you always talking in riddles? I know you've had losses and hard times, and I'm sorry for that. But why push everyone away?" Hallie moved her hand off my arm, and I felt the loss of her warmth immediately. She folded her arms over her chest. "We *all* go through shit, but that's when we lean on one another." I didn't open my mouth. No one outside of my family knew the truth. Hallie shook her head, exasperated. "Fine, Jasper. Have it your way."

"I'm truly sorry," I said, meaning every word. "Keep doing what you're doing, and you'll dominate in this tour."

I went to walk away when she reached out and took my arm again. When I glanced back, all the fight had fled from her perfect body.

"Thank you," she whispered. Her Texan accent was thick in this moment. She was unreserved, and I knew she meant what she was saying. "For everything." She looked up at me through thick lashes, pupils wide. "Despite what's happened between us, if I hadn't seen you all those years ago . . ." She shook her head. "I wouldn't be here now, living this dream." Her hand slackened on my arm, and she began to run her fingers up and down my skin, gently . . .

"Hallie . . ." I growled, my cock practically pushing through the zip in my jeans under her touch.

Hallie stepped closer, and closer, turning me until she was only an inch away. She was almost a foot shorter than me, but in this moment, she held me under her control. When her big turquoise eyes met mine again, I fucking stopped breathing. Hallie put her hand on my chest and said, "Thank you for coming to see us ride here in Doha." I clenched my jaw, hands fisted at my side to stop from crushing her to me and slamming my mouth to hers. "Thank you for coming to me in the warm-up ring and calming me down." I glanced down and saw her nipples hard and scraping against my shirt. I swallowed a groan, then Hallie cupped my cheek with soft hands and said, "I'll miss you." Hallie lifted to her tiptoes, then pressed a kiss on my cheek.

As her lips grazed my cheek, suspended for several seconds, I grasped hold of her biceps and growled, "Hallie . . ." It was a warning, a clear sign that I was about to fucking snap.

"Jasper," Hallie whispered back, meeting my eyes. There wasn't goodbye in her eyes, there was an invitation, clear as day. I couldn't . . . I shouldn't . . . The tension built and built between us, static thickening the air, until Hallie rolled her shoulder, the thin strap of her camisole falling . . . and dragging the material with it, revealing her full breast and hard nipple . . .

Control snapping, restraint fallen, I crashed my mouth into Hallie's, pushing her back into her room. Slamming the door closed behind us, Hallie's back hit the wall as I turned her and plunged my tongue into her mouth. Hallie moaned and I lifted her leg around my waist to grind my hard cock against her warm pussy.

I broke from her mouth, kissing down her cheek, her neck, saying, "I'm fucking addicted to you." Hallie shivered as I pulled her head back by her hair, her hips rocking forward as I did. "I can't fucking stay away, no matter how hard I fucking try," I said. And I bent down, ripping the top of her nightwear in two, and not giving a fuck as it fell to the floor. I instantly sucked on a nipple, Hallie's back bending farther as she pushed her tit into my mouth.

"Jasper," she moaned, and I sucked even harder. I bit down, and Hallie shuddered against me.

"You like it rough, don't you, Angel?" I said, looking up at her to see her eyes fluttering closed and her cheeks flaming under my touch.

"Yes," she said, arching as she clawed at my back.

"Mark me," I ordered. Hallie's nails dug into my flesh harder. When my shirt blocked Hallie from giving it to me like I needed, I stepped back and ripped it open too, tossing it to join hers on the floor. Hallie leaned against the door, tits bare, skin flushed, her bright-turquoise gaze fixed on me.

"Get your shorts off," I said, and licked my lips as Hallie placed her hands on the waistband of her shorts and slowly pulled them down. Her bare pussy was revealed to me in seconds, and I almost dropped to my knees so I could take her in my mouth.

"Kick them to the side," I said when her shorts fell to pool at her feet. Hallie did as ordered, and I unbuttoned my jeans, pulling down my zip. I lowered the waistband of my boxers until my cock sprang free, and I took it in my hand. "I want you to touch yourself." Hallie went to do exactly as instructed. "Uh-uh, not just yet." I tipped my head to the side as I took her in. "When I tell you to."

Hallie's eyes widened at my command. I loved this side to her. When the feisty cowgirl became my tame little show jumper who did anything I asked. I stepped closer. Her breathing was choppy, tits rising up and down with each erratic inhalation. I stopped mere inches from her perfect fucking naked body. "Tell me," I said, softly running my fingertip over her chest. Hallie went to move, but I shook my head. "No," I ordered, and she stopped, which had my hard dick throbbing. "Hands above your head," I said, and Hallie immediately lifted her hands, clasping them together against the wall. I moved my fingertip to her breast, circling the flesh. Hallie moaned, fighting to keep her body still. "Tell me," I repeated, running my finger around her nipple but not quite touching the hard flesh. I kissed her cheek, a barely there kiss, my bottom lip dragging over her blush. "Have you touched yourself since our night in the trailer?"

Hallie whimpered, and when I met her eyes, she nodded. "To the memory of us?" I asked. Another nod. "Show me," I said, and Hallie's eyes widened. Reaching up, I unthreaded her clasped fingers and pulled one hand down to her side whilst keeping her other hand above her head and pressed against the door. Hallie's hand moved over her stomach, and I could feel precum leaking from my cock.

"*Show* me," I said again, harder in voice this time. Hallie liked that, if the rocking of her hips was any indication. "Show me how you fucked your hand to the thought of me pushing you over the saddle rack and eating your perfect pussy from behind until you fell apart on my tongue."

Hallie's eyes fluttered closed, then rolled back open like she couldn't take any more, and she put her hand between her legs and began to play with her clit. "Good girl," I praised, and another cry slipped from Hallie's lips as I did. I held on to my cock again, slowly stroking it back and forth as Hallie circled her clit, her breathing getting faster. I kissed along her jaw, keeping a hand over her head. "Did you come thinking of how I tied you up with the reins and put a bit in your mouth to stop you from screaming as I fucked you?" I said, and Hallie cried out so loudly there was no way somebody passing outside wouldn't have heard.

"Jasper, please . . ." Hallie begged, shaking her head back and forth.

"Please *what*, Angel?" I asked, pinching her nipples between my finger and thumb. When she cried out again, her body shuddered.

"Do you want me to make you come?" I asked.

Hallie nodded. "Yes! *Yes!*"

I kissed her jaw, then her mouth. Hallie tried to kiss me back, but her cries and moans were coming faster and faster the harder she circled her own clit. "That's not what polite ladies say, Angel," I said, and looked down, stroking myself harder as I saw how wet Hallie had become.

"Please!" she cried out, meeting my gaze. "Please, Jasper!"

Crushing my lips to her again, I released her wrist and dropped to my knees. Yanking her leg over my shoulder, I dove straight in and licked along her pussy, dick pulsing as her taste immediately exploded on my tongue. Hallie cried out and her hands fastened into my hair.

I was fucking relentless.

Sucking her swollen clit into my mouth, I pushed my finger into her entrance . . . and that was all it took. Hallie screamed, her pussy clenched around my finger, her clit twitched, and she came on my tongue.

I licked and licked her, completely addicted, until Hallie began to push me off her. I kissed down her smooth thigh, licking and nipping at her skin as I did. I wanted to mark her, show any fucker that dared look at her who she belonged to and how I'd claimed her.

Getting to my feet, I met Hallie's glazed gaze. She fought for breath, skin flushed and body shuddering with the aftershocks of her orgasm. But I'd just begun. I stroked my cock when Hallie looked down and watched me.

"You like that? Watching me?" I asked, and Hallie nodded.

"I want to taste you too," she said, and looked to me again for permission.

I groaned, teeth gritted together, then cupped her cheek. Hallie leaned into my touch, then I said, "On your knees, Angel."

Hallie knelt on the floor, her palms sliding down my chest as she did. My cock was aching and harder than I'd ever been in my life, and just the sight of Hallie on the floor before me, waiting for my instruction, almost had me coming on the spot.

"Open your mouth," I said, my voice like cut glass.

Hallie placed her hands on my thighs, her eyes meeting mine, never looking away. She opened her mouth wide and waited. "Fuck, Angel, you're beautiful," I said, brushing my thumb over her bottom lip, and I stepped forward, pushing the tip of my cock between her lips. I threw my head back and growled when Hallie immediately swirled her tongue around me, the feel almost bringing me to the floor too.

"Good girl," I said, voice strained, then, "Can you take more?"

Hallie nodded, and before I had a chance to push farther into her mouth, she leaned forward and swallowed me to the root. *"Hallie!"* I groaned, my hands slamming against the door as my body pitched forward at the feel. I widened my legs and tipped my head back as Hallie sucked me deep, her tongue running up and down the sides of my cock as she swallowed the tip.

"Christ," I said, and gritted my teeth together to keep from spilling down her chest. I peered down, and Hallie was still looking up at me as she rocked back and forward, taking hold of the base of my dick and stroking that too. I couldn't take it. The most beautiful woman in the world was on her knees for me, sucking me to the back of her throat while I still had the taste of her come on my tongue.

"Can you take more?" I asked, hurriedly. I needed it faster. I needed . . . Fuck, I didn't know. Hallie slipped off my cock and said, "Yes." Bending down, I clasped her cheeks and crushed my mouth to hers. I kissed her hard and fast, then keeping my hands on the side of her head, pushed my cock into her mouth and thrust forward. I growled at the feel of her wet hot mouth, then withdrew. I pushed in again, Hallie's hips beginning to rock forward as her body began to beg for more. Hallie held on to my thighs as I rocked in and out of her mouth as I held on to her face. Seeing my cock disappearing into her perfect mouth was euphoric. I moved faster, deeper, and Hallie took it all, every fucking inch. Pressure began to build at the base of my spine, and my balls began to ache.

Fuck!

I yanked myself out of her mouth and put my hands under her arms. As if she weighed nothing at all, I lifted Hallie off the floor and took her to her bed, the lights of Doha making a glittering backdrop through the window. The curtains weren't drawn, and I didn't give a fuck. Let the entire world know I was about to fuck Hallie Oakley, and that I'd never wanted anyone more. Hallie's lips were swollen and thoroughly fucked. Her tanned skin was flushed and marked by my teeth, and I wanted to fucking devour her, consume her.

Hallie lay on her back, and I took a moment to drink her in. Her pretty eyes were leaden, turned-the-fuck-on, and then she opened her legs. Her pussy glistened, and her hole clenched around nothing, just begging for my cock. Hallie put her hands on her tits, playing with her nipples.

"Fucking perfection," I said, and pushed my jeans and boxers down my legs, kicking them to the side. I walked toward where Hallie lay, stroking my hard cock as I approached. It was still wet from her hot mouth, dripping precum.

"Jasper," Hallie said, "I need you inside me."

I groaned as those words left her mouth, and I placed one knee on the bed between her legs, then the other. Hallie's attention flicked between my face and my hand stroking my cock, like she couldn't decide which she wanted to watch more. She dropped one of her hands between her thighs, her fingers moving to her clit, but I pushed it away.

"Your pussy is mine," I said, and crawled above her. Hallie's hands moved to my chest, and she ran her soft palms over every inch of my skin.

I groaned, and Hallie looked me square in my eyes and said, "Fuck me, Jasper. Please."

Leaning down to my elbows, I lined my cock up with her pussy and slammed inside in one hard thrust. Hallie's hands slapped onto my back and her nails dug into my flesh as she cried out, her voice echoing around the suite. I slammed my lips to hers, my tongue slipping into her mouth. Hallie kissed me back as I began to push into her faster and faster, her pussy choking my cock. "Yes!" she cried out, breaking from our kiss on a gasping breath. But I didn't stop. I kissed her anywhere I could reach as Hallie's hips began to rock against me, taking me even deeper.

"Hallie . . ." I growled, changing my angle until her head threw back and I knew I'd hit her G-spot. I pounded against it, watching in awe as Hallie lost all composure, completely falling apart beneath me. "Fucking scream," I said as I thrust harder and faster inside of her. Hallie began to shake, and I was transfixed, watching her fall apart. I didn't even feel her nails raking at my back, too busy watching the most beautiful woman in the world begin to come. Her gaze clashed with mine, and her body stilled as she shouted, *"Jasper! I'm coming!"*

Hallie broke apart beneath me, around me, her pussy clenching so tight around my cock that my orgasm slammed into me so fast and hard that my chest fell against Hallie's tits, and I spilled inside her on a harsh groan.

Hallie moaned and moaned, her pussy squeezing my dick like she was going to come forever. I rocked inside her, needing this to last as long as it could. I licked along Hallie's throat, her skin damp from our fucking and her hair curling into waves. When Hallie's grip on my back lessened, I lifted up slightly, and she met my eyes.

In that second, as her turquoise gaze met mine and she smiled, I knew I was fucked.

So I kissed her again. Hallie's hands threaded into my hair, and I kissed and kissed her, staying inside of her for as long as I could. When I finally slipped out, I sat up, widening Hallie's legs, watching my cum spill from inside her.

Hallie's breathing was erratic as she watched me, only to moan when I traced my finger up her thigh, then pushed my come back inside her pussy, her body jumping as I pressed against her G-spot, the area too sensitive from just orgasming.

"Jasper," Hallie said breathlessly, but smiling, "do you have a breeding kink?"

I smirked. "For you? Abso-fucking-lutely."

Hallie smiled, and my chest caved in when she laughed. I crawled above her again, kissing her, then I lay beside her. My fingers found her pussy again, and I switched between playing with her clit and pushing my finger inside her. "Fuck, Angel," I said. "I'm addicted to you. I never want to leave this bed. Just want to fuck you for eternity."

Hallie turned her head to face mine, barely an inch between us. "Then that makes two of us," she said, and my heart just about stilled.

Hallie's forehead touched mine. When she moved back, she stayed locked on my gaze. "So," she said, breaking the silence. "That happened again."

I laughed. My spent cock twitched to life when Hallie moaned as I circled her clit. "Jasper," she said, body shaking from oversensitivity, but I didn't stop. Shifting closer, I applied more pressure and sucked her nipple into my mouth. "I can't," she moaned.

"You can," I said, and watched her as her eyes fluttered, as her body built back up to coming again. Only this time, Hallie met my eyes and never looked away as she broke apart. Even as her legs widened, her clit swelled, and she cried out for the third time, back arching, only to collapse on the bed, completely spent.

"No more," she said, then rolled into me, trapping my hand between her thighs. Hallie laid her cheek against my chest, and I felt something switch inside of me. Something move, like a displaced puzzle piece suddenly being found and slotting back into place.

I kissed the top of her head, stroking her dark hair, trying to wonder why the fuck she had such an effect on me, such a hold. I shifted, and Hallie looked up. "Oh, my gosh, Jasper. Your back. I've made you bleed!"

I didn't even look, but I could feel the deep scratches. "Worth it," I said, then lowered Hallie back to lie on my chest. My legs were hanging off the end of the bed, but I couldn't care enough to move.

Hallie settled down on me, then played with the hairs on my chest. "That shouldn't have happened again, should it?" I hated hearing the dejection in her voice. I held her tighter. I didn't want to answer. Because it shouldn't have, but I was sure as fuck glad it did. "Do you really have to leave tomorrow?" she said. Hallie's voice held a note of apprehension within it. Like she shouldn't be asking me to stay. If anyone on this earth had the right to make me stay anywhere these days, it was this raven-haired, blue-eyed angel.

But I didn't answer. Because, the truth was, I didn't. But fuck . . . I'd decided to stay away, and now she was lying in my arms with my cum inside her. I was clearly shit at keeping my word.

"Jasper?" Hallie asked, and lifted up, resting her forearms on my chest so she could see my face. The hope I saw in her expression fucking felled me.

How much have you told her? Forrest's words circled my head. *She's a twenty-five-year-old woman, she can decide for herself.*

I ran my fingertip over her dark, perfectly manicured eyebrows, down over her high cheekbones, over a spattering of freckles on her nose, then to her full lip with a perfect bow.

Fuck, I had to leave. I did. But as I lay here right now, I couldn't think of a single reason why I had to go. If I stayed on the tour, we could have this. Every night. I could have her *exactly* like this. But that was my selfishness talking.

The angel and devil on my shoulder argued, and I couldn't fucking take it.

"Come on," I said, needing to move, and lifted her off the bed. I kept her in my arms as I walked us to the bathroom. Setting Hallie down on a chaise longue that sat in the center of the large bathroom suite, I walked to the huge, jetted bath and turned on the taps. Without looking back, I poured oils into the water and watched the vanilla-and-amber-scented steam cloud and billow upward. When I turned around, Hallie was stretched out on the chaise, watching me. She had a slight crease between her eyebrows, and I knew it was because I hadn't answered her.

I bent down and lifted her in my arms. I went to move to the bath when Hallie's hands cradled my face and she stopped me in my tracks. Her bright eyes searched every inch of my face, and she asked, "What's holding you back, baby?"

The "baby" almost had me dropping to the floor and vowing I wasn't going anywhere. I pressed a long kiss to her forehead, then lowered Hallie into the water, switching on the jets. I went to sit on the ledge, when she grasped hold of my hand and said, "Join me."

Unable to say no to this woman, I climbed into the bath, slipping behind her. I pulled her against me, her back to my chest. Hallie sighed as she laid her head on my shoulder. I lifted my foot when the bath was full and turned off the tap with my toe.

Steam licked at our skin and the jets massaged our muscles. I ran my fingers up and down Hallie's arms until at last, she said, "Jasper?" I knew she wanted answers. I felt a boulder in my chest when I thought of all I kept inside. I had kept too much to myself for so long that it felt too heavy to endure. I had taken on the burden as leader of my family . . . and I was so fucking tired of shouldering all the weight. Grief of my father still pressed on my chest, of Genny, of all the businesses, the threats . . . I was fucking drowning.

Hallie turned until she met my eyes. One glance at her had all my high walls falling, and Hallie was stepping straight over the rubble. I closed my eyes, then ran my hand down my face. "I'm trying to protect you," I finally confessed.

Her eyebrows pulled together in confusion. She shook her head. "I don't understand. How and why are you protecting me? From *what?*"

A lump built in my throat at the question. My father's face drifted into my mind, then the crash site and my father's dead body on the ground before me. My hero . . . my favorite person, broken before me.

"What do you mean there's been a crash?" I said into the phone. I grabbed my car keys and ran out the door. I'd been in a meeting that had run far too late. It was cold and wet and freezing outside, the rain lashing down in torrents. We were in the thick of winter, and the weather was harsh and unforgiving.

"Jas, it's . . . it doesn't sound good. The police have got in touch as you're his next of kin. They called here because they couldn't get hold of you personally." Forrest's tone was too soft, too filled with emotion. "The first responders are at the scene. They're trying to get him out as we speak."

I stumbled as I slipped on mud and righted myself to climb into my Range Rover. The phone connected to the car's speaker. Forrest was still speaking, but it became white noise in my ears as I skidded out of the car park and hit the country roads that led home. The wipers were on their fastest speed, and I squinted as I drove, trying to navigate the labyrinths that were England's dark country back roads, made worse by torrential rain and lack of lampposts.

"Is he dead?" I found myself blurting, chest aching as I awaited the response.

Forrest was silent, and I felt my heart physically begin to crack. "I don't know, Jas," Forrest said carefully. "The police said they'd know more when they had got to him." Forrest swallowed loudly. "The car sounds like it's in a really bad way."

A choked sound ripped from my throat as my mind conjured up what that could look like. My father, the man who raised me and the best man I knew, trapped in his car under a prison of rubber and metal.

"I'll meet you there," Forrest said. "I'm about ten minutes behind you."

I hung up on Forrest without another word and drove more recklessly than I should to get to a car wreck. But this was my father. *I didn't even remember the journey to the crash site. The only sign that there was even an accident up ahead was the sudden flashing of emergency vehicle lights and the road closed off by the police. I stopped in a long line of cars and threw my door open. I didn't even turn off the engine as I ran forward. I pushed past the temporary barriers that had been used to close the road and shouldered past the policeman who tried to stop me.*

I choked on a sob when I saw my dad's treasured vintage Defender up ahead . . . or what was left of it anyway. Right now, it resembled a mashed-up silver piece of metal.

"Dad!" I screamed, as arms wrapped around me from behind. I didn't know who they belonged to, but I threw them off me and made a rush for the car. But when I got there, firemen were cutting off the door. As one of them pulled it from the broken frame, I dropped to my knees.

"Dad!" I shouted again, but my body began to tire, all the life draining from me. Because when I looked through the crushed frame of the car, my father's lifeless eyes stared back at me, blood marring his face. He was still strapped in the driver's seat.

But he was gone.

My father was gone.

And there was nothing I could do about it . . .

I blinked back to the here and now as the memory played out in my mind, the smell of charred rubber, metal, and blood, and the feel of thrashing rain still so prominent in my mind. Hallie's hand was on my cheek, keeping me grounded. I stared into her searching eyes, her open, kind, beautiful eyes, and I found myself saying, "I don't think my father's car crash was an accident." Those words seemed to slice right through the steam around us in their heaviness.

Hallie froze, lips parting in shock. Clearly, whatever she guessed I might have said, it wasn't that. I brushed a wet strand of hair off her shoulder. Before she could say anything, I kept going, a dam broken down. "We also believe Lady Dahlia was drugged in Saint-Tropez and Genny's fall was orchestrated on purpose."

"Jasper . . ." Hallie said, shock and pain flickering on her pretty face.

"And the day Dahlia got loose and you helped us?" Hallie nodded. "Her stable block's electrics were hacked so she could escape." Hallie swallowed. "And I've been getting letters," I blurted. Now I'd started speaking, I couldn't stop. It was like a tidal wave, all my pain pouring out of me in one devastating blow. Hallie turned fully in my arms and sat between my legs. Her hands landed on my chest, and all her concerned focus was on me.

"What kind of letters?" she asked, softly.

I followed a droplet of water as it ran down Hallie's neck and over to her shoulder. Leaning forward, I kissed the drop, her skin silky soft beneath it. Hallie shuddered. I lay back, placing my hands over hers on my chest and said, "Threatening ones." I inhaled deeply. "Ones that vow to destroy me, my family, and . . . anyone I love."

As those final words slipped through my lips, sympathy flooded Hallie's face. She shook her head, as though she couldn't believe it. But I wasn't finished. "Whoever is threatening us claims responsibility for my father's death. They said he was an immoral man and needed to be punished." My heart ached at that thought. To me, my dad was anything but. I had no idea why they claimed he was corrupt. Phillip had never been able to find anything that my father had done wrong, but whoever was targeting us certainly felt they had reason to murder him.

"They claim they are targeting Genny and want her dead too." I laughed a humorless laugh. "Genny! My sweet little sister who doesn't have a bad bone in her body." My voice wavered and I felt like my throat was closing in. "They nearly killed her, Hallie. My little sister. When she went down that day, in front of me and my cousins . . ." I choked. "I thought she was dead. In that moment, I thought I'd lost the last member of my nuclear family."

Hallie lurched forward and wrapped her arms around my neck. I held her to me, threading my hands through her hair. I clung to Hallie like if I didn't, she would turn to vapor and slip away from me too. *"Ssh,"* Hallie soothed, stroking her hands down the back of my head. "It's okay."

I shook my head and pulled back. I met her eyes so she would know how serious I was. "It's *not* okay, Hallie. Don't you see?" My breathing was choppy. "We have no idea who is doing this. The police are good for fuck all. I hired the best private investigator money can buy, and even he can't find a trace. It's dust in the fucking wind when it comes to the bastard who is after my family." I slammed my hand into the bath water, making it splash over the sides. "I can't defend all I love because I'm fighting a fucking ghost! No trace, no trail. Just fucking stress and threats and the fear that someone else I love will be taken from me. *Hurt*, because of me."

Hallie straddled my legs, pressing her chest against mine to rip me from my spiral. She dropped her forehead to mine. Her hands cupped my cheeks as I fought for breath. The minute she wrapped herself around me, my body lost its fight, and I was drained. All the tension in my muscles evaporated, and I held on to Hallie so tightly I feared I'd hurt her. But she stayed still, letting me breathe her vanilla scent in.

I didn't know how many minutes passed before I pulled back and met Hallie's sad and shocked gaze. "I want you, Angel. Fuck, do I want you. But I couldn't live with myself . . ." I lowered my chin. "How the hell could I live with myself if I put you in harm's way?" Hallie's eyes dropped. I cupped her face and said, "No, Angel. This is serious." She met my gaze again. "You are just at the start of greatness, Hallie. The way you ride, you and Huxley . . . the world is *yours*." I pulled her closer. "I couldn't fucking live with myself if whoever is targeting my family found out about my feelings for you and turned their attention your way."

Hallie swallowed, and her eyes widened. "What feelings do you have for me?" Her voice was a whisper.

I stopped breathing, replaying what I'd just said. I inhaled a stuttered breath as she waited on a precipice for me to speak. Chest caving, and truth spilling out, I said, "I fucking adore you, Angel." I laughed a humorless laugh. "I spend my days wondering how to fucking see you without putting you in danger. I go to sleep thinking of you, and when I wake up, your face is the first thing I see in my mind." Hallie's chest rose and fell. She licked along her lips with her tongue, and I said, "I'm falling for you, Hallie. *Hard.* I tried not to. I tried to be cold, to push you away, but there you were, wherever I looked, and you broke through my shields day by day until all I could see and feel was you."

"Jasper," she hushed out and pressed her lips to mine. But this kiss wasn't hurried or hard. It was soft and . . . fuck. It was a kiss that told me things were changing between us.

Had changed.

Hallie broke from my mouth, then said, "I'm falling for you too." The effect that had on my heart was all-consuming. I'd been lonely so fucking long, and in walks an angel from Texas to fill the void I believed would never close.

I lit up inside, but immediately a dark cloud rushed in to smother any light. My shoulders sagged and I knew devastation shadowed my face. "But it's because of that I can't see you in danger." Hallie tensed. "The letters . . . they mention everyone I'm close to. Who I love." My voice was rasped and exhausted. "Even Henry . . ." I sighed.

Understanding shone from Hallie's pretty eyes. "That's why you stopped competing," Hallie said, knowingly. I nodded. "Jasper," she said. "These people, or person, they've already taken everything from you."

I pushed my hands through Hallie's hair, and said, "Not everything. Not the best thing. Not yet." Hallie's worried expression grew soft.

"That's why I can't risk you, Angel. You're too fucking important to me to put in harm's way. As much as I want you, I can't have you."

Hallie lay down on my chest, and I peppered kisses wherever I could reach. She lifted her head after a few silent minutes and said, "Could we keep this quiet? Just between us?" The burst of warmth that exploded in my chest at that point was off the charts. But it was still too risky, and I shook my head. "No, please," Hallie said. "Listen to me." Hallie wrapped her arms around my neck, imploring me to hear her out. "No one would need to know outside of our family and friends. And even they wouldn't need to know if you felt it wasn't safe." My heart began to race. I loved what Hallie was saying. But it felt impossible. "Like you said, I'm at the start of my professional career. Keeping it to ourselves would keep us from gossip too. Accusations that I was using you to get ahead. The likes of Camille and Alexis would get nothing on me."

My blood boiled with instant anger. "No one would fucking *dare*," I spat.

At my reaction, lust built in Hallie's gaze. "Keeping this to ourselves, it wouldn't allow any of those rumors to spread. I could keep my focus on the Grand Prix, you wouldn't have to worry someone would target me . . ." Hope pulsed off her in waves. "And we could still have this. *Be* like this."

"I couldn't ask you to do that," I said. "Sneaking around . . . It wouldn't be fair."

"You're *not* asking me. I'm suggesting it," Hallie said. She traced invisible words on my chest. "I . . ." A blush burst on her cheeks. "I want this, Jasper." I stopped breathing as she met my eyes. "I want *you*. However that must be."

I dropped my head to Hallie's forehead and just breathed her in. Her strength, her affection, the fucking peace I felt when I was with her. I wanted what she was offering. I wanted it so fucking badly I was dying to say yes, to agree.

"Whoever is after me has managed to infiltrate every area of my life. As much as we wish we could keep this quiet, they might find out." I shook my head. "Then they'd be after you."

"You're worth the risk," Hallie said, determination in her turquoise eyes. Then she smiled and said, "And I'm a real good shot with a gun."

Despite the heaviness pressing down on us, I laughed. It felt good.

"I don't doubt it," I said, kissing her cheek.

"Sleep on it," Hallie said, hope remaining in her blue stare. "Just . . . just don't throw us away without taking some time to think it all through. I've . . ." Hallie blushed and simultaneously destroyed me. "I've never felt this way about anyone before."

Right then, I wanted to burn down the fucking world just so whoever was targeting me was taken out. Because I felt the same way for Hallie, probably more.

"Please . . . don't give up on us just yet."

I nodded, then just lay with her until the bath water was cold and Hallie's breathing had slowed to a relaxed, steady pace. I glanced down to see she had fallen asleep. A knife sliced through my chest. I wanted this too. I wanted *her*.

Lifting Hallie, I stepped out of the bath with her in my arms. I wrapped her in a towel, then took her to bed, tucked her underneath the duvet, and closed the hotel curtains. For several long minutes I sat beside her, just watching her sleep. She was perfect. If someone had told me a few months ago I'd be here now with a woman I was more than infatuated with, one who clasped onto my heart harder each day, I would never have believed them. But here I was, contemplating throwing all my self-imposed rules into the wind to have secret stolen moments during the day and long nights by her side.

Leaning down, I pressed a kiss on her cheek. I didn't know yet what I was going to do. Seeing her like this, peaceful and happy . . . I couldn't imagine doing anything to hurt her. And sadly, that included being with me. But a damn magnet with the force of gravity was keeping me at her side. I kissed her again, then got up to go back to my room.

I looked to the floor for my clothes, only to feel soft fingers hold on to my hand. I glanced down, and with sleep-filled half-lidded eyes, Hallie whispered, "Stay." I needed to go back to my room to think. My flight was first thing in the morning. I had only hours until I had to be at the airport. Hallie blinked slowly, and said again, "*Please.* Stay."

Her fingers squeezed my hand, and that was all it took for me to lift the duvet and slip underneath. Hallie immediately curled against me, and I wrapped her in my arms.

I turned off the lamp beside the bed and didn't sleep one wink, just listening to her breathe and internally debating what was for the best. But as Hallie turned and laid a kiss on my cheek, I wasn't sure there *was* a debate anymore.

My heart had already made its choice.

Chapter Sixteen

Hallie

"What's up your ass?" Sage said as the people carrier drove her, me, and Atticus to the private hangar at the airport. Our destination: Mexico City. We were taking the private plane again. It seemed this was the Knighton treatment, one I wasn't sure I'd ever get used to.

I stared out the window and tried my hardest to not feel the fact that my chest had caved in and sadness was dragging me down. "Nothing," I said. "I'm just tired. I . . . I didn't sleep." That was a lie. I had never slept better than I did with Jasper holding me to his chest.

"You can take the bed on the plane, Hals," Atticus said. "I'm wired. I had a late night last night too, but I'm still on a high."

Sage rolled her eyes but stopped herself from saying whatever barb was on the tip of her tongue. I was proud of my best friend. She'd been doing well at keeping her jabs to Atticus at a minimum.

Atticus looked disappointed that Sage had kept to the ceasefire. Sometimes I wondered whether he really slept around as much as he said he did, or whether he just said it to get a rise out of Sage. If that was the case, he'd have to find another way to rile her up. She was being a true professional these days and keeping her mouth closed.

When silence fell in the car, Jasper's handsome face immediately filled my head. Followed by the ache in my heart from finding my bed empty this morning.

I'd asked him to stay, *begged* him. He had slept beside me, held me, cherished me, but when I woke this morning to my alarm, he was gone. I had gone to his suite to see housekeeping already cleaning it out for the next guest.

I'd asked him to give us a chance if we kept things private. He'd agreed to think on it, and I was sure his leaving without even a goodbye was my answer. I understood his reasoning, I did. I heard the racking pain in his voice last night when he told me about the person who was trying to hurt his family, what he believed about his father's crash. But I still wished things could be different for us.

I meant what I said—I was falling for him. And not in a superficial way. I was falling for him in a way I had never fallen for anyone before. The way my heart swelled when he was near . . . the way my pulse raced . . . and the way we made love, fast and hard and him in total control. It set me on fire, gave me something I didn't even know I needed.

"Hallie!" Sage's shrill voice cut through my heavy thoughts.

"What?" I snapped.

Her eyes filled with confusion. "I've been calling your name for the last minute." She pointed to the open door of the minivan and the Gulfstream jet that was waiting for us to board. "We're here."

Sage eyed me strangely but let me off without a grilling. I was sure it'd come soon. I gathered my hand luggage and followed her up the airstairs with leaden feet. At the top of the stairs, Atticus spoke to Emma, the lead air hostess, before ducking inside. Sage kissed Emma on her cheek, and I followed, wanly greeting Emma as I stepped into the cabin.

Then everything in my body froze. Sitting in his usual back seat was Jasper. My heart kicked into a sprint and the caved-in hole in my chest was instantly filled with light. Jasper lifted his head, and his midnight eyes met with mine. They softened, and I could read everything he wanted to say to me.

He wanted this.

He wanted us.

He was giving us a chance.

"I can't believe you're coming to Mexico!" Atticus said to Jasper and kissed him on his cheek. But Jasper didn't take his eyes off me.

"Hallie?" Emma said. "Can I please ask you to take your seat for takeoff? And turn your phone to airplane mode."

"S-sorry, of course," I stuttered, then moved to the seat beside Sage. My body suddenly felt wired, buzzing with happiness. He wanted us. We . . . we were together? I couldn't wrap my head around it. Sage narrowed her eyes on me, then looked back to Jasper.

When she looked at me, she said, "And just like that, you're out of your mood."

"Sage . . ." I warned under my breath.

She batted her hand at me. "Shut up, Hals. You know I won't say shit to anyone." She leaned in close. "But maybe work harder at covering your love bites and the teeth marks all over your neck and chest next time you have a secret fuckfest with the boss, huh?"

I blanched and yanked my compact out of my bag. I quickly powdered the red marks Sage was referring to, then picked up my cell. I went to turn it off, when a new message sat in the center of the screen.

JASPER: I WANT TO TRY. I WANT YOU.

As soon as those words stared up at me, I fought the need to jump from my seat and run into his arms. Instead, I ran my thumb over the words of the message and let my heart thud loudly.

I hadn't had Jasper's number before, and I assumed he'd programmed it into my cell last night while I slept. Turning back to see him, he was already watching me. Waiting, I realized. I smiled at him and nodded.

Jasper smothered his returning smile with a hand, then looked out the window as we taxied to the runway. I inhaled and felt like since I'd woken up this morning, it was the first *full* breath I'd taken.

As the plane took off, I felt a lightness pass throughout me. Jasper hadn't left. He was coming to Mexico City with me—*for* me. And we were going to try. In secret, we were going to try.

I didn't think it was possible for more of my dreams to come true. Apparently, I couldn't have been more wrong.

Mexico City, Mexico

"I have to go," I said against Jasper's mouth. The minute we'd arrived at the hotel last night, Jasper had knocked on my door and proceeded to make love to me until we'd passed out, exhausted in the early-morning light.

I pulled on my riding tights and straightened the collar of my base layer. Today we were practicing, getting the horses warmed up and ready for the competition tomorrow. Jasper's arms came around my waist, and he pulled me back against his chest. "Stay with me," he said, and kissed down my neck.

I laughed, and though I should have pulled away, I offered more of my neck for him to kiss. "Mr. Knighton! You are the owner of the stud and brand that I ride for, and you're encouraging me to miss a vital practice for the Grand Prix this weekend?"

I turned in his arms and became breathless at the smile that took up Jasper's handsome face. "Exactly," he said, and pulled my chest to his. He kissed my lips, then slipped his tongue into my mouth.

"Mmm . . ." I moaned, then broke away. "No! *No,* I must go!"

Jasper smiled again. "I'm the boss, Angel, so I decide if you can skip the practice or not. I'll tell Leon you're spending the day in bed with me, being tied up so I can lick your cunt so hard you pass out from the many orgasms I'll give you." I squeezed my legs together at the thought of that.

"I'm sure he'd love that," I said breathlessly. "And our trainer may be employed by you, Jasper, but even you can't tell him what to do."

"Eh," Jasper said, dismissively. "Leon's bark is worse than his bite." I playfully slapped his hand away from me.

"To you, maybe, but to us mere mortals who actually need his coaching, he's a hard-ass—in the best way possible, of course."

"Fine," Jasper said, and let me go. While I braided my hair, he pulled on his slacks and shirt. Walking to him, I moved his hands away and began fastening his buttons, inhaling his sandalwood and mint scent. I could feel Jasper's gaze on me, and I felt so light and happy I worried I could float away.

Jasper's hands landed on my hips. When I'd fastened the final button of his shirt, I said, "There." Jasper had been staring at me with pure adoration on his face, and I felt my heart melt in my chest. I was concerned about my ability to ride today, as my legs felt weak under this much affection.

Since we'd gotten off the plane yesterday and checked into our hotel, Jasper hadn't left my side. We had a five-star-hotel floor to ourselves, like we'd had in Doha, and just like in Doha, my room was right next to his.

A knock suddenly sounded at my door. *"Ssh,"* I said to Jasper as I threw on my boots, bouncing on the spot as I tried to zip them up. I quickly grabbed my riding hat. "That'll be Sage," I said.

I found my purse and my cell thrown on the floor and gave Jasper a quick kiss. He held on too long, and I hoped this playful side of Jasper would never fade. It was as though he had opened the gates of his heart up to me and, along with it, let in some light. "Get to your meetings. You have businesses to run, Mr. I-run-the-entire-equestrian-world-CEO."

"Fine," Jasper said, face stern. "But after the competition, you're mine again, and I'm going to fuck you so hard you won't be able to walk for days."

I rolled my eyes but was immediately on countdown for that time. I loved riding; I never wanted competitions or practices to end. But right now, I was ready to forgo the practice. This was a first for me.

"Hallie!" Sage's frustrated voice came through the door again. I kissed Jasper one more time, then ran for the door. I opened it and slipped through the small crack I'd created before shutting it behind me. Sage stared at me strangely, and said, "Ready?"

"Yes." I nodded and quickly moved to the elevator.

Once we were inside, Sage said, "So you're together now or what? Like, in a relationship?"

Blood drained from my face. I went to open my mouth, to maybe deny it, but I never lied to Sage, and I couldn't find my voice to do so now. I never kept anything from her.

Sage held up her hand. "Do not even think about lying to me, Ms. Oakley," she warned.

My shoulders sagged, and I said to her, "Please don't tell anyone," I begged. Sage's pissed-off scowl turned into one of concern. "*Please* . . . We need to keep this quiet."

"I won't," she said, and seemed to think on things. "Is it because he owns Golden Oaks and Knighton Equestrian? Fuck anyone who accuses you of sleeping your way to the top. Your performance speaks for itself."

I shook my head. "It's not just that." I sighed in exasperation. "I know you're my best friend, my *sister*, and I tell you everything, but I really can't go into why we've decided to keep this secret. It's . . ." I trailed off. "It's not my story to tell."

Sage studied me harder, and for a moment I worried she could read my soul. "Okay," she said, and reached for my hand. Squeezing it, she said, "I'm not going to lie, that worry in your gaze is kinda concerning me, but I trust you to be safe—and if you ever need to talk about anything, you know I'm a vault."

I kissed Sage on the cheek. "Oh, I *know* you are." I raised my eyebrow at her knowingly, and Sage stuck her tongue out at me. But to be fair, she *was* a vault. After all, she had her own drama concerning another member of the Knighton family, and her rude gesture told me she knew that I was onto her. I was sure there was more to their story than she'd divulged. She didn't really have a leg to stand on.

Watching the floors descend on the elevator panel, I said, "You ready for this one?"

Sage nodded her head. "As long as there's no fucking water jump, my queen of darkness will kick ass this weekend." I laughed. Fefe was quite the drama queen, but when she was on form . . . the world had better watch out.

Sage stepped closer and closer to me, until she said, "*Sooo . . .*" I turned to her. She put her hands out, palm facing palm, lips pursed, and said, "Just tell me when to stop." She began moving her hands apart, an inch, two, three . . . and I slapped them down.

"Sage! Can you stop?" But I laughed under my breath.

"For fuck's sake, Hals. Inquiring minds just wanna know." She leaned closer. "I've seen numerous pictures of Jasper in breeches over the years, and let's just say they leave *nothing* to the imagination."

"Sage," I said, "I'm warning you. *Stop.*"

Sage shrugged and leaned back against the elevator wall. She played with her hat and hummed along to an instrumental piano rendition of "Albatross" by Taylor Swift. I stretched out my neck, relaxing my muscles, trying to ignore her, but it was no use. Eventually I sighed and said, "It's fucking huge."

"I knew it!" Sage shrilled triumphantly. She cackled, then wrapped her arm around my shoulder. "You go, girl! Get that massive *D*!" The doors chose that exact moment to open, and Atticus was waiting just outside. I felt my face flame. Atticus covered his smirk with his hand.

"Ladies," he greeted, then jumped on the elevator as we exited.

Sage nodded her hello, just as I said, "Hi, Atticus."

"I left my hat upstairs. I'll see you at practice," he said.

As the doors closed, and we walked outside to our car, I said, "Inquiring minds want to know if large endowments run in *all* the Knighton men?"

Sage choked. "Don't, Hals. I've managed to block all memory of that particular cock."

She quickly changed the subject to talk of this weekend's course.

"Yes, baby boy!" I said, as Huxley got us another clear. I stroked his neck and kissed his mane. "I'm so proud of you, baby. You are such a good horse."

I was the anchor rider on our team today. Sage had gone early in the class and had set the time for the fastest round on Fefe. They had flown over the course like bats out of hell. No one came close all class until Atticus, riding eleventh, smashed her time by three seconds.

I glanced at mine and Huxley's time and smiled. Once again, we Knighton riders were dominating the top three, only with Sage in second place this time, and me and Hux in third. Atticus, of course, was firmly in first place.

By the time the final few riders completed the course, we still held all the top spots. After receiving our trophies and ribbons, and taking our victory gallop around the arena, we dismounted and led them to the stalls. I had just finished kissing Huxley and giving him a treat when I saw Jasper in the distance. He was chatting to some other riders, and I couldn't help but want to throw him into a stall and ride him too.

Like in Doha, Jasper came out of his private box before I rode and stood with me to keep me calm. But I was better this time. Now that I had a Grand Prix under my belt, my nerves were low level. Still, having Jasper beside me before every ride was certainly something I could get used to.

I had just taken off my hat and unbuttoned my riding jacket when someone covered my eyes from behind me. "Guess who?" I couldn't help the beaming smile that pulled on my face when that familiar gruff voice and strong Texan accent drifted into my ears.

It couldn't be . . .

"No way!" I said and turned around. Canyon Hayes stood there in all his Texan cowboy ruggedness, and a lump clogged my throat.

"Hey, short stack," he said affectionately, pulling on the end of my braid. I threw my arms around his neck and hugged him tightly.

Canyon hugged me back and a few stray tears fell from the corners of my eyes. When he put me down, I stepped back to look him up and down. A rush of homesickness washed through me, seeing him dressed in his typical red plaid flannel shirt and well-worn jeans with battered cowboy boots. His light-brown, shoulder-length hair was as thick and wayward as always, and he looked just like he always had when we grew up side by side on my daddy's ranch.

"What are you doing here?" I said, holding on to his arms. I chuckled. He was still as muscled as always. But I hadn't seen Canyon in over a year, our schedules not allowing us the time. Seeing him now before me, I realized just how much I'd missed him.

"What?" he said, his tongue wrapping around his vowels. "You think I wouldn't come and see my Hallie-girl kick ass in her fancy-ass horse competition just south of the border?" He balled his hand into a fist and pretended to punch my arm. "I wouldn't have missed it for the world."

Gratitude hit me like a tidal wave. I hugged him again, tighter this time, and Canyon pulled back and asked, "You gonna introduce me to your new man?" My heart fluttered at that, and I naturally sought out Jasper. He was nowhere to be seen. But when Canyon pointed to Huxley, I realized he meant my new man of the equine sort.

Get your head on straight, Hals.

I turned to my beautiful horse and ran my hand down Huxley's nose. Huxley huffed his warm breath in my face. "This is Lord Huxley, the current main man in my life."

Canyon ran his hand down Huxley's neck, and like all horses, he leaned into his touch. "Howdy, boy. You better be keeping my girl here safe." I lost myself in studying Canyon's movements. He continued running his hand all along Huxley's body, studying his build, sizing him up, while my horse relaxed under Canyon's touch. The sound of a throat clearing behind me made me jump.

Jasper stood behind me, a furious look on his face. My heart raced at his expression—nothing, and I meant *nothing*, was as hot as Jasper Knighton going all alpha and claiming me as his, whether it be with words or body language alone. And when Canyon turned around and glanced between Jasper and me with a raised eyebrow, I knew I'd have to have a talk with Jasper about his obvious jealousy. We were meant to be keeping our relationship secret, but if he kept acting like this, we wouldn't stay a secret for long. And that couldn't happen.

I rocked on my feet. "Jasper, I didn't see you there," I said with a forced laugh. Jasper continued glaring at Canyon, arms crossed over his broad chest.

Jasper tipped up his chin. "Who's your friend, Hallie?" Jasper's deep and savage voice had my stomach clenching. It was so hot. With his dark hair, eyes, and stubbled cheeks, he looked menacing.

Taking hold of Canyon's arm, I said, "This is Canyon. We grew up together as kids, until . . ." A wave of sadness immediately swept over me. When I looked up, Jasper's hard stare had switched to one of concern, clearly sensing my change in mood. "Until I had to leave Texas for Florida."

"Canyon Hayes," Canyon said, and put out his hand for Jasper to shake, giving me time to gather myself from the flash of grief that had just wrapped around my heart.

Jasper shook Canyon's hand, then tipping his head to the side, said, "Why do I know your name?"

Canyon hooked his thumb at me. "No doubt from Hals." Canyon put his cowboy hat on his head and tipped the front at Jasper. "I remember hearing about you when Hals was growing up in Florida."

"And we'll stop there, thank you, Canny," I said, my cheeks beginning to burn.

"No, I'm keen to hear those stories," Jasper said, but then studied Canyon again. Recognition hit his eyes. "Canyon Hayes . . . as in Canyon Hayes, the natural horseman?"

Canyon wasn't good with recognition or praise, so he just nodded his head. "At your service, sir."

"I've read articles about you," Jasper said, his jealousy dropping and a hint of awe lacing his voice. "You're a horse whisperer."

"None of those articles were sanctioned by me," Canyon said about the press. "But yeah, horse whisperer is a good an explanation as any for what I do." He faced me. "I'm down here working with a barrel horse and rider who were in a road accident. When I saw you were stopping here on the tour, I shifted some things around so I could see you." Softness flashed over his stubbled face. "You were incredible out there, Hals." Canyon used his index finger to gesture around us. "This ain't my world, far fucking from it, but you kicked ass. Even a cowboy like me could see that." I cuddled him again, smelling the soothing scent of Texas dust on his clothes. I would always associate Canyon with home. With the young, carefree Hallie before her world was destroyed.

"Canyon?!" Sage's excited voice came from across the yard. "Canyon freakin' Hayes, is that you?" When we looked up, Sage ran at Canyon and threw her arms around him. Suddenly, Atticus appeared next to Jasper, the same scowl on his face as Jasper had been wearing earlier. I rolled my eyes at these incredibly possessive Knighton men.

"Atticus," I said, when Sage pulled back, "this is my childhood best friend, Canyon." I nudged Canyon's arm. "But he may as well be my brother. He's a good friend of Sage's too."

Sage laid her hand on Canyon's shoulder. "Canyon's a *true* horseman, Atticus. You could learn a thing or two from him."

Canyon looked at me in confusion, then stepped away from Sage. "Okay, whatever is between y'all has nothing to do with me. Sage, I know you too well to be lured into whatever rivalry you have going with Atticus here."

Sage scowled at Canyon spoiling her fun. "Pussy."

Canyon turned to me and under his breath said, "I see she hasn't changed."

I laughed. "What are you doing tonight? You don't have to leave yet, do you?"

"Nah. I've got a hotel here for the night." Excitement burrowed within me. "There's a bar I know, just up from my hotel. Was gonna see if y'all fancied a night dancing." Canyon winked at me. "It's been a while since we two-stepped, Hallie-girl."

"Yes," Sage said, answering for us both. She rubbed her hands together. "Yes to dancing. I've missed a rugged cowboy bar; these

pompous show jumpers don't know how to get down and dirty. Sign me the fuck up."

"Sage, you have the team competition tomorrow." Leon joined our group, stopping Atticus from saying whatever was about to come out of his mouth. "You *all* do." When I faced Leon, my heart sank. I knew he was right, but Canyon was my *family*, and I hadn't seen him in far too long.

"What if we didn't drink and were in bed by midnight?" Sage asked Leon, batting her lashes at him.

His hard expression was impossible to read, and even Sage, with her stunning good looks and sensual charm, couldn't break him. Then Canyon said, "Y'all are welcome to come too. I promise, the bar is a good time, and if y'all like authentic Mexican street food, there's food trucks outside that are amazing. We could go there first." Canyon shrugged. "Y'all gotta eat, right? What's a lil' dancing on top of that?"

Jasper met my eyes, and I could see disappointment shining within them. Not because he didn't want me going out, but that we couldn't be seen out together as a couple. "Just how local is this bar?" I asked Canyon. "Is it off the beaten track?"

Canyon laughed. "Put it this way, Hals. I can't imagine any of your fancy show jumping peers drinking there tonight. It's the type of place you only know because you've lived among the locals for a while."

I met Jasper's eyes again. We could maybe be a little more relaxed there. Hide a little in plain sight. "That sounds perfect." I turned to my trainer. "Leon? Is that okay? We won't go if you're really against it. The competition comes first."

Leon was silent, debating this out in his head. But then Jasper put his hand on Leon's shoulder, and said, "Let them go, mate. They deserve a night off." My heart fluttered. "And we'll tag along, keep an eye out that they don't party too hard." Jasper threw me a covert wink, and I wanted to reach across and kiss him. I managed to hold myself back as Sage began to whoop.

Canyon looked to Leon, Atticus, and Jasper. "Y'all got casual clothes, or don't they exist in your world?" He pointed at their breeches, shiny boots, and Jasper's designer shirt and slacks.

I couldn't hold back my giggle. "We'll scrub up well, don't you worry," Atticus said, still eyeing Canyon. I probably should tell him that there was absolutely nothing between Canyon and Sage. Canyon was too sweet and introverted for someone like her. She'd eat him alive.

"And you?" Canyon said to me, pulling on my show jacket's collar. "You got anything but your fancy riding clothes with you?"

I leaned into my best friend. "Canny, if you think I go *anywhere* without my old Ariat boots, jeans, and hat, you don't know me at *all*."

"It's all she wears outside of competitions," Jasper said, the heat in his eyes making me melt.

"Just as I thought," Canyon said, then put the bar's whereabouts into Jasper's phone, with the plan to meet in a couple of hours.

Once back at the hotel, I showered and changed, smiling at my reflection in the mirror. I wore my perfectly worn blue jeans that fit me to perfection, a blue plaid shirt that I tied at my waist to show an inch of skin, and my brown Ariat cowboy boots that were so broken in they felt like slippers.

Going to the hat box I took everywhere, I opened it up and gently removed my Stetson from its protective lining. My heart ached at the worn edges and scratches that had been there for years. I brought it to my nose and inhaled.

I could still smell him—smoke, leather oil, and horse.

A lump clogged my throat, and I closed my eyes. *"Wake up, Hallie-girl. Canyon's at the door with his daddy. We got some cattle to move on before breakfast." I groaned, cracking open an eye to see the sun only just rising outside my bedroom window. Daddy knocked again, then opened my door. He had a steaming mug of black coffee in his right hand, another mug in the other, and a smile on his face.*

"I don't wanna get up," I said, pushing my face into my pillow.

Daddy sat on the side of my bed and set one cup down on my nightstand. The sweet scent of hot chocolate drifted into my nose. Daddy took off his hat and placed it on my head. "Come on, cowgirl. We gotta move."

The memory was both a blade and a balm to my heart. "I miss you, Daddy," I whispered to the heavens, then put his hat on my head. Moving to the mirror, I swiped red lipstick on my lips and was ready to go.

I left my room just as Sage was leaving hers. Sage winked at me and tipped her hat. She was in double denim, her jeans skintight to her long legs, a snug denim vest with nothing underneath, and a leather cowboy hat on her head.

"Hottie Hallie is out tonight!" she said and kissed me on my cheek.

"Same to you, Sexy Sage." My best friend laughed, then linked my arm with hers. We stepped onto the elevator, and I cast a glance at Jasper's room. We'd agreed to meet in the hotel lobby to avoid suspicion.

As we stood against the elevator's back wall, our reflections stared back at us from the polished doors. "Ever feel like we live in cosplay most days?" Sage asked. She pointed to her outfit. "This is us. Plaid and denim and cowboy boots. Yet we've both found ourselves in breeches, show shirts, and thousand-dollar riding boots." She laughed. "We were raised in dust and dirt, and now we're all fancy arenas and horses that cost more than most people's homes."

I got what she meant. "We wouldn't change it for the world, though, right?"

Sage shook her head. "You know I wouldn't." She stepped forward and turned to face me with her hand on her hip. "But I have to say, it's nice to be reminded how fucking hot I look in this getup."

Sage Miller, everybody, my humble best friend.

The doors opened, and I linked Sage's arm, pulling her from the elevator. "Come on, hot stuff. We have food trucks and a bar to get to."

There had been low-level chatting from near the elevator when we exited, but sudden quietness made me glance up. Atticus, Leon, and

Jasper were all staring at us. "Um . . . hi," I said, feeling a blush burst on my cheeks.

Atticus was looking at Sage with blatant hunger in his eyes. Sage ignored him like he wasn't being obvious in lusting for her.

Leon was smirking at Atticus, covering his amusement with his hand. And then I looked to Jasper. If any of our competitors were to see the way he was staring at me now, pure lust in his midnight gaze, people would instantly know there was something between us.

"You boys like?" Sage asked, twirling around.

"The car's here," Atticus said, abruptly turning around. Sage's expression shuttered a little, and she followed him out, a little less pep in her step. Leon nodded at me and went next. Jasper stepped beside me, not too close, and said, "When I fuck you tonight, you'll be wearing nothing but those boots and hat, got it?"

Heat built between my legs. "Yes, sir," I said, and Jasper gestured for me to get in the car first. I made a show of that too, making sure Jasper got a good view of my ass. If his strained breathing was an indication, I'd say I'd been successful.

"What's he doing here, I wonder?" Atticus said when we were all in the car. I looked out the window to see Jake McGowen walking into reception, looking around him as if he didn't want to be seen.

I immediately turned to Jasper, whose eyes were locked on his rival. They narrowed when he shook hands with a man I didn't know. Clearly Jasper did, as he said, "Danny McGuire?"

"Who's he?" I asked.

Leon was staring at them in interest too. "Irish horse dealer, but of the dodgy kind. Even served time. He has his hands in everything—gambling rings, match fixing, you name it."

"What did he serve time for?" Sage asked.

"Attacking rival stud farms," Jasper said, and he quickly took out his cell and texted someone. His private investigator, I supposed.

"The security are at the stables with the horses. I checked in with them not long ago," Leon said, his suspicious eyes following McGowen's and McGuire's retreating backs.

"Since when are they in bed together?" Atticus asked to no one in particular.

"He was close friends with Jake's father." Jasper breathed deeply. "I'd have thought Jake would have cut all ties after McGowen senior was sent to prison."

"Asshole," Sage said. "What was his father thinking? Why would anyone want to hurt a horse? Especially if it's your business."

"Money," Atticus, Jasper, and Leon all said at the same time.

I sighed, feeling a little antsy. We were the only riders staying at this hotel, aside from some of Team France. And to my horror, Camille Dubois was on the third floor. I didn't dislike people often, but just knowing she'd been with Jasper killed me.

"The fucker is pissed off," Atticus said from the back of the car. I smiled at all the men in our little gang wearing plaid shirts and jeans. Their polished brogue shoes weren't exactly on theme, but it warmed my heart that they'd tried.

Jasper looked hot, of course. He always did. None more so than when he had nothing on at all.

"Why's he pissed?" Sage asked.

"Because we're fucking crushing it!" Atticus said, his usual cheeky persona back in place. "Arsehole thought he only had me to go against this year, then two American cowgirls rocked onto the scene and started kicking his arse and stealing all the prize money."

I couldn't help but laugh, and I caught Sage smothering her (reluctant) laugh too.

"Look," Leon suddenly said. We looked to the entrance of the hotel, and Jake and Danny McGuire were there again. Danny was smoking a cigarette, but that's not what got Leon's attention. Alexis Hobbs and Camille Dubois walked up to join the men. Jasper had gone rigid. He lifted his phone and took a picture of them together.

We watched them for several minutes, until they walked into the hotel together and entered one of the restaurants.

"Nothing good will come from those four sharing company," Atticus said.

"Are you worried?" I asked Jasper.

He tipped his head to the side in thought. "More like concerned. They might be just meeting up for a meal, but I want this documented just in case."

"Have Phillip watch for them," Leon said. "Tell security to be extra vigilant too." The car behind us was filled with security. Jasper had decided to assign us all a personal guard. They kept their distance, but they were always watching. Jasper had assured me they had signed NDAs. If they caught or suspected anything between me and Jasper, at least it wouldn't be the end of the world.

Jasper signaled to the driver to go, and we made our way to the bar deep in Mexico City. I'd been to Mexico a few times as a child. Daddy would buy cattle here sometimes, and we caught the odd rodeo down this way too. Even as a kid, Canyon had a magical connection with horses. He would enter all the competitions where cowboys raced to be the fastest to back an unbroken horse. Canyon used to clean up there. It was how he began helping others with troubled horses. Fast-forward a decade later, and he was so sought after, he spent much of his time traveling around the US and South America, helping people who had unruly horses or worse, had been traumatized in accidents. His wait list was a mile long.

As if reading my mind, Leon said, "Jasper told me about Canyon, Hallie." I turned to face my trainer. The movement made my thigh press against Jasper's. The others were unable to see when he placed his hand on my leg and left it there. Shivers broke out along my spine. Hell, even just holding my leg elicited an erotic response.

"Yeah, he's incredible," I said, forcing myself to speak when Leon looked at me expectantly. "We grew up together. He's a year older than me, but his daddy was my daddy's right-hand man on the ranch I grew up on." I saw sympathy flash in Leon's eyes. He knew my whole story, of course. "When my daddy passed, Canyon's daddy took over the ranch. Canyon helps too when he can, but he's more in demand than ever." I shook my head. "He hates the fame he's acquiring in the horse world and the press that he's been reluctantly getting, but hell, seeing him work with damaged horses is awe inspiring."

Leon and Jasper shared a long look. "What?" I asked.

"We were wondering, if he had time, if he would maybe look at Dahlia?" Jasper said.

I exhaled quickly. "How did I never think of that?" But then my heart sank. "Only, Canyon barely leaves the Americas. He's only just started taking on work in South America." Disappointment swirled in my gut. "He's a rancher through and through. Doesn't like to leave his home for long. His parents are getting on and struggle to run the ranch without him. Plus, the amount of work he gets here is more than he can handle anyway."

Jasper's hope fell if the dropping of his shoulders was any indication. "Nice thought, though," he said, but then left it at that.

I glanced at Leon. "We'll figure something out. I'll speak to Canyon. He might know someone closer to home who could help us." I thought of Genny and Lady Dahlia, and my heart sank. I could see the pain on Jasper's, Atticus's, and Leon's faces as another prayer for Genny and Dahlia's recovery was shattered.

"I know Canyon, he'll help in any way he can," I said, knowing it was true. Canyon would be able to recommend someone. I was sure of it.

The car came to a stop, and suddenly the door was being opened. "Howdy, folks," Canyon said, playfully putting on his thickest country-bumpkin accent. He took my hand and led me out of the car. I gave him a hug, and he whispered, "Nice to see you in real clothes again, Hals."

Everyone else got out, and I followed Jasper's gaze as he took in the sight before us. Music was playing, the night was balmy warm, and local ranchers wearing cowboy hats milled around, eating the most delicious food from the food trucks that made a *u* shape, with benches for dining in the center.

"Move aside, boys," Sage said. "There's some tacos al pastor with my name on them and a Mexican Coke bottle I'm about to wrap my expert lips around." Sage made her way to the taco truck, causing a wave of men to follow her pendulum hips as she did. When I flicked a glance to Atticus, he was smirking at her antics. They were the definition of cat and mouse.

"Fajitas, Hals?" Canyon asked.

"You know me so well," I said. Jasper and Leon followed Sage to the taco truck, and Atticus beelined for the burritos. In seconds, he had two beautiful Mexican women laughing at whatever he said. I swear, the English accent was an aphrodisiac to most people.

Jasper and Leon talked, heads together, with Jasper looking up and checking on me every two minutes. I bit my lip to stop smiling when the hunger in his gaze made my nipples hard.

"Hallie Oakley," Canyon said, as we waited for our fajitas. "You and the bossman, huh?"

"Wh-what?" I stuttered.

Canyon laughed, so loud it drew people's attention. I slammed my hand over his mouth. "Hallie, I never knew you had it in you!" he teased, throwing my hand away. Canyon accepted our plates and put them down on the table nearest to us. Everyone else was still waiting on their food, or in the case of Sage and Atticus, flirting with their many admirers.

"*Ssh,* no one can know," I said, and Canyon shook his head. "What?"

"Just fate, I guess, or something like it."

"What do you mean?" I asked. I groaned as I took a bite of my fajita and a myriad of flavors burst onto my tongue. I held it up to him. "Okay, ten points to you for bringing us here."

Canyon tipped his hat to me, smirking. But then leaned forward. "What I meant," he said, "is that it's funny how you're madly in love with the man who inspired you to ride all those years ago." His voice dropped. "And by the look of it, he's crazy about you too."

"I'm not madly in lo . . ." I went to say, but something inside of me stopped me from saying those words. Madly in love. *Was I?* My heart kicked into a sprint.

Canyon laid his hand on my arm, pulling me from my panic. "It's a good thing, Hals. After everything you've been through, you deserve someone to love, who clearly loves you in return."

I turned; Jasper was taking his food off the vendor, and Canyon's words rang true. Fucking hell. I was head over heels in love with Jasper Knighton.

My heart melted. "He deserves it too," I said, and turned back to my friend. "His family has had a run of bad luck of late. Really bad luck." I told Canyon about Jasper's father, Lady Dahlia, and Genny's accident.

"Shit, that's awful," he said, and sat back. "I know someone in Denmark who travels to the UK. He trained with me back in Texas, and he's really good at what he does. I could give him a call and see if he could help?"

Leaning over, I kissed Canyon's cheek. "You're a star." I sat back down, just in time for everyone else to come and join us. Sage sat on my left and Jasper sat beside me to my right. He pressed his thigh against me, and I leaned into him, drinking in his comforting warmth.

My pulse still raced. I *loved* this man. I truly did.

"So Canyon, what are you doing here?" Leon asked. It was the most animated I'd ever seen Leon. But horses were his entire life, just like they were Canyon's, so I wasn't surprised they would get along.

"Barrel racer coming back from a rodeo was in a car accident. She lost an arm. The horse broke a leg but had surgery and was saved. Though now that the leg is better, she's permanently scared. Can't be ridden, can't be touched, can't even hear the sound of an engine without freaking out so hard she needs sedating." His expression grew sad. "But we're making progress. It's gonna take a long dang time, but we're getting there."

"How do you even go about starting that career?" Jasper said.

Canyon thought about it. "I suppose this is where the term horse whisperer comes from," he said, "because I can't really explain it. I just spend time with the horse and learn to read them, to speak to them, and they reveal their trauma. It's a language, I suppose. One that I'm lucky enough to comprehend. It's in the way they move or react, their personalities shine through . . ." He shrugged, like his talent wasn't incredible. "Once I understand them, I can start the healing. It's always a slow progress, and sometimes there's a limit to how much we can do. But horses are worth trying for, right? They help us, care for us unconditionally, so it's only right that when they need help, we be at their service."

"I couldn't agree more," Jasper said, tapping his Coke bottle to Canyon's.

"Amen," Leon echoed.

Seeing Jasper and Leon bonding with Canyon gave something to my soul I didn't know I needed. This was my old and new life colliding, and to me, it was beautiful.

"Canyon is all about natural horsemanship. He rides with a bitless bridle," I said, and immediately felt the rush of heat pass through my veins at the memory of a rubber bit clenched in my own teeth.

Jasper must have been thinking of it too, as he discreetly placed his hand on my thigh, then slowly crawled his fingers inward until they pressed against my clit, beginning maddening circular motions.

What was he thinking?

"Are we ready to dance?" I said, jolting to my feet before Jasper made me come right there at the table. Jasper hid his smirk with a napkin, and Canyon got to his feet too.

"Let's show these Brits how it's done on this side of the pond," Canyon said, and I followed him to the building next door. Night had fallen and the string lights around the food trucks looked like fireflies dancing in the night sky. The sound of country music quickly lured us downstairs.

As soon as we entered, the feel of sawdust under my feet and peanut shells discarded on the floor soothed my soul. Luke Combs and Lainey Wilson blasted from the speakers, and Canyon held out his hand. "Miss Hallie, may I have this dance?"

"You may," I said, and let him lead me to the dance floor. It was packed, but we found a clearing with enough room for Canyon to spin me. I laughed as he threw me around the room.

"Don't look now, but your man can't take his eyes off you," Canyon said a few minutes later, and I looked over my shoulder to see Jasper holding a beer, leaning against a nearby wall with Leon. Leon was animatedly talking into Jasper's ear, but Jasper's eyes were locked on me. He scraped his teeth along his bottom lip. It was heady, the power that I had in this moment. Jasper was dominant, and I was happy to be submissive to him in bed. I *lived* for those moments. But right here, right now, the way he was watching me, his empty hand balling at his side as he fought the need to hold me . . . It was addictive.

"Let's tip him over the edge, hey?" Canyon said, as Willie Nelson played next and the tempo increased. As Canyon spun me around the dance floor, he said, "I think it's working." I looked behind me to see Jasper handing his beer bottle to a confused Leon and heading toward me.

He wasn't . . .

He couldn't be . . .

"She's all yours," Canyon said to Jasper, and gave him my hand.

"What about you?" I said to Canyon.

A woman placed her hand on his shoulder, pulling him her way. "You're practically my sister, Hals, so I won't go into it, but . . . I do okay."

I laughed as he was dragged into the center of the dance floor by a dark-haired beauty and he spun her like he'd just spun me.

When I turned to Jasper, he placed his hand around my waist. "Jasper," I said, and checked around us. Leon smirked at us and shook his head. There was nothing but amusement on his face. Atticus too, if his wink at me from across the dance floor was any indication. Turning back to Jasper, I said, "We can't, someone might see."

"My security team have checked and we weren't followed. No one here knows us. We're safe."

I looked to our friends again. They were completely unbothered by our closeness. "I feel like the team may be onto our secret relationship."

"Good," he said, without looking around. "Then I don't have to hold back in doing this." Before I even knew what was coming, Jasper pushed me into a dark corner of the room and crushed his mouth to mine. Safely out of sight, I moaned, gripping onto his muscled biceps before melting into his embrace. People on the dance floor spun around, the music pounding out a fast beat, but we stood suspended in time, still, and falling into one another's arms—our own pocket of peace in the chaos.

Jasper eventually broke away, and I wrapped my arms around his neck. "Are you here to two-step with me?" I asked dubiously.

"I have no fucking clue how to do that, or even dance in general, so I thought I'd just hold you instead." His face shone with jealousy. "If one more of these fucking cowboys drools your way, there's a real danger that I'm going to commit murder tonight." I threw my head back, laughing. Lifting my hat from my head, I placed it on his.

I stepped back and looked my fill. Jasper Knighton in a cowboy hat should be illegal. "Fuck," I said, and I squeezed my legs together when heat built between them. Then my gaze softened. "This was my daddy's hat," I said, and even over the music, I knew Jasper heard the bittersweet tone of my voice. Jasper lifted the hat off his head and placed it back on my own.

"Then it belongs on his little girl's head." Jasper kissed me again. In fact, he kissed me so much that I was ready to leave the bar and go back to the hotel so I could bend over and get fucked in just my hat and boots. I must have groaned out loud at the visual, because Jasper kissed along my cheek, whispering into my ear, "I'll fuck you here and now in front of all these people if you don't stop."

"Okay," I said, and Jasper's nostrils flared with need. He squeezed my ass, hard.

"You're a fucking siren," he said, then added, "Dance with your friend, Hallie. You only have tonight with him." Jasper looked across to Leon, who tapped his watch, like the strict coach he was. "Or about an hour before your keeper makes you go home." With one last kiss, he left me on the dance floor, where Canyon found me and danced with me again. Then Atticus cut in and gave two-stepping a go. For a complete novice, he wasn't too shabby. Canyon claimed the final few dances.

When Leon approached us, my skin was damp with sweat, but I was bursting with happiness. "I hate to be the bearer of bed news," Leon said, leaving it there.

"No, you fucking don't, you sadist," Atticus said to Leon.

Leon shrugged. "You're right. I don't. But it's time to leave."

My shoulders sagged in disappointment, but I'd been grateful for this time with my oldest friend tonight. Plus, when I found Jasper near the exit, his blown pupils told me what lay ahead of me back at the hotel.

As we emerged into the balmy night air, I turned to Canyon. Wrapping my arms around him, I said, "I miss you, Canny. Thank you for coming to see me."

"You're doing it, Hallie-girl," he said, pride thick in his voice. "You're really fucking doing it." He pulled back and with a choked voice said, "Your daddy would be so proud."

"Yeah?" I rasped.

"Yeah." He kissed me on my cheek and said, "Come to the ranch soon, okay? Your house is waiting for you. I keep on top of maintaining it."

"Thank you," I said to him.

"My mama and daddy want to see you real bad too, Hals. Make time for a visit when you get a break from being a jumping superstar."

I laughed a watery laugh. "I will."

Reluctantly, I let Canyon go, and he shook hands with the men and gave Sage a hug too. Turning to Jasper and Leon, Canyon said,

"Hallie told me about your sister. I'm truly sorry I can't come myself; I'm completely booked out for the next year and can't be too far from the ranch back home. But I know a guy based in Denmark. I'll speak to him about coming out to help y'all."

The relief and appreciation that took over Jasper's body made me breathless. "Thank you," Jasper said, and he shook Canyon's hand again. "I really mean that."

"You ever want a job in the UK, you know who to call," Leon said to Canyon.

My friend laughed. "Kind of like coffee over tea," Canyon said, "but I appreciate the offer." With a final kiss on my cheek, Canyon waved his hand. "'Night all. See you soon, Hals. Best of luck on the rest of the tour."

I watched my oldest friend walk into his hotel and immediately missed him. A hand suddenly splayed across my lower back. "We'll arrange some time off for you to visit him in Texas." I looked up at Jasper and saw the sincerity in his gaze.

"Thank you," I said, but when our eyes lingered on one another, my melancholy quickly faded and pure need took its place.

The ride back to the hotel was torture. Sage fell asleep and was therefore a moody demon on the ride up to our floor. Atticus was his usual happy self. Leon fought yawns, and I had to laugh at how this type A trainer had let his hair down for a night just so we could have a bit of fun.

Personally, I couldn't look at Jasper. The tension pulsing between us was almost overwhelming. The minute we made it to the floor, everyone went to their rooms. Will, Jasper's security guard, nodded at us as we passed, before sweeping the floor for any signs of danger.

I discreetly passed Jasper my key card. "I'll be no more than three minutes, Angel. I need in your cunt so badly I can't take it." He squeezed my ass. "Be ready for me."

I choked on a breath, but then let myself into my suite and immediately stripped, putting my boots and hat back on once I was naked and taking myself to the chest of drawers on the side of the room. I leaned over the top until the polished wood scraped against my nipples.

I spread my legs, my pussy dripping wet from all the teasing tonight . . . and I waited. The minute I heard my door open, my clit throbbed in tandem with my racing heart. I knew the minute Jasper saw me splayed out for him—the groan that left his mouth was illicit.

The sound of Jasper's zip sliding down and his shirt hitting the floor was like thunder in the silence of the room. I felt him approach, only turning my head last minute and looking back at him under the brim of my hat. Jasper's expression was hungry, and when I widened my legs some more, I screamed out loud as he slammed inside of me, the motion causing the drawers to bang against the wall.

Jasper leaned over my back, blanketing me with his cut torso when he filled me and said, "I'm going to fucking ruin you, Angel."

Ruin me he did . . . four times.

And the hat and boots never came off.

Chapter Seventeen

Hallie

Madrid, Spain
One month later

"Girls' night!" Sage hollered the minute I opened the hotel door.

I whooped when I saw she was holding a bottle of champagne. "Come in!" I said, and Sage stepped forward but slapped her hand over her eyes. "What the hell are you doing?" I asked in confusion when she smacked her shoulder on the doorframe.

I shut the door as she said, "Just making sure I wasn't walking into a sexfest and a naked boss in your bed." Sage lowered her hand. "Actually, on second thought . . ."

I pushed Sage and then dragged her into the living area of the hotel suite. As always, Knighton had put us up in the most insane five-star hotel. At this rate, I'd never be able to stay in normal accommodations again.

"You're such an idiot," I said, and Sage waggled her eyebrows.

"Mr. Bite-on-This-Bit not back yet?" she asked.

I held back my laugh. Sage just loved the details of our first night in the trailer. "No, he gets here later tonight," I said. Jasper had been back at Golden Oaks for five days now. He'd had meetings and returned home to check on things. We could have gone too, as we had a few days before the next competition, but Sage and I had decided to come to Spain early and have some downtime relaxing in the sun. Leon was here looking at some horses, and Atticus was around too, though we hadn't seen much of him.

Sage bopped my nose. "You've caught the sun, Hals," she said. "Your freckles have popped out on your nose and cheeks." Today, we had lain in the sun by the hotel pool for hours. After the nonstop craziness of the tour, it felt heavenly. Next up was a night on the town.

Sage popped the champagne and I grabbed two glasses. She filled them to the top. "To kicking the rest of this tour's ass!" Sage said, and I burst out laughing.

"Sage! Shut up! You'll jinx us!"

"Fuck off! No, I won't, we've got this." She clinked my glass with hers. Shaking my head, I drank too. Sage pulled out her phone and checked her email. "Your lover boy came through for us and booked a VIP table at the best club in town." Sage winked. "It's freakin' great having friends in high places."

"It is . . ." I said, cautiously, waiting for whatever joke she would add next.

"And certain *low* places," she added, licking her lips salaciously.

"There it is," I said dryly. Sage sat on the bed and laughed, finishing her champagne in one go.

"You might wanna go easy on that, lady," I said as Sage poured herself another.

Her hand froze and she stopped her pour. "Who are you and what have you done with my best friend?"

I shook my head. "I have no idea," I said, in disbelief that I would ever say such a thing, and held out my glass. "I think I've been spending too much time around Leon."

"There's no trainer here tonight, Hals. We're free! And we have two whole days to recover from our hangovers. We're golden," Sage said, and we sank the bottle in ten minutes.

When the front desk called to tell us our car had arrived, I wobbled getting to my feet. "Whoa," I said as I steadied myself on the coffee table, and Sage laughed at me like I was a world-class comedian. We were in that glorious place between being absolutely trashed and sober, and thinking about my life—my career, doing it alongside my best friend and, of course, Jasper—everything felt pretty damn perfect.

I stumbled to the mirror and smoothed my hand down my black-halter-top mini dress and my black cowboy boots with the pink accents.

"You look fucking *hot*!" Sage said and smacked my ass. She was dressed in a strapless bright-red jumpsuit that made her blond hair look impossibly bright. Besides fancy dinners, I couldn't remember the last time we had dressed this way. Horse girls got used to grass stains on our riding gear and mud on our faces.

"You look awesome too," I said, and grabbing our purses, Sage linked arms with me as we jumped on the elevator. We stumbled through the foyer, and the doorman helped us into the back seat of our car.

As soon as the car pulled away, a text lit up my phone.

JASPER: On flight now. Will be there soon. Get that pussy ready. I have a pair of handcuffs with your name on them.

"Fucking hell," Sage said, and I looked up from my phone to see her reading the message.

"Nosy much!" I said, and pulled my phone away while trying to stop my body from igniting in flames at just the thought of Jasper tying me up. It was something we did often, and I had zero complaints.

Sage fanned herself with her hand. "Hallie, what kind of freak have you unleashed in Mr. Prim and Proper, and how do I find a clone?"

I laughed, and Sage busied herself with grabbing another bottle of champagne that had been provided for us by the car company. As she poured our glasses, I replied to the text.

ME: I'll be ready and waiting.

I posed for a selfie, making sure it was a full body shot showing my short dress and boots, and fired it off. Only seconds later, Jasper texted back.

JASPER: Angel . . . fuck . . . you look incredible.

I smiled when he added:

JASPER: It's a good job I'm not out with you tonight. I would murder anyone that even turned their head your way.

ME: That shouldn't make me hot, but my nipples just got hard.

JASPER: Stop, or I'll be hiding my hard-on from the flight crew.

I clenched my thighs together and fought back a moan.

JASPER: Have a good night and behave. I'll be waiting for you later.

"You done?" Sage asked, and thrust a glass of champagne under my nose.

I flopped back on the seat behind me. "That man has me under his thumb."

"And frequently wrapped around his dick, if the moans coming from your suites are any indication."

Panic suddenly rushed through me. I snapped my head to Sage. She burst out laughing. "I'm joking!" she said and cackled some more. "I swear, I haven't heard a thing." She shrugged. "When you told me y'all's relationship was staying a secret, I didn't believe y'all could do it. But it seems you have." Sage clinked her glass with mine. "Kudos."

I smiled, but my heart stuttered a beat in disappointment. Nothing had changed for us, but the letters were still coming for Jasper. Thankfully, there'd been no new incidents of late; the amount Jasper was spending on security must have been eye watering.

No one had found anything out about us, which was good. But sometimes, in my dreams for the future, I wish we were able to be open. The number of times I'd had to still my hand as I went to push his hair from his face or simply kiss him before I jumped in a competition.

But I'd rather have Jasper this way than not at all.

"Hals, we're here." Sage's voice broke me from my melancholy, and I looked outside to see a massive club with a line of people waiting to get in. It wrapped around the block. Thank God for VIP tickets.

Sage took my hand when we exited the car, and she showed the email to the doorman. Our security followed behind us, but far enough away to not be our shadows.

Electronic dance music slammed into our ears as soon as we walked down the hall that led to the VIP section. The minute we arrived in the lounge, we were assigned a table and bottles of every liquor imaginable were laid out for us, along with every kind of mixer and, of course, champagne.

My eyes brightened when they landed on my favorite tequila. "LALO!" I shouted over the heavy rhythmic beat and poured a shot for me and Sage.

"You can take the girl outta Texas . . ." she said and winked as we picked up a lime segment each and sprinkled salt on our hands.

"To handcuffs!" Sage toasted and I stopped myself from smacking her.

I rolled my eyes and knocked back the tequila. I closed my eyes, allowing myself to remember all things Texas. Until Sage grabbed my hand and said, "Dance floor, now! This girl needs her pussy pounded, and I'm done with DIY."

"I did not need that visual, Sage," I said, rolling my eyes.

"Says the cowgirl who's saddle sore from too much cock," she retorted. I swear, I was going to wire her jaw shut. But I couldn't disagree with what she was saying. Jasper was insatiable. Again, no complaints from my corner.

"Ladies," a voice interrupted. Atticus stood before us, dressed in his signature all-black. His dark hair was stylishly tousled, and I wondered whether God had sent the Knighton men to womankind as an apology for the many douchebags they had to endure daily.

I went to say hello when I caught his smirk. Great. He'd heard my loudmouth friend. "Zinc oxide is good for saddle sores, Hals. I'm sure I know someone who could rub it on for you." Atticus checked his watch. "I think he lands in an hour." Then the bastard winked.

"Thanks for the advice, Atticus," I said dryly.

He nodded, then his attention dropped to Sage. She was looking at the dance floor over his shoulder. She'd gone from arguing with him at the drop of a hat to seeming completely indifferent to his presence. Anything Atticus said that once would have triggered Sage's usual fire now just slid off her like Teflon. He was good at hiding his disappointment, but the slight sagging of his shoulders and his fake happy-go-lucky grin were a dead giveaway.

Sage pulled on my arm. "We're going to dance," I said. "You coming?" I flinched when Sage dug her nails into my hand.

"No, but thank you," he said, and pushed past us to the lounge. Sage watched him go from the corner of her eye but then dragged me through the crowd until we reached the center of the dance floor. Green laser lights flickered over the massive room and a crowd of bodies moved around us to the beat. I smiled and let the alcohol and music carry me away. Lost to the freedom, I felt like I didn't open my eyes until Sage's mouth met my ear. "I need a drink!"

I looked around. The dance floor was crammed, and a bead of sweat ran down my face. We'd been dancing awhile, if the increase in capacity was any indication.

Sage held my hand and pulled us across the dance floor until we arrived back at our VIP table. She glanced over at the bar and froze. When I followed her gaze, I saw Atticus talking to a striking Spanish woman in a gold dress. The woman said something to Atticus, and he put his arm around her waist, then left through the back of the club.

Acting like she hadn't seen anything, Sage grabbed a new bottle of champagne and quickly poured us each a glass. "Sage?" I said, checking she was okay, when people sat down at our table.

I looked up in confusion, only for annoyance to fill my veins at the sight of Alexis Hobbs, Camille Dubois, and Jake McGowen. Sage stilled and narrowed her eyes at them. As much as Jasper and others had warned us against them, they hadn't had much to do with us. A few snide comments here and there when in the practice ring, but we never socialized anywhere they did, so we'd managed to avoid them.

Up until now.

"Ladies," Jake said, nodding his head. Jake was Switzerland to me. Jasper hated him; they had history. But he'd only ever been kind to me and Sage. His choice in friends, however, left a lot to be desired.

"Jake," I said.

Sage was less amiable. She scowled at them all, showing exactly what she thought of them joining us.

"Hallie, Sage," Alexis said, her posh English accent grating on my last nerve. I adored most British accents, but for some reason, I hated hers. "Fancy seeing you here."

Camille looked anywhere but at us. She almost seemed bored by our presence.

"Alexis," I said in return. Sage still said nothing. Alexis didn't seem to care and made herself a gin and tonic from the drinks laid out at our table.

"Say," Alexis said, sipping her drink and relaxing back on her seat, "Did you all hear that Devon Smith was caught fucking his eighteen-year-old groom? Too bad his wife turned up to surprise him in Shanghai."

Jake shook his head. "Devon has been cheating on that woman with anything that moves for years. That's not exactly groundbreaking."

Alexis raised her eyebrow at Jake. Leaning forward, she said, "I guess." She paused, then said, "How about Gemma Montgomery from Canada sucking Roger Sykes's cock under his desk just so she didn't lose her place on his team?" I hid my shock at that. If that was true, it was awful. Gemma Montgomery had just turned twenty years old. Roger Sykes owned a stud farm in Montana, a really good one, and was at least three times her age. And married with kids.

Jake ran his hand down his face as though he was tired of this type of conversation. Camille was now playing on her phone, completely checked out. I couldn't help but admire her beauty, but it made me sick to think that Jasper had been with her.

"Actually," Alexis said, pulling my attention again. This time her gaze slammed to mine. "It seems Montgomery isn't the only one fucking her boss to climb to the top." I stilled. The breath left my lungs, and my heart quickened to double speed. Sage leaned into me, a silent signal that she had my back.

Alexis fought a smirk, and Camille lifted her head from her phone, only to place it in front of me on the table. When I looked down, there was a grainy picture of me and Jasper walking one evening beside the Huangpu River. We weren't holding hands—Jasper had his in his pocket. But I was smiling at something he said. And the way he was looking at me . . .

Like he loved me.

In any other circumstance, I would have asked for this picture to keep. But right now, fear raced down my spine. I wanted to hit myself. I was strong, goddammit. I wasn't shy and meek, and I certainly wasn't scared of bitches like Alexis and Camille, but having my biggest secret at risk of being exposed . . . it made a statue of me.

"What?" Sage said, laughing. "You think some grainy picture of Hallie walking with Jasper one night in a public place is somehow evidence of them fucking?" Sage flicked her hand in dismissal. "Y'all need to get a life."

But Alexis never moved her eyes off me. This woman had a reputation for being a tyrant in the industry, and she'd clearly set her sights on me as her next target.

Finding my voice, I said, "We were discussing the course, Alexis," keeping the wavering out of my voice. "Nothing more. There's no juicy story for you here."

"Now kindly, or not so kindly, fuck off from our table," Sage added, pasting a sugary-sweet smile on her pretty face.

"This might be the only picture there is, but people have been talking," Alexis said.

"Alexis," Jake warned. She ignored him.

"Jasper's sudden appearance at this year's tour when he'd made it clear he was staying away." I kept my face neutral. "The way he comes to see you before you jump." Then Alexis smiled. "And the fact that he sneaks into your room most nights, not coming out until morning."

Blood rushed through my head, creating deafening white noise in my ears. I opened my mouth, but nothing came out. Alexis wasn't done. "The riders we have spoken to have made it perfectly clear that if it wasn't for your Knighton sponsored horse, you wouldn't have even made it to a five-star event, never mind a tour."

"But you're pretty, exotic even," Camille said, her French accent wrapping around the vowels. "And Jasper Knighton has a weakness for pretty, exotic things." She shrugged nonchalantly. "I should know. I was that for him too once."

"Hallie is one of the best riders in the world and you bitches are just jealous," Sage said.

I wanted to scream, I wanted to tell them to eat shit and die, but their words had paralyzed me. I never thought it would bother me if people thought I got to where I was in any way but through talent, but right now, it felt like they'd burrowed into my soul and put my biggest insecurity on display for everyone to judge.

I said nothing, but Sage jumped to her feet. She held the bottle of champagne. I saw our security guards begin to approach. "Get the fuck out before I smash this over your butt-ugly faces."

Jake jumped to his feet. "Alexis, Camille, let's go. You've done your damage." Jake walked toward the exit without looking back. How had he just sat there like that and let them say this shit?

Sage stepped forward, and I honestly believed she was going to strike them with the glass bottle in her hands. As the guards reached the table, Alexis waved them off like they were nothing. She got to her feet, as did Camille, and smoothed her dress down like she hadn't sat at our table just to shred me—and I think threaten me too.

"He'll tire of you soon enough," Camille said. "He always does. You're not the first pretty face that's caught his eye. You certainly won't be the last. He'll cast you aside. You'll lose your sponsorship, and without a horse that can do everything for you, you'll be back at auntie's equestrian center in Florida, watching those of us with talent conquer the world while you're teaching eight-year-olds how to trot."

"I'm not with Jasper," I eventually said, some bite in my tone.

Camille smiled. "Of course you're not, Cherie." She walked away.

"See you in a few days," Alexis said, and left too. I remained seated, stunned.

Sage sat down beside me. "You okay?" she said, searching my face. Lowering her voice, she said, "They have no evidence. That picture was innocent." I nodded, but I was taking nothing in. I never thought I'd care if rumors started about me, but hearing other riders on the circuit were saying it too made me feel sick. Like every clear I had achieved so far meant nothing.

"Hallie," Sage said, sternly. "You're a fucking amazing rider. Do not let those hags make you think otherwise. They're jealous. And it's not Huxley that makes you a good rider. It's *you*."

"I know," I said, but without conviction.

In this moment, I felt like that little raggedy ranch girl again, looking at an unattainable dream I never knew I had. I had fought tooth and nail to get where I was, but now with a few rumors, all that was diminished?

I hadn't realized Sage had spoken to our guards until she came back to the table. "Our car is outside. We're going home."

I didn't argue.

As we sat in the car, Sage tried to talk to me, but I shut down. We'd been careful, right? That picture was innocent enough, like Sage had said. "She said someone has been saying he sneaks into my room at night."

Sage rolled her eyes. "She doesn't know shit. Anyone could pluck that accusation out of their ass without proof. She had nothing concrete. She's just trying to fuck with you, with our team, in any way she can."

I turned to Sage. She held my hand. "We're winning, Jasper won't sell her Golden Oaks, and she's pissed. She's trying to take us down. It's what she does. She's a bored bitch who gets her kicks being a dick to others." I nodded again, but there was still a sinking feeling in my chest.

We arrived at our hotel and took the elevator to our rooms. When we got to my door, Sage followed me inside. She wasn't leaving me alone. But when I got to the living area, and saw Jasper sat on my couch waiting, I froze.

Jasper's welcoming smile faded as I just stood there. "What's wrong?" he asked, instantly aware of my mood.

Sage spoke for me. "Alexis Hobbs, Jake McGowen, and fucking Camille Dubois."

Jasper's face clouded with thunder. "What did they do?"

Sage squeezed my upper arms. "I'll let Hallie tell you." My best friend came to stand in front of me. "You okay?" I nodded, but I could see she knew it was bullshit. "Nothing they said was true. You know this." Sage kissed me on my cheek. "Call me if you need me."

Sage left the room and shut the door behind her. Jasper was unmoving, watching me. When he made to come to me, I held out my hand to stop him. "Please," I said, embarrassed by the tears I felt building behind my eyes.

"Angel," Jasper said, panic in his tone. "What the hell did they say?"

I looked into his dark eyes. He was so fucking beautiful. "That we were fucking. That it was the talk of all the riders, and you only sponsored me because I was a pretty face—that one came from Camille."

Jasper's teeth gritted together, and his hands clenched into fists at his sides. "That's bullshit—"

"And that I'm a shit rider, and the only thing that keeps me on this tour is Huxley."

"I told you not to listen to them! They're poisonous. Everyone in the industry knows it. You told me you could handle it if they said anything to you."

He did tell me that, and I did say that too, but it didn't mean that they hadn't hit some kind of hidden nerve within me.

"They have no proof we're together," he said, inching closer. I could see he wanted to hold me, but I couldn't, not right now. I needed space. Ever since I came to England I'd been consumed by this man. This was the first time I didn't want to fall into his arms.

"They had a picture," I said.

"Of what?"

"Us walking along the river in Shanghai."

Jasper frowned. "What were we doing?" he asked.

"Talking. That's all."

"Then they don't have shit!" he said, voice raised. Jasper came closer still, and I could smell his cologne. Usually it comforted me, but not right now. "I'll protect you. I'll get more guards for you. Is that what you're worried about? Someone coming for you because of the rumors? I swear nothing will happen to you. I won't let it."

I shook my head. An attack from whoever was targeting Jasper hadn't even crossed my mind. No, it was my pride that was hurt.

"Hallie—"

"They said everyone thinks I've fucked you to get my place. And that you do this often." I met Jasper's eyes. "Do you? Will you tire of me once you've fucked me enough times and throw me aside? Will you take Huxley from me and leave me to find another sponsor?"

Jasper reared back like I'd just hit him. "Did you honestly just say that to me?" His voice was cold, and his posture became shuttered.

"I did. Camille was only too open with how easily you brushed her aside."

Jasper laughed without mirth. "I didn't give a flying fuck about Camille! It was a stupid one-night stand that I immediately regretted. You . . ." He trailed off, then lost his anger to say, "You were the game changer." Jasper shook his head, then said, "If you think all this between us has been some twisted game for me, me playing with some younger woman to get my kicks, then what the fuck, Hallie. You don't know me at all."

Jasper left my room, and I stayed standing in the same position for God knew how long. My chest squeezed, just replaying that devasted look on his face. The disappointment that I'd believed anything those two had said to me, when I'd been warned numerous times what and who they were.

Needing air, I left my room and climbed the staircase to the roof. There was a twenty-four-hour pool up there, which I was hoping at this time of night was deserted.

I opened the door and let the humid Spanish air stick to my skin. It felt like the Texas and Florida heat and made me feel like I had a little bit of home with me. Thankfully, the pool was empty, and I turned to the rail that overlooked the city of Madrid. I leaned over and closed my eyes.

What the fuck, Hallie? I thought to myself.

I felt someone beside me. I exhaled, knowing who it would be. But when I opened my eyes, it was to find Atticus. He leaned over the rail too, looking just as despondent. "Hallie," he said, smiling. But his grin didn't hold any of its usual spark. It looked kind of sad. "Fancy meeting you here."

I huffed a laugh. "I needed air."

Atticus nodded and looked out over the city. Silence stretched between us until I said, "I had a run-in with Alexis Hobbs and Camille Dubois tonight at the club. Jake McGowen was there too but didn't really get involved."

Atticus turned to me. "What did they say?" Like Jasper, fury immediately engulfed his face. It was clearly a Knighton trait.

"That I was fucking Jasper to get to the top on a Knighton horse." I relayed everything else they said too.

"They're a plague on this tour," Atticus said. "And we're all convinced that Alexis is into dodgy business, just none of us can prove it yet." Atticus narrowed his eyes at me when I didn't say anything back. "You didn't let them get to you, did you?"

"I didn't intend to," I said, but shrugged. "Apparently the thought of being accused of sleeping my way to the top was nothing to being told it in reality." I sighed. "I'm thinking I might have a little bit of impostor syndrome." I smirked. "Who knew?"

Atticus looked utterly confused. "Hallie, I say this because I mean it, you're one of the best riders I've ever worked with. And I've been doing this my entire life. We have seen the best of the best walk through Golden Oaks' gates, and you're one of the top. Easily."

The tightness in my chest began to slacken, only to be replaced by intense guilt. "Thank you," I said, and meant it. I dropped my head to my folded arms on the rail and said, "Jasper saw me when we came home, and I pushed him away."

Atticus faced me. "I'm going to say something that Jasper would most certainly kill me for. And as a younger cousin with residual trauma from the way Jasper and Forrest used to bully me as a child, that's saying something." Atticus smiled, and I could see the love for his cousin in his expression. "But Jasper . . ." Atticus thought of what to say. "He is the rock of our family, you know?" I waited for him to continue. "He's the one who has always shouldered the heaviness of our family business, our name, and reputation. He was the best rider, the best son, and the best big brother. Because as much as he's my cousin, I see him as my brother. We all do." My heart began to melt.

"We've had a lot of loss in our family." He shrugged. "Felix says it's because the universe must balance out. We have a lot in material wealth and success, so those privileges must come with bad things too." He sighed. "I don't know. But for whatever reason, we've lost too many loved ones, and the man who held us all together? Jasper. He helped raised us, cared for us, taught us to ride. If we had a problem, we had one hundred percent faith that he would fix it."

I could see that. He'd been that way for me too. "But as I've grown older and lived my own life, I've realized what that had to have cost him, you know? Who is there for Jasper when he needs help? Who is there for him when he crumbles?" Atticus tilted his head in my direction. "I've never seen him relax like he does when he's with you." My throat clogged and tears built in my eyes. "With the attacks . . . He didn't trust anyone, he fell into a dark place that none of us could pull him from. But you did," he said, and a tear tracked down my cheek. "I know he's worried he's put you in harm's way, but Hallie, you've changed his life." When more tears fell, Atticus said, "Shit, I didn't mean to make you cry."

"No," I said. "You didn't . . . I . . ." I shook my head and wiped my cheeks. "He's changed my life too."

Atticus gave me a small smile. "I know he comes off all cold and brooding, but under that hard shell is a man with a big heart who would die to protect those he loves." Atticus stared up at the sky, but said, "But he's the biggest star in this industry, and with it comes pressures that we couldn't even imagine. And people who would do anything to bring him down."

Guilt and shame shrouded me. I must have hurt him so badly. He'd warned me of what Camille and Alexis might do, and I played right into their hands—at the expense of his heart.

"Thank you," I said, and wrapped my arms around Atticus. He hugged me back, then said, "No problem."

I went to walk away, when I said, "You didn't go back to that woman's hotel, did you?" The woman he'd been with at the bar. The one Sage watched him leave with, a flicker of hurt in her eyes.

Atticus shook his head and gave me a sad smile.

"She has a big heart too," I said to Atticus. "The biggest."

He knew who I meant. His expression softened as he said, "I know . . . I know she does." Atticus turned back to look at the view, and I climbed down the stairs. Making sure the floor was clear but for our guards, I knocked on Jasper's door. When he didn't answer, my heart sank. I opened my door and walked into my suite, only to find him pacing the living room. He froze when he saw me, caution in his expression. But when I ran to him and sank into his embrace, he held me and lifted me in his arms. Carrying me to the bedroom, he stripped me of my clothes and laid me in my bed. He climbed in beside me, and I said, "I'm so sorry."

"Ssh," he soothed and kissed my hair. "Are you okay?"

I nodded. "I am now."

I breathed in his mint and sandalwood scent, and any concern I had for Alexis and Camille's gossip melted away. I felt foolish that I'd let them hurt me this way—*us* this way.

"Sleep," Jasper said, and my eyes grew heavy. "I'm going to keep you safe, Angel. I promise." As I drifted off to sleep, I thought I heard him add, "Just don't give up on me, please. Stay by my side. Because I don't know what I'd do anymore without you."

Chapter Eighteen

Jasper

Cannes, France
Two months later

"Yes!" I said under my breath and clenched my hand into a fist as I watched Hallie deliver another clear round. Today was the team event for the Knighton Cavaliers, and her clear had just catapulted them to the top. They were fucking doing it. For the past few months, our team had dominated most of the Grand Prix on the circuit—Madrid, Shanghai, Prague. And now Cannes. Yesterday saw Sage with the winning round. We were sweeping both the individual and team events with ease.

Even after Alexis, McGowen, and Camille had tried to rattle Hallie in Spain, we had stayed strong and kept dominating. The gossip mill had moved on when no more evidence of my and Hallie's relationship surfaced—and there was always another scandal waiting for the spotlight.

After a small hiccup, life was . . . hell, it was *good*. I never thought I'd be able to say that again.

I rushed from the stands and headed to the stalls to meet Hallie. Jean Pierre, the owner of one of the biggest studs in France and a close friend of mine from the circuit, met me en route.

"You fucker!" he said, but he was smiling. I laughed as he hugged me. "Can you leave some room at the podium for the rest of us?" Jean Pierre backed away, but said, "I'll be up front with you, Jasper. I'm planning on poaching Sage and Hallie from you next season."

"You can try," I said, but there wasn't even a flicker of doubt in me that it would be possible. I couldn't fucking believe it, but week by week, month by month, my life had gotten lighter. I'd mainly stayed on the circuit, doing most of my business on the road. I'd flown home several times for important meetings, to check on Henry, and to see my sister, but mostly I was here, with my woman and my team, and although I wasn't riding, I still felt it. That comradery, that buzz you got from this nomadic life.

But most all, I'd felt *peace*. Months of being with Hallie every night, seeing my team ride . . . just peace. I knew the threatening letters hadn't stopped, but Forrest had shielded me from most of the drivel they spun.

Our security was solid, and for the first time in a very *long* time, I felt like I could breathe. And dare I say . . . I felt happy. The reason for that appeared at the far end of the yard, riding back to our stables on Huxley, fresh from her victory gallop for the Knighton Cavaliers, with Sage and Atticus following behind.

A sudden crash came from the opposite end of the yard, and I turned to see what it was. I heard things being thrown around and frustrated snarls. As at all the venues, I'd organized for our stables to be separate and off limits but to those in our employ. The rest of the competitors were kept beyond a bolted gate. Curiosity won out, and I moved to the gate and looked through.

Just as I was about to turn away, Jake McGowen came from a tack room, face flushed and yanking opening the button of his collar. He was muttering expletives under his breath, and he slumped down on a bale of hay that was outside of an empty stable and put his head in his hands.

"Throwing a strop, McGowen?" I said, curtly. I fucking hated this guy. Years of him being a dickhead on the circuit could never redeem him in my eyes. And the fact that he hadn't stopped Alexis and Camille from piling on Hallie and Sage made him a complete outcast in my opinion.

His head snapped up at the sound of my voice. "Oh, fuck off, Knighton," he said, venom in his tone.

I shook my head. He was pathetic. I turned to walk away when he said, "Bet you're smug as shit, huh? Lapping up the prize money with your shiny new riders and your arsehole of a cousin." My blood turned red hot.

"Watch how you fucking talk about my riders," I said, my voice ice cold. I stepped close to the gate, having to keep my hands at my sides so I didn't throw open the lock and punch this fucker in his face.

He laughed, but there was fuck all humor in it. "Piss off, Jasper. I don't have the energy for you today." His eyes were narrowed and threatening as he looked back to me and said, "Just get back to your perfect life and your perfect fucking business and count your billions." He laughed again, and I swore to myself that if he did it one more time, I'd end the bastard. "You wouldn't know hardship if it hit you in the mouth. Fuck off back to your easy life and get out of my face."

Was this prick serious? Easy life?

No, I told myself. Let him sulk. He wasn't bloody worth it.

I should have ignored him, but I couldn't help but say, "You might want to watch yourself, Jake. This community is small. And people have seen you sneaking into hotels and meeting unsavory characters on almost every stop of the tour." I'd had it on good authority from Phillip's men that he'd met with Danny McGuire numerous times, not to mention his continued association with Alexis and Camille. The blood drained from his face. I had no idea what that group was up to, but it was stealthily doing *something*, I was sure of it. Once I found out what that was, I'd be going straight to the FEI and the authorities. If I could get them all banned, the industry would be a better bloody place.

"Wh-what? I don't know what you're talking about!" he snapped and jumped to his feet. Nice to see I had him on the ropes.

I stepped up to the gate again. "If I find out you're up to anything below board, or anything remotely like the shit your dad was doing, I'll fucking bury you so far beneath the ground you'll never step foot in this industry again."

With that, I walked away and back toward my team. Atticus, Sage, Leon, and Hallie were with their horses, having just dismounted. They waved when they saw me coming, then my phone began to vibrate in my pocket.

When Forrest's name came on the screen, I answered and said, "Another fucking double win, can you believe it?"

Forrest's usual celebratory response didn't come. Instead, he was silent, which caused me to stop in my tracks. "Forrest?" I pushed.

"You're going to need to come home, Jas. There's been an attack on the stud."

My heart crashed to the ground, and when I looked up, Hallie came rushing toward me, concern on her face. Atticus was next. "What?" he pushed. "What's happened? Who's that? Forrest? Felix?"

"Forrest," I said, and then said to Forrest, "I'll be back as soon as I can. Give me a few hours."

I hung up, and now Leon and Sage were with me. I glanced around me, making sure it was clear, but quietly said, "There's been an incident at the stud."

"No!" Hallie cried, "Fuck!" Atticus hissed, "Oh my gosh," Sage whispered, and Leon's and Atticus's faces filled with rage—I imagined I looked the same. Atticus and Leon knew of the attacks. Sage might have assumed, but she didn't know details.

"What's happened?" Leon said. "Is anyone hurt? The horses?"

"I don't know," I said, then began to head to the exit. "I must go. Forrest is going to sort things until I'm there. I . . ." It all came crashing down then—the fear, the fury, and the fucking stark truth that things hadn't settled and gone away at all. The threats were still real. The happiness I'd just been finding it impossible to have felt of late . . . It all turned to dust.

Some fucker was truly coming for me.

"I need to go," I said.

"We'll come," Atticus said.

"No!" I said. "Go to Paris. Don't give any indication to anyone outside of this team that something's wrong." I was breathing quickly, my head racing with a million thoughts.

"Jasper," Hallie said, tears filling her big turquoise eyes. It fucking destroyed me. Taking her arm, I checked the coast was clear and pulled her into a private tack room. I shut the door and crushed my mouth to hers. When I pulled back, I said, "Stay here. Carry on to Paris. I'm going to double security." I cupped her face, smoothing my thumbs down her cheeks. "I'm going to make sure you're safe, that you're protected. I promise—"

"Jasper—"

"I'll fix things, I promise, Angel—"

"Jasper—"

"You don't need to worry, you—"

"Jasper!" Hallie's raised voice cut me off. I stared down at the girl who had completely taken hold of my damaged soul and knew I didn't deserve her.

Hallie held my hand and kissed my fingers. "I'm not worried about me," she said, her accent thickening. "I'm asking about *you*. Are *you* okay, baby?"

I stared at Hallie, the woman I was pretty fucking sure I loved, and said, "No, but I have to go anyway."

"What did Forrest say?"

"He didn't elaborate," I said. "Which makes me think it's really bad." Nothing had hit the news yet, so I was glad for small mercies.

Hallie kissed me again. I wanted to go to a hotel room with her, lock the door, and bury myself in her all night and forget about what I might face back home. But . . . "I have to go, Angel."

"Call me," she said. "When you can. Or if you need me. Any time of the day or night."

A glimmer of warmth broke through the tension coiling inside of me. "I'll always need you." I kissed her again, then said, "Kick arse in Paris. Don't let this spoil your focus. You're doing too well. And I'll get back to you as soon as I can."

"Okay," she said, and I burst from the tack room and headed for the car that was waiting for me at the entrance of the stables.

"Jasper." Atticus caught up with me. "Keep me informed, yeah?"

"I will," I said, then gripping my youngest cousin's arm, said, "Keep them safe. Please." My throat thickened, and I said, "I can't fucking believe it's happening again."

Atticus wore his concern on his face for me to see. "You know I'll take care of things here." I nodded and hugged Atticus, then rushed to the car, waving at Leon, who was trying to comfort Sage and Hallie. I texted back and forth with my pilot—the only good thing about this situation was that it was less than an hour's flight to get back home. If I'd been somewhere like Shanghai, I'd have been crawling out of my skin.

When all the arrangements had been made, I stared out the window of the car, and the images of my father's "accident" came firing into my mind with the force of a million bullets. Of Genny falling, Dahlia crushing her in front of a packed crowd. Now *this*.

What or who the fuck were we facing?

One thing was for certain: Over the past few months, I'd fooled myself, believing that I could have any kind of normal life while this threat hovered over our heads. It was a fantasy, a mistake I wouldn't—couldn't—make again.

I had to find out who wanted me destroyed, once and for all. I couldn't put anyone else at risk. I couldn't put Hallie at risk. I hadn't told her, but I fucking loved that woman with everything I had left within me. She owned my soul. I had to find a way to keep her safe.

I'd do whatever it took.

I ran toward the house, seeing black smoke billowing in the air as I did. Forrest opened the door; Felix was standing behind him. "What happened?" I said, not even saying hello. Was our stud on fucking *fire*?

Forrest's expression was livid. Even the quiet and introverted Felix looked murderous. "They attacked our family barn," Forrest said.

I blanched. "The horses . . . Henry . . ."

"They're shook up," Forrest said. "But . . . they're okay." I smelled smoke again and looked toward the stables.

"Jesus . . ." I said, rubbing my forehead and saw that our private arena was in shambles. The roof had caved in and the exterior of the stables beside it were blackened by the flames.

"The police have just left," Felix said. "The fire chief is still here if you want to talk with him?"

"Yes, immediately," I said, wondering how the hell this could happen to a state-of-the-art barn.

"What have they said?" I questioned as Felix and Forrest led me in the direction of the fire chief. "Arson?"

Forrest nodded. He threw me my wax jacket. He and Felix put on their coats too, and I followed them outside, where an older man who I presumed was the fire chief was waiting.

"Mr. Knighton?" he said as I shook his hand. I nodded. "Sorry about your barn. But I was doing my assessment and wanted to flag a few things up to you."

"Of course," I said.

"We've got the inspector out here, and he was checking over the barn. You have the best fire-suppression materials, but on initial testing, it looks like someone painted on some kind of accelerant." My stomach dropped to the ground.

"What?"

The fire chief nodded. "Luckily, because your barn was so high tech, the materials underneath the accelerant slowed it enough for your horses to make it out okay."

I looked to Forrest and Felix. "It was an internal job?" They looked as furious as I felt.

"I can't verify that. Seems you have a lot of day workers and deliveries et cetera coming to the farm. It could be anyone. Or," the fire chief said, "it could be an inside job. The police will take over that investigation."

I would also be talking to every member of staff myself. If someone was working here under nefarious reasons, I'd flush them out and try my best not to kill them.

"It seems as though someone took an open flame to a concentrated area of accelerant that quickly spread. Again, the saving grace was that the alarm and sprinkler system worked, and the treated wood and insulation underneath slowed the flames enough for your staff to get the horses out before they inhaled too much smoke." The fire chief held out his hand again. "When we have the final report, we'll be in touch."

"Thank you," I said, and turned back to my cousins. "Gather all the staff, we need to vet them all. Immediately."

Forrest nodded and turned away to make a phone call to Victoria, our estate manager.

"Where are the horses?" I asked Felix.

"This way," he said.

We headed for the stables to the west of our house. "We got one of the fuckers who started it," Forrest said, catching up to us, and I stopped dead in the field we were crossing.

"One of the arsonists?" I asked.

Forrest nodded. "The police have him in custody."

"He stabbed one of our security team, but we managed to subdue him until help arrived. We're pretty sure he wasn't working alone, but there was no one else on the premises, and the twat isn't talking."

"I need to tell Phillip," I said, and pulled out my phone.

"I've already done it," Forrest said, and I exhaled. Fuck. "Here. Read this." Forrest passed me a photocopy of a new threatening letter.

It read:

If I can't get you, I will destroy what you love most: your horses.

Lord Henry and the rest of the family's pets will fall, as will your empire.

"When did this arrive?" I asked Forrest. My voice had lost its edge. What they'd done to poor Dahlia—*twice* now—was terrible, but to burn down an entire stall block with all the horses inside was on another level of evil. Thank God for the security team, the yard staff, and the fire-suppression upgrade on the barn, or they would have killed them all. I needed to make sure the injured guard and his family were well compensated for what had happened.

I rubbed my head. It was throbbing.

"It came yesterday. The police have taken all the previous letters. I shared our concerns that the last officer on our case was too dismissive. I may have also been a privileged cunt and reminded them of our social standing." Forrest hated pulling that shit, but I agreed, needs must. "I've pulled some strings for our concerns to be taken much more seriously, and let's just say that our case will now be in the hands of Scotland Yard."

"Fuck, Forrest," I said, and put my hand on his shoulder. "Thank you."

He dropped a kiss on my head. "Look what happens when you let your family help." Forrest pointed at Felix. "But it was Felix here who got us an in at Scotland Yard. We're a family, Jasper. We *all* face what comes our way. End of story."

Felix's phone rang. "It's Atticus," he said. "I said I'd call him to explain once we'd spoken to you." I nodded and Felix stepped away to catch up Atticus on everything.

"Fuck," I said, when the stables came into view. "This was a close one."

"*Too* close," Forrest said. "Whatever fuckers are coming for us . . . I want their heads to roll." Forrest blew out a long breath. "The horses were so scared, Jas. I keep thinking of what could have happened if the perpetrator hadn't been stopped. He was clearly a paid assailant, but he's keeping mum about who hired him. Someone has something over his head that's assured his silence, for sure. I gave Phillip access to his phone details before the police got here. Hopefully he'll be able to pull something from it. Though it looks like a burner, so I'm not sure how much information that'd hold."

Several security guards were patrolling the stable block. I nodded at them as we passed the barn to arrive at the field that the horses had all been turned out in temporarily. The first person I saw was Genny, who was at the nearest fence around the paddock.

"Jasper," she said, tears in her eyes. She was next to Forrest's horse, Aurelia, running calming strokes down her face. The mare leaned into Genny's touch for comfort.

I rushed to my sister and wrapped my arms around her. She was in her wheelchair, and she broke apart when I held her. "Why is all of this happening to us?" she cried. A lump built in my throat, and when I pulled back, I kissed her on the forehead.

"We'll find out who is responsible, Gen. I swear it." I felt the weight of endless threats bearing down me again. I wanted Hallie to be here so badly, but I also wanted her in Paris. I'd already doubled the security on the team. At this point, it was ridiculous—other riders must be wondering what was happening with our team, but right now, I didn't give a fuck. Safety first. Leon had confirmed the new guards had arrived, and he and Atticus had given them their orders. Every one of our traveling staff members now had a personal detail, and the stables were completely covered, day and night. From the horsebox drivers to the grooms, everyone was being protected. The security team would also be keeping a close eye on our staff in case they were ever acting suspicious. The staff didn't know that, of course, but I couldn't take any risks.

A familiar huff had me turning, and my beauty of a horse was tossing his head at the paddock's fence, trying to get my attention. Henry was restless, that much I could see, so I went to my prize stallion and put my hands on his cheeks, pressing my forehead to his. "I'm sorry, boy," I said, and felt the emotions I'd pushed down clog my throat. I stayed there for several minutes, patting his neck and checking him over. It was him they wanted, because whoever wanted to take us down, they wanted me destroyed most of all.

"They won't get near him again," Forrest said. I turned around, and Forrest, Felix, and Genny were there, watching me.

I nodded, then sat down on a bench that overlooked the paddock. Felix sat down beside me, then Forrest, and Genny pulled herself closer to us too. The mood was solemn as we watched our equine family in the field. I checked over every horse with my eyes.

"Has the vet been?" I asked. I felt exhausted. Everyone did.

"Yeah, none of them had smoke inhalation, so that was lucky. He set the fire in the arena," Forrest said. "By the time it spread to the stable block, we'd got the horses out before the flames could cause them any physical harm."

"Atticus was furious when I told him," Felix said. "He's desperate to come home."

"There's no point," I said. "Plus, I need him out there with Leon to keep an eye on Hallie," I added. "And Sage."

Felix nudged my arm. "You know Atticus has a big mouth, don't you?" My heart started beating faster. My shoulders sagged, but I couldn't help but laugh.

"He told you all?"

"About Hallie Oakley stealing your heart?" Genny said, sadness clearing from her eyes and a playful glint taking its place. "Well, he might have started a WhatsApp group, excluding only you, to spill the beans. It's called *Jasper and Hallie Sitting in a Tree.*" Genny laughed, and I loved seeing her this way. "He even sent pictures of you with her in a cowboy bar in Mexico. And you were *dancing*?" Genny asked incredulously.

"More like standing completely still and scowling at anyone who dared check Hallie out." I shook my head. "I'm going to kill that little shit when I see him again. Whenever that may be."

"Soon. Go back on the tour," Forrest said. "This place is Fort Knox now. We found a stolen ID card on the assailant that allowed him access to the stud. He told the gate he was delivering some feed. So we have something to go on."

"I can't go," I argued, but I couldn't deny I longed to get back on my plane and back to Hallie. Forrest was right, this place was as secure as it could possibly be now. Besides hiring the actual SAS, I wasn't sure how much more it could be guarded.

"You're better off on tour, making sure they're protected there too," Felix said. "Most of our competitions are here in the UK for now." He gestured to himself and Forrest. "Come home when we're away."

Every part of me wanted to refuse. That was what old Jasper would have done, the man who took everything on himself.

"We're all sharing the load, remember?" Forrest said, and I nodded. It was going to take me a long time to shed the need to be the only one in control.

"I'm staying a few days, at least. I want to make sure things are okay here. I have some meetings too. Then maybe I'll think about rejoining the tour."

"Go spend time with Hallie. Watch her compete," Genny said. "You deserve happiness, Jas. And Hallie is lovely."

I smiled at my sister. It was actually nice, all my family knowing. A relief, really. These were the closest people I had in my life. Everyone who mattered to me now knew Hallie and I were together. It felt . . . right.

"What's the tour like this year?" Genny said, and I studied her. There was an air of sadness around her that had been with her ever since her accident.

"The same, I suppose," I said, but then added, "And not. Us two aren't there, for one. It's bothering Atticus."

"Yeah," she said. "Maybe one day we'll have that again," she said with positivity that I could see was forced.

"How is Dahlia?" I asked, and only silence met me. "That bad?"

"She's no better, if that's what you're asking," Genny said. "I think her getting trapped in the wire fence has put her progress right back." She looked to Henry, Sebastian, and Aurelia. I could see that my sister wished Dahlia was back here with the family horses too.

I reached out and held her hand, saying, "I think I've found someone who can help us. He was recommended to me by an excellent source. He's from Denmark. I'm talking to him about coming to help Dahlia heal from her trauma. He thinks he can be of assistance."

"You have?" Genny asked, her voice a whisper. Tears built in her eyes. I stood and hugged her again. "I just want her happy. I don't care if I can never ride her again. My wish is for her to be at peace in herself and not so afraid."

"We'll do everything we can, I promise," I said. *For you too,* I wanted to add, but Genny didn't like being fussed over. I kissed her head and sat back down.

"Fucking hell," I said and ran my hand down my face. "I remember the days we would sneak into these fields with our fathers' booze and get drunk. Now, we gather in them to plan how to defend ourselves against an unseen enemy." I raised a pretend glass. "Here's to getting older and having responsibilities. It's bloody terrible."

"Dickhead," Forrest said, joking. Then he got to his feet. He went straight to Aurelia and kissed her on the nose. Sebastian came over and began kicking the gate at the lack of attention, and Felix laughed.

"His majesty is demanding a treat and affection too." Felix got up to get him one—them all, really. One could not give a Knighton horse a treat in this place without the rest demanding one too.

I squeezed Genny's hand, then made my way to Henry. Genny came with me. "He misses you," she said.

"Way to make me feel even guiltier for not being here, Gen."

She hit me on the arm. "I didn't mean it like that," she said. Then she watched Henry. "It's as though he knows there's a competition happening out in the world and he's not there to show his prowess. He keeps jumping the fences between the paddocks as if to remind us how impressive he is."

I laughed, but it broke my heart. I was dog tired, strung out, and wished I could teleport Hallie here from France just to hold her.

"You really like her, don't you?" Genny asked, reading my mind.

I glanced down to my sister, leaning against the paddock's gate. "That's an understatement, Gen," I confessed.

Genny held my hand and squeezed my fingers. "Finally," she said, smiling. "It's about time you let someone open that caged heart of yours. You deserve to have someone care for you in the way that you have cared for us all for so many years."

Guilt consumed me. "I couldn't protect you all, though, when it mattered. I failed. What if I fail her too?"

Genny's expression hardened. "You're not omnipotent, Jas. You can't prevent bad things in life from happening. Even when we seem to get hit from all sides." Genny shrugged. "We are *blessed* in life. Always have been. We can't be happy for those blessings, then moan when we experience the bad. It's a balance, Jas. We're British, and we must keep calm and carry on, regardless," she joked, but it was the truth too.

I was so proud of my little sister in that moment. I kissed her on the cheek. "Mum would be so proud of you, Gen. And we know Dad was."

"Thank you," she said. "Now, will you take me back to the house? I'm exhausted and want to stress-eat chocolate until I'm sick."

"We'll come back with you," Forrest said, and Felix followed behind him. We walked down the path to the house. I pushed Genny, and she told us all about her progress in rehab. I truly was proud of her. She was so strong, and so positive where I feared most people would crumble. The scent of smoke lingered in the air, a heavy reminder of how close we came to disaster. With every step that it invaded my lungs, I vowed to double down on looking for who was hurting us.

Humans were one thing to injure. But our horses?

Those evil fuckers had just declared war.

Paris
One week later

I ran into the venue, passing hundreds of women dressed to the nines and men decked out in suits, all drinking champagne. The sun was shining, the air warm. It was a great day for riding. I pulled out my phone and called Benjamin, flashing the security guard my pass as I rushed down to meet Jean Pierre, who had invited me to watch the competition from his private box.

"Hey, Jasper," Benjamin, my groom, said.

"Hey, Ben. How is he?"

Ben laughed. "I promise he's good, Jas. I've just ridden him and he's great, not shying or spooking. Jumped well. He seems back to normal. A true professional." I relaxed, exhaling in relief. Ben had been with me for years at this point. Henry loved him, and I didn't trust anyone else to take care of him.

Henry and the other horses had been shaken up for a few days after the attack. I'd decided to stay the week at home to help settle him back down and be there if the police or Phillip needed anything. I felt immense guilt about leaving him right now, but Hallie, Sage, and Atticus had swept again in the individual competition yesterday here in Paris, and I was going to make it just in time to see Hallie jump in the team event with Huxley.

"Perfect," I said to Ben. "Keep checking in. Let me know if he's safe."

"I will, I promise," he replied.

"The extra security is with him, yeah?" I asked.

"Yes," Ben said. "All ten of them." There was a note of dry humor in Ben's voice, but I knew he would keep Henry as safe as I would.

"Okay, talk to you later," I said and hung up. I searched for Box Ten, all the time thinking about home. The fucker that had been caught committing arson had been arrested and was going to be charged, but he still wasn't talking. Phillip was working on the burner phone. He'd indicated last night that he might have something, a lead, *finally*, but he wasn't telling us more until he knew it was concrete.

As bad as the entire situation was, a lead would at least bring hope that this shit show was about to be blown wide open.

Reaching Box Ten, I knocked and let myself inside. Jean Pierre was stood against the rail, watching whoever was jumping. "Jasper!" he said and came over to shake my hand. He put a glass of champagne in my hand and gestured to the balcony. "You're just in time to watch your new superstar."

I sipped at the champagne and looked out to the arena. The venue was at the Champ de Mars, and every time I came here, I would look up to the Eiffel Tower, the arena at its feet, and think how bloody lucky we were in this industry to jump at such an epic place.

Camille Dubois cantered out of the arena, waving to her home crowd. She was smug, as always, but on one of Jean Pierre's horses she'd made good time and was clear. I wasn't a fan, but she was an excellent rider. I couldn't fault that. She'd stayed far from Hallie thus far. I'd promised Hallie I wouldn't interfere for now, but if she said anything to her again, I'd make my feelings known.

"Can Hallie beat that time?" Jean Pierre said and nudged me. In that second, Hallie was introduced, and I fixed my gaze on my woman trotting out into the ring. She was dressed in her olive-green Knighton Cavaliers show jacket, her raven plait hanging down her back.

Fuck, but she was beautiful.

Hallie had no idea I was here. I wanted to surprise her. The bell sounded and Hallie pushed Huxley into a canter. I gripped the champagne glass so tightly that I worried it might smash. But as soon as Hallie cleared the first fence, I relaxed. Huxley looked good. He was calm and moving steadily. Hallie, as always, was as fluid as water.

I pulled out my phone and couldn't resist taking her picture as she sailed over fence five directly in front of the Eiffel Tower. I had the exact same framed picture of me on Henry on my study wall from a few years ago. I looked down at the picture, running my thumb over Hallie's face. When I refocused on the round, it was to see Huxley stumble badly after fence seven. He had cleared it, but I saw Hallie pull him back slightly. Even from here I could see the look of concern on her face.

I focused on Huxley's front right leg. He was limping. Hallie must have realized it too, as she held her hand up to the officials and gently brought Huxley to a walk, retiring him from the ring.

My stomach fell and Jean Pierre said, "Are you seeing his right leg too? Strained, perhaps?"

"Shit," I hissed. "Looks like it." I handed Jean Pierre my half-full glass and patted him on the shoulder. "I need to go check on things."

"What a shame," he said. "That partnership has been incredible this season. Let's hope it's nothing serious."

I left the box and rushed to the stables. It took me ten minutes to get there, and by the time I did, Hallie, Sage, Atticus, and Leon were already in the yard. Mila was holding Huxley as the vet assessed his leg.

Leon looked up at me and subtly shook his head. *Fuck.* It clearly wasn't good.

"Jas?" Atticus said, frowning. "Fuck, I didn't know you were coming back today." He pulled me in for a hug.

When I turned, Hallie was looking up at me, tears in her eyes and devastation on her face. She'd removed her jacket and hat and had her arms across her chest. Her bottom lip wobbled when she saw me, and I wanted nothing more than to pull her close. But Mila and the vet weren't among the people who knew we were together, and after the arson attack and the rumors that had only just died down, I didn't dare expand that tight-knit group.

"It's ligament damage," Hallie said, and the crushing sadness in her voice made me want to yank her to me and make sure she was okay.

The vet stood. "Mike," I said, shaking his hand. "It's good to see you again. Though I wish it were under different circumstances."

"Same, Jasper. It's nice to see you around here again."

"What are you thinking?" I asked.

"Ligament. He'll need some scans and X-rays to rule out everything else, but he must have landed on it badly. It's a strain, or at worst, a tear."

A tear fell down Hallie's face, and she moved to Huxley, throwing her arms around his neck. She bloody loved this horse.

"Anything you need to do, you have carte blanche," I said. "No penny spared."

Hallie lifted her head from Huxley's neck and turned to me. "Thank you," she mouthed, and I nodded. It was the least I could do.

"I'm going to give him some injections now for pain and to reduce the inflammation. We'll keep him stalled, iced, and rested, then we can get to those scans."

"I'll call Liz, our vet back at Golden Oaks, and tell her he'll be coming home." I met Hallie's eyes and said, "We'll get him better and back on the circuit in no time."

"Good man," Mike said, then shook my hand. "Let's get Lord Huxley resting in his stable, and I'll be back with the meds."

Hallie went with Mila, rugging Huxley up and getting him settled. Leon moved beside me. "I'm going to contact Danielle at the stud and see who looks ready to jump now. Lady Marjorie was the most promising when we left for the circuit. Danielle told me she's been making excellent progress with our trainers since then. We can have her flown over today. She's on the list of registered horses for this season."

"Okay," I said, but I couldn't take my eyes off Hallie, who was whispering in Huxley's ear.

"You listen to me, milord," she said, and my chest ached at the affection in her voice. As they always did, Huxley's ears flicked back and forth, listening to his rider. "This is just a little bump in the road for us." She kissed his nose. "You're going to go home and heal, then I want you to come right back to me, and we'll finish what we started. Okay? The tour is far from over for us."

"This'll kill her," Sage said under her breath, coming to stand beside me. "She's totally fallen for him."

I made a vow right then that I was gifting Huxley to Hallie. When you found your heart horse, the one that attaches itself to your soul, there's no separating you. Hallie waxed lyrical about Canyon, about his ability to connect to horses on another level. But whatever magic lived at the ranch they both grew up on had rubbed off on her too. I'd never seen horses connect to anyone as quickly as they did to my girl.

Mila left the stable with a bucket in hand. I assumed she was getting Huxley food. Making sure the coast was clear, I snuck into the stall with Hallie. She didn't look up from Huxley's neck. She must have thought I was Mila as she didn't turn around.

"Angel?" I whispered, and Hallie's head whipped up. The minute our gazes connected, she fell apart. Throwing her arms around my waist, I held her to me and let her cry.

My shirt became wet with her tears, but in this moment, I didn't give a fuck. *"Ssh,"* I soothed, kissing her hair. "He'll be okay, I promise. I'll have only the best vets working on him."

"Thank you," she whispered. "I just . . ." Hallie backed away and ran her hand down Huxley's neck again. "I just feel so guilty." She shook her head. "I must have approached the fence wrong or pushed him too hard."

"It was *far* from your fault," I said sternly. "I was watching. In this sport, these things happen."

Hallie laid her cheek against Huxley's neck again. "I'll miss him."

I stepped back when Mila came back into the stable. With a nod at her groom, I left Hallie with Huxley and went to Leon and Mike, who were talking in the yard.

"No suspicion of foul play, right?" I said to Mike. I'd like to say Mike looked shocked by my question, but after the past few years and

McGowen's father's stunts, plus the sordid history of this sport, none of us were. The sad truth was, it was rife in our industry.

But Mike shook his head. "No, I just rewatched his landing online. It is genuine. No foul play."

I exhaled in relief. "Thank God."

"I'll just give him the medication, then we can see if the swelling goes down. From there we can discuss him traveling back to Golden Oaks." I nodded again, then Leon came to stand beside me.

Sage had gone in the stable with Hallie to keep her company. Atticus was brushing down Barnaby, giving them some space. I'd check in with him later.

"Marjorie is the best option," Leon said, and showed me Danielle's text confirming that. I stared back at Hallie, and the devastation on her face—it cut me where I stood. When the person you loved was hurting, the pain you felt for them was debilitating.

"Actually, Leon," I said, taking his elbow and pulling him far from anyone else. "I need to run something by you."

Chapter Nineteen

Hallie

I slumped down in the scalding water of my bath and tried not to let the cavernous feelings of disappointment fill me. Huxley would be flying back to England tomorrow night, and we were moving on to Saint-Tropez. Atticus told me it looked like I would be riding Lady Marjorie until Huxley was healed. Leon had left the yard with Jasper to sort it. Maybe I would have her for the rest of the season. She was an amazing mare, one I'd had the privilege to ride at Golden Oaks. She was beautifully natured and nowhere as crazy as Fefe. But . . .

She wasn't Huxley.

Together, my gentle stallion and I had formed an unstoppable team, and I adored him. I inhaled, the scent of sandalwood filling my nose, which only reminded me of Jasper. I had no choice but to carry on. This was my career, and things like this happened all the time.

The clicking of the bathroom door opening had me jumping up in shock. I held my hand over my racing heart, only to see Jasper walk through. "Jasper," I said, breathlessly. "You scared the hell out of me!"

I sank back into the water, and Jasper sat down on the ledge. He ran his hand down my cheek, so affectionately it brought butterflies to my chest. But the careful touch also made my sadness barrel back. "I'm okay," I said honestly. "Just sad." I frowned. "How do you always get a key to my hotel rooms?"

Jasper smiled wide and my heart skipped a beat at how handsome it made him look. "I have my ways."

For the first time since Huxley was injured, I laughed. "You mean you just asked the girl at the front desk to have it, and so affected by your stunning good looks, she handed it straight over, no questions asked."

"Something like that," he said. I stared at him a little longer. "Joking! It's my name on the booking so it wasn't hard." I laughed again. It took me a second to absorb how he was dressed, in a Knighton Equestrian black base layer top, matching breeches, and . . . his riding boots? I blinked and blinked again.

It made me realize that apart from the night I caught him jumping Henry in the family barn, I hadn't seen him in riding gear at *all.*

"Why are you dressed like that?" I asked, and sat up. I could smell the scent of horse on him too.

Where had he been?

Jasper got to his feet and grabbed my towel from the heated rack. He held it out to me. "I've come to take you somewhere."

My pulse kicked into a sprint. "Where?"

"It's a surprise." Jasper cast me a flicker of a smirk, and I decided right then that I loved this playful side of Jasper. I checked my watch. "It's ten o'clock at night. And it's dark," I said.

"You'll be fine," he said, and flicked his head. "Come on, Cinderella, I promise I won't have you back too late. There'll be no turning into a pumpkin on my watch."

I laughed, but confusion ran thickly in my veins. But I trusted Jasper, allowing him to drink his fill. He'd been gone for over a week, and I'd missed him so much. But mostly, I'd missed those heated midnight eyes on my body and having him inside me. I rubbed the oil from the water into my skin.

"I know what you're doing, Angel," Jasper said, his voice growing raspy. He stepped closer. "And just know that when we get back, I'll give you exactly what you want." His teeth raked over his bottom lip as he roved his gaze over me. "I've missed the taste of your pussy."

Breathlessly, I said, "Do we really have to go out?" Him tasting my pussy sounded like a much better plan.

Jasper groaned. He put the towel around me, and I noticed the bulge in his breeches. "I can help with that," I said, and stepped out of the bath. He leaned in and kissed me. I moaned as he did, realizing that the phrase "missing him" wasn't a strong-enough explanation for what I felt.

"You're tempting me to stay, Angel. But we have somewhere to be first." Taking my hand, he led me from the bathroom and into the main area of my hotel suite. Waiting on the couch was the turquoise base layer and riding leggings set that I modeled all those months ago for Knighton Equestrian at his warehouse.

I turned to Jasper, heart swelling. He shrugged. "I've called it Hallie Blue." He stepped close to me, and leaned in, kissing my cheek. "To match those turquoise eyes of yours."

I was so gone for this man.

Jasper pointed to the set. "Put them on."

"What?" I asked, completely confused. I'd just had a bath.

"Put them on, grab your hat and boots. You're coming with me." I stared at him with an eyebrow raised. Jasper glared back in silence. After a strained few seconds, he said, "Don't make me get the handcuffs."

"That sounds like a good time," I said, and watched his lips twitch. But then . . . nothing. I got it. He was sticking to his guns and wasn't telling me shit.

"Fine! You win," I said, dropping my towel to the floor. I reached for the set, only to feel Jasper's hand graze my ass as I bent down.

"Fuck, Angel," he groaned, sounding like he was in pain.

Heat traveled straight to my clit at the sound of desperation, but I stood straight, moved to my drawers to get my panties and a sports bra, and said, "No, no, Mr. Knighton. We're apparently in a rush." I pointed to his hard cock showing through his breeches. "Get yourself under control until we're back from . . . wherever it is we're going."

I strutted past him, but Jasper stood in my way, and lifting my head with his finger under my chin, said, "Just know I won't go easy on you when we get back."

I rose to my tiptoes, kissed him on the cheek, and said, "I'm counting on it." Jasper growled as I went back into the bathroom and got dressed. I threw my hair back in its usual braid and exited the bathroom.

When I reached Jasper, he took hold of my hand, twirling me around. "My favorite color I've ever created," he said, and I couldn't stop the blush that rose to my cheeks. With another long, passion-filled kiss, Jasper pulled back only an inch and said, "I missed you so much, Hallie."

I melted. "I missed you too." Jasper's responding smile was blinding.

Taking my hand, he led me from my room. Will was there, alongside Debbie, my personal bodyguard. I tried to drop Jasper's hand so they wouldn't see, but he kept tight hold, shocking me.

"Jasper," I said, gesturing to our hands when they walked ahead of us. "They'll know."

"Good," he said, acting completely out of character. He smirked, but then whispered, "Plus, they've signed NDAs so can't say anything without the might of my legal team coming down upon them."

I laughed and held on to his hand as we took the elevator down to the basement, where two cars were waiting. There was no driver in the blacked-out Land Rover Defender at the front.

Jasper opened the passenger-side door and held out his hand. I slipped into the seat and relaxed when I discovered it had a massage feature. Jasper got in the driver's seat beside me and smiled. In the side mirrors of the Defender, I saw Debbie and Will get into the car behind us.

"Are you going to tell me yet where we're going?" I asked as Jasper pulled out onto the Parisian streets. The city was as vibrant at night as it was during the day.

I smiled when the radio came on and my favorite country music station was playing. Lainey Wilson sang about whirlwinds as we cut through the busy roads. It wasn't until we made our way out of the city that I turned to Jasper. "Okay, this is getting ominous," I joked.

Jasper smirked and put his hand on my thigh. It was a little thing, a small sign of affection, but it was one of my favorites. "You're onto me, Angel. I'm taking you to my secret château that has a sex dungeon, where I'm going to tie you up and have my wicked way with you."

I squeezed my thighs together. "Don't promise me a good time and not deliver, baby."

Jasper laughed, and when city limits gave way to rolling fields, we made a right turn. We were entering a horse farm—an expensive one, if the outbuildings were anything to go by. "I have literally no idea what's happening," I said, but Jasper, maddeningly, kept silent.

When we stopped, Leon was waiting for us outside of an arena. I waved at my trainer. I looked to Jasper for answers, but he was getting out of the car, then opened the passenger door for me.

"Hallie," he said, offering his hand. It was clear he wasn't going to tell me what was happening either, so I just kept my mouth closed and waited for it all to be revealed.

"Jasper, Hallie," Leon greeted. There was a playfulness to his expression too, and nerves began building within me. "Let's go," Leon said, leading us through the pedestrian door of a truly impressive indoor arena. I flinched under the bright overhead lights after having been inside the dark car for so long; as my vision cleared, I could see the arena filled with a Grand Prix–level jumping course. It was expertly designed and, judging by Leon's smug expression, I knew it was he who had set this up.

"*Okaaaay,*" I said, "I'm suitably confused, so can you please . . ." My words trailed off to nothing when a large door at the end of the ring slid open to reveal Golden Oaks' Benjamin leading a huge, bright-gray stallion. My heart leapt to my throat as they approached.

"Henry," I whispered.

I whipped my head to Jasper and said, "You're joining the circuit?" To say I was excited was an understatement. He was going to ride with us, by our side?

Jasper stood in front of me and cupped my cheeks. I searched his face for an answer, but he shook his head, making me more perplexed than ever. "I'm not joining the circuit." Jasper pointed to Henry, who was now standing behind him. Every time I saw this stallion, I was awestruck. Jasper nodded in the direction of his prize horse. "Henry is."

"I . . . I . . ." I went to ask what the hell *that* meant, when some light bulb went off inside my head. I glanced down at my riding gear, and my hat in my hand. *"No,"* I whispered.

"Hallie Oakley," Jasper said, holding my hand tightly in his. "Will you do me the honor of riding my horse?"

I was having an out-of-body experience, I was sure of it. *No,* I'd fallen asleep in the tub and was drowning, hallucinating as I did. They could be the only explanation for what was happening right now.

"This isn't real," I said, meeting Henry's dark eyes over Jasper's shoulder. He stood still and proud, like the king of horses he was.

Jasper chuckled at my reaction. Leon and Ben led Henry toward the mounting block, giving Jasper and me some privacy.

I met Jasper's eyes that were already locked on mine. "I can't ride Henry, Jasper. He's *yours*."

"Hallie," he said, but I was still shaking my head. I *couldn't* ride Henry. I wasn't good enough, hadn't enough experience. *"Hallie,"* Jasper repeated, with firmness this time. When he had my full attention, he said, "There is no one else, and I mean *no one*, who I would trust with my boy more than *you*."

Butterflies fluttered through every inch of me. "Why?" I whispered.

Jasper smiled but then stepped closer until our chests met. He cupped my cheeks, making sure our gazes were glued together, when he said, "Because I'm madly in love with you, Hallie. That's why."

His words hit me like raindrops, gently sinking into my soul. "Jasper," I said, and I pressed my lips to his. "I love you too," I returned against his mouth, kissing him until the smile spreading on my face made it impossible.

Jasper hesitated just a moment, and said, "The rumors about us have died down amongst the other riders." He let those words dance around us, and I knew what he was saying. If I rode Henry, they would come back tenfold. "There would be no proof of our relationship, but it's common knowledge that no one rides Henry but me." He ran his finger down my face. "And now you."

"I know," I said, and truly searched my heart and soul. Would it upset me if the likes of Alexis Hobbs and Camille Dubois began giving me a hard time again? They had really upset me before. But now, as Jasper held me, telling me he loved me, and Henry stood behind me waiting for my decision, there wasn't a choice at all.

"I don't care," I said, and meant every word. "I want Henry."

"Come on, then," Jasper said, a hint of excitement in his voice, taking my hand and leading me to his treasured horse.

Jasper released me and ran his hand down his stallion's face. "Henry," he said to his horse, "Hallie is going to ride you for a while, okay?" I listened to his words, but I couldn't believe this was real, even pinching my own arm when no one was looking. It hurt like a bitch, so I must have been awake. "She's very good at what she does, and you must be as good for her as you are for me. Okay, boy?" Jasper winked at me. "She's been doing well in a lot of Grand Prix, and we all know how much you love to do that. But she wants a first place, and I know you're the man to help her get that. Okay?"

"Hat on, Hallie," Leon said, interrupting the moment, trainer mode in place. I did as he said.

Jasper pointed to the mounting block. "Up you get, Angel." Jasper took hold of Henry's reins from Ben, holding him still for me. "I rode him earlier tonight and he's in great form. He's settled, and he's ready for his queen." That explained why Jasper had to leave with Leon earlier. He was here. It was also why he was in riding gear. They must have flown Henry out as soon as Huxley went down.

As I climbed the mounting block, I felt like I was floating. Lord Henry was the most famous show jumping horse in the world. His stud fees alone had brought in millions of dollars, and I, a girl from the Texas boonies, was about to get the chance to ride him on the most prestigious stage in global show jumping. We wouldn't be in the team competition tomorrow but could be registered for Saint-Tropez.

None of it seemed real.

Placing my foot into the stirrup, I swung onto Henry's back and took my seat in the saddle. I smiled, and the dreamlike trance I had been wearing like a veil fell away from my body—leaves leaving their branches in fall.

"He's huge," I said as I looked down at the ground. It seemed real far away. Henry was eighteen hands and built of pure muscle, easily the biggest horse I had ever ridden. I reached forward and ran my hand through his platinum mane. It felt like silk. I wrapped my arms around Henry's thick neck and said, "You're perfect, baby. More than I could have dreamed."

"He suits you," Jasper said, his voice husky. When I looked to him, Jasper's gaze was shiny. He'd just told me he loved me. And he'd given me his heart horse to ride in the Sandings Global Champions Tour. It was clearly emotional for him.

This man . . .

Seeing Jasper all those years ago at my aunt's equestrian center, riding a young Henry, had inspired me to ride English. To show jump. Now I was madly in love with that very same man, and he was with me. Fate or some other higher power had guided us to this point, right here. I could feel it in the static around us.

Jasper, Leon, and Ben stepped back, and Jasper said, "Go on, then. Give him a go." My heart took off into a sprint, and I had to breathe slowly to calm myself down. I didn't want Henry to mistake my excitement for nerves.

I clucked to the stallion and Henry began to walk. He was bouncier than Huxley, and I could feel his incredible strength through the reins. I moved to the arena's outside track, smiling when Henry looked at the fences and sped up in anticipation of jumping them.

"Not just yet, boy," I said. "I have to get used to everything else first." His ears moved back and forward, listening as I spoke. I walked him around once, and knowing he was already warmed up, moved him to a trot. I couldn't stop the happiness radiating from me as I passed a mirrored wall and glanced at me riding Henry. It was a dream—all of it. Henry, the tour, and Jasper Knighton telling me he loved me. What was my life?

I passed Jasper, who was leaning against the wall with a look of pure pride and joy on his face. "Get him in a canter, Angel. Let him show you what he can do." Henry was soft on the bit, allowing me to navigate around the arena with the gentlest of nudges.

When I made it to the next corner, I clicked my tongue, and Henry effortlessly transitioned to canter. He was smooth, and I felt like a child on a carousel, imagining I was on the real thing. But I *was* on the real thing. The best real thing. And I knew I'd never ride another horse like Henry.

"You're beautiful," I said to Henry. "What a gentleman."

Henry looked to a fence again, and giving him what he wanted, I turned and headed for the Pantheon-themed vertical, with two columns as the wings. Henry didn't even bat an eye at the fence's design. He sped up for the jump, head high and determined, and sailed us over. Time felt suspended as he went airborne. I smiled as we cleared the fence, landing as soft as a feather.

Jasper clapped and his responding smile was blinding. "Perfect, Hallie," he said. But I couldn't speak. The lump in my throat stole any words I could muster. When I turned Henry to the next fence, the wind of our jump dried the falling tears off my cheeks. And the tears didn't stop until we'd cleared the course and I'd brought Henry to a halt near the men.

Jasper was at my side in seconds. Seeing me smiling through my grateful tears, Jasper's eyes shone too. "You approve?" he asked, gravel in his voice.

"I approve," I said, laughing. I felt high with happiness.

"We need to have several sessions with you on him before Saint-Tropez," Leon said, his no-nonsense attitude slicing through the sentiment of this moment.

I nodded. He was right.

We had work to do.

And I had a dream horse to get to know.

Will and Debbie rode with us in the elevator, and when we left them at their posts for the night, Jasper and I beelined straight for my room. Only this time when the door shut behind us, there was no urgency. Even though we hadn't seen each other for a week, the raw need to rip one another's clothes off in seconds wasn't there. Instead, the air was thick between us, like it had its own life force, its own heartbeat. I held Jasper's hand tightly and we stopped in the middle of the room. Our gazes caught, and my breathing was stuttered.

I wanted to say a million things to this man, this incredibly sweet and broken man, but no words would do it justice. The gift he had given me tonight . . . and I wasn't even just talking about Henry. I was talking about *him*. Jasper, over the past few months, had slowly let me in. But tonight, telling me he loved me . . . He had finally given me what I wanted most—his heart, his soul . . . all of *him*.

"I love you," Jasper said again, his raspy voice like a lullaby to my ears. I soaked those words in, letting them fill whatever cracks still lay in my heart.

Jasper reached for the quarter zip on my shirt and then lifted it over my head. Leaning down, Jasper kissed my lips, but before I could push for more, he withdrew. Reaching behind me, he unclasped my bra and dropped it to the floor.

"Beautiful," Jasper murmured, as his gaze ran over my breasts. He kissed me on my cheek, gentlemanly, softly. I shivered, goose bumps breaking out all over me, not from the cold, but from anticipation of what tonight held—what it meant for us both. We'd never gone slow in our lovemaking. Always hot and heavy and full of commands and domination.

Tonight was different, we both knew it. *We* were different.

We were in love.

Jasper got down onto his knees and pressed a single kiss to my torso. Taking hold of the waistband of my riding tights, he pulled them down my legs. One at a time, he tapped each of my legs, signaling for me to lift them so he could remove the tights completely. My riding socks came next, until I stood in only my panties.

Running his palms up my bare calves, then thighs, Jasper looked up at me and said, "That night in the barn, when I first saw you, I thought you were an angel." His palms created warm paths as he ran them up and down my skin. "You were so fucking beautiful, I didn't believe you could actually be real." I felt tears prick my eyes.

Hooking his fingers into the waist of my panties, he dragged them down my legs, never breaking eye contact with me as he did. Like he didn't want to miss a moment of this night.

When he'd tossed them aside, Jasper rose, but not before leaning forward and laying a chaste kiss on my pussy. I gasped, craving more, but then Jasper was already on his feet. I stayed still as he shed his shirt, his boots, then his breeches and boxer briefs.

My heart thudded like a drum as he stood before me, naked. His cock was hard, but I didn't rush to take him in my mouth. As always, I let Jasper take the lead. Stepping forward, Jasper pulled the tie from my braid and shook out my hair until it flowed in waves to my waist.

"Perfect," he said, and threaded his hands through my hair. When his lips met mine, I sank into his embrace. Going on my tiptoes, I clasped my arms around his neck and allowed his lips to move against mine, slowly, meaningfully, showing me without words how much he adored me. I understood the sentiment because I adored him too.

Jasper slipped his tongue into my mouth. It met mine, but it was tranquil in its exploration. I moaned into his mouth, and Jasper's hands ran down my back until they grazed over my ass. Reaching my thighs, he lifted me off the floor, guiding my legs around his waist.

My eyes were closed as I reveled in the kiss, but I felt us move across the room. The softness of the mattress pressed against my back as Jasper laid me down. His lips didn't break from mine. His cock ran against my clit, but again, there was no urgency. Just gentle rocking back and forth—a promise of what was to come.

Breaking from my mouth, Jasper met my eyes and smoothed stray hairs from my face. "I love you, Angel," he said again, like he would never tire of telling me what was in his heart.

It felt hedonistic.

"I love you too, baby. So much I feel like I can't contain it," I said, and Jasper kissed me again, but then began to move down my body. He kissed me everywhere, each one feeling like it was branded into my skin. He kissed over my chest, then around my breasts. My back arched as he licked across my nipples, but then he moved south. When he reached my pussy, he pressed my knees to either side until they hit the bed, exposing me to his midnight eyes.

Jasper ran his thumb straight down my center, from my clit to my entrance, and I inhaled a shaky breath. Leaning down, Jasper licked along the path his thumb had just made. Not hurried, not frantic, but calm and measured. Shivers made a tidal wave down my spine as they accosted my body. I pushed my hands into his dark hair as Jasper took his time, treasuring every second of tasting me.

The room was silent but for my quiet moans and labored breathing. Sex had never been like this. This moment told me that, up till now, I had never made love. And being madly in love with the person you were sleeping with . . . it was like nothing I ever thought I'd have.

"Jasper . . ." I moaned as I lifted my thighs, unable to take the pressure that was building in my clit. But Jasper didn't stop, he also didn't speed up. He was torturing me slowly, making me feel every second before he blew me apart. I rolled my hips, trying to chase the orgasm I could feel building, but Jasper pressed down on my thighs, trapping them so I couldn't move.

"I need to come," I pleaded, my back arching again. Still, Jasper didn't hurry. He lapped at my clit and hole until I worried I'd go insane from the slow pace. But then he took my clit into his mouth and began to suck. The climax that felt too far in the distance collided with Jasper's mouth, and I cried out loudly into the silent room as stars burst behind my eyes and the most intense orgasm I'd ever experienced shattered through me.

My eyes closed and I held my breath, feeling every nerve in my body come alive. Jasper didn't stop; he licked me through my climax until my hips began to jerk, and I crashed down on the mattress.

My breathing was erratic, but my body felt completely sated.

Jasper kissed my inner thighs, occasionally brushing over my clit. Every time he did, I'd gasp. "Jasper," I said, "I need you," and Jasper kissed up my stomach, my torso, and my breasts until he was above me. Holding his stubbled cheeks in my hands, our eyes met, boasting all the love we felt inside. Pulling him down, I kissed him and kissed him until he rolled us. Now I was above him, and Jasper guided me back, tearing his lips from mine. I straddled his waist. Jasper ran his thumb along my still-sensitive clit.

"Baby," I moaned.

"Ride me," he said, and positioned me above his cock. I sat up, and Jasper held his hard length, putting his tip at my entrance. I bit my lip, never breaking from his heavy gaze as I sank down, taking him inch by inch, just as slowly as he had licked me.

Jasper gritted his teeth. "Fuck, Angel," he rasped. "So tight." I tipped my head back as he filled me completely. It felt so right, so perfect. Leaning forward, his eyes never leaving my face, I pressed my hands to his chest and began to rock back and forth.

"I love you," I said, as I gradually built up the pace. My clit rubbed against his groin as I moved, and his cock hit my G-spot inside me. "Jasper!" I cried, feeling his hips begin to lift, spearing himself inside me more. Jasper gripped my hips, using the leverage to increase the tempo.

"I love you too," he hushed out, voice tight. I shook my head, unable to take the feeling of coming again. "Come, Angel," he said, and I rocked back and forth two more times before my entire body tensed and I lit up from my toes to my scalp. I cried out and rode Jasper faster and harder, feeling every bit of my overwhelming orgasm, only for it to sweep through me further when Jasper grunted and came inside me. I opened my eyes and looked down at the man who had captured my heart.

His cheeks were flushed, his body cut with lean muscles and flexing as he poured himself inside me. Using his grip on my hips, he thrust into me three more times before he roared and I dropped to his chest, spent.

Jasper's breathing was fast, and I let his racing heartbeat beneath my ear lull me into a blissful calm. Jasper's cock twitched inside me in the aftermath. His hands stroked through my hair.

After a few minutes of silence, Jasper pulled me up to his face. He kissed me, and I sank into him. Moving me beside him, he wrapped his arm around me until we were sharing the same pillow, limbs entwined.

"I can't believe we're here, like this," I said, running my fingers through the dark hairs on his chest.

"I can," he said. "The minute I knew you were real, not a figment of my drunk imagination, I think my soul knew who you were to me." He smirked. "I fought it, of course, because I'm a stubborn bastard." Jasper's humor dropped. "But mostly, because I think I knew how I would feel about you, given the chance, and with all the threats against my family, against *me* . . ." He sighed. "I didn't want you tangled up in that."

My heart broke for him. He'd already told me about the arson attack, of course. And the family horses being targeted. "Are you sure Henry is okay to be ridden after the break-in?"

"More than," Jasper said, smiling again. "Wait until you enter the arena on him." I smiled too, just witnessing the nostalgic happiness spread on Jasper's face. "He loves the crowd and being the center of attention." He shook his head. "He's something else." Jasper met my eyes. "I want you to show him, Hallie. He deserves it and so do you."

I kissed him, then asked, "Did he fly in today?"

Jasper shook his head. "We came yesterday." I frowned in confusion, so he explained. "I didn't want to leave him behind anymore. Didn't want to risk it. So I brought him with me. I have friends' stables all lined up for the tour, secure ones. I wanted him where I could protect him—close by." Jasper wrapped a strand of my hair around his finger. "But then Huxley went down, and Leon was getting one of our other horses sent over. And I saw it in my head. *You* riding Henry. He was already here, and I've been depriving him of what he loves most—competing." Jasper shrugged. "There was no debating it. I just knew it was meant to happen. You were meant to show my boy."

"Thank you," I said, beyond grateful for this gift.

"Always," he said, and then added, "We'll keep it quiet until we get to Saint-Tropez. Just in case."

I'd been thinking about our next stop on the tour. "How are you feeling about going back to Saint-Tropez?" I asked carefully.

Jasper tensed, but then said, "Not great. I think all I'll ever see when we go there is Genny being crushed." He shook his head. "But it's always going to be on the tour, and we must attend, so my plan is to replace it with good memories. Of you riding and killing it on Henry."

I laughed. "Not that you're biased, of course."

"Never," he said back, smiling.

"Seriously, thank you," I said again, curling into Jasper's broad chest. I closed my eyes, feeling sleep pulling me down. "You've made more than one of my dreams come true."

Sleep began to lull me into unconsciousness, but not quick enough to miss Jasper say, "You *are* my dream come true, Angel." Then he kissed my head, and my heart filled with light.

So this was how it felt? I mused. *To find your soulmate.*

It was serene.

Peaceful.

Utter bliss.

Saint-Tropez, France
One week later

"What the ever-loving *fuck*!" Sage's shrill voice cut through our private section of the arena's stalls. I smiled, seeing Ben lead Henry toward us. He had been kept at Jean Pierre's stud here in Saint-Tropez until today. Jasper followed behind them.

Sage snapped her head to me again. "*This* is your new horse?" Sage slapped my arm. "You bitch! You told me you weren't sure who you were getting yet!"

Atticus brushed past us and went straight to Henry. He gave the stallion a huge fuss. "Hello, mate. I bet you're happy to be here again." It was strange, because Jasper was right; here at the stalls, Henry *did* seem to have a new aura about him. He was a showman through and through, and he was eager for the stage.

Jasper came to stand beside me. "You ready?" he said.

"Absolutely," I replied. And I was. In the week between tour stops, I had been training on Henry every day. It didn't take me long to find our rhythm. Huxley was safely back at Golden Oaks getting treatment, and in the meantime, I had the best horse in the world to ride.

No big deal.

Leon appeared and clapped his hands. "Okay, team. Time for the practice ring."

Sage gave me a big kiss on my cheek. "You lucky fucking bitch!" she said, then slapped my ass. "You must be a really good fuck if he's given you his pride and joy to ride." Sage's eyebrows danced and I flipped her off. The echo of her cackle followed her as she mounted Fefe.

"You got this," Atticus said to me, hand on my shoulder. He nodded to Henry. "There's no safer horse."

"Thanks, Atticus." Since our talk on the rooftop in Spain we'd grown closer.

"Doesn't mean I'm still not going to beat you, though!"

I rolled my eyes. "Would expect nothing less."

Mila helped Ben get Henry sorted, and I put on my hat. I went to put on my show jacket when Jasper stopped me and said, "Follow me." Confused, I did as he said and followed him to a tack room. Jasper shut the door behind us and moved to a portable clothes rack where a garment bag hung. He handed it to me. "For you."

"What is it?"

Jasper folded his arms over his chest. "You're riding a new horse," he said. "I thought that occasion deserved a new jacket too."

I unzipped the suit bag, and gasped. "Jasper . . ." I said, and took out the perfectly tailored and pristine Knighton Equestrian show jacket in Hallie Blue. I had to blink away appreciative tears. "I adore it," I said, and crossed the tack room to throw my arms around his waist and whisper, "Thank you." I pulled back and shook my head. "Jasper, you have to stop spoiling me."

Jasper smirked. "Hallie, I'm a billionaire. If I want to spoil you, I bloody well will." I always forgot that about him. Not that he was rich, because his property and horses showed that. But he wasn't arrogant or selfish with his money or love. He was genuinely a lovely man. A bit cold and moody to those not close to him, but never to me anymore.

"Put it on, then," Jasper said. He took the jacket from me and held it out. I turned and slipped my arms into it, then spun around for Jasper to button up the front.

"It fits perfectly," I said, then moved to the mirror. I ran my hands down the premium wool fabric. The black velvet collar was a perfectly traditional touch and made the bright color pop more.

"Your eyes," Jasper said, moving behind me.

For once, I understood what he meant. The oceanic blue of the jacket made my blue eyes blaze. Turning, I looked up at Jasper and said, "I love you."

Jasper kissed my lips. "I love you too."

When we broke apart, I asked, "Are you going to watch from Jean Pierre's box again?"

"No," he said, surprising me. "I'm walking out with you and Leon and watching from the viewers' plinth."

"But . . ." I went to argue.

"I'm not missing my two loves taking center stage." I melted again and went in for another kiss, then . . .

"I'm not afraid to come in there and interrupt whatever is happening!" Leon said from the tack-room door. "Hallie is needed at the practice ring, now!"

Jasper sighed and dropped his forehead to press against mine. "I'm going to fire him."

I burst out laughing. "Yeah, like that would ever happen." I headed for the door, only for Jasper to pull me back and take the promised kiss anyway.

"Ride safe," he said when we broke apart.

"You got it," I said and left the tack room. Ben and Mila had Henry ready. Sage and Atticus had already gone. I threw on my hat and mounted Henry.

Jasper walked out of the tack room and headed for the practice ring. I took a deep breath. "You'll do great," Ben said.

"You look incredible on him," Mila said also.

"Thanks, guys," I said, and clicked my tongue for Henry to move.

Once we had left the safety and privacy of our private section of the stalls, I heard the gasps and whispers coming from the staff around us.

"It's Lord Henry." I saw their disbelief and excitement. I braced myself for the comments that would no doubt be thrown my way. I wouldn't let anything bad penetrate today.

Henry's head was high and it made me smile, but nerves ran like rapids through me, the more notice we attracted. I had banked on attention, but this was on another level. Then again, I didn't know what I'd expected. Henry had been my dream horse growing up; it stood to reason he was most other riders' too. People believed Jasper had retired him, and here I was, bringing him back. It was bound to raise eyebrows.

Jasper was waiting at the warm-up ring with Leon. He watched me approach, and Leon opened the gate. Sage and Atticus were cantering around, Sage coming to a stop beside me when I entered.

The other riders in the ring were staring. "Oh, this is *fun*," Sage said, watching all the awestruck expressions.

"Walk beside me for a while," I said to Sage. "I don't want to be gawked at on my own."

We began walking around the ring, only for Camille Dubois to trot up to us. "Not fucking him, hey?" she said, turning her nose up at me. "You tried to be so convincing too," she said. "Well played, I suppose." She shrugged. "You fuck so well that you gained the best horse in the process." She laughed. "I'm impressed."

Camille went to trot off when Sage said, "How many Grand Prix have you won this season so far, Camille?"

Camille scowled at my best friend, and I held back a laugh. "Thought so," Sage sang. Camille cantered off angrily, leaving me numb from her barb. She pulled up next to Jake McGowen, who was glaring our way. They talked in low whispers, but I could imagine what they were saying. And oh, goody, Alexis was watching me from behind the barrier.

Let them fucking look.

"Cunts," Sage said. Then turned to me. "Remember, you have earned your place here, Hallie. The best thing you can do is go out there and kick ass. That'll shut the haters up." Sage glared at Camille, who was still shooting me death stares. "Jealousy makes even the most attractive people ugly."

We approached where Jasper and Leon were standing ringside. Jasper caught my attention. "What did she say to you?" His voice was cold, like the Jasper I first met.

"That I've fucked my way to the top, the same old, same old." Jasper's jaw clenched. But his eyes were narrowed on McGowen et al.

He took out his phone, and I heard him say to someone, "Tail McGowen and Dubois. I don't like the way they're watching Hallie." He was so overprotective, and I loved that side of him.

"Head down and carry on," Leon said, making me refocus. "Warm him up, ignore the noise, and pop him over the practice fences." I nodded and took Henry out to the rail.

I was riding last today in the timed individual, which no doubt would piss off people even more. But I did as Leon said and shut out the noise. As I kept Henry warm, I visualized the course. I pictured us getting a clear round.

I pictured us *winning*. There was something in the air today, I could feel it.

Camille and Jake probably thought they were getting to me by saying those things. But the joke was on them—their shitty comments were only fuel to my fire.

A half hour later, I winced, watching the big screen as Sage came out of the ring with four faults. She'd knocked down a pole on the second-to-last fence. "Next time," I said when she returned, and Sage just nodded her head.

Atticus made good time as always, and then Camille got a clear too. Jake McGowen was jumping before me. Jasper stood beside me in the tunnel and watched his rival with venom in his expression. I completed my prejump ritual—chin strap, girth, and water—before smoothing the front of my new jacket.

"Give him lots of rein," Jasper said, as we watched Jake soar over the fences. "Make sure to give him enough room on the tight corners; he's a big horse and needs that extra space. He'll make up the lost time on the approach and over the fence. Give him extra leg on the oxers and keep him steady through the triple. He can get too excited and rush if you're not careful." I smiled. We'd been through all these points at practice this week. But I loved Jasper for making sure I was prepared.

"I've got this," I said, risking a glance down at him.

Jasper exhaled. "I know you do, Angel."

The crowd lifted with applause. "Fucker," Jasper hissed.

Jake patted his horse's neck, his time knocking Atticus from the top spot. Jake came out of the ring, a smug look on his face. He passed by us. "Good luck," he said flippantly.

"Concentrate," Leon said sternly, and I nodded.

The camera must have flashed to me, because suddenly a wave of gasps and excited murmurs rolled over where we were standing. Leon patted Henry's neck. "They know you're here, boy. Show them what you can do."

"Last to ride is Hallie Oakley, from Ocala, Florida, riding Lord Henry of Golden Oaks Stud," the commentator said, and the crowd roared.

I took a deep breath, and keeping my attention straight forward, trotted into the arena. The sun was beating down, and the stands were jam-packed. The minute we picked up our trot, my heart thudded with the roar of the crowd. People were on their feet, and a million cell phones were taking pictures.

I struggled to hear anything over the commotion, but then the crowd quieted, and the atmosphere went from raucous to completely silent. The bell sounded, and I pushed Henry into a canter. He was so comfortable to ride, his strides long and his gait smooth.

Turning into the first fence, I felt Henry's excitement pulling on the reins. "Steady, boy," I said as we took flight. I flashed back to a twelve-year-old me watching this exact horse show me a dream I didn't even know existed.

When he landed, a smile broke out on my face. No matter what happened this weekend, I was riding Henry, and that was winning in itself.

Like Jasper had advised, I gave Henry enough rein to go, giving him more leg on the oxers. And exactly like Jasper had said, as we turned into the triple, Henry became headstrong and fought to go faster. My arms ached as I held him back, keeping him steady so he didn't get too under the jump and risk knocking it down.

My heart beat faster as we approached the final fence. I had no idea how fast we were going. Henry moved like the wind, making his speed unreadable. The final fence was a spread, a jump Henry was famous for mastering. The red and white poles called our name as we cantered toward them, then Henry took off and I closed my eyes for a moment, just drinking in the moment, only to open them as we landed . . .

A clear round.

The crowd lifted in volume, rising to their feet. I turned to the scoreboard and whooped in excitement when I saw us soar to the top spot. Leaning down, I hugged Henry and said, "We did it, boy! We did it!"

I looked over to the viewer's plinth, and Leon was clapping, Jasper beside him, the only emotion he displayed his wide smile. I made my way toward them, meeting Jasper's eyes. He was beaming at me. I slowed Henry to a trot, then a walk when we got out of the tunnel. Ben was there to get Henry, and I dismounted, Sage flying into my arms.

"Fucking hell, Hals! That was the best riding I've ever seen!" I squeezed my best friend. I was shaking from adrenaline.

Atticus hugged me, spinning me around as he lifted me off the floor. "Fuck Jasper, you can have Henry from now on."

"Thanks, Atti," I heard Jasper say dryly from behind us. I wanted so badly to jump into his arms, but we were surrounded by too many people. Leaning in, he whispered, "I'm so proud of you, Angel. So fucking proud."

"Thank you."

Leon was next, giving me a brief one-armed hug. "Well deserved, Hallie."

"Thank you, everyone," I said, then moved to Henry. I kissed his cheek and hugged his neck. "You were everything I dreamed of and more," I whispered for his ears only.

"Atticus, Hallie," an organizer said, "it's time for the podium." Sage squeezed my hand, and I felt my stomach fall. It didn't feel right, her not being up there with me.

"Go on!" she said, reading my mind. "The day is yours."

I walked beside Atticus. He had his arm around me. Jake McGowen was in the tunnel already, ready to claim his second place. He watched us approach, any niceness he'd ever showed me evaporate. "Atticus," he said coldly.

"Jake," Atticus said. All his playfulness had gone, and in its place was one scary bastard. Atticus glared at Jake, and I wondered if they suspected it was Jake making all the threats. Jasper was sure he was up to something.

"Follow me, please," the organizer said, and each of us took the podium. When I was handed the winner's trophy, I held it high and just drank in the moment. The crowd roared with applause and my heart felt so full. I knew my aunt and uncle would be watching from Florida, and it made me so happy I thought I would burst.

As we descended the podium, the organizer was chatting to Atticus. I suddenly felt someone move to my side. Jake McGowen. "What?" I asked, walking faster in heading back to the stalls.

"You got in bed with the devil, huh?" he said in a shitty tone.

I turned on him. "Shut up, Jake. Don't be a sore loser."

"That's not it," he said, and I stopped dead.

"Go on, then. What is it?"

Jake checked around him. "Just know that your man has a lot of enemies."

My heart skipped a beat. "I don't have a man," I argued, hating how I had to deny us. But this conversation was exactly why.

"Okay, Hallie. Whatever you say. But no one believes that Jasper would just let any random rider compete on Lord Henry." I kept my mouth firmly closed to that. Jake sighed in annoyance. "Fine, keep your secrets, but be warned that people talk, and the gossip mill is rife."

"Your friends, you mean?" I snapped back. "Funny how you're trying to help me now when you sat there and let them rip me to shreds."

"You have no idea what people in this industry are like, Hallie. They can be vicious."

"Tell me something I don't know, Jake."

"People are out for Jasper, okay? I'm warning you to be safe," he said again.

I narrowed my eyes on him. "Are you one of the people I have to look out for? Or is it just those two hags you keep hanging out with? Are they making threats against Jasper?" I rolled my eyes and went into full bitch mode. "Forgive me, Jake, but the company you keep, along with your family's less than stellar reputation, doesn't make you the kind of person I can trust."

Jake laughed a humorless laugh. "Think what you want of me, but I don't hurt people or horses." I wasn't sure whether that was true, so I didn't reply. "Heed the warning or not. I was just giving you a friendly heads-up."

"Then *who*?" I said, as he walked away. Jake turned around. "Who are his enemies? Give me names. Information, not hushed rumors and speculation. And the reason why."

"Power? Jealousy? Take your pick. I have no idea who is after him," Jake said, and his face did look earnest. "I just know someone is." With that, he walked off.

I saw my team and Jasper waiting for me beyond the tunnel. I lifted my trophy over my head, dismissing Jake's warning as jealousy, and they all cheered. Sage linked arms with me, and Atticus slung his arm over my shoulder.

"One glass of champagne is all you get in celebration," Leon said, and Atticus rolled his eyes.

"Yes, Daddy," Atticus joked.

"We have the team event tomorrow, and we want to win that too." I smiled as my friends all celebrated around me. Looking over their shoulders, I met Jasper's eyes.

"Love you," he mouthed.

"Love you too," I mouthed back.

This would be a day I would always remember. A dream came true; I had a newfound family that I adored and a man that I was madly in love with.

I wasn't sure how I got so lucky, but one thing was for sure, I was never going to take it for granted.

Chapter Twenty

JASPER

The sun was hotter today, so hot that riders were allowed to ride without their jackets, and our team was clad all in white but for their boots. I stood beside Hallie, as always. She was the last to ride again today. Henry was stomping his feet, ready to go.

She pulled at her collar. “I’m boiling,” she said. But like she always did, she conducted her precompetition ritual: chin strap, girth, water. Mila handed her the water bottle. Hallie downed it in one. “That’s better,” she said, and smiled at me. It was normally just a sip, but today the weather clearly required more.

“Remember . . .” I said, but Hallie cut me off before I could finish.

“*Lots* of rein, hold him back on the triples, and lots of leg on the oxers.”

“Smart arse,” I said, smirking at my attitude. I leaned in closer. “Just for that, I’m going to make you wait to come tonight, Angel. Delayed gratification.”

“Sadist,” she sniped.

I shrugged. “Perhaps.”

Hallie swallowed her laugh, and Leon patted Henry's neck, just as Dillon Matthews from Team USA came trotting out.

As he passed by, he said to Hallie, "Keep riding like this, Hallie, and you'll be called up to Team USA in no time!"

"Thank you, Dillon!" she said, and beamed at me. My heart squeezed. She was getting all the acclaim she deserved, and she was amazing on Henry. I didn't think I'd been prouder of anyone in my life.

The announcer called Hallie's name, and she trotted out into the ring. Leon and I walked to the viewer's plinth, Atticus and Sage coming too now that their rides were done.

She cantered around the outside, waiting for the starting bell to sound. When it did, Hallie approached the first fence. As Henry cleared it, I suddenly narrowed my eyes on Hallie and the hairs on the back of my neck stood on end. By this point, I knew exactly how she rode. I knew her tells and her movements as if they were my own. And right now, her seat wasn't as good as it usually was.

Sage moved beside me, as did Leon. Even Atticus wasn't speaking—we were all too busy staring at my girl. As she approached fence two, Hallie's hands dropping too low with her reins, I said, "Something's wrong."

As Henry landed, the crowd murmured as Hallie nearly lost her stirrups, swaying in the saddle. "She's too unsteady," Leon said, a slight urgency in his voice.

"What's wrong with her?" Sage said. "Is she too hot?"

As always, Henry picked up speed as he approached the triple, the triple that was directly in front of us. I leaned over the railing to get a closer look and watched as Hallie approached. My heart nearly stopped dead when I saw her eyes were rolling and her head was dropping forward.

"Stop her!" I suddenly shouted and ran past Sage and my cousin. I never took my eyes off her as I darted toward the ring, Hallie began to tilt, seemingly losing consciousness.

But I knew my horse, and there was no stopping him as he gunned for the triple. Somehow, Hallie was able to stay seated over the first fence, but when I saw her eyes close on the approach to the second,

Henry lifted off the ground, and Hallie's body went completely limp. I made it into the ring just as Hallie slipped from Henry's back and slammed with a deafening thud onto the spread poles before falling into the wing. Henry jumped the third fence alone, Leon rushing from behind me to stop my stallion from taking off.

My heart was in my throat as I beelined for Hallie. The crowd was silent, so silent that only I could be heard in the still arena. "Hallie!" I shouted, not seeing her move. The fence had fallen, Hallie taking the full brunt of the poles and tall standard on her backbone. "HALLIE!" I screamed, just as I reached her, throwing all the broken lumber and fiberglass aside.

She was out cold. I leaned over her injured body. "Hallie, baby, talk to me," I begged. My heart was thundering in my chest, and panic took me in its hold. There was a moment of relief when Hallie opened her eyes, her gaze trying its best to find me, I squeezed her hand, seeing medics running toward us in the distance. "Look at me, Angel," I said, but when she tried, her pupils were blown, and my stomach fell, all the blood draining from my face. There was a suspicious-looking substance gathered in the corners of her mouth.

Had she been given something?

Had she been *drugged?*

"Hallie! Talk to me. *Look* at me!" I demanded, unable to keep any kind of calm, but her eyes rolled back again and she lost consciousness. "Hallie!" I pushed, but she wasn't fucking waking up. "Hallie!" I tried again, my heart ripping in two.

"NO!"

To be continued . . .

Playlist

"Florida!!!" (feat. Florence + the Machine)—Taylor Swift, Florence + the Machine

"Spotless" (feat. The Lumineers)—Zach Bryan, The Lumineers

"I Am Not Who I Was"—Chance Peña

"Thinking 'Bout Love"—Wild Rivers

"System"—Foy Vance

"White Horse"—Chris Stapleton

"Wait Up for Me"—Amos Lee

"Things a Man Oughta Know"—Lainey Wilson

"Temporary Tears" (feat. Foy Vance)—NEEDTOBREATHE, Foy Vance

"Fire It Up (The Silver Spear)"—Foy Vance

"My Home Is You"—The Strumbellas

"Lay By Me"—firekid

"Grow into Love"—Half Moon Run

"Back to You"—WILD

"As We Ran"—The National Parks

"King and Lionheart"—Of Monsters and Men

"Guiding Light"—Mumford & Sons

"She Lit a Fire"—Lord Huron

"You're Gonna Go Far" (with Brandi Carlile)—Noah Kahan, Brandi Carlile

"Wildflowers and Wild Horses"—Lainey Wilson

"Before You Leave Me"—Alex Warren

"The View Between Villages"—Noah Kahan
"Wild Horses"—The Sundays
"Nobody Knows"—The Lumineers
"Little Bit Better"—Caleb Hearn, ROSIE
"The Prophecy"—Taylor Swift
"Goliath"—Smith & Thell
"Detour"—Maren Morris
"You Should Probably Leave"—Chris Stapleton
"I Can Do It with a Broken Heart"—Taylor Swift
"The Bones" (with Hozier)—Maren Morris, Hozier
"New Moon" (with Kacey Musgraves)—Brooks & Dunn, Kacey Musgraves
"Broken Halos"—Chris Stapleton
"Tequila"—Dan + Shay
"I Can't Make You Love Me"—Teddy Swims
"Whirlwind"—Lainey Wilson
"The Stable Song"—Gregory Alan Isakov
"Burn, Burn, Burn"—Zach Bryan
"To Be Free"—Dylan Gossett
"Blue Eyed Constellation"—Max McNown
"How"—Marcus Mumford, Brandi Carlile
"Grow Old with Me"—Sunny Sweeney
"Worst Way"—Riley Green
"Good Thing Going On" (feat. Abbey Cone)—Mat Kearney, Abbey Cone
"Indigo" (feat. Avery Anna)—Sam Barber, Avery Anna
"Blink Twice"—Shaboozey, Myles Smith
"Brunette"—Tucker Wetmore
"The Roads"—Jonah Kagen
"Comin' In Cold"—Bailey Zimmerman

Listen to the Break Me (KE 1) *playlist on Spotify: authortilliecole*

Acknowledgments

I was six months old when I first sat on a horse (there's pictorial evidence, and it was a Shetland). My early childhood and teens were filled with endless days at the stables, summer horse shows, and pony club. In my teens, I would sneakily read Jilly Cooper novels (God rest her soul), devouring every page. Horses were my first-ever passion in life, and even in adulthood, they still are. I have been fortunate to own horses all my life (and yes, I had a feisty chestnut mare just like Fefe—one I spent more time on the floor with than on her back!). I currently have two young geldings who are my heart.

I knew one day I would write a romance based on the horse world. I had to. I was raised on a saddle, hacking out in the English countryside every chance I could, and I wanted to do this part of my life justice in written form. I was simply waiting for the perfect storyline to spring into my mind. Then one day, out of the blue, Jasper and Hallie appeared to say hello and demanded their story be told. Who was I to refuse?

Break Me is part one of their story, and I deeply apologize for leaving you with such a brutal cliffhanger! But their story is so detailed and intricate that putting everything down in one book was impossible. I promise I won't have you waiting forever, though. As I write these acknowledgments, I am well into writing *Tame Me*, book two, and I promise, it'll be well worth the wait. More Jasper and Hallie are on their way soon!

To make this book happen, it has taken a team of people. Liz, my super-agent and friend, thank you for helping me fulfill my Jilly Cooper fantasy and bring a book based on show jumping to life. Twelve years together and counting. I can't wait for what's to come. To the entire team at McIntosh and Otis, thank you so much for being my biggest hype squad. Love you all!

Thank you so much to my lovely editor Lauren Plude for taking a chance on me and inviting me into the Montlake family. It has been amazing to work with you, and I cannot wait for more projects in the future. Abby Zidle, my fellow horse girl, thank you for helping me whip (get it? 🙂) this manuscript into gear. Your American horse-girl experience has been invaluable, and it was a dream to bounce ideas off someone who lived in this world too.

Liz Gluck, thank you for all your support and for keeping on top of my chronically disorganized self—I know I'm a mess to work with! To everyone else at Montlake who helped get this book out into the world, I appreciate it more than you know.

To Rebecca Hilsdon at Penguin UK and the whole team. Thank you for always supporting this British girl and giving my books homes on shelves I used to hunt through as a child. I would never have imagined this to be my life. I love my Penguin family so much. Onwards and upwards!

On to my family. Stephen, my partner in crime, hubby, and best friend. You weren't a horse boy growing up, but thank you for helping me with mine when the winter hits and the mud is at my knees. I love you to the moon and back and so do my horses, who you never asked to be involved with but put up with anyway!

To my children. You're the best thing I have ever done and I love you more than life. Thank you for sharing in my love of animals and horses, and M, I can't wait until I'm watching you in show jumping competitions too! Maybe Team GB is in your future!

Mam, the OG horse girl. Seventy-one and still mucking out daily. You are a superstar. I love you lots and couldn't be without you. Sam, thank you (I think 🙂) for throwing me back into the horse world after my time galivanting abroad for a decade. They were meant to be a form of therapy for me, which most days they are, not so much when

I'm falling off and slamming to the floor like a bag of bones! You're the biggest supporter of my books and the one who pushed me to write about Jasper and Hallie, mainly so you could read it. I hope it was worth the wait!

To Pat, my nephews, and the rest of my family, thanks for all the support. I love you all.

To The Coven, thank you for all the love and support you have given me. You lift me up like no one else, and I thank God every day that you came into my life. *Coven for life!* To my mam friends, thank you for always reading my books, even if it makes me cringe when you do!

And last, my readers, my Tillsters. I say this all the time, but you changed my life and I will be forever grateful to you for that. Your support has been unwavering, and I hope you know how much that has meant to me over the years. Here's to more stories in the future and many more broody men and feisty women to come!

About the Author

Photo © Lauren Watson Perry at Perrywinkle Photography

Tillie Cole is the *New York Times* bestselling author of numerous novels and series in many genres, including contemporary romance, dark romance, young adult, and new adult fiction. She graduated from Newcastle University with a BA Hons in religious studies and taught high school social studies before putting pen to paper and finishing her first novel. After several years of living in Italy, Canada, and the US, Tillie is back in her hometown in England with her husband and two children. When she is not writing, Tillie enjoys spending time with her little family, curling up on her couch watching movies, drinking far too much coffee, and convincing herself that she really doesn't need that last square of chocolate. For more information, visit https://tilliecole.com.